LOST CURSE

T. LYNN ADAMS

THE LOST CURSE

T. LYNN ADAMS

SWEETWATER BOOKS,
AN IMPRINT OF CEDAR FORT, INC.
SPRINGVILLE, UTAH

This is a work of fiction. The characters, names, incidents, places, and dialogue are products of the author's imagination, and are not to be construed as real.

The views expressed within this work are the sole responsibility of the author and do not necessarily reflect the position of Cedar Fort, Inc., or any other entity.

ISBN 13: 978-1-59955-955-1

Published by Sweetwater Press, an imprint of Cedar Fort, Inc.
2373 W. 700 S., Springville, UT 84663
Distributed by Cedar Fort, Inc., www.cedarfort.com

LIBRARY OF CONGRESS CATALOGING-IN-PUBLICATION DATA

Adams, T. Lynn (Terri Lynn), 1962–, author.
  The lost curse / T. Lynn Adams.
      pages cm.
  Summary: Teens Jonathan and Severino travel to Kanosh for a vacation and end up getting involved in a plot to plunder the lost Carre Shinob mine.
  ISBN 978-1-59955-955-1
  1. Gold mines and mining--Utah--Fiction. 2. Treasure troves--Utah--Fiction. 3. Paiute Indians--Fiction. I. Title.

  PS3601.D397L67 2012
  813'.6--dc23

                        2012009718

Cover design by Angela D. Olsen
Cover design © 2012 by Lyle Mortimer
Edited and typeset by Emily S. Chambers

Printed in the United States of America

10 9 8 7 6 5 4 3 2 1

Printed on acid-free paper

ACKNOWLEDGMENTS

S O MANY people have helped make this book a reality. I owe my thanks to Kevin Buxbaum, who had faith in the characters and wanted to see more of their adventures. I also am grateful to Jennifer Fielding, Emily Chambers, and the rest of the crew at Cedar Fort. They took a risk with a new author, and I truly appreciate it.

To Martin McAllister, who owns Archaeological Damage Investigation and Assessment, a big thanks for your help and expertise. Also to the BLM officer who works undercover on archaeological investigations, thank you. Both of you were tremendous resources, and I appreciate your willingness to share your experiences and your knowledge.

Finally, and primarily, my family—they deserve a big thanks. Troy, your support is wonderful, and your cooking and laundry skills have been greatly appreciated. Aaron, I love bouncing ideas off you. Thank you. Go write your own book. Brandon, Cayden, Danielle, Elyse, and Hunter—your names are finally in print in one of my books! You are among my greatest fans.

Also, David, thank you so much for showing me the Spanish turtle and all the Spanish shadows around Kanosh. You opened my eyes to a piece of history few people know about and planted in me the seeds that grew into this story. To Tom and John, your stories about Kanosh and the Death Light are legendary. I appreciate you sharing them with me! Maybe one day I'll have my own Kanosh stories to tell.

PROLOGUE

GUNFIRE EXPLODED through the remote canyon, filling the air with a thunderclap of gunpowder, bullet, and primer. Even as the sound bounced and echoed its way across the cliffs, a single brass casing ejected from the pistol. Still hot, it spun through the air, flashing in the setting sun. The light ricocheted off its metal jacket like ball lightning.

Birds, startled from their evening roosts, erupted with disapproval. Their protesting wings beat the cooling air as they lifted out of the canyon, cackling their alarm. But the bullet did not pursue any of them. It had already found its target.

When the projectile penetrated him, the young Paiute Indian stiffened in protest. The man crumpled to the ground, his face and torso landing in the cold water of a thin stream.

From across the creek, a young dog heard the sound and saw the outcome. Fury at the attack drove the dog, without hesitation, through the water and toward the shooter. Teeth bared and hackles bristled to their fullest, the animal rushed to defend his slain master.

A second bullet pierced through the dog's face and neck, exiting out its shoulder and stopping the dog just short of its target. Seventy pounds of remains crumpled to the stone-strewn earth in a heap.

As the second casing fell to the earth, three men remained standing. Two stood, shocked at the sudden turn of events. The other, stilled by hatred, breathed deep and waited a few moments. Then, not wanting even the animals in the canyon to find the man's body, he ordered the frightened pair to lift the corpse and carry it deep into a crevice in the side of a cliff.

The dog they left for the scavengers and maggots.

ONE

SHOOTING THROUGH the sky at 510 miles per hour, the A320 cut through the icy atmosphere and left a contrail dissipating behind them. Somewhere below, a child or adult saw the white line spreading across the blue expanse between Los Angeles and Salt Lake City. They didn't see the killer on board the plane.

Most of the hundred and thirty passengers inside the plane's cabin—oblivious of the contrail, the killer, or the people watching them from below—read, slept, or stared out the windows. None of them knew of the deadly cat-and-mouse game taking place.

Halfway back in the plane, vivid blue eyes watched a tiny cell phone screen. A special app tracked every keystroke and recorded every word that passed through the "mouse's" cell phone a few rows ahead. Still, the cat didn't want to miss a thing.

Sitting in the business section, Cole Matthews didn't know he sat so close to the claws of a hungry cat that tracked his electronic moves. Instead, he remained focused on a valuable chunk of cheese waiting for him in Utah.

Dressed in a Valentino business suit and Berluti shoes, Cole worked his smartphone. A large gold ring, with a tiger's-eye stone, encircled his left thumb. The ring only fit his thumb, but he liked it that way. It reminded him of a business deal that went bad a decade earlier. That's when he discovered, the hard way, that everyone has a different motive for working, and sometimes their reasons interfered with his plans. Now, every time he hired a new employee, he let the ring remind him to be cautious.

Cole's thumbs pressed the keys of his phone. *I'll be on the ground in twenty minutes.* The ringed thumb pushed Send.

A minute later, the response came back. *I'm waiting at the baggage claim.*

The plane slowed its airspeed and descended half a mile in the atmosphere. Though no cabin lights indicated their descent, the passengers felt the shift and knew it signaled the end of their two-hour flight. Zippers sounded as passengers placed items back inside their carry-ons; seatbelts unclicked for last-minute trips to the bathroom.

Next to Cole, a handsome Hispanic teen straightened and glanced at the overhead indicator lights with deep brown eyes. For Cole, who spent his time more worried about making money than making conversation, the teenager had been a perfect seat companion. The youth had spent the entire flight watching the landscape out the window. Now, however, the teen's movement distracted Cole from his phone. Looking at the change in cabin activity, Cole glanced back down and sent one final text. *No mistakes this time. I have several buyers waiting.*

A few rows back, in the economy seats, Ryan Polson intercepted a copy of the final text and then saw that Cole had shut off his cell phone. Punching in a few commands, Ryan closed his own phone and slipped the still-active device into an inside suit pocket. His jaw worked a piece of gum while he finger-combed his blond hair. Intense blue eyes tracked the stewardess making her final walk through the aisle. If she asked to see his phone, it would appear turned off even though it still recorded everything the "mouse" did electronically. As soon as Cole Matthews reactivated his phone when they landed, Ryan would know.

The plane slowed and descended further until individual buildings came into view, sitting like gray and brown cubes on the landscape. Flaps lowered on the plane's wings. The aluminum bird rocked gently on the air currents as it came closer to the earth. Through the window, cars came into view on I-15.

Now the man-made bird lowered its landing gear, the hydraulic system humming through its belly and locking into place with a deep, powerful sound. Trees came into focus and the flight attendants took their seats. A few horses appeared in the fields. The runway came into view and the plane swept in, one hundred feet above the ground, fifty, twenty. Lights and signs appeared on the runway, whisking by at one hundred thirty miles an hour.

On the runway, the rear wheels touched earth, followed by the nose wheel as the plane settled to earth.

Resting from its flight, the airplane exited the straight runway and rolled toward its numbered gate. Across the cabin, the sound of seat belts unlocking filled the air in staccato announcements. A few impatient passengers stood up to retrieve their bags from the overhead bins even before the plane stopped.

Once the covered walkway had been extended to the cabin door and the secure portal released, passengers left their seats, threaded together, and moved up the narrow aisle toward the Salt Lake International Airport.

Lifting a backpack to one shoulder, eighteen-year-old Severino stood, anxious to be finished with sky travel for a while. It had been a long journey of airplanes and airports since he'd left Cusco, Peru, almost twenty hours earlier.

Bent under the overhead compartment, Severino waited for his older seatmate to rise from his seat and, again, noted the tiger's-eye ring on the man's thumb. Tiger's-eye stones increased focus and promoted balance. To hide a smile, the teen looked away. Even though the man had stayed focused during the two-hour flight out of Los Angeles, anyone who spent that much time texting had to be out of balance. Someone needed to tell him the ring wasn't working.

The older man, with silver streaking his dark hair and business deals filling his mind, didn't know or care about the teenager's thoughts. He rose from his seat without looking at the youth and pushed his way into the line of people shuffling toward the exit.

Without moving, Severino watched him leave and then turned his attention back to the still-crowded aisle. People moved by, shoulders hoisting luggage, bags jostling other people. One passenger smiled and waited, creating a slot for the teenager. Severino nodded his gratitude and entered the aisle. Mimicking the short steps of those in front of him, he moved with the crowd toward the door. Passengers moved out of the crowded, warm plane and entered the ramp's cool interior.

Ahead of him, the line of people moved up the ramp and spilled into the openness of the terminal, breaking apart—wanting more distance between them than normal. Their actions were a common response to the confines of the airplane and Severino felt the desire for more space wash over him. As he moved from the passenger seating area into the large corridor, he rolled his shoulders in appreciation of the reclaimed freedom.

He followed the crowd ahead of him, knowing they would lead him to the baggage claim area where, he hoped, the Bradfords would be waiting for him. In Los Angeles, Spanish had been as prevalent as English, but here, in the center of the United States, he doubted he would hear much Spanish and not a word of Quechua.

Coming down the escalators, his dark eyes searched the sea of faces below him. Then he made a visual connection and smiled.

On seeing the Peruvian descend the escalators, Jonathon Bradford returned the smile and stepped forward. The last time he'd seen Severino had been at midnight beside a river in the Andes Mountains while terrorists searched the jungled slopes for him. Severino saved his life that night and Jonathon hoped, in some small way, to be able to repay him.

Still, he wasn't sure how to greet the teen.

Jonathon's mother answered that question for him. She surged passed Jonathon and swallowed Severino in a full hug as soon as he stepped off the moving stairs. *"Mi hijito precioso,"* she breathed, "my precious son—you are finally here."

At the emotional welcome, the backpack slid from Severino's shoulder and he hugged the woman he had never met, holding her tight. For a full minute they embraced, Rosa murmuring her gratitude over and over, and Severino whispering that she did not need to thank him. He would do it all over again.

The words and the scene filled Jonathon and his father with their own sense of emotion and they waited, respecting the union and not wanting to intrude.

When Rosa stepped back she wiped the tears from her eyes, speaking in fluent Spanish. *"Es increíble* to finally have you here."

A smile emerged from the Peruvian. *"Sí,* it is incredible. I can't believe it. Thank you so much."

A hand to the shoulder and a grin became Jonathon's greeting to Severino. "Well, believe it, *hermano.* You're here in the U.S. You made it."

The group spoke in Spanish, the language flowing from all of them like water. The luggage carousel began to turn, a metal whirlpool that pulled everyone toward its slow, circular current. Though Jonathon's parents still chatted with Severino, they drifted with the others toward the carousel's pull. In the slow human current, Severino moved with them, nodding quiet replies, his answers polite.

This hesitant side of Severino intrigued Jonathon. In Peru, Severino held a rifle with ease and risked death by the Shining Path terrorists to free Jonathon from their grasp. Now the Peruvian stood on foreign soil for the first time in his life, holding a backpack instead of a gun, his gaze downcast instead of elevated with fury.

Through light brown eyes, Jonathon watched Severino, withholding his own questions. There would be time later to get to know him. For now, Jonathon would let his parents claim Severino's attention. He understood their need and the instant bond they felt. Twice last year, the eighteen-year-old saved Jonathon's life in Peru—once by getting him out of the sacred tunnels of the Incas and, a second time, by helping Jonathon escape from the terrorists. That made Severino an instant and cherished member of their family.

As an expression of gratitude, his parents paid for Severino's visit to America. For the next month, they wanted to get to know the Peruvian and let him experience a world different from his own. Jonathon also knew his parents hoped that if Severino saw opportunities beyond his impoverished mountain home, then he would accept their offer to pay for a college education. So far, Severino refused to go to school.

They extended the same offer to Severino's sister, Delia, who nursed Jonathon back to health after finding him in the tunnels. It took a while for the shy sixteen-year-old to accept their offer, but she now lived with her mother in Lima and attended a private high school. Through emails and Skype calls, they saw her adjusting and growing in confidence and ability, adapting to life in a metropolitan area. Most important, she no longer lived in fear of the Shining Path terrorists.

Jonathon lowered his gaze at the discomforting thought. Though he hadn't told his parents, he knew Severino refused to go to school because of his association with the Shining Path terrorists. Severino had not given up his quest to find his father's killer, and Jonathon doubted he ever would. By posing as a terrorist, Severino planned to discover the man responsible for killing his father and bring him to justice. Whether that justice would be legal, Jonathon didn't know.

A drinking fountain became Jonathon's temporary oasis, and he moved there to distract himself and give his parents more time to visit. The steel bar responded to his push, and cold water hummed out of the belly of the machine, arcing over the drain. Several mouthfuls of water moved down his throat before Jonathon straightened and turned, colliding with a man engaged in a quiet cell phone conversation.

"If you're sure he's found a real Spanish turtle, I want a photo *now* . . ."

Startled and apologetic, Jonathon stepped back, out of the man's path. "I'm sorry, sir. I didn't see you."

Anger at the unexpected collision lifted the man's face. Beneath a crown of blond hair, the man's vivid blue eyes displayed fury. The man's expression pushed Jonathon back even more. He saw enraged muscles work along the man's jaw and Jonathon braced for a verbal barrage; then the voice on the other end of the cell phone reclaimed the man's attention. Returning to the conversation, the man cursed the jostling, pressed the phone tighter to his ear, and walked away.

Uncomfortable with the entire moment, Jonathon watched him go.

"Type A personality," a quiet voice commented. Startled, Jonathon turned to find Severino standing beside him. The Peruvian nodded, motioning toward the man walking away. "I saw you bump into him."

"It was an accident."

"I know. You okay?"

"Yeah."

"He chew you out for it?"

"I think he wanted to, but he went back to his phone conversation instead. Something about a Spanish turtle. Do you know what that is?"

Unfamiliar with the term, Severino frowned and shook his head. "A turtle that speaks Spanish, I suppose. He probably won't find too many of those around here."

The remark brought a smile to Jonathon's face. "Well, apparently someone has. The guy said he wanted to see a photo of it *now*."

"*Classic* Type A personality—very impatient. They make great terrorists but rotten friends."

With his last comment hanging in the air, Severino bent and got a drink from the fountain. Next to him, Jonathon's gaze followed the Peruvian, thoughts spilling through his mind like water. Would a month with Severino prove the youth to be more of a friend or a terrorist? Jonathon didn't know, but for his family's sake, he hoped Severino would be more of a friend.

If Severino knew the thoughts his comment provoked, he didn't show it. Finished with his drink, he nodded toward the carousel. "They might pick the wrong bags if I don't help."

At the baggage claim, the pair joined Jonathon's family and watched the luggage drop out of the square portal and onto the conveyer belt. Backpacks, duffel bags, garment bags, soft-sided and hard-sided suitcases of all colors circled in front of the flight's passengers. Hands emerged from the crowd and claimed each piece.

A press against his shoulder turned Jonathon's attention. Severino stood close, his eyes on the carousel. "There's your angry friend. He is more interested in his phone right now, not the luggage. Maybe the photo of his Spanish turtle is coming soon."

Though Severino did not point, Jonathon knew where to look. The blond man stood next to the baggage claim, watching the luggage but holding his phone in his hand.

A duffel bag fell out of the portal and landed on the silver conveyer belt. It would pass in front of the blond man before it reached them. Severino nodded. "There's my bag."

"Want me to go get it?" Jonathon asked.

"No. I'll get it. Maybe I can spot what a Spanish turtle looks like while I'm there," he grinned.

Before Jonathon could protest, Severino moved through the crowd, working his way between people until he stood on the opposite side of the man. Positioned next to him, Severino pretended to watch the passing luggage but Jonathon saw his focus stay on the phone. Bags passed in front of them, including Severino's duffel. Checking the tag, Severino let it move on by and waited for the next duffel. When it passed, he checked the tag. The man glanced at his phone then back at the conveyer belt. More luggage passed, more duffel bags. Severino's bag began to come around again.

Through the sounds of a busy airport, Severino heard the quiet hum of a phone on vibrate. The blond-haired man turned his hand over and checked the phone. Wanting a bit more privacy, the man shifted away from the Peruvian and opened his phone. He worked a few buttons and an image uploaded to the screen. As it did, the man's blue eyes scanned the image and the muscles in his face went slack. Stunned, the man looked up, trying to process what he had just viewed.

When the opportunity to view the picture appeared for that split second, Severino reached in front of the man and apologized. "*Con permiso.*" Checking the tag, Severino locked his hand around the duffel's straps, lifted the bag from the belt and pulled it across, in front of the man. "*Discúlpame.*"

Annoyed, the man stepped away, glanced again at the picture on his phone, and exhaled under his breath at the image. Though only a whisper of sound, Severino heard it and knew the photo had a powerful impact on the man.

With his duffel bag in hand, Severino turned and threaded his way back through the crowd to the Bradfords.

"Is that it?" David Bradford reached for the duffel.

"*Sí, es todo,*" Severino confirmed.

"Great, then we can head home. We have three other children waiting at home who are very excited to meet you," he said and smiled. Holding the duffel in his left hand, David slipped his right arm around his wife and led the way to the exit.

Jonathon hung back. "Pretty slick move. Did you see the photo?"

"I saw something, but it didn't look like a turtle to me. It looked like a rock."

"A rock?"

"*Sí,* a very big rock." Severino shouldered his backpack, his eyes scanning the crowd, his voice conveying disappointed. "And I had been hoping a Spanish turtle was an American term for a really cute girl."

He brought his gaze back to Jonathon's and smiled.

For that brief moment, Jonathon saw a typical teenager, not a terrorist, in Severino's dark brown eyes. Relief and surprise brought laughter from him. "Oh, don't worry. You'll meet plenty of American girls this summer, I promise."

"If they look like rocks, I'm not interested," the Peruvian teased.

"Hey, all the girls I run with look like models."

Dark eyes canted sideways, and the Peruvian looked at Jonathon. "Did I tell you all terrorists can spot a liar?"

The comment froze Jonathon's smile even as the doors opened and they stepped out of the terminal into the hot, dry air of a Utah summer.

TWO

WHEN THE wall of heat fell against him, Severino sucked
in a gasp of surprise. "It's like an oven out here. Is it always
this hot?"

"During the summer, yes. During the winter, we get snow. Lots
of snow."

Ahead of them, David turned back. "Someone has some money,"
he muttered in Spanish, as a chauffeur helped a skycap load luggage
into the back of a black four-wheel drive Cadillac Escalade limousine.
A man with graying hair and a tiger's-eye ring oversaw the process.

Recognition rolled through Severino. "That was my seat partner
coming in from Los Angeles. I thought he looked rich."

Jonathon laughed. "That guy flew coach? I don't think so."

"I don't know about flying coach, but he sat beside me the entire
time."

A frown crossed Jonathon's face. "Did you sit where there are three
seats across or only two?"

"Only two seats."

"The whole way?"

"Sí."

Jonathon held out his hand. "Let me see your boarding pass." Not
concerned, Severino withdrew it from his back pocket and passed it to
Jonathon. A quick scan of the information increased Jonathon's frown.

"Hey, Dad. This says Severino flew in the business class. How come? You never pay for more expensive seats."

"I didn't have to. I used my frequent flyer miles to pay for the upgrade. I figured, since it was Severino's first time flying, I'd let him enjoy it. Why, are you jealous?"

"A little. I hear all the cute flight attendants work business class."

David laughed. "Well, Severino was there. Ask him what he thought of them."

"Rocks," Severino dry-panned without waiting.

"Yeah, right. You're just trying to make me feel better."

"Is it working?"

"No." Raising his voice again, Jonathon called to his father. "I want to fly business class next time."

"Okay, just use your frequent flyer miles and you can."

"I don't have frequent flyer miles!"

"Then save up your pennies. No, wait, I take that back . . . save up your dollars."

Shoving the boarding pass back to Severino, Jonathon scowled. "I think he likes you better."

A shrug rolled off Severino's shoulders. "*Es probable*. Most people do."

Beneath the hot sun, the two teens looked at each other for a second. Then they both started to grin.

No one heard the gun erupt with deadly force. The custom silencer muffled the pistol's blast, but the .410 shotgun shell found its mark. In the sand, the snake's rattled warning spiked before fading into the hot Utah air. Once again, death had come to the desert west of Kanosh.

The warm wind rippled Ryan's T-shirt, dampened by sweat and streaked with desert dust. The wet material absorbed the breeze and felt cool on his chest. Ryan settled the two-pound Judge pistol back into his shoulder holster. Angered by the snake and the entire afternoon, he kicked the headless corpse away from the truck and jerked open the door. A quick grab across the seat allowed him to retrieve a topographical map.

Ryan scowled. "He obviously marked the wrong spot on the

map. Maybe he's working for Cole."

Still unnerved by finding a deadly snake coiled in the shade of the truck, another man shoved the bloody remains further away with his hiking boot. The body coiled and writhed in futile protest. "I don't think he's working for Cole. The guy is old and had never read a topo map before. It was probably just an accident."

With the map laid across the sun-seared truck hood, Ryan studied its ridges and valleys. A curse of frustration lifted his gaze to the rugged landscape it depicted. Sagebrush and wild grass dotted the ground, knots of pale color left on a tapestry of sand. Boulders, remnants of violent volcanic activity millennia ago, protruded from the earth like angry scar tissue.

Ryan tiredly rubbed his tanned face, feeling two days of stubble on his cheeks. "Didn't the old man say it was on a ridge and you could see both the Pahvant Mountains and the Crooked Mountains from there?"

"Yes. So, it has to be in the area."

"If it even exists."

Dismay at the comment caused Steven's shoulders to lower. "You saw the photo."

"Yeah, I saw it, but you said the photo was at least five years old. Maybe Cole beat us to it. Maybe someone else did. It could be long gone by now."

In the ninety-eight-degree heat, sweat rolled off Ryan's brow and left wet streaks through the dust and stubble that darkened his cheeks. Still, his sharp, blue eyes swept across the horizon, alert, studying the two mountain ranges until he made his decision. Folding the map, Ryan shoved it into a small daypack. "We need to keep looking."

Relieved, Steven gave a nod of agreement and removed his hat and raked his hand through his dark hair back against his scalp, spreading the sweat through the thickness to cool his head. Then he replaced his cap and followed Ryan across the sand and shale.

Heavy snake-proof boots crunched over small cacti and broken sandstone. Desert insects harassed them with a constant assault, attacking their skin, flying at their eyes, and tormenting their mouths and noses. Grasses, dried from the heat and heavy with stickers and seed heads, scratched at their skin and impaled their clothing. Both men stopped often to drink warm water beneath the cloudless sky or scan the terrain ahead with their binoculars, studying the rock formations. Each area searched received a red check mark on the map.

Three hours of hiking brought Ryan to a stop, breathing hard in the heat. He wiped dirt from his mouth with the back of his hand before taking a drink of water. Sweat soaked the front of his shirt and glistened on his tanned skin. Even through sunglasses, he squinted up the next ridge.

Two more swallows of water were gulped down before Ryan took a second break to suck air into his tired lungs. Looking back to the east, he saw the Pahvant Mountains. To the west lay the Crooked Mountains. Too tired to speak, he nodded to Steven, and the pair began to weave their way through the sage-dappled lava flow and up the next ridge.

The sun burned down on them from its two-o'clock position. A hawk flew silently overhead and a jackrabbit bounded away in fear. The flight of grasshoppers, startling away in the dry grass, sounded like the buzz of rattlesnakes. As they moved, the men kept their eyes shifting from the terrain around them to the ground at their feet, not wanting to mistake the rattle of a snake for the sound of a grasshopper.

Both men studied the land, their gazes devouring each rock and boulder as they climbed. On top of the rock-strewn ridge, they slowed their search—recrossing the ridge, looking at the formations around them again and again—trying to locate just one formation in a lava flow of thousands.

Then Ryan stopped, smiled, and tipped his head back to the cloudless sky. An incredulous laugh came from between his dry lips as he caught the gaze of his partner and pointed to the north. "What does that look like?"

Steven followed the direction of Ryan's point. A four-foot-tall rough stone emerged from the desert floor like a turtle emerging from its shell. Stunned, Steven's eyes widened. "It's a turtle!"

With a widening arc of his hand, Ryan pointed around them. "And there are the Pahvant Mountains and the Crooked Mountains. I think we found it." As he moved through the landscape, drawing closer, a sound of appreciation rolled out of Ryan. "I think we have us a genuine Spanish turtle."

This time, neither man heard the dry grasses crunch beneath their passing or felt the small rocks and shale shift under their boots. Both remained focused on the rock, its features emerging with more clarity as they drew closer. The rock had been carved by human hands centuries earlier.

A few feet from the figure, Ryan stopped and combed his fingers through the sides of his blond hair. Uncertain now, anxious and overwhelmed, he stared at the turtle carving, letting the magnitude of his find settle in his mind.

"Oh, it's beautiful," he whispered. Ryan circled the rock, afraid to touch it, as if the carving would fade like a mirage. His eyes noted the large shell, four legs, raised head, and tail. "It's all here. A perfect Spanish turtle, hand carved by the Spanish explorers—and we beat Cole to it!"

A smile lightened Steven's face as he studied the carved stone. "So, what are you going to do with it?"

"I am going to use it to sucker punch Cole. He has wanted one of these for years, and I'm going to drop it in front of him like chum. Then, I'm going to take him out of the picture for good."

Steven pressed his lips together and nodded. "Sounds like you've planned this for a while."

"For twelve years."

"That's a third of your life."

"Tell me about it." Now Ryan squatted beside the turtle, touching it for the first time. The direction of his voice shifted and he spoke to the rock. "But you've been waiting for five hundred years for someone to come and listen to your story. What kind of story do you have to tell us?"

Strong hands stroked the rough shell and ran over the carved head. "Look at you. Your head is up. That means they carved you looking at the mine." Ryan followed the direction of the turtle's head, to the Pahvant Mountains. "Is that where the mine is, huh?"

In the desert sun, the stone turtle remained silent.

"What else do you want to tell me?" Ryan continued to let his hands travel over the stone, prying the features, feeling for clues his eyes might miss. At the front of the turtle, an unexpected find caused him to lift his gaze in astonishment. "I've never seen this before. Both forelegs are tucked into the shell."

"Does that mean something?"

"It means there are at least two traps at the front of the mine."

Stunned, Steven looked back at the distant mountains. "It must have been a very valuable mine to protect it with a double-trap system."

Concern sent Ryan back around the turtle, feeling, searching. Near the back, his face sagged and he shook his head. "One back leg is tucked too. They even booby-trapped the rear entrance."

"They didn't want anyone getting in or out of it, did they?"

"No. They wanted to protect this mine." Needing a break, Ryan backed away from the turtle. "You know, ancient Spanish records tell us the Spaniards left over seven billion dollars in gold bars tucked away in mines throughout Utah. They hid even more than that in silver bars. They had to leave it and get out fast because the Indian slaves were revolting and killing the Spaniards."

The Pahvant Mountains lifted Ryan's gaze from the turtle, and Ryan shook his head, continuing. "And that's just the processed stuff they left behind. There's no telling how much un-mined ore is left in those mines. Did you know Spanish records made about the Lost Josephine Mine, just south of here, said before they had to flee they were uncovering slabs of virgin silver that weighed over a hundred pounds each?"

"No."

"And the Lost Rhoades Mine, which is somewhere in the area, is said to have a vein of gold in it over four feet wide."

A soundless whistle escaped Steven, and he too looked at the Pahvant Mountain range. "Do you think this turtle points to one of those mines?"

Ryan shook his head, frowning. "I don't know. For all we *do* know about those lost mines, nothing has ever indicated they were marked by a turtle or guarded by a double-trap system on the main tunnel and a trap system out the back. This turtle may be pointing to a mine that makes the Lost Rhoades Mine look like a piggy bank."

Steven held motionless, private thoughts rolling over in his mind.

Not able to stay still, excitement drove Ryan to his feet, and he circled the turtle. "So, where is the mine, girl? You gotta tell us more. You know *exactly* where it is."

To uncover answers buried by time, Ryan brushed dust and dirt off the rock and lifted debris from ancient carvings. A strong, careful touch carried his hand over the turtle's head, his fingers playing and prying across the crown while he read the stone's silence. Within a minute, Ryan's face brightened. "It has a notch!"

Anticipation brought Steven forward a step while Ryan dug debris from a small, V-shaped notch in the crest of the turtle's head. Hope moved a smile onto his face. "They only notched the head to show direction," Steven offered.

"I know, I know." Ryan brushed at the large pieces of debris and blew away the finer silt. "They had to have carved a second notch into the shell somewhere to line them up."

Both men searched the carving, their trained eyes scanning every inch, their fingers feeling every ridge and divot in the stone, yet the sun-baked rock held its clues beneath centuries of caked dirt. Fingertips and nails scraped, lifted, and flaked away the layers.

"I got it. I got it!" Steven smiled, brushing dirt from a crevice in the turtle's back. "It's not just a notch, it's a line—a perfectly straight line. Look at that."

Stepping beside him, Ryan looked and a smile pulled across his face. A straight furrow ran for five inches down the back of the turtle, exactly over the center of its shell. "That line is too straight to be natural."

"I know."

"They carved it."

A smile of agreement came from Steven and he pulled out a piece of string. "Now let's see where it points."

Together, the men pulled the string taut, placing it in the furrow and then running it out through the notch. Sighting along the string, they focused on the mountain ridge sitting silent twenty miles to the east. The string pointed both men to the same mountain face, and they sat back against the turtle, studying the distant blue-gray slope beneath the sunlight.

Minutes slid off the clock, and then Ryan suddenly removed his sunglasses. The expression on his face told Steven he saw something. Careful not to shift his position or his gaze, Ryan lifted binoculars and peered through the magnifying lenses. "There's a heart up there!"

"What?"

"Gold was at the heart of everything the Spanish did. They used gold to rule nations, win wars, find new lands, convert people to Christianity, perform good deeds, and buy their way into heaven. That's why a heart became one of their most common symbols for gold." A smile appeared beneath the black-framed binoculars, and

Ryan shook his head in amazement. "Those Spaniards carved a heart across the whole face of the mountain!"

"You're kidding." Next to him, Steven lifted his own binoculars, scanning the area until he too saw the deep shadow of a symmetrical heart. "That thing must be close to a mile wide! Are we seeing this right, or are we just wanting to see something so badly we're making it up?"

"I think we're seeing it right, just like the Spaniards wanted to see it when they returned." Then Ryan smiled. "*Thar's gold in them thar hills*, and, if this turtle and that heart mean anything, there's going to be an awful lot of gold up there."

"So, what are we going to do?"

A lopsided grin passed from Ryan. "Find the gold!"

"And what about the turtle? Are we going to leave it here and risk Cole finding it?"

"No. We came to find the turtle and we're going to take the turtle. Besides, I think Cole would offer us a pretty penny if we take the turtle and then show him photos of it and tell him we know where it was pointing."

"How much do you think he'll offer you?"

"I'm betting he'll go six figures for the turtle. If we go up on that mountain ourselves and find evidence of Spanish mining activity, he'll throw down more without a blink."

"And if we find the mine?"

"What do you think?"

The thoughts dropped Steven to his seat on the rocky earth, his eyes locked on the distant mountain. Soon laughter filled his expression, and he rubbed both sides of his head with excitement, leaving streaks of sweat and dirt. "This is big. This is really big."

"It doesn't get much bigger. How long will it take you to get this turtle out of here?"

Turning back to the rock, Steven studied the creature, taking new care in his examination. "It looks like rhyolite. Seems to be all one piece. The stone is probably buried deep in the earth. To dig it out may take days . . . weeks, depending on how much of it is underground."

"Like an iceberg."

"Yeah, but if you want it out fast, I could cut through the base of the stone with a turbo blade and take it off right above the ground."

"Would it damage the turtle?"

"It could, but if I use soft-bond diamond blades, it probably won't."

"What about noise?"

"I could use a three-layer blade—copper in the middle. It cuts down on noise, but it will still be loud. Sound out here could carry for a mile or more."

"How long will it take for you to cut it off?"

"Three, maybe four hours, but you can see several miles in any direction. If you keep an eye out for company and give me a warning, I can shut off the saw before someone gets close enough to hear it."

"What about moving it? How much will a piece like that weigh?"

An inhale of breath showed Steven's mental calculations. "Rhyolite is lighter than it looks, but you're still talking almost two-thousand pounds, give or take a few hundred. We'll need to use the hoist to lift it onto the back of the truck or onto a trailer."

Ryan frowned. "People will see it."

The statement did not concern Steven. "We'll build a special crate to protect it during shipping and load it in the crate right here using hydraulic pulleys and the hoist. We won't bring the truck and trailer up here until the stone is cut and ready to go."

"How long will it take to load?"

"A couple of hours, if everything goes right."

The news settled with other thoughts into Ryan's mind. "And you have all the gear you need to cut, crate, and load this thing?"

"I can get it here in a day."

"And how long will it take you to build the crate?"

"Two days."

"So, we're talking three—maybe four—days total to get this thing out of here, right?"

"About that."

The full time line did not please Ryan and he frowned. "Can you work at night?"

"I wouldn't want to cut the stone at night. I need to see what I'm doing and what the rock is doing. But I could build the crate at night, and we can load it at night. "

"If you build the crate at night, you'll be tired during the day and could make a mistake cutting."

"Possibly."

Ryan removed his cap and rubbed his hair hard, thinking, before hooking the cap over the back of his head and tugging the bill back into place. The decision made, he nodded. "I don't want to risk a mistake. This turtle is too valuable. Let's get the stuff here and the crate built, then we'll worry about cutting and loading. If it takes three, four, or even five days, that's fine. I don't want the turtle damaged."

"So, how are we going to protect it from Cole until we can get it out of here? You know Cole is looking for something in this area. He could be here looking for the turtle."

"We'll have to stay out here at night. We can camp down there, in the valley, where we can keep an eye on the ridge. This is public land so, if anyone asks, we're just hunting jackrabbits and scouting for the deer hunt."

"That will explain the guns."

"And the binoculars."

A grin lifted both sides of Steven's mouth. "Sounds good. I don't mind camping for something like this."

A confident finger pointed to the topographical map. "What if Severino and I go camping in Hell Hole Canyon?" Jonathon said, smiling.

The frown from his father preceded David's disapproving headshake. "I don't think that's a good area. It's not the safest place to take a first-time camper."

"But no one will bug us there."

David laughed. "There's a good reason no one will. It takes hours to get there, and hell holes and rattlesnakes are everywhere."

"What are those?" Severino asked.

The question turned Jonathon away from the map on his father's desk. "A hell hole is like a sinkhole—it's a deep, open hole in the ground. The canyon has dozens of them. Some of them are natural. Some of them are man-made. The Spaniards used to mine for gold in the area and dug lots of holes up there. We may find some."

"Gold or shafts?" Severino asked.

"Both. You just have to be careful not to fall into a hole. A lot of them were hidden on purpose."

Shifting his weight, David leaned back in his chair and looked at the Peruvian teen. "Rattlesnakes are poisonous serpents we have here in the United States, and you'll definitely find lots of those if you go to Hell Hole. Bob Morton killed thirteen of them in one afternoon when he had to ride in there looking for stray cattle a couple of years ago."

"But it doesn't really matter where you go around Kanosh, Dad. There are rattlesnakes all over the place."

"Yes," David grinned. "So pick a place close to the hospital. That way, if you get bit, you don't have to travel as far."

With his lips pressed into a tight line, Jonathon turned back to the map. "Okay, so where do you think we should go?"

The chair creaked as David leaned forward to study the map. "How about here?"

David's selection caused Jonathon to protest. "Up Kanosh Canyon? No way. Everyone goes there."

"No, head up Kanosh Canyon but take the right road above Corn Creek and go here, to Horseflat Canyon." David pointed to a narrow canyon that passed between the rippled lines of two towering ridges. A blue line indicated a small creek in the bottom of he canyon. "You'll need to hike or pack in on the ATV. Since no motor vehicles can get up the trail head, hardly anyone goes there, so you won't be bugged," he teased. "But once you are there, you can follow the trail on up to Spring Canyon, which is fairly open. There might be some good flat places to camp there, but you'll probably have to build your own fire pit and dig a latrine. Or if you don't want to do that, you can loop out of Spring Canyon to the right. It takes you down through Hollow Ridge Canyon and right back into Kanosh Canyon, where they have some nice campsites, with bathrooms. Just don't head north through Crazy Ridge."

"Why not?"

David smiled. "It will dump you right into Hell Hole Canyon, and I'm trying to keep you out of there. There are a lot of other canyons and trails to explore, okay?"

A nod and smile affirmed Jonathon's consent. "Okay. We'll stay out of Hell Hole." With another glance at the map, Jonathon tapped the site he liked. "I think we'll try to find someplace in Horseflat. If not, then we'll try Spring Canyon further up, but I'll call and let you know where."

"I'd appreciate that. You'll probably have to call from your grandma's house, though. I doubt there's much cell phone service that deep into the mountains, so be careful."

"We will."

David stood from his chair, and the trio moved out of his office. "You have everything all packed?"

"Yup. We're taking off in just a couple of minutes. Should be down to Kanosh before dinner."

"So you'll be gone a week?"

"Maybe a week and a half, but I'll let you know that too."

"Sounds good. Have fun."

The computer screen reflected several minutes of data inputting. Relieved to have his monthly task finally done, Tate prepared to push Save. Just then a new hand reached around in front of him and pushed Backspace. The information from the screen began to disappear in a rapid string of erasing keystrokes.

Tate saw the hand, saw the disappearing information, and did nothing about it. He couldn't. The tiger's-eye ring on the man's thumb told him exactly who stood behind him, and Tate wished he could disappear like each vanishing letter.

THREE

BEEN HERE long?" the man behind Tate asked.

"A while," Tate responded.

"That's too bad." Cole removed his finger from the Backspace key and leaned forward, peering with interest at the partially destroyed information. "Who ordered a diamond turbo blade?"

"I don't know. Some guy asked if I could get one in for him."

"When?"

"Just today."

"How'd he pay for it?"

Uneasy with the questions, Tate hesitated. "Cash."

At the answer, Cole stepped away and let Tate rise from the chair. The young shop owner did, but hesitated to face the older man. Cole questioned him some more. "Did you get his name?"

"I don't remember." Tate avoided looking Cole in the eyes.

Not in the mood for lies or memory lapses, Cole stepped close and lowered his voice. "I suggest you remember."

Uncomfortable, Tate shifted, nervous. "Steven Smith, I think he said."

"Steven Smith. That's a generic name. Is he from around here?"

"No, I don't think so."

"So why is he ordering a high-quality rock blade? What is he going to cut with it?"

"I don't know. He said he already had two but wanted a backup, just in case. A lot of people quarry rocks around here. I order blades all the time."

"Three blades. He either plans to do a lot of cutting over a long period of time, or he's going to be doing a lot of cutting real fast and pushing those blades at high speed." Cole rubbed a hand over his lower face and looked at the man half his age. "When is the blade coming in?"

The question made Tate wince. "He paid for priority shipping."

"Priority? Well that tells me he's planning on pushing those blades at high speed. When will it get here?"

"Tomorrow afternoon."

"He order anything else?"

"No." Tate spoke the truth, though he left out information about the man also paying cash for two sleeping bags.

Cole turned away from the computer. "Well, when he comes in, I want you to find out more. See if he'll tell you what he's cutting and where. And get his license plate; I'll run a check on it and find out who Steven Smith really is."

Without looking up, Tate nodded, though his consent came with duress. In the stiff silence, he fingered the back of his chair. "When did you get to Kanosh?"

Dressed in jeans and a comfortable polo shirt, Cole adjusted the ring on his thumb. "Just now. I came straight to your place, but I've spent the last two days at the University of Utah, researching."

Tate didn't move away from the computer desk. It gave him a small sense of protection and security—two things he'd never felt around Cole. "So, why did you come see me first?"

Gray eyes lifted and Cole watched the uncomfortable man. "You should know that."

"Yeah, I guess I do."

"So, why don't you close down your shop and come with me? We have a few things to do. One of them is to find your cousin, and another is to find that map."

Though emotion twisted and knotted inside of Tate, he moved to the window of his hardware and variety store and turned over the sign to read Closed. Afternoon sun glowed gold through the window-pane, and Tate let an exhale slip through his lips, his eyes closed. Deep inside, he wondered if the sign would ever read Open again.

Jonathon's grandmother met them on the porch, throwing open the door and her Kanosh home to the teenagers. She greeted both of them with a hug and ushered the pair into a house filled with the rich aroma of roast beef.

"I've been so excited for you to come. I've been cooking a roast in the crockpot for you today. I also baked an apple pie for dessert, and there's homemade bread too. I figured that was about as American as food gets for Severino. I hope you are both hungry. You can bring your suitcases in here." The older woman motioned them down the narrow hallway, speaking as she moved. "Jonathon, you can stay in your dad's old room, and Severino, you can stay in the guest room."

Though Jonathon translated for Severino as they followed her, she did not wait for each phrase. Instead, she continued her energetic monologue, her hands talking almost as much as her mouth. "This is the bathroom, and here are clean towels. The toilet paper is under the sink. If you need me to do any laundry for you, just put it in here, and I'll do it. I check it everyday," she lifted the lid to a hamper.

More words and excitement tumbled out of her. "The kitchen is in here but I thought we'd eat in the dining room, since you're company. Dinner will be ready in about half an hour." She paused long enough to give both of them another hug. "Oh, I'm so glad you're here!"

A quick wave of her hand beckoned them through the dining room and back to the living room. "You can bring the rest of your personal things inside and then put your camping gear in the garage or just leave it in the truck. I don't think it will be stolen if you want to leave it in the truck."

"Can we back the truck into the garage?" Adept at conversing with his grandmother, Jonathon managed to slip the question in somewhere between the piano and the sofa.

"Oh, of course, dear." She hugged them each again. "Just go ahead and do whatever you want. Don't let me interfere. I'm going to go finish dinner. Be sure to wash your hands when you're done." Moving on her feet as fast as she spoke, the woman disappeared back into the kitchen.

For a moment, Severino stared after her in stunned disbelief.

"Now I know where your little brother gets it from."

Jonathon laughed and led the Peruvian out of the house, down the front steps, and across the driveway to their truck. "Grandma will talk your ear off, but she's fun . . . and she's a great cook. She'll probably give you a dozen more hugs before the night it through too. She loves to hug."

"Americans hug too much."

Jonathon laughed as they reached the truck. "And Peruvians kiss too much."

"Hey, a *beso* on the cheek is our hug or handshake. It's how we greet each other, and that's not a bad thing if she's cute."

"Yeah—but if she's ugly or has acne, *yuck!*" A mock shudder rolled through Jonathon. It brought a smile to both of their faces and lightened the load of the gear they pulled from the back of the truck.

The whine of an approaching ATV engine interrupted their task and lifted their gazes from the laden truck bed. A machine hummed along the road, the helmeted rider intent on an unknown destination. When the four-wheel-drive vehicle pulled into the driveway, curiosity pushed Jonathon away from the truck to get a better view. The rider dropped the machine into park and cut the engine. Before the motor purred to a halt, hands unsnapped the helmet's chinstrap and removed the fiberglass protection. Long, black hair fell free and tumbled down in a thick, silky curtain across the driver's shoulders and back. Hooking the helmet over the handlebars, the rider stepped off the machine, a smile bright on her brown face.

The two rapid steps that carried her forward closed the distance between them and she gave Jonathon a full-bodied hug. "Jonathon Bradford! You're here!"

Instant recognition filled Jonathon's face and he dropped his duffel bag, thrilled to return the embrace. "Tallie! What are you doing here?"

The question caused her to blend a scowl and a smile on her oval face. She smacked his shoulder, scolding him. "I live in Kanosh, remember? No, you don't remember because you haven't come to see me for a couple of months!" Without giving Jonathon time to respond, Tallie turned toward Severino. "And you must be that really cool Peruvian who saved Jonathon's life. I gotta get a hug. *Mucho gusto.*" Before Jonathon could translate, Tallie stepped forward and gave Severino a welcoming embrace.

A bit uncertain at the domino of events, and with his other hand still holding his duffel bag, Severino responded with a light, one-armed hug. "*Mucho gusto, tambien*," he managed.

Over Tallie's shoulder, Severino lifted his gaze to Jonathon, surprise holding his dark brown eyes. He mouthed a soundless question to Jonathon. "Does she speak Spanish?"

Laughter came from Jonathon. "Hey, Tallie. *¿Hablas Español?*"

Tallie stepped back from the hug and shook her head. "*No mucho.* Not much. Just a little bit." She held up her thumb and forefinger to indicate a tiny amount.

"You are not Spanish?" Severino asked in broken English, his dark eyes taking in her brown complexion.

"No, I'm Paiute."

Confused, Severino looked between the girl and Jonathon. "What is Paiute?" he questioned with care.

An answer, in Spanish, flowed from Jonathon. "Paiutes are Native Americans, indigenous people to the United States, like your Quechua people are to Peru."

A nod of understanding came from Severino and his handsome eyes returned to her. More English came from him slow and careful. "But you speak some Spanish?"

This question Tallie understood. "*Sí.*" A turn to Jonathon shifted her back to English. "There are a lot of Spanish workers that come into the café to eat. They teach me some words, but I don't think all of them are good."

"Why?" Jonathon asked.

"Because when I say them back, they all laugh."

A ribbon of a smile lightened Jonathon's face. "Maybe it's just the way you're pronouncing them—your *acento.*"

"Maybe." Now she tugged on Jonathon's baseball cap. "So, why didn't you tell me you were coming down?"

"I didn't know it myself until last night."

"Your grandma called me when you got here. You should have called or texted or something!"

"It all happened so fast."

"Only emergencies happen too fast for a text, and then you should be able to at least Twitter the details." Tallie lifted the duffle bag Jonathon had dropped. "*Es todo?*"

Reverting to Spanish, Jonathon nodded. "I think so. We'll leave most of it in the truck and just park it in the garage tonight."

"Keep your words *simplé*," she warned him in Spanish then, searching her mind for more Spanish words she knew how to use, Tallie formed another simple question. "How long are you here?"

"Oh, a week, maybe ten days."

Not liking the answer, she shook her head and held up two fingers. "*Dos semanas*, two weeks," she bargained. A shift back to English allowed her to speak with clarity. "Stay two weeks and we'll hang out together when I'm not working at the café. I'm on my dinner break right now."

"That'd be fun."

"We can go fishing . . . you know, *pescado*." She motioned as if casting an imaginary fishing line in front of Severino. Proud of herself, she smiled at Jonathon. "I know that one because the Mexican workers come into the restaurant all the time and order *pescado*."

"Um . . . that's because *pescado* means a dead, cooked fish," Jonathon whispered. "If you want to go fishing and catch live fish from the water, you need to say *ir a pescar*."

"Oh, my bad, *puedo ir a pescar* . . . ."

"Say *podemos*," Jonathon corrected.

"*Podemos ir a pescar*," she announced.

With the success of her Spanish offer, Severino nodded and smiled.

"And we can go horseback riding too," Tallie announced. Not wanting to make a mistake, she turned to Jonathon, her voice whispered close to his ear. "How do you say that in Spanish?"

Jonathon whispered back. "*Montaremos a caballos*."

Turning back, Tallie blurted out the sentence with a smile. Severino lifted startled eyes and looked from her to Jonathon for confirmation or denial of what she'd just said.

Shocked, his own face red with sudden embarrassment, Jonathon covered Tallie's mouth with his hand. "Um . . . you don't say it like that."

"Like what? You told me to say—"

Again he clamped his hand over her mouth before she could repeat her mistake and he spoke to Severino in rapid Spanish. "She's trying to invite you to ride horses this week. She has horses."

Relief washed across Severino's face. "I'd like that, *sí*." Yet, the more he thought about her mistake, the more difficult it became to hide a smile and his dark eyes shifted to hers, laughter sparkling in their chocolate depths.

Cautious, Jonathon released Tallie's mouth but still kept his arms around her, holding her close in case she tried to say it again. "He said it would be fine."

"I know that's what he said. I know what *sí* means. I want to know what *I* said," she countered.

"No, you don't want to know. *I* don't want you to know!" The more Jonathon thought about it, the more startled he felt until he shook his head in amazement and blew out his surprise. "Whew, it's going to take me a moment to recover from that one."

"It was an innocent mistake," she protested.

This time a playful grin accompanied Jonathon's response. "Mistake or not, I didn't know someone could mangle Spanish like that. Yup, I'd say it's definitely your accent." With his arms still enchaining her, Jonathon lifted Tallie off the ground and physically turned her toward the house. "Let's go see if Grandma has enough food to invite you to dinner—it will keep your mouth doing something besides trying to speak too much Spanish for a while."

A quick elbow to his ribs caused Jonathon to *woof* and wince at the same time.

After dinner, Jonathon and Severino walked with Tallie out to her truck. "I gotta get back to the café. Stephanie is covering for me."

"When do you get off?"

"Not until eleven . . . then we have to clean and do the money, so I won't be out of there until midnight. But I have the whole day off tomorrow. What are you guys doing tomorrow?"

At her ATV, Jonathon grinned at her question. "Spending it with you, if you'd like."

"I'd like that. We could show Severino around Kanosh, maybe go shooting or fishing or . . ."

"Don't say it," Jonathon warned.

Tallie giggled. "Okay, but we could spend the whole day together, if you want."

"That would be fun."

As they spoke mostly in English, Severino bent and retrieved a rock from the gravel. The stone entered his hold, and he rolled it over in his hands, looking at it closely before lifting his gaze to the valley around them. "*Riolita*," he said in Spanish.

Stunned by a Spanish word he had never heard before, Jonathon turned. "What?" he questioned.

Severino showed him the red-ribboned rock in his hand and repeated the word. As Jonathon took it in his hands, Tallie stepped forward. "Oh, you found a piece of bacon rock, *tocino*—bacon. I know that word is right, because of the café."

Jonathon turned to her. "What's bacon rock?"

She shrugged. "It's just some rock we have around here."

"*¿Aqui?*" Excitement brightened Severino's eyes and face as he followed enough of their English to understand.

She smiled. "*Sí.* Here. Well, no, not *right* here. We have it out in the desert, but it's all over out there." She lifted the rock from Jonathon's hand and showed them the stripes of brown, red, and cream. "We call it bacon rock because it looks like a piece of raw bacon. See?"

Enthusiasm brought a nod from Severino and Spanish tumbled from his mouth. Then his eyes lifted and his hand swept across the horizon. He looked back at her for confirmation.

"Ahh . . ." Stalled in their communication, Tallie looked at Jonathon for help.

"He says this kind of rock comes from volcanoes, and wants to know where they are."

"The volcanoes or the rock?"

"Both"

"Ummm . . . well, the rocks are everywhere and volcanoes are all dead. *Muertos.*" Tallie managed.

"*Inactivos,*" Severino nodded his understanding. "*¿Puedo verlos?*"

Startled by the question, Jonathon and Tallie exchanged glances. Hesitant, Tallie shrugged. "You want to see the volcanoes? *Bueno, sí,* if you want," she responded.

"I do," he responded. "*Gracias.*"

"We could go see them in the morning, before it gets too hot. What time do you guys want to leave tomorrow?"

Jonathon answered the question. "How 'bout we pick you up around nine?"

She retrieved her helmet from the handlebars. "Sounds good, but don't go to my old house. I am living on my own now. I'm renting the Dunbar place; well, actually, I'm not renting it. They wanted someone to keep up the yard and maintain the place this summer, so I'm just trading work for rent until I go to college this fall."

"Sounds great."

"Do you know where it is?"

"Yup."

"Good. I'll see you tomorrow morning at nine." She gave them each another hug and deposited the rock back in Severino's hand. Shorts and lean brown legs swung onto the ATV. A deft move of her hands captured her glossy black hair and secured it into a ponytail. She then bent forward, poured the entire length into her helmet, and tugged the protective gear on over her head, snapping the chinstrap back into place. Finished, she lifted her gaze to them and her eyes and face smiled. "See you *mañana*."

The ATV awoke and she backed it out of the driveway before a final wave of her hand sent her back down the road to work.

Severino rolled the stone over in his hand. "Bacon rock, I like that."

"What did you call it, *riolita*?" Jonathon asked.

"*Sí*, it is a common rock around large volcanoes. Rhyolite lava comes out very thick and slow, like toothpaste being squeezed from a tube, so it piles up in tall ridges and bands instead of spreading out into flat lava flows. When it cools, the minerals separate into layers, according to weight, and it looks like this."

"Like bacon," Jonathon teased. "How do you know that?"

A shrug lifted Severino's shoulders. "There are a few volcanoes in Peru." Now he nodded in the direction Tallie had taken. "So, are you and Tallie a couple?"

The question caused Jonathon to laugh out loud. "Not at all."

"She hugged you."

"She hugged you too, and she hugged my grandma. She hugs everyone. She's American. We hug too much, remember?" A smile came from Severino but he remained quiet waiting for Jonathon's answer. "Nah, I've known Tallie all my life. We played together every summer growing up. Now we get together every time I come down. She's a year older than me and more like a big sister. She just graduated from high school in May."

"You have a cute big sister," he teased.

"Yeah, well—even if your sister *is* cute, you still don't date her. You know that."

Agreement nodded Severino's head. "*Sí.* My sister, Delia, is cute but I'd never date her. I *know* her!"

Laughter slid out of Jonathon. "Exactly. I feel the same way about Tallie. She's cute, she's really fun to be with, but someone else can date her."

Rather than go inside, the two sat down on the front steps, content to watch the quiet town settle in for the evening.

"So, do you have a girlfriend down in Peru?" Jonathon asked.

"No."

"Why not?"

With his forearms resting on his knees, Severino glanced down the street, his eyes somber as they watched a dog trot into a neighboring yard. "I run with the Shining Path, remember? The girls know that and they are all afraid, as they should be."

Jonathon saw and heard the strain. "You need to get out," he offered.

A sad smile partnered with Severino's headshake. "It's not that easy."

"Go to school in Lima. You know my family wants to pay for your education."

Now the Peruvian laughed. "The Shining Path is in Lima too. How do you think they found you so fast when you were in the hospital?" He toed at a small rock on the step. "I'm not sure I can get out. Besides, I'm getting close to him."

The news surprised Jonathon. "The man who killed you father?"

Looking up, Severino nodded. "He's called *El Cernador.*"

Unsure of the term, Jonathon rolled it around in his mind. "The Sifter?"

"*Sí.* It is because he sifts out those who will live and those who will die."

"That doesn't sound too promising. What if he finds out about you and decides you will die?"

A shrug of shoulders became Severino's first response. "Then I die. Thanks to your family, Delia is in a good high school in Lima and getting good marks. Already the University of Cayetano Heredia is watching her, as are several other universities. She may even get a *beca* to attend. I think you call them scholarships. Then she will get a good job and can support my mother."

Frustration drove Jonathon's gaze aside for a moment, then back again. "Severino, you should be going to college too. Then both of you can help your mother. Forget this obsession to catch your father's killer. Do something with your life. You're too smart to do nothing."

The words Jonathon chose did not settle well with Severino and he turned hardened eyes at the American. "I am doing something. Just because you do not agree with what I am doing does not make my choice, or my life, *nothing.*"

The realization that he had offended Severino came with clarity and Jonathon sat back. "I didn't mean that. I'm sorry. It's just that I see how intelligent you are. You speak two languages fluently and are picking up English fast. You remember *everything.* Good grief, you even know about rocks! It just seems to me there must be something else you can do besides having *El Cernador* point a gun at you and decide if you will die. I'm betting if your father was here, he'd want you to go to college."

The final comment moved deep inside Severino. He lowered his voice, picking up a broken blade of grass laying on the step between his feet. "If my father was here, I wouldn't need to find his killer."

FOUR

DARKNESS POSSESSED the spaces between the trees and turned gnarled branches into demons, rocks into specters. Thick shadows draped over the mountainside and shrouded the landscape. A few sounds managed to pierce the heavy blackness— the moan of trees, the scrape of movement on rock. Above the ground, an occasional bat broke through night's obscurity, the clicking sound of its sonar leading it around ghoulish images and dangers.

On the shale-shattered surface, Tate did not look up. The sight of darkness, thickening around him, choked out his nerve. Any other mountain, any other canyon would be fine. A night in the woods did not bother him—his current location did. He never wanted to go into Hell Hole Canyon and avoid the sink holes and the rattlesnakes.

Mostly, though, he wanted to avoid the spirits interred within the canyon's steep walls.

People who spent the night here told of ghostlike figures and beings moving across the canyon. They also heard eerie sounds: like Indian chanting—Ancient Ones summoning up unseen powers to drive away unbelievers from their sacred mountains.

Though not a Native American, Tate respected their beliefs and legends, and he worried about angering them—and the spirits of their ancestors. The Native Americans around Kanosh did not go up into the Pahvant Mountains after dark. They left that mountain range to the spirits of their dead. They especially did not go near Hell Hole Canyon. Now Tate stood alone in the Pahvants, in the grasp of Hell Hole Canyon—at night. The combination did not allow his nerves to settle.

Of course, Cole Matthews didn't fear ghosts or people. That's why he sent Tate into the canyon that afternoon to take current pictures of the area. Though Tate didn't want to be there, he knew his position, and the fear of repercussions—even jail time—drove the twenty-six-year-old into the mountains.

A long hike from the nearest vehicle access point into the canyon took more time than he had daylight. Now the sun had settled into its western bed, and Tate found himself imprisoned by the dark.

A lifetime spent in the mountains left Tate confident in the out-doors, even at night, but the energy that flowed through Hell Hole Canyon eroded all that. He knew the history of the canyon, and he did not want to see a ghost or spirit from that past emerge out of the shadows to haunt him.

The camera hung like a noose around his neck and a pistol rode, heavy and clumsy, against his hip as Tate continued his treacherous passage out of the canyon. The camera came for Cole, the gun came for rattlesnakes, but Tate did not even bring a flashlight for himself. Of course, he had not intended to be in the canyon after dark. He had told himself he would be back in Kanosh long before night fell, but he didn't realize the hike would be so long or difficult.

A distinct noise, like a growl of deep hate, roiled up through the night behind him, startling the blood in Tate's veins. Fear brought his abrupt turn on the steep slope, and he lost his footing. Shale shifted away beneath him and he fell, sliding several feet down the rocky face. Dead limbs and protruding rocks grabbed and cut at him, ripping his clothes and leaving bloody trails on his skin. Frantic, his hands found a cedar branch in the darkness that became his anchor, ending his slide with a sudden stop. A roll brought him to his knees, and he scrambled to his feet, afraid of whatever just made that sound. With eyes terrified of what he might see, Tate's gaze pried the dark night, trying to open the blackness.

For several seconds, he nervously scanned the shadows. When his frightened search found nothing, temporary relief cooled his back and neck. Then the fear of the unknown heated his nerves, and he contin-ued down, faster now.

Then he heard it. Not the howl of a wolf or the scream of a mountain lion—a strange, inhuman wail that echoed off the canyon walls until the flesh on his body tightened with fear and he could not move. The eerie sound, like the cry of a banshee, deepened in pitch to an ominous rumble—so low and powerful he couldn't determine the creature's location in the darkness. He did know, however, the sound of a predator.

The growl circled around him, only a few yards away, held in the black throat of night. Frightened, he slid his pistol out of the leather holster and pressed off the safety. In the darkness, the action made a small *click* and he heard a large animal shift through the brush. The pistol tracked the movement, and Tate dropped down the slope, side-stepping the steep face. Having a ready-to-fire gun in his hand made the descent more dangerous, but Tate no longer cared about finding easy steps down the canyon. Safety inside the cab of his truck waited only several hundred yards away.

The growl returned, this time to his right. He yelled at it, hoping the sound of a human voice would chase the creature away, but the beast, and its growls, raised into another inhuman wail of fury. Though Tate pointed the gun in its direction, a lifetime of training prevented him from pulling the trigger until he could see his target. For several seconds he held a blind point on the creature and then, frustrated, Tate tipped the muzzle toward the sky and resumed his descent.

Buried from Tate's sight, the large animal continued its own, controlled path down the slope, keeping pace with him a dozen yards away. Sometimes it growled as it tracked him. Other times an eerie silence fell over the canyon, and then Tate would jump and spin as the thing growled again, in a different location.

Or maybe more than one creature tracked him.

Twice Tate saw movement between the trees, but by the time he swung the pistol there, the shadow had fled. He needed light, just enough to spot the creature—then he could shoot.

The camera swung against his chest, and Tate remembered its built-in flash.

Lifting the camera with his free hand, Tate pointed it in the direction he'd last sensed the beast. His finger depressed the shutter, and light exploded through the night, freezing the trees and bushes into gnarled phantoms that disappeared back into darkness. Yet the light had been enough and Tate caught a glimpse of yellow hair as something bolted away.

For that second he wondered if a mountain lion followed him. The Pahvants had mountain lions—but then the growl returned and he knew no mountain lion sounded like that.

That realization frightened him even more. He could deal with a mountain lion. The unknown felt more terrifying. Tate hastened his step and passed from the trees out into the open slope. Relief flooded through his veins. Moonlight reflected off his truck, still three hundred treacherous feet below. He quickened his descent until he careened down the mountain, rocks and pebbles sliding and tumbling down the slope ahead of every step.

The creature behind seemed to know time and distance were fading. It moved closer, decreasing the distance between them. Tate could smell it. The thing reeked of an open tomb—of earth and death—and Tate knew it was no normal predator.

This time, a rock caught his boot, and he sprawled forward, landing face first, skidding down the slope. The jarring fall knocked the pistol from his hand, and the gun fired. Gunpowder illuminated the darkness as it spat out of the end of the muzzle, sending the bullet into the night.

The noise first startled then enraged the beast, and the animal's fury filled the canyon.

Behind him, Tate heard the sound of the creature exit the trees, advancing with full speed down the slope. Yelling in fear and protest, Tate twisted on the ground, scrambling to his feet. Then he saw it.

Behind him came a hideous creature. With glowing eyes and a half-human face, it snarled rage as it flashed down the mountain after him.

At the awful, surreal image behind him, everything inside of Tate stopped functioning—his lungs, his heart, his feet, even his mind. No wolf, no cougar, no human looked like that. The beast combined all of them in its awful visage.

Then Tate roared in terror and grabbed for the only thing he had. The camera flashed and illuminated the night, blinding the creature and giving Tate a chance to turn toward safety only a few more yards away.

Cursing in terror, leaving his pistol lost to the night, he sprinted the last few feet down the slope, hitting the side of the truck with both hands to stop his rapid descent. Fear filled him and escaped in a panicked cry as he fumbled with the door. All around him, the awful smell increased. With a jerk, he flung open the door, threw himself into the cab of his truck, and pulled the door shut just as the hideous creature slammed against the truck.

He screamed and fell back against the seat. The half-human face that attacked the window had blue eyes.

Terrified, Tate turned the engine to life, and it responded instantly. Throwing the truck into gear, he accelerated down the mountain, but the creature did not leave. Racing beside his truck, it kept pace, trying to break through the glass, trying to get to him. Gnarled teeth and fangs snapped at him through the glass, leaving streaks of saliva down the window. Yellow fur rippled over sinewy muscles, and the otherworld beast threw its powerful body at the door. Tate felt the truck shake, heard the hideous clawing of nails as the fiend scraped at the door handle, tearing through the paint. Determined to get inside the cab, the monster ran beside the truck and attacked the door with fury.

More fearful of the creature than of the mountain, Tate accelerated to dangerous speeds until the thing fell behind, disappearing into the night.

Not many customers came into the diner just before closing. Fewer still came in torn and bloodied and shaking with fear. When the door chime sounded and Tallie saw the battered man stagger through the doorway, she dropped her broom and grabbed a clean towel, horrified by the sight.

"Tate! What happened?"

"Tallie, I'm so sorry."

At his side, she slid her brown arm around his waist and pressed the rag against a nasty cut on his forehead. "Sorry for what?"

"Sorry for everything. It's all my fault."

"What's your fault?"

"All of it."

"Sit down, Tate. You're not making any sense. What happened?"

He sank onto the cushioned seat of a booth and caught his head in his hand. For a long time he shook—hard—and could not speak.

"I'm going to get some water, Tate. I'll be right back." Tallie returned behind the counter and filled a tub with warm, soapy water. She also gathered some more towels. The other worker filled a glass with cold water. Both returned to the booth with their items. Tate took the glass of cold water and swallowed it, still shaking.

In the booth next to her injured friend, Tallie began to sponge the blood and dirt off his wounds. "Tate, were you in a fight or a car accident?"

"Neither."

"Then how did you get so hurt? Have you been drinking?"

"No!" He sat back in the booth and ran trembling hands over his face. Fear and shock painted age on his features. "I upset them, Tallie."

"Upset who?"

"The spirits of your ancestors!"

"What?"

"In Hell Hole Canyon."

The location stunned Tallie and she slowed for a minute. "Why did you go there after dark, Tate?"

"I didn't go there after dark. I went there during the day and got stuck there after dark."

Tallie moved away his blood-soaked sleeve to reveal a gash on his upper arm. She pressed a clean towel against it. "What were you doing up there?"

Unwilling and unable to give her an answer, Tate could only provide her with a nervous shake of his head. "I shouldn't have gone at all but I had to take pictures of the canyon. When it got dark, it was there. It came after me. I saw it. I looked in its eyes, and now it's going to kill me. It has blue eyes, Tallie. Blue eyes!" He rocked forward and swore in anguish. "I'm a dead man." The words emerged as torn and disjointed as the man.

"You're not making any sense, Tate. I think you ought to go the hospital in Fillmore."

Hazel eyes shifted to hers, filled with fear and regret. "Maybe I should just go back and let it kill me. If I died, things would be better for you and for me."

Frustrated, Tallie tucked her silken black hair behind one ear. Using one hand, she continued to hold the cloth tight against his arm.

With her other hand, she dipped a second towel into the warm water. This she used in gentle movements against his face, trying to clean up the old blood without causing new blood to spill from the cuts that littered his features. "You're talking nonsense. Nothing would be better if you died."

A swallow wrenched down his throat. "Yes it would, Tallie. You don't know everything. If you did, you'd never forgive me. It's here, and I brought it here."

"What's here, Tate?"

"A Skinwalker," he breathed, "and I saw it. It has blue eyes and blond hair and it tried to kill me."

At his words, Tallie stopped working on him and lifted horrified eyes. In the small space of the booth, their gazes locked, and the rest of the world ceased to exist. Unable to hide the shocked expression on her face, Tallie stared at him while thoughts bled through her mind.

As a young Paiute, Tallie had never been frightened of the boogie-man, but let her brothers whisper that a Skinwalker was coming and she could not sleep for days. Even the name frightened her—for even a whisper could draw their attention and their hatred. They would come, crossing thousands of miles, just to silence the whispers and destroy the one who spoke of them.

Even Native American legends spoke in hushed ways of the Skinwalkers, evil men bent on vengeance and destruction. She knew they spent years mastering the darkest magic so they could change at will into animals and take on the traits and abilities of their chosen creature. To achieve that level of malevolence, Skinwalkers had to kill someone in their own family and then make oaths with the Dark Warrior. Only then could they prove their souls black enough to become Skinwalkers. When a Skinwalker appeared, they always had a reason—a specific human target. Always people died or disappeared at their arrival.

Now Tate sat in the café, bleeding and upset, telling her had seen one in Hell Hole Canyon.

Time slipped by in silence, and Tallie struggled to piece together her shattered world. She'd known Tate all of her life, known him to be quiet and strong, but he had obviously experienced something that shook him to his soul. Had he really seen a Skinwalker? Did they really exist?

She couldn't answer that question. She only knew the legends: if a Skinwalker revealed himself to a white man, things were going to go very bad for everyone.

In the café, only the quiet sound of Tate's blood dripping to the table punctuated the stillness. Finally, Tallie swallowed and braved a question. "Tate, are you sure?" she whispered.

"I have a picture of it, Tallie. Yes, I'm sure." With trembling hands, he lifted the camera from around his neck and set it on the table in front of him. He shook but managed to activate the images. When the last photo loaded onto the screen, he turned it toward her, and Tallie choked in horror. A half-human face, blurred by speed, charged the camera from above, but the hideous creature could still be seen. Tallie recoiled.

Understanding her fear, Tate withdrew the camera from her vision and turned the image back toward him. Numb, he stared at the photo, willing himself to face the terror he felt. In disbelief, Tate shook his head. "It attacked my truck, Tallie. My door is all torn up on the driver's side. I'm not making this up. It's real. A Skinwalker has come to Kanosh."

A hand shook Steven from his sleep. At two in the morning, Steven had to force open his eyes, blink, then force them to reopen wider than before. His body did not want to wake up.

Above him, Ryan straightened his blond hair and returned his cap to its position. "It's been quiet tonight," Ryan whispered, looking around, the intense blue of his eyes well-adjusted to the dark. "Not a living soul or farmer's truck out this way since midnight." He rolled his shoulder muscles, stretching them.

Steven sat up and pushed back his sleeping bag. "I'm not worried about souls or farmer's trucks. I'm worried about rattlesnakes."

"Haven't seen any of those pass by either." Ryan nodded toward the edge of camp. "You can sit on that rock right there. It's uncomfortable, but it will keep you awake and gives you a good view of the entire area."

The two traded positions in the sparse camp. They had no campfire and no lanterns, and their flashlights lay untouched in their packs. They'd set up camp in the dark and remained in the dark to avoid attracting attention.

Used to the night's light from his four hours of watching the ridge, Ryan deftly moved to his sleeping bag. Adrenaline pumped through his veins and he knew it would take him a while to fall asleep. It always did on nights like these.

From his perch on the rock, Steven yawned and tried to draw more oxygen into his body. It would take him time to wake up.

To help Steven and give his own body time to unwind, Ryan spoke in quiet tones. "Are you married?"

"Yeah. Got two kids and one on the way."

"So, what does your wife think about your playing antiquities thief this week?"

"I didn't tell her."

The comment stunned Ryan and he turned to look at the man. "So where does she think you are?"

"Training for my desk job."

Ryan flinched at the answer, remembering his own share of lies—lies he told his wife to cover his real life. In the dark night, Ryan said nothing.

Steven lifted the night vision binoculars to his eyes, scanning the ridge several hundred yards away. He took his turn at making conversation. "So, are you married?"

"For two more weeks."

Surprised, Steven turned to look at the blond laying on top of his sleeping bag. "Wanna explain that one?"

"About the time you get back from your 'job training,' my wife will have all the divorce papers drawn up and ready for me. All I have to do is sign them."

"I'm sorry."

On the bag, Ryan shrugged. "It happens." A moment of thought passed through him. "About three years ago, I made the mistake of telling my wife what I really did for a living. She put up with it for a while, until she decided she couldn't tolerate me, or my job, any longer. Who knows, maybe I should have kept quiet about everything, let her keep thinking all I ever did was go to a nice, safe office from nine to five every day, with a week or two away for occasional 'job training'."

Steven lowered the binoculars. Ryan seemed sad—almost

human—tonight. Quiet thoughts rolled through Steven's mind. "You two have any kids?"

"No, so that's good, I guess."

"Yeah, I guess. So, how long have you two been married?"

Ryan stared up into the star-strewn sky. "Nine years. And you?"

A shift on the rock turned Steven in a different direction and he resumed scanning the dark landscape. "We're going to be celebrating our sixth anniversary next month."

"Three kids in six years? You have been busy."

With the binoculars still pressed to his face, Steven chuckled. "Yeah, they keep us busy. Our oldest is four, and he's all boy. We also have a two-year-old girl who has me wrapped around her little finger just like her mama. Then my wife told me just last week she's due again, in February."

Ryan canted his eyes to look at him. "And what did you think about that news?"

A smile crept out from beneath Steven's binoculars, his eyes still focused on the dark terrain. "I enjoy being a dad."

The comment forced Ryan's gaze away from Steven and he stared up into the star-filled night. Above him the heavens stayed still as the earth moved. Finally, Ryan's voice grew serious. "Maybe you need to consider doing something else. You play this game long enough and you're going to wind up dead in a ravine somewhere."

"I need the money."

"No one needs it that bad."

"Maybe, but right now . . . it pays the bills." Moving his binoculars south, across the valley, Steven questioned his partner. "So, why do you do it?"

One word emerged from Ryan's mouth. "Cole."

"I guess I should have known that. Why the vendetta?"

For a long time, Ryan lay still on his sleeping bag, not sure he wanted to answer. Silence settled over their camp. Night sounds drifted across the darkness.

Then, from the rock, Steven tensed. "We got company."

Without prodding, Ryan retrieved his own night vision binoculars and rolled to his knees. "Where?"

"About two miles to the southeast."

The blond did not have to raise his optics to see. A light

glimmered on the front of South Twin Peak.

From the view of his binoculars, Steven queried the source "Is it a truck?"

"If it is, it only has one headlight and that would be the brightest headlight I've ever seen." Ryan joined Steven and the two watched the light through their binoculars.

"Think someone's out spotlighting?"

Ryan shook his head. "No. The light isn't casting a beam. It's just . . . there."

"I don't remember a road being over there," Steven whispered.

"There's not." Together the pair watched the brilliant white glow then Ryan felt a surge of tension. "It's moving toward us."

Steven's brow frowned over his optics. "How can you tell? It's still too far away."

"The light has a faint blue glow."

Dumbfounded, Steven lowered his binoculars and started at his partner. "What?"

Without removing his eyes from the light, Ryan spoke in hushed explanation. "Doppler's Blue Effect. All color is transmitted on light waves. When the distance between you and any moving light source shortens, the light waves shorten and that releases a faint blue tint. That means, if you have good eyesight, you can pick up a slight blue color in the light."

"You're kidding."

"Dead serious. That white light has pale blue glow to it. That means it's moving toward us."

Puzzled, Steven returned his attention to the light and felt cold move through his body. The light had indeed developed a pale, barely perceptible blue glow.

Crouched in the desert beside him, Ryan continued to speak, his voice low. "When a lighted object moves away from you, the light waves between the object and your eyes lengthen, and the light picks up a golden glow. That's called Doppler's Red Effect. Watch a train's headlight next time one passes. You'll see it."

"How do you know this stuff?"

"Spend enough nights alone in the dark, waiting for someone to ambush you and you'll start noticing every detail, even color differences in light."

Out in the desert, the light continued to move in a slow, straight path toward them.

"Think someone knows we're out here?"

"I don't know." Ryan shifted and checked his pistol nestled close in its holster. The movement caused Steven to do the same.

"See anything yet?"

"No, just the light." Frustrated, Ryan lowered his binoculars and listened. Through the night, no sound of a motor approached his ears. He settled lower over the sagebrush and returned the optics to his eyes.

The bright light reached the bottom of South Twin Peak and then moved out onto the flat. The men could now see it swaying slightly, back and forth, as if being carried by someone walking. Without a word, Ryan scooted backward across the camp and retrieved a heat sensing scope from his bag. Skill kept the sound minimal in the night.

"This should tell us what's around that light," he whispered. Lifting the device, he looked through the lens, questioned what he saw and looked at the light with his own eyes.

"What did you see?"

"Nothing," Ryan replied. "It isn't showing any heat readings at all."

Steven frowned. "That's impossible. That light is too bright. It has to be producing heat, and, if someone is carrying it or riding in a truck, that will produce heat too."

To test the optics, Ryan viewed Steven through the lens, and the man's image erupted into a rainbow of colors. He returned the device to the light. "I got a jackrabbit hopping away out there, but the light still isn't registering."

"Let me see."

In the dark, they passed the scope. Steven sighted in through the lens, readjusted his location, sighted again, and breathed out a quiet curse. "This is weird."

"Get down. Whatever it is, it's coming this way."

Both men lowered themselves to the earth, trying to follow the light with their binoculars as it crossed the valley, in a slow, straight line, to their camp, appearing to pass right over the top of the sage.

"I'm not hearing anything yet," Ryan growled.

"Me neither. What *is* that thing?"

"I don't know. It isn't even illuminating the earth around it. It's like it is just a light."

"A very bright light. I don't like this," Steven whispered.

When the light approached to within a hundred feet, the men fell silent, watching the orb. At their silence, the light held still, no longer advancing. For two full minutes, nothing moved on the desert floor.

The stationary light now fed a whiteness into the night that did not hurt the men's eyes and they could stare directly at its epicenter. In silence, the men tried to figure out what generated the glow and why the light did not cast a beam or create heat.

Ryan motioned to Steven, pointing to the left, his mouth forming his thoughts but no sound. "Stay here. I'm going to circle around."

Steven shook his head in warning, but Ryan had already left, keeping low in the bushes. Turning his attention back to the light, Steven watched, horrified, as the light reacted to Ryan and turned to track his movements, watching them.

The light *knew* they were there.

FIVE

O H, YOU look terrible."

"Gee, thanks, Jonathon. Good morning to you too." Tallie moved across the living room, her long hair swinging free and loose down her back. She wore hiking boots with thick socks rolled over the tops of her boots, khaki safari shorts, and a white T-shirt. Near the front door, Severino stood silent, watching.

"That's not what I meant," Jonathon apologized. "It's just that you look like you had a pretty rough night last night."

She rolled her eyes. "You're not dazzling me with your compliments, Jonathon." Dark eyes shifted their gaze to the quiet Peruvian and Tallie smiled, circling her forefinger near her temple. "Jonathon is *loco*." The unexpected words and actions brought a laugh from Severino, his face lifting into a handsome smile.

Frustrated, Jonathon threw out his hands. "Okay, fine. You look absolutely gorgeous! *¡Preciosa!*"

She stopped. "Well, thank you. It's about time you said something kind."

At the door, Severino smiled and lowered his head. He understood only part of their banter, but he knew they were playing with each other.

"Yes, you're beautiful, *bonita*, breathtaking." Jonathon fired a string of compliments in quick succession, alternating between Spanish and

English, until his voice changed. "So what's different this morning?"

She laughed out loud. "Ah . . . honey stops fast when it's cold; so do compliments when they aren't sincere." Smiling with tease, she retrieved a key and inserted it into the lock on a gun safe.

"Tallie!"

The tone of his voice seemed to be the key she needed, and, as the safe's lock opened, she opened up too. Her voice sobered. "I didn't get much sleep last night. I had to take a friend to the hospital."

"What happened?"

"He had an accident up in the mountains. He's fine, though. They stitched him up, gave him something to stop the pain and help him sleep, and then I took him home. I didn't get back to my place until four thirty this morning."

"I'm sorry. I didn't know. We can do this later, if you'd like."

"Nope. Now is fine. Here, take this." She lifted a rifle out of its cradle. She passed it to Jonathon as she used a second key to unlock a cabinet and retrieved a couple of boxes of ammunition.

"What's the gun for?" Jonathon asked.

"You never take off around here without one. You never know what you might need it for . . . a tin can . . . a rattlesnake . . . something bigger. You ready?"

"Sure," Jonathon offered.

From across the room, Tallie caught Severino's gaze, and her smile warmed. "Let's go, then." Severino returned the smile and bowed his head in agreement.

The bark of a gunshot echoed across the valley. In protest, the final tin can flew up into the air, catching the sunlight. Watching the trajectory of the rusted target, Tallie smiled. "Nice shooting, Jonathon."

Tipping the muzzle up, he reloaded the rifle and passed the weapon back to her. "Thank you. Now see if you can beat that."

"Five shots and only three cans hit . . . yeah, I can beat that, no problem." Settling over the hood of Jonathon's truck, she snugged the rifle against her shoulder, sighted in on her target, and pulled the trigger.

Click.

The tiny noise sounded ominous and filled the gravel pit. Knowing what the sound meant, Tallie held still, her gun still on target, waiting to see if the bullet would hang fire. When enough time passed, a frown crossed her face. "Jonathon Bradford. What did you do to my gun?"

"Nothing."

She rolled the gun to the side to look at the action. "You just don't want me to outshoot you."

Before she could explore the misfire further, Severino's hand closed around the rifle's action. "*A ver*," he offered. "Let me see." He lifted the gun out of her surprised hands.

"No," she protested. "It's dangerous. You can't pull the trigger . . ."

His dark eyes held hers, and, by feel, he opened the action and ejected the jammed shell. Now his gaze shifted and his eyes checked the primer on the cartridge, noting the small dent left by the firing pin, telling him the gun worked properly. The shell had been defective. Discarding the misfired round, he checked the chamber visually and with his finger, and then reloaded a fresh shell.

Working the action, he pumped the shell into the chamber. With a quick lift to his shoulder, he found the next target then pulled the trigger, shooting the rifle without using the truck's hood as a rest. The bullet blew across the gravel pit and into its mark. With rapid movement, Severino worked the action again, fired again, and a second bullet hit its target. Reloading and firing in rapid succession, three more bullets slammed through three more targets.

Stunned, Tallie straightened and looked at Severino. "Where did you learn to handle a rifle like that?"

Emotion did not appear on his face. "Peru."

Turning back to Jonathon, she questioned him. "Did you know he could shoot like that?"

Amazed, Jonathon shook his head, recalling the rifle Severino held on him the first time they met. "No. I had no idea . . . and that may have been a good thing."

Trying to sort through many puzzling questions, Tallie looked straight into Severino's eyes, but she did not remove the rifle from his hold. Never shifting her gaze from his face, Tallie spoke in English, letting Jonathon translate. "Sometime you're going to tell me how a kid, from the mountains of Peru, learned to handle a rifle like an expert."

With care, Severino placed the rifle back into her hands. "Maybe sometime," he returned in broken English, "but not now."

The trio climbed into Jonathon's truck and headed west, on Black Rock Road to show Severino volcanic remnants. Plumes of dust from the gravel road spat up behind them. An occasional jackrabbit zigged and zagged away from the road, and once they saw a lone antelope turn its head to watch. Fifteen miles, then twenty, passed under the truck tires as the three talked. With Severino's broken English, Tallie's little Spanish, and Jonathon's translations, conversation flowed easily between them.

Jonathon angled the truck to miss a large rock on the road. "So, how come you are interested in volcanoes?"

A shrug came with Severino's answer. "The Andes Mountains were formed by volcanic action and tectonic shift."

"Tectonic shift?"

"*Sí*, you know—when two land plates slide together. Peru sits on the edge of the Nazca plate and the South American plate. When the two plates slide together, it causes earthquakes, or *terremotos,* and volcanic activity. We have a lot of both in Peru."

Startled, Tallie joined the conversation. "You still have volcanoes in Peru?"

"*Sí*, Peru has about three dozen, but Chile has almost one hundred active volcanoes. In fact, more than fifty volcanoes have erupted in South America in the last decade alone."

Jonathon whistled. "That's at least five eruptions every year. That's a lot."

"The most powerful eruption in all of South American happened in Arequipa in the 1600s. That volcano is less than two hundred miles from my home. There are volcanoes all around me."

So, how did you learn this stuff? Do they teach it in school?"

Severino looked away, watching the landscape pass outside the passenger window. "I didn't go to school very much. I had to help provide for my family."

The unusual comment turned Tallie to look at Severino. Though he could feel her gaze on him, he continued to stare out the side window. She tucked strands of hair behind her ear but the wind, rushing into the cab, continued to free them. "So, you learned most of this stuff on your own, then."

"I studied books when I could find them and asked a lot of

questions. My friend Carlos taught me a lot. You have to be able to read the earth and the rocks to stay safe in the Andes Mountains." Not wanting to mention the hidden Inca tunnels that crisscrossed Peru, Severino chose his words with care and shifted a glance at Tallie.

As one of the only Americans to see, and survive, the ancient tunnel system, Jonathon understood Severino's caution. Built by the Incas, the empire had used those tunnels to escape the conquistadors centuries ago. They had taken their families, herds, gold, and sacred mummies into the tunnels and disappeared, becoming known to history as the Lost Inca Empire.

Jonathon stumbled into the ancient secret when he fell into a tunnel and became lost. He had seen their sacred mummies and baskets of gold and could have claimed instant wealth and fame by telling the world what he discovered; but Jonathon had also seen the Inca culture and promised Severino he would not be the one to reveal the tunnels to the world. The secret of the Incas, their survival, their tunnel system, and their mummies would be revealed through a descendant of the Inca Empire. Severino and the other tunnel runners would be the ones to tell the world the truth . . . not Jonathon.

"So, how do you read the earth and the rocks?" Tallie questioned, letting Jonathon help her with words she did not know.

"There are signs. If you watch for them, you can tell when an earthquake or volcanic eruption is coming."

"And you know how to read them?"

"Some."

Before Tallie could ask more, Jonathon swerved the truck and then braked hard. The sudden skidding over gravel threw everyone forward and changed their focus. "Rattlesnake on the road," Jonathon explained.

With a shift of the gears, Jonathon put the truck in reverse and backed down the road, looking out his window for the errant reptile. Finding it, he maneuvered the truck around the creature, placing the snake on Severino's side of the vehicle.

"Look out your window. That's a rattlesnake. You want to stay away from them. If you see one, go in the opposite direction. If you hear one, find out where it is before your next step."

Severino looked down at the three-foot rattler increasing its speed, trying to get off the gravel road and reach the safety of the desert foliage. "What does it sound like?"

The question brought a grin from Jonathon. Locking the truck in park, he opened the driver's door. The movement startled Tallie and she placed a hand on his forearm. "What are you doing?"

"I'm gonna let Severino hear what it sounds like."

"That's stupid. You'll get bit."

"No, I won't. If Severino is going to spend any time in this country, he needs to know what a rattlesnake looks like and sounds like." Dropping to the graveled road, Jonathon walked around the front of the truck, bending to scoop up some small rocks as he moved. As he came into view of the snake, he tossed the pebbles at the reptile, hoping it would coil in response. The rocks only propelled the snake faster across the gravel and toward the edge of the road.

"Oh, no you don't!" Jonathon rushed to the shoulder, grabbed a broken sage branch from the small barrow pit and raced the serpent to its retreat. With the branch as his prod, Jonathon poked the poisonous snake. This time, the disturbance worked and the rattler coiled its body into a serpentine position to face the threat. The tip of its tail rattled a warning.

A grin lifted Jonathon's face toward the truck. "Hear that? Sometimes insects in the grass can sound like that, but you always want to be careful when you hear the sound because it may be a snake."

"Jonathon, leave it alone and get back in here," Tallie urged.

Now the passenger door open and Severino stepped to the ground. With his dark eyes on the serpent, the Peruvian moved around the creature to stand by his friend. Tallie groaned her frustration from the protected interior of the truck. "Oh, you guys are crazy . . . *loco*." Yet she too climbed out of the truck.

"Got your gun?" Jonathon asked.

"Yes, but I'm not going to shoot it."

"Then I will."

"No! It's not doing anything except being threatened by you. Let it go."

"Not yet."

"When?"

"After I show Severino how it bites."

Horrified by the comment, Tallie pulled on Jonathon's arm. "You're being stupid."

"No, I'm not." Light brown eyes sparkled with tease, and Jonathon smiled at Severino. "Wanna see how far it can strike?"

"Sure."

Jonathon pushed the branch toward the snake and the serpent struck. The speed of the strike caused them all to jump back. "They can strike up to two-thirds of their body length, so this guy can bite you if you get within two feet. Bigger snakes will strike farther."

"I'd treat them all as really big snakes and stay a long ways away from them," Tallie advised.

Maneuvering the stick, Jonathon touched the snake on the back of the head. The reptile bit at the branch, leaving a streak of dark liquid on the dried wood. "See that? They can strike from any direction, even if you're behind them, so never think you're safe around a rattlesnake."

Tallie reached for both of their arms. "Come on, guys. Let's leave it alone to go hunt little mice and baby birds."

This time it worked, and the three backed away from the creature. The coiled serpent snaked the top of its body around to face them as they retreated, its tail vibrating in defense.

A toss of the stick returned it to the small gully that ran beside the road and Jonathon let Tallie pull him back to the truck. "You know, there are some guys that wouldn't let you back into Kanosh if they knew you let a rattlesnake live."

"Yeah, but I'm not worried about those guys. I'm worried about you two. Let's go. Remember, we're out here to show Severino volcanic rocks, not rattlesnakes."

"Aren't the rocks out near those Indian writings your dad showed us?" Jonathon swung up behind the wheel and watched Tallie climb into the truck from the passenger side. Severino held the door for her in silence.

"My dad never called them Indian writings," Tallie countered as she slid across the truck seat and settled next to him.

"Sorry," Jonathon corrected, "Native American writings."

A smile accompanied her hard shove against him. "That's not what I mean."

With his own counter grin, Jonathon rubbed his shoulder. "Then what do you mean?"

"My dad wasn't sure what kind of writings they were, but he did say they were *not* Paiute."

"Oh, and you guys were the only tribe around?" Jonathon teased. With Severino in the truck and the door closed, Jonathon returned the vehicle to drive and headed down the road. Gravel, once again, crunched under the wheels.

"Yes! We took up all this land, from Northern Utah out to Colorado, clear down to Arizona and all the way out to California and clear up into Oregon. Just because we're small now doesn't mean we were small then. All the tribes knew about the Paiutes and wouldn't dare come into our land and mark it up with graffiti."

He smiled. "Well, someone did."

"That's right, and no one knows for sure who that someone is, but they are gone and the Paiutes are still here. Learn from that, Jonathon. Don't mess with a Paiute or I'll dump your sorry butt right here on this road and let you walk back to town, rattlesnakes and all."

"I believe you." Laughing, Jonathon lifted his gaze to Severino. "See why I don't date her?"

This time she punched Jonathon in response.

The truck continued to head south and Jonathon scanned the rugged landscape around them. "Boy, I haven't been out here in years. You'll have to tell me how to get there."

"Just follow this road for about three more miles until it forks, then take the left fork," Tallie instructed.

Continuing down the road, Jonathon looked at her. "Isn't this where the Jack-o'-lantern Light is?"

Curiosity filled Severino's voice. "What is that?"

Anxious to tell a new set of ears the story, Jonathon did not hesitate. "It's this really bright light people see out here on the desert at night sometimes. People who have seen it say it follows them and looks like a lantern but no one is ever holding it. Some people think it's the ghost of a brakeman who fell off a train out here."

A scowl on her face, Tallie shook her head in protest. "Every strange light in the world is said to be the ghost of a brakeman who fell off a train but they're crazy. The Jack-o'-lantern Light was around long before trains were even invented."

"How do you know that?"

"Because they have written accounts of pioneers seeing it over one-hundred and twenty years ago—before trains arrived in Utah. And my tribe knew about it even before then." She turned to Severino. "They called it the Death Light—*La luz de la muerte*." Her knowledge of its Spanish name surprised both of them, and she shrugged and explained. "The Mexicans who come into the café see it a lot out in the desert when they're herding cattle or sheep. They talk about it all the time. They don't like the light because it follows them and, before it shows up, the animals start acting strange—like they can sense its coming and they're scared of it. In fact, the light ran Ron Grasky's horse to death a few years ago. He and some friends were trying to rope it."

The story caused Jonathon to laugh. "How do you rope a light?"

"I don't know. They were drunk and decided to go after it on their horses, but the light wouldn't let them surround it. It kept turning and moving so they couldn't get behind it. That kind of freaked them all out, to think the light was intelligent."

"It doesn't take much intelligence to outwit four drunk cowboys who think they can rope a light."

The comment brought a smile to Tallie. "Well, Ron's horse got scared and threw him. It took off across the desert and the light started chasing it. They found the horse the next day, dead. It had been run to death."

"That's too bad."

"Yeah, it was a good horse."

Beyond the truck's open window, Severino watched the terrain pass. "The light, does it just come here or to another area?"

"Mostly here—around Sink-a-Beaver and the twin peaks. There used to be an old guy who lived out here on a ranch and he saw the light all the time on his property. When he finally died, they found a dozen locks on the inside of his cabin door because he was so scared of the light getting him."

"Have you seen it?" Severino asked.

Jonathon shook his head. "I'm not out here enough. Tallie, have you ever seen it?"

"No, but I know people who have. No one wants to see it because they say it means something bad will happen."

"Is it true?"

Hesitation from Tallie caused both Jonathon and Severino to look at her. A sadness held her eyes. "My dad saw it just a few days before he disappeared."

"Disappeared?" The word bothered Severino.

Silence rode with Tallie as she stared out the window. Aware of the situation, concern lifted Jonathon's hand off the steering wheel and he rubbed her shoulder but said nothing. This was her story to tell, if she chose to.

More dust and heat and desert rolled under the truck tires before Tallie made a decision, her voice quiet. "Will you help translate, Jonathon?"

"Sure," he whispered, "anything you want."

Relying on the language she knew best, Tallie began to speak in English, her eyes fixed out the windshield at the road in front of her, her mind far away from the west desert.

"My dad disappeared ten years ago. A lot of people think he just took off and left his family, but he wouldn't do that. He loved us too much. About a week before he disappeared, he got home really late and was talking to my mom. He sounded upset. He was working with some guy he didn't like from out of town and the guy said he'd pay my dad to find a *pekai*."

The Paiute word drew the attention of both Jonathon and Severino. "What is a *pekai*?"

"From the way he was talking, I think he found a desert tortoise, but I'm not sure. I never really learned Paiute. Anyway, my dad left it out in the desert and wasn't sure he wanted to tell the guy where it was. I don't think he trusted the guy. On the way home after finding it, my dad's truck got a flat tire, and he got out to fix it. That's when he saw the Death Light."

She pressed her lips together at the memory. "At first he thought someone was just walking toward him carrying a really bright light, but when he called to it, no one answered. The light just kept coming, kind of swaying back and forth. When it came within fifty feet, he thought maybe someone bad was following him because he'd found the *pekai*; so he quickly grabbed a crowbar out of the back of the truck. When he did that, the other tools banged against the side of the truck and the light reacted."

She looked out the side window, and Severino could see pain in her expression. "I heard my dad tell my mom the light hadn't been afraid of his voice or the truck motor, but when it heard the sound of metal, it jumped, like it was startled or scared. He said it then took off and disappeared in just a couple of seconds. It spooked my dad that a light would react to sound like that and move that fast. As soon as he finished changing the tire, he came home. He told my mom it was an omen. He wasn't going to tell the guy about the rock."

"Wait, you said it was a *pekai*—a tortoise. Now you're saying it's a rock. What did he find?"

Air huffed out of Tallie as she thought. "I don't know. I told you I didn't learn Paiute. Maybe *pekai* means rock because I definitely heard him say rock that time. Anyway, he was scared about the light and about the guy who wanted it. I heard him tell my mom that he loved her and he was going to make some phone calls in the morning and not risk it anymore." Now her shoulders lifted in a sad shrug. "A week later, he was gone. He went up into the mountains to fish one evening and never came back. We know where he went fishing. We found his gear, but everything else was gone . . . his dog and his truck. We even found his favorite fishing pole, still leaning against a tree, but we never found a trace of him."

SIX

WITH HIS elbow resting on the window frame, Severino looked out across the desert and rubbed his lower face. A collection of thoughts raced through his mind, yet he could not seem to find a word of response, in Spanish or English.

For Jonathon, his mind turned through several possibilities like the road twisting across the desert. It was the first time he had heard this much of the story, and it raised questions in him he hadn't asked before. The truck powered through a series of small hills and low valleys, passing a truck parked on the side of the road.

"Do you think the guy who wanted that rock killed him for it?" Jonathon managed.

The question was one she had not had to answer before and Tallie struggled. "I don't know. All I know is that my dad's been gone since I was eight years old. Something happened to him, I know that . . . I just don't know what." To change the conversation, she nodded to the road. "There's a fork up here in the road. You need to take the left one to get to the petroglyphs."

Jonathon did, turning now to drive southeast across the desert. The rarely traveled road bounced them back and forth, rocking their bodies against each other in the interior of the cab. Soon, on the right side of the road, great walls of black lava rock erupted above the earth. The ancient flow stood sixty feet high, rippling over the landscape for as far as they could see, like a black serpent. Tremendous boulders of lava, some the size of a house, speckled the earth around the dark reptilian wall.

The road swung close to the lava flow, and Jonathon chose that spot to settle the truck into park and silence the engine. There, the three took another look at the mighty intrusion on the land before climbing out into the July heat.

Still lost in her story, Severino stepped out of the truck and held the door for her. As Tallie slid across the seat and stepped to the ground, the Peruvian quietly shifted his body in front of hers. Surprised, Tallie lifted her eyes and his deep gaze held her there, between the door and the cab. "I am sorry about your father. I would give you the answers if I could." Then, not sure she understood his English, Severino spoke again, his voice quiet. "Do you understand?"

She understood his concern perfectly and nodded through her emotions.

On the opposite side of the truck, Jonathon dropped to the ground and closed the door. Coming around the hood of the vehicle, he saw Tallie and Severino, standing close. The focus in their eyes and the movement of their lips told Jonathon they were talking intently, quietly about something, and he knew it had to be about her father. Somehow, it felt right to give them the privacy they needed, and he slowed his approach, giving them time.

Severino saw him. With a step back, he let her move past him and lifted his gaze to Jonathon. When their eyes met, a smile danced across Jonathon's face. "Hey, you two, try not to get bit, okay?"

Not aware of Jonathon's playful meaning, Tallie unsnapped her holster and made it easier to retrieve her pistol. "Yeah, snakes love this place, so you'd better let me go first."

Advancing around the hood of the truck to stand beside his friend, Jonathon lowered his voice to a whisper. "That's not what I meant."

A grin of understanding lifted the muscles on Severino's face.

Tallie turned back to Severino, not hearing them. "Do you know what type of rock this is?"

The question required Severino to shift his focus and he looked toward the top of the ridge. "*Sí, es basalto*, basalt, and those are tremendous flows."

Hearing the translation, Tallie smiled. "Wanna see the basalt up close?"

"*Por supuesto.*"

"Then follow me, but watch for snakes," she warned.

Weaving through the dry grass and grasshoppers, the trio made their way to the ancient wall of black stones. The boulders canted and stacked on each other as if a giant force had thrown them into a haphazard line that ran for miles.

Reverenced by the size, Severino touched the sun-heated rocks with his hands, feeling the strength, almost sensing the rock. His gaze swallowed the mighty wall that went for as far as he could see. "It must have been a huge eruption for a volcano to melt and send out this much lava. Think of what it must look like underground."

The comment puzzled Jonathon, and he looked at Severino, but Tallie called to them. "I found them. They're over here."

The beckoning of her hand flagged them toward an outcropping of lava rock. There, on the south side of several rocks, carvings in the black surface showed the discoloration of centuries. The silent etchings spoke to them across time.

Amazed, Jonathon looked at them and smiled. It had been a decade since he'd last seen them, and his eyes scanned their surfaces as if seeing them for the first time. "These are so cool!"

"They are. I just wish I knew what they meant."

With careful steps, Severino approached the etchings and looked at them. His dark eyes examined each carving, reading the silent marks. Puzzlement showed on his face as he moved around the first rock to peer at other carvings in the area. The same careful examination took place.

Tallie saw the unusual look on Severino's face. "Are you okay?"

He looked back at her, his brow furrowed with concern, and she felt his eyes prying deep, trying to pierce the rocks for answers. Uncertain, her voice hesitated. "Severino, what's wrong? You look bothered."

Her question caused him to straighten and he pointed back at the symbols, struggling with his words. "We have these same carving down in Peru."

"What?" The announcement stopped Jonathon from taking photos of the glyphs with his phone. Turning to Tallie, he frowned. "I don't care how big you think your tribe once was there is *no way* Paiute territory extended all the way to Peru."

She shook her head in confusion. "It didn't."

Overwhelmed, Severino turned back to the images. "No, but the conquistador territory did. These aren't Indian carvings. These are old Spanish markings."

Tallie and Jonathon looked at Severino, stunned. Anxious to explain himself, the Peruvian pointed to a symbol. "This means gold. There were Spanish here, looking for gold and they found it."

He pointed to another. "This symbol is the king's sign. It means they were sending the gold from this area back to the king—for Spain and for glory. This one is the sign for food. There was plenty of food here."

Now his voice softened and sorrow filled his expression as he touched another symbol. "And this one means slaves. There were plenty of slaves in the area too." He looked at Tallie, aching to communicate with her, piecing his words together in Spanish and English. "That's why your people are small now. The Spaniards enslaved them to work in their gold mines. Your Paiute nation died in those mines."

The words knocked her back a stride, stunned. "How did you know that?"

Sorrow claimed his eyes. "I can read this same symbol in Peru, for my people." He looked at her. "I am not just Peruvian. I am Inca and my people were enslaved for gold and silver too."

Shock captured her face. "You are Inca? I thought the Inca Empire disappeared five hundred years ago."

Silence claimed his mouth and his mind searched for the words he wanted to say. Feeling inadequate, he lifted his eyes to her, speaking in Spanish, letting Jonathon quietly translate. "The empire disappeared because of the Spanish thirst for gold, but some Inca people managed to escape and survive. I am descended from those survivors."

Now emotion flickered across his face and his voice quieted even more. "I think you lost much of your Paiute empire because of the same gold thirst. Am I wrong?"

"No," she whispered.

Hearing a piece of history he had not heard before, Jonathon stopped translating and looked at Tallie. "Whoa, wait a minute. Is this true?"

Without taking her eyes off Severino, she nodded. "Yes. The Spanish came into this area and enslaved tens of thousands to work in the mines."

"Then how come we don't hear about it?"

Angered now, she turned to Jonathon. "Because it's a piece of history no one wants to hear about, okay? By the time the Spaniards left and the white man came here, there were only a few Paiutes left, hiding out in the desert. All of our strongest warriors had been killed and most of our men, women, and children had died in those mines or were sold into the slave trade and shipped to Mexico, California, or Spain."

Sensing deep hurt, Jonathon held up his hands. "I'm sorry. I didn't know."

She softened. "Most people don't." Now she looked at Severino. "I'm sorry to know it happened to your people too."

The concern in her voice and eyes caused Severino to straighten with pride. "Today my people have strong hearts because of their hurts."

The comment brought a gentle smile to her face. "I think the hurts have strengthened my people too." They stood a few feet apart, watching each other, linked by shared history, the silence between them communicating beyond their language barrier. Finally, Tallie lifted her gaze to the carvings. "So, my dad was right, they're not Paiute carvings."

"They're not even Native American," Jonathon agreed.

A few more private thoughts held each of them there, then the trio made a quiet return to the truck. No one spoke as they crossed through the grass. In gesture of understanding, Severino gave Tallie's back a quick rub. The gentle touch caused her to lift her eyes, and she looked at him, smiling her own gesture of friendship.

Now, when the truck left the area, they did not feel the jostling of the vehicle over the rough roads. The dirt trail merged them back onto the main gravel road; the truck took them up small hills and down low valleys, and still they let only the sound of gravel passing beneath their tires join them in the cab.

Several miles ahead, human movement near a parked truck caught Tallie's attention. People had returned to the vehicle.

She nodded at the movement. "We always stop when we see people out here, to make sure they're okay," she offered. "It's a long walk back if they're not."

Jonathon nodded in agreement and he slowed down, pulling along side the truck that claimed the shoulder on his side of the road. "You guys okay?"

Stepping back away from the driver's door, a man looked up, startled to see another vehicle on the remote road. Though exhaustion showed in his hazel eyes and his dark hair carried desert dirt, he managed a smile. "Ah . . . we're fine. Thanks."

Another man walked around the front of the truck, and he too was surprised at the second vehicle. Blue eyes made a quick scan of the three young passengers inside the cab, and, as he made visual contact with Jonathon, he lowered his gaze, tugged the bill of his cap down further over his blond hair, and passed quickly between the two trucks. Puzzled, Jonathon followed the man's movements in the side-view mirror, watching as the man disappeared to the far side of the vehicle.

From the middle seat, Tallie leaned forward. "You out here hunting?"

The dark-haired man shrugged. "Scouting, actually."

"Seen anything?" she asked. Beside her, Jonathon continued to watch the second man in the mirror.

Now the first man looked back toward South Peak, as if considering his answer. "No," he hesitated, "not really. Just lots of snakes. They seem to be all over out here. Is that normal for this area?"

She smiled. "Yeah, but there seems to be a lot more snakes all of a sudden. I don't know where they're all coming from but I've seen more on the roads in the last couple of days than I have all summer"

Jonathon continued to watch the second man in the mirrors.

The first man motioned back to the south. "Speaking of roads, do you know of any out on South Twin Peak?"

Tallie frowned. "Not *on* the peak, but there is a road that will take you around the base."

"How close does the road get to the peak?"

"Half mile. If you want to get on the peak itself, you'll have to hike. Same with North Twin Peak."

"So there's no way I could drive a truck up there?"

"No. It's even tough with an ATV, but you can do it."

The man seemed to digest Tallie's comment before stepping away.

"Well, thanks," he offered, and then waved a farewell, signifying the end of their roadside conversation.

Jonathon eased the truck away, hoping to get a final glimpse of the other man behind the truck, out of sight.

"What are you looking at?" Tallie questioned.

"The second guy. I've seen him before, but I'm having a hard time placing where."

"You mean the guy who acted like he didn't want to be seen?" Severino questioned, his eyes also watching the side mirror for another look at the blond.

"Yeah. I'm remembering his eyes, but for some reason, I don't think he had a beard when I saw him."

Tallie shrugged. "It only looks like his beard is a few days old."

The comment gelled Jonathon's thoughts. "That's it! That's where I saw him. He was the guy I bumped into at the airport when we picked up Severino."

"You mean the guy with the photo of a Spanish turtle?"

"Yes."

Confused, Tallie looked at Jonathon. "What's a Spanish turtle?"

Severino smiled. "I hoped it was a cute American girl, but it is not. It's just a rock."

"Oh, it has to be something else."

"No, I saw a photo on his phone. It is just a rock."

Behind the wheel, Jonathon's face showed shock as his mind pulled two thoughts together. "Tallie, you just said your dad had found a *pekai* out in the desert and you thought he meant tortoise . . ."

The same merging of thoughts stunned Tallie and she drew in a breath. "I did, but later I heard him say rock. Could there really be something called a turtle or tortoise rock?"

At the question, Jonathon shifted in the seat and pulled his cell phone out of his front jeans pocket. He passed it to Tallie. "Look it up on the Internet. See what it says."

A search for turtle rock or tortoise rock returned empty, and she shook her head.

"Try Spanish turtle," Severino suggested.

Within seconds Tallie had the new words typed into the search box and pushed Enter. Choices loaded onto the screen, and Tallie scrolled through the options. "I don't think these are going to work, either . . . Oh, wait, here's something." She opened the link and lifted her eyebrows. "You aren't going to believe this. Apparently Spanish turtles exist."

"What are they?"

She started to read in English while Jonathon translated. "*Spanish turtles were stone directional markers carved by early Spanish explorers. The carved turtles indicated the location of, and distance to, working gold mines.*"

Stunned, Jonathon looked at her. "Gold mines? That's just what those petroglyphs said!"

Tallie continued. "*In many ancient cultures, the turtle was thought to carry the world on its back, and gold certainly held up the Spanish world. Furthermore, in almost all cultures, the turtle is the symbol of wisdom and knowledge. However, the most probable reason the Spaniards used turtles as directional markers was that the native tribes of America considered the turtle sacred. For that reason, the Spaniards could leave a carved turtle in the area for years and come back to find it had been left alone, its directions to their mine still true.*"

For several seconds, silence filled the cab before Jonathon spoke. "That guy back there is looking for gold."

Severino refuted him. "He's looking for an entire gold mine!"

Excited, Jonathon turned to Tallie. "So, are there any Spanish gold mines in the area?"

She shook her head. "Everyone thinks so, but no one has ever found one, and that's fine with me. There are spirits protecting those mines."

Jonathon looked at her hesitantly. "What kind of spirits?"

"The spirits of my ancestors and all those who died in the mines." Tallie looked out at the passing desert. "When the Indian tribes rebelled and were able to drive out the Spaniards, they worried the Spanish would return and enslave them again. They also wanted the spirits of those who had died in the mines to rest in peace, so the different tribes buried the mines on their lands—to hide them and to sanctify them. Now they are sacred burial grounds and should be left alone."

Severino nodded his approval. "There is not enough gold in the world to make me disturb the final resting place of my ancestors. Sometimes the past should remain buried."

Jonathon looked across the cab at Severino and nodded in agreement. His time in the Peruvian tunnels had taught him that money and fame were never an appropriate exchange for family and heritage. "Men shouldn't be so caught up in gold that they forget family."

To guard herself, Tallie folded her arms tight across her chest. "I hope those men back there never find the mine."

Silence held the three in their own private thoughts during the long drive back to Kanosh. The hot summer roads began to coax fatigue into Tallie's frame. With the rocking and vibrating of the truck, and beneath a lulling blanket of desert heat, her mind grew heavy. Rich, dark eyes stayed closed longer and longer, until, soon, they did not open. Deprived of sleep the night before, she found it in the cab of Jonathon's truck.

At first, Tallie's body tried to remain upright, but eventually her head listed to the side and settled on Severino's shoulder. He shifted to give her a better resting place and felt her weight on his shoulder deepen.

"Is she asleep?" Jonathon asked.

"Finally."

"Good. She needed it." With a smile, Jonathon looked over at her asleep against Severino. "So, are you two a couple now?" he teased.

A quiet laugh came from the Peruvian. "We can barely communicate."

"I don't know . . . I think she's communicating pretty well right now, don't you think?"

Severino looked down at Tallie. "I don't think she is communicating. I think she's sleeping."

With his eyes back on the road, Jonathon's voice grew serious. "Actually, she is saying she's very comfortable with you."

The comment made Severino smile. "She's comfortable with my shoulder."

"That may be true, but she wouldn't be leaning on your shoulder if she wasn't comfortable with the person attached to it. No . . . I'm pretty sure it's *you* she's comfortable with."

This time Severino moved his back against the truck door and let more of her weight shift onto him. "If she feels comfortable with me, then that's fine. I don't mind. I understand what it's like to lose a father and a large part of your culture. She can lean on me in more ways than one if she needs to."

The comment increased Jonathon's respect for the Peruvian, and he looked over at his friend in appreciation. The two exchanged silent glances and then said no more, letting Tallie sleep and the truck roll over the miles of gravel road.

Half an hour later, Jonathon pulled into her driveway and shut off the engine, looking at the two. Tallie still slept deeply, her head pillowed on the Peruvian's shoulder and chest. "Wanna wake her up or let her sleep?"

Severino glanced down at her. "If she keeps sleeping, she won't sleep tonight."

"True."

Leaning forward, Severino brushed her long black hair off her face. "Good morning," he teased in English.

Tallie's dark lashes moved, then opened and she peered into his eyes. "Good morning," she murmured back.

"You are home."

Though simple English, his sentence worked. Tallie's mind brightened and she sat up, embarrassed, chattering in English. "Oh my gosh! Did I fall asleep on you? I am so sorry! I hope I didn't drool. Did I drool? That would be so embarrassing!"

Confused, Severino lifted his eyes to Jonathon for help.

"*Babear*," the American answered, a chuckle coming from his voice as he pointed to his mouth and pantomimed drooling.

Understanding Severino laughed. "*No mucho*," he teased. "Not much."

Hands covered her face and she rocked forward in the truck. "Oh! I can't believe this! This is so embarrassing."

Laughing now, Severino leaned forward and rubbed her back. "It's okay. It's just a *chiste* . . . a joke. Look." He sat back and showed her his shirt where she had been resting. "No drool. It's dry."

The dryness of the fabric surprised her, and her gaze raised to his. "It is dry."

Delight danced in Severino's eyes and sparkled over his smile, dimples deep on both sides of his face. He cocked his eyebrows and waited for her response.

Realizing he had been teasing her, Tallie sat up and smiled. "Well, I can change that." Before Jonathon or Severino could react, she'd opened her water bottle and poured it down the front of Severino's shirt and turned toward Jonathon.

"Hey!" Startled, Jonathon bailed out of the cab of the truck, trying to escape the dousing. Tallie bolted after him, sloshing him with the last ribbon of water, laughing as he clamored to safety. Severino left the other side of the cab.

"It's a *chiste*," she taunted.

Seeing a hose lying near the driveway, Jonathon caught Severino's gaze and motioned toward the water weapon with his eyes. *"Venganza,"* he mouthed.

Tallie saw the movement of Jonathon's mouth, saw the hose, and knew their thoughts. With the focus shifted back on her, she turned and fled for safety from the hose.

Jonathon didn't have to suggest it twice. When Tallie sprinted away, Severino bolted after her with surprising speed. Lean arms, hardened by a life of physical labor, wrapped around her and twisted her to face Jonathon. Jonathon had already retrieved the end of the hose and lifted the handle on the spigot. The hose bucked with water pressure, stopping at the closed nozzle.

When she saw Jonathon's intent, Tallie squealed her protest. "You wouldn't dare."

"Yes, I would."

"You'll get Severino wet too!" she stammered.

"He'll dry off."

"Jonathon, don't!" With her attempts failing, she pushed back and tried to break free, but Severino held her tight, laughing as she fought to escape.

When the first blast of water hit her straight in the face, she sputtered and spat a giggling protest. "I can't swim!" A second blast of water drenched the front of her shirt, and her body twisted with more laughter, fighting the spray of sun-warmed water. "Truce!"

"You don't believe in truces!"

"Yes, I do when someone else holds the hose!"

Now, Jonathon stepped close and unleashed the water's full force over the top of her head. Sheets of liquid rolled down her long hair and obscured her vision. Still trying to catch her breath between the laughter and the water, Tallie let her legs buckle, but Severino refused to let her drop, holding her upright. All three wore dark stains of wetness on their clothes. Water glistened on their bodies, and they laughed together in the hot sun. None of them heard the truck door close behind them.

"I thought they gave Indians indoor plumbing years ago."

The new voice and cutting comment stopped the teens. A man in his late twenties walked over to the water spigot and cut off the flow. A second man stood a few steps behind him.

In his arms, Severino felt Tallie tense and helped her straighten to meet the arrivals. Pushing back her wet hair, Tallie stepped toward the first man. The smile had vanished from her face. "Halden, what are you doing here?"

"Obviously interrupting your bath time."

Angered but not wanting to answer, Tallie shifted her gaze to the second man, his face cut and swollen. The sight softened her expression. "How are you feeling today, Tate?"

The second man gave an uncomfortable nod and looked at the ground. "I'm fine. Thanks."

"Tate, what are you doing running with Halden? He's not your type."

Halden locked Tate into a neck hold and messed up the quiet man's hair. "What do you mean, Tallie? We're cousins!"

She frowned. "Everyone knows that a horse and a jackass may be cousins, but that doesn't mean they should be hooked to the same plow or run on the same track."

The comment did not please Halden, who narrowed his eyes. Releasing his cousin, he took a quick, threatening step toward Tallie. "We need to talk . . . *now.*"

At the aggressive approach, both Jonathon and Severino stepped in front of Tallie, their bodies becoming a shield. From behind them, her hands made gentle contact with their arms, and she stepped between the two friends. "I'll be fine."

Stunned, Jonathon let his eyes shift away from Halden. "Tallie . . ."

With water still dripping from her clothes and body, she gave a strained smile. "*Está bien.*"

Concerned, Severino looked at Jonathon. He didn't need to understand a word of English to read the man's body language and he didn't like what it said. Nor did he like Tallie's response—things were *not* fine, and he could sense it.

When Severino tensed, ready to move forward again, Jonathon leaned his head and whispered in Spanish. "Let her go. Tallie's tough."

Severino hesitated, but a final, silent plea from Tallie released his muscles, and he let her pass. Still tense, Severino watched Tallie join Halden, and the pair walked away, leaving everyone else behind on the gravel driveway.

Near an empty corral, Halden turned to face her. "So, who are the two *kids*?" he questioned.

"They're friends. Listen, Halden, go home. I told you, you're wasting your time."

"And you're being stupid. Your family needs the money. You know they do."

"I won't make money that way."

Lifting a boot, Halden rested his foot on the lower rail of the fence while his upper frame leaned against the top rail. "Tallie, if it will help you pay the bills—"

"I *am* paying the bills, without doing something like that!" Angry words bit through the air.

"Tallie, I know you're getting the bills paid, but that's about it. You're working long hours at the café, giving anything extra you have to your family, but, in this economy, it's getting harder and harder. This is easy money, Tallie. All you have to do is give me what I want. You know I'll pay well for it. Double my last offer." A smile accompanied his actions and he withdrew an envelope from his pocket.

The sight of the envelope filled her with fury, and she shoved him. "Get out of here."

Before Tallie could turn to leave, Halden caught her arm, gripping it hard and pulling her around. Anger had steeled his eyes and set the muscles on his face into hardness. "Don't make a show . . . not here, not now."

"Or else what?" she hissed. "You'll force me to give it to you right here, right now? I'd like to see you try."

Without hesitation, Halden pulled Tallie against him, his lips finding hers in a heavy kiss.

Across the driveway, a frown lowered Severino's brow at the aggressive move. "Does Tallie have a boyfriend?"

"Um . . ." Confused, Jonathon puzzled over the sight.

Crack!

The sound of her slap against Halden's face echoed up the driveway and brought a smile to Jonathon. "Nope."

Fury drove Tallie back a step, and her dark eyes flashed at Halden.

"Don't you ever touch me like that again! You are *never* going to get what you want!"

Though his cheek had reddened from her brutal slap, Halden laughed. "You're lucky I'm offering to pay you for it, Tallie." Then he leaned close, his voice dropping to a whisper. "Just so you know—I can *take* anything I want . . . including that. I'm offering to pay you for it because I care about you and your family."

A vicious shove became her response and she propelled him backward. "You jerk! You don't care about me or my family. Get out of here now!"

At the sound of escalating tension, Jonathon, Severino, and Tate moved to the corral, breaking between them. "I think you'd better leave right now," Jonathon warned.

Angered that someone a decade younger would try to tell him what to do, Halden turned to Jonathon. "Are you going to make me?"

As he stepped toward Jonathon, Severino slammed his forearm against Halden's throat and shoved back, turning so his arm wrapped around the man's neck. With a swift move, Severino twisted Halden into a choke hold and wrenched the man's wrist behind his back. "*¡Déjala sola!*" The growled warning carried menace in its tone.

With his hands up in a display of peace, Tate moved toward his cousin. "Tell your friend to let Halden go, and we'll leave."

Seeing Tate approach and not understanding him, Severino tightened his hold, forcing Tate to stop his advance. Jonathon stepped in front of Tate, preventing any more forward steps. "You better get in the truck now." He spoke it not as command but as a suggestion.

Agreeing, Tate retreated to the vehicle but Tallie stepped after him. "Tate, don't get involved with this."

At her words, he turned pain-filled eyes to hers. "I already am. I'm sorry, Tallie. I didn't know Halden was going to do that."

"It's okay, Tate."

"No, it's not. It's wrong. This whole thing is wrong, but I can't stop it."

With Tate out of the way, Severino forced Halden to walk, bent sideways, toward the vehicle. A few feet away from the truck, Severino released him with a shove and a string of Spanish. Halden sprawled to the ground then scrambled to his feet, holding his neck. He wanted to rush the Peruvian, but the look in Severino's eyes stopped him. Halden had never seen eyes that hard, that experienced, or that ready to face threats. "What's he saying?" he demanded.

Jonathon shook his head. "You don't want me to repeat it. Just get in the truck and leave now."

In anger, Halden cursed a racial slur at Severino. Severino understood the derogatory comment and advanced in anger, but Halden climbed into truck, shut the door, and started the engine. With the metal barrier between them, Halden's boldness returned. "Keep the money, Tallie. You earned it today."

As he drove away, gravel spitting out from beneath his tires, Tallie found the envelope Halden shoved into her back pocket when he'd kissed her. Furious, she hurled the envelope at the disappearing truck, then turned and walked into the house.

Stunned by the events of the last moments, Jonathon looked at Severino before walking over to the envelope. Retrieving it from the ground, he opened the packet, stared for several seconds, and lifted his head in shock. "There's almost two thousand dollars in here!"

SEVEN

THEY FOUND Tallie in the kitchen, peeling carrots. Shards of orange flung into the sink with each furious pass of the peeler. Jonathon felt her anger and, his own muscles tense, stopped near the table. "You wanna tell me what's going on?"

"I'm making dinner; that's what's going on."

"I'm not going to play with you, Tallie. I want the truth. Why did that creep force a kiss on you and then shove almost two thousand dollars into your back pocket? Just what is he trying to buy from you?"

Startled by the comment, she turned and looked at him. Jonathon extended the envelope to her view and her complexion paled. "That's blood money. Get it out of my house!"

"What do you mean, *blood money*?"

She didn't answer but turned back to the sink, striking the carrots with more aggression. Anger shook her body. "I have to get these carrots cooking for dinner, and then I need to start the potatoes and . . ."

A different approach came from Severino. A step closer put him behind her and he reached around, placing his hand over hers, stilling the peeler. "Tell us everything," he whispered in Spanish.

Tallie didn't need to understand his words. The quietness, the smoothness of his actions, told her what he said and softened the rage she felt, bringing her to stand motionless. She answered him in English, her Spanish inadequate for the answer. "He wants the wire map."

"What's a wire map?" Jonathon translated.

"It's a map my great-great grandfather made over a hundred and twenty years ago by burning it onto some leather with a piece of hot wire. That's why we've always called it the wire map."

"What's it a map for?"

A struggle with private thoughts and decisions filled her face. Then, tired before her story began, Tallie sank into a chair. "The Spanish weren't just here looking for gold and silver mines. They were looking for *Carre Shinob* and they didn't care what it cost in human lives."

Easing his body into another chair, Jonathon watched her. "What is *Carre Shinob*?"

"It means house or temple of Shinob. It had been built by seven different tribes to honor *Shinob*, the god of love. Because the temple was made of pure gold, the Spaniards wanted to find it—only they thought it was seven cities made out of pure gold."

The explanation lifted Severino's attention. "You mean *El Dorado*, the gilded place?"

"Yes, and they spent a century and a half looking for seven cities of gold, the Seven Cities of Cibola, when, in truth, the temple was right under their noses, inside the Sacred Mountain."

Stunned, Jonathon and Severino stared at each other. "So the wire map is of *Carre Shinob*?"

She ran her hand across the table top, hesitant. "Because we have always considered the stones of the earth sacred, the seven tribes built *Carre Shinob* deep beneath the earth so it would be completely surrounded by the strength and spiritual power of stone. The temple is pure gold and filled with sacred gold objects—records of our people and precious items that represented our gifts and love for Shinob. When the Spanish heard about it though, they searched for seven *cities* of gold and never found them. Instead, they enslaved the Indians and forced us to mine for new gold. Thousands of Indians, from all the tribes, died in the mines while thousands more were sold into the slave trade."

The story became difficult for Tallie and she stopped for a long time, struggling with her thoughts. "In time, the Indians saw the Spanish getting close to *Carre Shinob*. To protect their sacred site, they rebelled and fought ferociously to drive them away. Many slaves died protecting its location, but it worked. The Spanish fled and never came back."

Hesitating now, Tallie breathed slow before continuing. "About a hundred years later, pioneers came into the area. We feared they would enslave us too, but for the most part, the pioneers lived peacefully with us. One man, by the name of Rhoades, developed a relationship of trust with Chief Wakara, a Ute Indian chief. Wakara's name means 'keeper of the yellow stone.' In appreciation for the friendship, Wakara took Rhoades to the location of a sealed Spanish mine on the condition that Rhoades use the gold for good and never tell others where it came from. That first trip, Rhoades came back with sixty-two pounds of already refined gold."

Jonathon sat back, shocked. "That's almost half a million dollars in gold! And that was his *first* trip?"

She nodded. "Their arrangement continued for the next forty years. Rhoades would go into the Uintah Mountains with an Indian guide and come back, several weeks later, with a mule train full of refined gold, never ore or rock. The Rhoades family gave away most of the gold for good, as promised, but they also kept enough to become the wealthiest family in the territory."

"I bet."

Tallie struggled to continue. "Years after Rhoades died, an Indian guide took his grandson, Caleb Rhoades, inside a sacred room deep in the mountains. Caleb said the room was massive and supported by seven giant golden columns."

"For the seven tribes that built it."

A nod confirmed Severino's statement. "Caleb said the walls, ceiling, and parts of the floor were pure gold, and he thought the room had been hollowed out of a single gold vein. He said it was filled with religious artifacts and treasures, but he didn't take anything. The guide told him it was the burial site of the great Indian leaders." Her voice softened. "Rhoades said the Indian called the place *Carre Shinob*."

"*He saw Carre Shinob?*"

"Apparently. If the Spanish had realized how close they were to *Carre Shinob* when our people rebelled and drove them out, they would have come back with all the armies of the world."

"Wow." Thoughts overwhelmed Jonathon, and he sat back in his chair. "A room hollowed out of solid gold—that sounds almost impossible."

Severino shook his head. "No, it's not—not in this area." The unexpected words caused both Jonathon and Tallie to look at him, questions written across their expressions.

With Jonathon's help, Severino explained. "Active volcanoes melt rock and metal ores into liquid. Since melted gold is heavier than the other materials, it stays at the bottom of the magma and will be the first mineral to settle into rock cracks or fissures. Sometimes the magma gets so hot, it melts all the other rock around it and leaves an entire hole or tunnel behind, called a lava chute. If there is enough melted gold in the magma, it will settle and stay behind in the lava chute. For a gold vein to be as wide as a room, Rhoades must have seen a lava chute filled with gold, and that is possible. They just found a gold-filled chute in Japan a few years ago, and it's a solid wall of gold almost ten feet across."

"Later, in another area, Rhoades claimed once to have seen a gold vein over seven feet wide," Tallie offered.

Not finished, Severino's head motioned toward the west desert. "This area is full of basalt lava flows on top of the ground—which means you had a lot of hot lava passing underneath the earth, melting the rock and leaving behind tremendous lava chutes and tunnels. These mountains here are mostly granite. Throw in some quartz, and you have the main rocks that indicate gold. If what I've seen is accurate at all, I'm betting there isn't just some gold in the area, there is a *lot* of gold in the area."

Jonathon looked at his friend. "So there really could be a single vein of gold somewhere in Utah that is seven feet wide?"

"Anywhere you have the right combination of volcanoes, granite, and quartz."

"Well, if there is, we'll never know where," Tallie interjected. "Shortly after Rhoades found that gold vein, he offered to share the gold with the U.S. government in exchange for their help and protection getting it out. He said there was enough gold to pay off the national debt and still pave all the streets of New York with gold, but the government decided they wanted all the gold for themselves."

"Figures. What'd they do?"

A sigh and a shrug moved out of Tallie. "The government created an Indian reservation everywhere they thought the gold might be, including the Uintah-Ouray reservation near Caleb's home. They knew the Indians wouldn't dig for gold—we didn't want anything to do with it. They also knew if the gold was on a government-owned reservation, they could keep Caleb Rhoades from digging for it, or anyone else who might dream of striking it rich."

A nod came from Jonathon. "Pretty slick move, actually."

"It was. So, the military sent in troops with mining experience to search for the gold, but they didn't find much. At one time, Caleb said prospectors could search all over the Uintah mountains, but they'd never find the gold because they were searching in the wrong place, and, even though gold hunters still search the Uintah mountains daily, no one has found anything of much value there."

The words seemed to hesitate in Tallie's mind and she looked up at a photo of her father. She had hung it in the short hallway between the kitchen and the living. The photo seemed to give her strength and she continued, a soft smile on her features. "My dad said the gold and *Carre Shinob* were never in the Uintah Mountains."

"Where were they?"

"On Paiute land."

Convinced she made the right decision to share the story, Tallie increased the strength of her voice. "When Rhoades and, later, Caleb would go into the mountain for gold, it would take them several weeks to make the trip, which means they weren't just running up their local canyon."

The new idea started Jonathon's mental calculator and he made the computations out loud. "That's right. Say a horse or mule can handle ten miles of mountain in a day. Give them ten days to go and ten days to come back—that means the actual mine could have been a hundred miles away from the Uintah Mountains." A smile of revelation came over his face. "They could have been making the trip over the mountains to Kanosh!"

"They were—my family knew them."

A dark brow lifted in surprise on Severino's face. "Why did your family know them?"

Nervous, Tallie fingered a necklace, sliding the pendant back and forth along the chain. "When *Carre Shinob* was built, each tribe assigned one family to care for the temple. My family was selected for the Paiute tribe."

Still trying to comprehend everything, Jonathon sat forward and made a confused wave with his hand. "Your family cares for *Carre Shinob*?"

Uncomfortable, Tallie nodded but did not look up. "We did until my father disappeared. He hadn't yet passed that knowledge on to his children, so now *Carre Shinob* is lost to the Paiutes forever. I don't know if the other tribes have also lost their knowledge of the temple's location or not."

Jonathon scooted closer anxiously. "But what about the map? Can't you use the map to find *Carre Shinob*?"

"No," she conceded. "Because my family knew the way, they never needed a map. I've never had a map to *Carre Shinob*."

"You've never had a map?" The announcement startled Jonathon and he pointed toward the driveway. "Then why don't you just tell him that?"

Frustration appeared on Tallie's face. "I have, but do you think he listens to me?"

Jonathon recalled the unwanted kiss and understood her emotion. "No."

Upset, Tallie pushed to her feet and crossed the kitchen. "Halden is such a jerk. He doesn't care what I say. He doesn't care about anyone but himself. Do you know what he said to me just now? He said he could take anything he wanted from me, including the map. What's he going to do, come in and ransack my home looking for a piece of leather?"

"He might," Severino warned.

"But I don't have a map to *Carre Shinob*!"

Sensing her growing distress, Jonathon stood and moved toward her. "Tallie, it's okay. Just calm down. He's not going to do anything."

"He already has, Jonathon! Besides harassing me, Tate is afraid of him. I don't know what he did, but Tate was never this way before."

"Is Tate the guy who was with him just now?"

"Yes, they're cousins, and Tate was always popular—everyone liked him—but then all that changed. My mom said it was because Tate missed my dad, but I knew it was because of Halden. Halden said or did something to upset him."

The comment surprised Jonathon. "Tate knew your dad?"

Tallie nodded. "Tate and Halden both. They were always rock hounding together, so they were over at our house a lot while I was growing up. At first, I didn't really notice the change in Tate because I was young and upset about my dad, but Tate stopped playing football in high school, stopped hanging out with his friends, and even stopped dating. His grades plummeted, and he barely graduated. He just went into a shell and has never come out of it. And it's always worse whenever he's around Halden. He doesn't talk, doesn't look up."

She sighed. "Tate's a really great guy, but he can't even see it anymore. He always helps my family. He's the first one there if Mom needs a new roof or some kind of home repair, and even though I know he can't afford it, he gives my family money every month to help with the bills. He'd bend over backwards for us and anyone else, but when Halden shows up, Tate just . . . well . . . you saw him."

"Yeah, he looked like he was close to tears."

"That's not like Tate at all. Something's wrong. I can see it in his eyes. Tonight he said this whole thing was wrong."

"What whole thing?"

Tallie reached for a cloth and wiped at the countertop. "Probably Halden's obsession with *Carre Shinob* and the wire map. I don't know what Halden's doing, but I bet it's illegal and I bet someone is bankrolling him. Halden never had fifteen hundred dollars in his life. Someone told him to give me that money, so what does he do? He decides to shove it in my back pocket during a kiss."

Sensing her anger returning, Severino covered her hand with his and let his eyes calm her, willing her to relax. "Don't think about that right now. *Cálmate. Está bien.*"

Jonathon joined the need to soothe her. "Listen, you've had a rough afternoon. Why don't you go get changed and we'll all head down to the warm springs." A roll of her head showed her uncertainty and Jonathon cut in before she could protest. "Severino has never been there, and we could relax. Come on, it'll be fun. Afterward, I'll treat everyone to dinner in Fillmore."

She sighed and nodded gratefully.

The warm springs lay snuggled against the earth, hidden by tall marsh grass. Flat volcanic rock rimmed the warm pool and held shallow and deep water together in one small, curving pond.

At the water's invitation, Jonathon pulled off his shirt, stepped out of his shoes, and propelled his body off the volcanic edge near the deepest part of the pond. A forward somersault completed his entry into the dark water. A second later he broke the surface, shook the warm water from his grin, and lifted his body and floated on the heated water. "I love this place!"

Next to the truck, Tallie laughed. Already she had discarded her sandals and now pulled her own shirt over her head, her swimsuit coming into view. She tossed the shirt onto the seat of the truck and unbuttoned her shorts. "Come on," she encouraged in English.

Severino watched her slide her shorts off over her hips, catching them with her toes before they hit the ground. She lifted the material on her bare foot and retrieved the shorts with her hand, placing them in the truck next to her shirt.

Still, the Peruvian hesitated. Tallie looked toward the pond. "Hey, Jonathon, how do you tell him to get undressed in Spanish?"

The question brought a burst of laughter from Jonathon, and he lowered his legs in the water, treading the warm surface. "You mean you didn't learn to say that at the café?"

She giggled. "No."

"Well, I could have fun with this. I could tell you a whole bunch of things to say to him that may or may not be what you intend him to hear." To tease her more, Jonathon treaded backward, moving to the other side of the pond.

Frustrated at Jonathon's obvious retreat, Tallie decided to handle the situation on her own. First, she motioned toward Severino's feet. "Shoes, take off your . . . *sapa* . . . *zapa* . . ."

"Careful," Jonathon warned.

Irritated, she looked back at her friend. "Then help me!"

In the water, Jonathon grinned. "Hey, I'm enjoying watching you try to figure this out."

"Oh, you are so dead when I get in there," she growled.

Turning back to Severino, she lifted her own sandal to show him, she then pointed at his feet. "Take off your shoes." Her bare foot moved against the back of Severino's shoe and held it while she motioned for him to step out of his shoe.

With a strange look, he complied, stepping out of both shoes.

"Good, great, okay . . . now your shirt." This time, she pointed to his shirt. Again, he didn't move. Without looking at the water, Tallie called again. "Jonathon, how do you say shirt in Spanish?"

"I forgot."

The response brought an exasperated huff from her and she turned. "You did not!"

Leaning back now, against a natural ledge, the water circling around his chest, Jonathon smiled and watched. "Hey, I'm enjoying this pantomime stuff. I want to see what you'll do next."

"Dead, Jonathon . . . you are so dead!" Turning back to Severino, Tallie smiled. "You need to take off your shirt. This thing." A tug on his sleeve marked the object.

A naïve expression followed Severino's gaze to her fingers, yet as his eyes crossed paths with Jonathon's, they sparkled. The Peruvian knew exactly what she wanted, and that realization made Jonathon smile even more.

"Your shirt, take it off." Tallie said a bit louder.

"He's not deaf, Tallie."

"I'm already going to kill you twice, Jonathon Bradford. Don't make it three times."

A show of confusion came from Severino with his raised eyebrows and extended hands, palms up. "*No entiendo.*"

To make it clear, she grabbed the logo on the front of his shirt. "*This thing.*"

Severino repeated the words slowly in English. "This thing."

"Yes, *this thing.*" For emphasis, she shook the front of his shirt.

Puzzled, Severino looked down at the logo and shrugged. "*No sé lo que dice.*"

Across the pond, Jonathon called to her. "He says he doesn't know what the shirt says."

The response brought a growl from her throat and she looked back at Jonathon. "You're translating for him and not for me? That's not fair!"

Jonathon grinned, cocky. "Hey, you're the one who wants his shirt off. Not me."

"You just lost lives three, four, and five, Bradford! Care to make it six?" Filled with frustration now, Tallie decided to show Severino what she meant. Her hands grabbed both sides of his top and began to pull it upward. "You need to take this off."

Severino did not make a move to help. Tallie lifted higher. "Oh, come on. You've got to understand what I want now!" She managed to lift the material up to his chest before a smile broke across Severino's face, and he took over, pulling it off over his head. By the time he slid both of his arms out of the material and emerged with his hair a bit tousled, laughter claimed his face. He spoke to Jonathon in Spanish and finger-combed his hair back into place.

From the water, Jonathon smiled and looked at Tallie. "He says you're good at explaining yourself. He knew what you wanted the first time you asked. He just enjoyed the pantomiming too."

Before Tallie could retaliate, Severino ducked and jumped into the water.

On the flat rocks, Tallie lay back, letting the sun-warmed surface heat her entire body. Her feet dangled over the rock edge. A colorful butterfly tattoo on the inside of her ankle danced back and forth over the water as she stirred the surface with her toes. Birds flitted across the sky, and an occasional evening breeze stirred the grass.

Hoisting himself out of the water, Severino climbed onto the rocks and moved to sit beside her. Water ran off his body and pooled on the porous surface beneath him as he sat, forearms resting on his knees. For a long moment, he said nothing, but then he looked over at her. "You okay now?"

Tallie understood his English. "I'm fine."

"Are you sure?"

She nodded.

Beside her, Severino remained quiet, but he picked up a small, broken rock—gray, red, and white in color. Red coloration filled many of the rocks around the naturally warm pond. Still silent in thought, he scraped the broken rock across the ground and saw the red streak it left behind. With a casual movement, he tossed the rock into the pond.

Swimming over to the side, Jonathon settled on the ledge in the water beneath them and caught Tallie's foot as it toed the water beneath her. "When did you get the tattoo?" he asked.

"A couple of years ago."

He turned her leg and lifted it to view the tattoo, noting the double butterfly image—a large one above a smaller one. Colors of teal green shared space with pink, yellow, and blue. "It's nice. I like it. How come you got it on the inside of your ankle and not the outside where everyone can see it?" He looked up at her.

"Because *I* wanted to see it whenever I crossed my legs. I can't see it if it's on the outside." With a lift of her leg, she demonstrated her reasoning by crossing her ankle over her knee.

"That's true." A strong surge lifted Jonathon out of the water, and he came to join them, sitting down on the other side of Tallie. "It matches your necklace. Was that on purpose?"

Thoughts pulled her back through time and Tallie fingered the small butterfly that rested on her chest, touching another part of her life. "Yes. Butterflies are kind of big in my family."

"How come?"

"I don't know. Family motif, I guess. I remember my grandpa had a really old butterfly drawing that I saw once, but I don't know where it is now. Then my dad made this necklace for me about a month before he disappeared. I guess they like butterflies. Anyway, I was worried I'd lose the necklace, so I had it copied onto my leg. Now, if I ever lose my dad's butterfly, I can get someone else to make me a new one by looking at the tattoo."

A motion from Severino indicated he wanted a chance to see the butterfly necklace. She lifted the pendant to him, and he took it in his fingers, studying the ornate silver creation with spectacular teal-green wings.

"I think it's some type of turquoise," Tallie offered.

Severino shook his head. "*No es.* It is variscite." Fingers caressed the brilliant creation. Four blue-green wings of stone lay cut and polished beneath delicate silver overlays. The vibrant, changing colors of the stones swirled and danced amid timid partners of gray and black veining, each wing joining to a small body of silver. "It is *bonita*, beautiful. The stone is from around here?" To help clarify his English, Severino used his other hand to indicate the land encircling them.

"Just north of here, in Fairfield."

He nodded in affirmation then gently laid the necklace back into place. Dark eyes shifted from the pendent to Tallie. "Your father said much with the stone. Variscite is a good stone. It has power."

"What kind of power?"

Now Severino's forefinger touched the pendant lightly, stroking it, his words silent as his mind struggled to answer. Legends borne of centuries said variscite was given to help the wearer remember deceased loved ones, and he wondered if her father knew he wouldn't be coming back.

Noting an unusual expression on Severino's face, Tallie wanted her answer even more. "Tell me," she encouraged.

Somehow, he managed a gentle smile and ended his contact with the stone. Careful to not hurt her, he shared its other powers instead. "The stone gives *valor moral* . . ." Unsure of the translation, he looked to Jonathon for help.

"Moral courage or bravery," Jonathon explained.

Listening, Severino gave a confirming nod and continued. "It gives the wearer the promise of great strength and success. It also makes the wearer independent and . . . and . . . *segura* . . ."

"Self-assured or confident," Jonathon translated, and then smiled and teased her. "Well, the stone got that part right. You are definitely cocky—excuse me—confident and self-assured. Ain't nobody gonna mess with you."

In response, Tallie struck her knee against Jonathon's side, popping his ribs hard with the motion. "Remember that, Jonathon, and don't mess with me."

After a laugh, Jonathon's voice gentled. "I also know you have great moral courage and inner strength. Your dad did pick the right stone."

"Thank you." A smile warmed her face and she fingered the necklace against her skin, thinking about her father, enjoying the knowledge she had just acquired. Silence, quiet, and comfort knit the three friends together.

Still lying on the warm rocks, Tallie rolled her head and looked between both of them. "So, where are you guys going to set up camp?"

"Don't know yet. We'll decide tomorrow." A playful smile lifted Jonathon's face and he looked down at her, speaking in fluent English. "When we find a place, you can come up and do some more pantomiming if you want."

The words brought Tallie upright and she smacked Jonathon's shoulder. When both boys started to laugh, she pointed a finger at Severino, startled that he understood their conversation. "I think you know more English then you are letting on."

"*Quizas*. Could be," he grinned.

"Oh, he knows more than he lets on about a lot of things. He's smart," Jonathon responded. "I just wish he was *smart* enough to change his mind about some things, college being one of them."

"Doesn't he want to go to college?"

"No."

The surprise on her face shifted from playful to serious and she looked at Severino. "*Por qué,* why not?"

At her question, an exchange of Spanish passed between the two boys. Words flew in a rapid cadence between them, too fast for Tallie to follow. Frustrated at Severino's reply, Jonathon shook his head. "You need to tell her the truth," he pressed in Spanish.

The suggestion brought a noticeable bristling to Severino. "She won't understand."

"Then let me explain it to her."

"No!" The word, the same in English and Spanish, turned Tallie's gaze to Severino, and she saw instant hardness in his eyes.

For a long moment, Jonathon and Severino stared at each other until, finally, Jonathon's gaze gave ground, and his eyes shifted to Tallie. "He, uh, has some personal issues he's dealing with right now."

Uncertain, Tallie leaned forward and wrapped her arms around her legs, closing herself up. "That's okay. I'm sorry I pried." She lay her brown cheek down against her knees and stared out across the pond, quiet.

Across her back, Jonathon sent a disapproving glare at his friend and motioned to Tallie, letting him know he did not agree with Severino's decision. A shift of his gaze brought Severino to look at her, reading her posture and her silence. Regret softened his anger, and he felt unsure about his decision. Then a new wave of irritation flooded over him, and he pushed to his feet, tension claiming his entire frame.

Not waiting, Jonathon climbed to his own feet and followed, catching Severino near the rail fence that encircled the pond. "Severino, you can tell Tallie the truth. She'll understand."

"No girl understands."

"*She* will! She knows what its like to lose a father."

"Yeah, well my father was murdered. She won't understand that—and she definitely won't understand what I'm going to do to *El Cernador.*"

The words chilled Jonathon, causing him to slow. "And just what are you going to do?"

EIGHT

J ONATHON STARED at his friend, daring him to respond. When Severino only stared back, horror took hold of Jonathon. "Severino, you can't be serious."

Severino responded low and in English, "I'm dead serious."

The response hit Jonathon like a wall and he ran a hand through his damp hair, thinking, frantic. "Are you stupid? If you fail, he'll kill you. If you succeed, everyone around him will kill you. If you try this, you're dead either way it plays out." Irritated, Jonathon looked away, then back at his friend. "And you know they won't let you die easily, either. They'll torture you to death."

"And the life they gave me isn't torture enough?"

Jonathon's voice raised in anger. "*Gave you?* You think they *gave* you the life you have? They gave you one event. You created all the rest! Every decision you've made, every thought you've had has created your life. If that life is torture, *you* made it that way, not them. That's why it's called *your* life, not theirs!"

Severino's jaw tensed, and he glared at Jonathon, his dark eyes flashing their fury.

Not finished, the American waved his hand behind them to Tallie. "Look at Tallie. She's been without a dad a lot longer than you have been. She was only eight years old when he went fishing and didn't come home. She hasn't seen him since. He never saw her grow up, never saw her first day of high school, never sent her out on her first date . . . or saw her dressed up for her first prom." The words made Jonathon slow. "And she was gorgeous, Severino. I saw the photographs." Sorrow moved Jonathon's head. "He should have been there to see her that night. He should have been there to see her walk across the stage at graduation and get her diploma. He should have been there to see all the scholarships she got, but he didn't see any of it."

Jonathon exhaled. "She still has no idea what happened to him or where he is, but after that one event, she made the decision to move on and make the best life she could. She made a decision to create a life her father would have been proud of."

The difference in Tallie's life lifted Jonathon's gaze, and he felt irritation return. "But what about you? Do you honestly think your father would be proud of you getting yourself tortured to death somewhere, while your mother and sister are left behind with no one to take care of them? If you think he would, go right ahead with your quest and on your tombstone, I'll be sure to write, "*Wonderful son and brother.*"

Severino cursed at him, hard. Unable to refute anything Jonathon said, he responded with the only word he could force through his lips, the only thought he had. Fury shook his insides and trembled his muscles; it knotted his mind and twisted his stomach, and he could do nothing but stare at Jonathon. Seconds passed in silent tension until Severino turned away and cursed again, this time at himself.

Sensing the change, the deep hurt in Severino, Jonathon's muscles released, and he turned back to the pond. As he walked by Tallie, he tapped her on the shoulder and made a silent gesture toward Severino. Then Jonathon dove back into deep water and swam to the opposite side. He didn't feel the warmth encircle him.

Unsure of what had just passed between the two, Tallie rose, brushing dirt and rocky sand from the back of her thighs. A few yards away, Severino leaned against the fence, his muscles tense, his face turned aside. Caution moved her forward. "Hey," she whispered her approach slow. "Are you okay?' He gave no verbal response so she stepped closer. "Can I help?"

"No. I am fine."

Not ready to leave, she drew close to the fence and rested her hands on the top rail. "*Lo siento*, I'm sorry you are upset," she managed.

"It's not your fault." Though his mind spun through a thousand words, his mouth could not release more. Frustration rolled out of him in a quiet groan, and Severino leaned his forearms on the fence, head lowered in defeat. Everything he had sought, everything he had wanted for so long suddenly seemed *wrong*.

A hand touched his shoulder, hesitant, gentle. Using her basic Spanish, Tallie spoke to him. "You can tell me what you want. Maybe I won't understand everything but I can smile and say *sí*."

The unexpected words made him laugh, and he straightened, turning to look at her for the first time. Dark chocolate eyes found her rich mahogany ones waiting. Nothing judgmental showed in her expression, just a willingness to listen and accept whatever he had to say. Finally, he nodded. "Okay," he said, his vision locked to hers. "I will tell you." For several seconds, Severino struggled to find the words in Spanish and English and managed to piece together a single sentence. "Smile when you do not understand but, *por favor*, smile more when you *do* understand because I really need a friend right now."

The sun settled toward the western mountains, washing the sky with pink, gold, and orange. Shadows lengthened around the pond. Still drifting in the warm water, Jonathon waited while Severino and Tallie spoke. He could not hear what they were saying, but he knew their conversation from their body language. Though Severino struggled to share things with Tallie, she never recoiled or retreated. Jonathon also knew when she spoke of her own feelings and hurts, for Severino watched her with that same commitment.

Eventually the pair stood close together, their foreheads almost touching as they spoke quietly, and listened and nodded their under-standing, piecing together the information they needed through two languages. Despite the verbal barrier, they shared a bond—a loss—that only the two of them understood. Somehow, it seemed right for them to come together.

Morning sunlight slid over the eastern mountains and down into the valley, waking the western desert. Leaves, green with summer, danced with the gentle dawn breeze. Already the day whispered of the coming heat.

Behind the steering wheel of the parked truck, Ryan shifted in the seat and tried to stay awake. He blinked hard. Neither he nor Steven slept last night because of the light. For the second night in a row, it reappeared, hovering only fifty feet outside of camp, moving and shifting each time they tried to circle around it.

At one point last night, Ryan fired his pistol to the right of the light, ripping up a wad of dry desert earth and pungent sage. Though the blast went through a silencer, Ryan knew someone could've seen the flash of gunpowder erupt from the end of the muzzle, and he considered that, but fatigue—and nerves—pushed him toward the rash move.

Even before the deadly bullet spat into the ground, the strange light reacted and jerked to the side. Then Ryan and Steven watched, horrified, as it circled around and followed the path of the projectile, growing brighter on the heat of the bullet's wake.

Neither man dared to move, unable to account for the light's ability to act, react, and even change. Only yards away, they watched the light shift from side to side, as if controlled by an unseen hand. Then the light lowered to the ground and sent out several candle-sized balls of light, startling Ryan and Steven backward. The smaller lights rolled and bounced along the ground, crackling through the night before they vanished and the orb of light disappeared, dimming away into the darkness.

Ryan and Steven sunk against the ground, their hearts drumming with adrenaline. When they felt sure the light had gone, the two men spent the rest of the night searching the area for signs—footprints, tire tracks, burn marks, residue.

They found nothing, not even a bent twig. By the time morning light returned to the west desert, the two men made their exhausted return to the hotel.

Now, sitting in the truck, Ryan blinked through his fatigue and stared vaguely out the windshield. Light from the rising day dressed the front of the motel in a warming glow. He knew Steven slept inside the motel room, gaining a few precious hours of rest before he left to make the long drive. Ryan, however, needed to stay awake and guard the truck. Their job had gone quicker than they originally planned. Now, with the Spanish turtle crated and secured to the trailer behind their vehicle, he couldn't afford to rest. He could sleep later.

Drained to the core, he shifted his gaze and made one call. Though he lifted the phone to his ear, his mind did not pay attention to how many times it rang. He'd been awake the last two days and two nights, and even before arriving in Kanosh, he hadn't slept well, not since learning of his wife's plans to file for divorce.

The phone rang one more time, and a man answered. "Hello?"

A surge of alertness returned to Ryan. "It's me."

"Did you have any trouble getting it?"

"No," he lied trying to forget the memory of the light and the feeling of unease it brought. "It's all crated up and ready to go."

"What does it look like?"

This time Ryan smiled inside the privacy of the cab. "It's beautiful. I've never seen one like it. And Steven did a great job of cutting it. It's a one-of-a-kind piece, a real treasure."

The man laughed. "Oh, I like to hear that. Just make sure nothing happens to it in transport. I don't want to have blame anyone—if you know what I mean."

"I do. Listen, Steven is crashed in the hotel room right now while I'm sitting in the truck, keeping an eye on things. He's pretty tired, and I didn't want him trying to deliver this thing until he got a few hours of sleep. We've had a rough couple of nights and some long days getting it out of there; but I need you to do me a favor."

"What's that?"

"When Steven gets there," Ryan looked at the hotel room and tried not to feel any emotion, "make sure he doesn't come back."

A hidden buzzer made its announcement as the café door opened. Tallie looked up and smiled at the two teenagers who entered, dirty and windblown. They returned her greeting with grins of their own and took seats at the counter.

"You look tired," she observed.

"Thirsty is more like it. Can we get a couple of strawberry lemonades, please?"

Tallie smiled and turned to fill the order. Frosted glasses emerged from a freezer filled with ice and dishes. The bottom of each chilled glass received a spoonful of crushed strawberries and thick red syrup. Next, she added crushed ice before filling the glasses with cold lemonade. The drinks finished, she set one down in front of each of them and added a couple of napkins. "It looks like you guys got your camp set up."

Jonathon reached for the straw dispenser. "We did, finally."

"Where is it?"

Unfamiliar with the drink, Severino watched Jonathon and used his own straw to stir the strawberries through the lemonade before testing the drink. Impressed with the flavor, he took several large swallows, gulping down the refreshing liquid.

Finished with his own, long draw on his straw, Jonathon lifted his eyes and finally answered. "We took the ATV trail up above Horseflat Canyon a couple of miles and are set up between Spring Canyon and Crazy Ridge. There's a stream only a few yards from the tent, and I've already seen some brown trout in there. You ought to grab a fishing pole tonight after work and come up with us."

She smiled. "I just might. How long did it take you to get up there?"

Jonathon looked at Severino and shrugged. "From my grandma's house it took us, what, an hour?"

"*Mas o menos*, more or less," Severino affirmed. "I don't go as fast as Jonathon. I am still learning the ATV."

"Don't let him fool you, Tallie. He's crazy on the corners. He's gonna be doing motocross in a few days."

Severino smiled but said nothing, taking another long drink of lemonade. Soon, both drinks were almost gone and the straws searched between the ice cubes for the last of the liquid.

"You guys are thirsty. Let me get you a refill."

Jonathon shook his head. "Naw. We just got back from Fillmore with some groceries. We've already loaded them onto the ATVs and need to get heading up the canyon. We just wanted to stop by and say hi."

Tallie ignored him and reached for two paper cups. "Then let me give you refills to go, it's hot out there." Before they could protest, she repeated the process, filling the paper cups with more strawberries, ice, and lemonade. Two plastic lids snapped into place over the cups, and she passed them across the counter to her friends.

"Thanks. What do we owe you?'

"How about you show me where those trout are tonight, and we'll call it even?"

Jonathon grinned at the offer. "Sounds great. We'll see you tonight." They took their drinks, slid straws through the lids, and left the café, walking by a full-sized truck pulling a flatbed trailer.

At the pump, Ryan finished filling dual tanks on the truck. He wiped sweat from his face and looked across parking lot. Tired, his energy drained from lack of sleep, he hung the nozzle and felt for his wallet.

Steven moved around the front of the truck and stood beside Ryan. "You're not going back to the motel to sleep after I leave?"

"No. I have some things I need to do."

A frown came from the other man. "You're wasted, Ryan. You need to get some sleep."

The blond shook his head and secured the cap over the second tank. "I don't sleep much anymore anyway."

"Then at least go inside and get something to eat, maybe something to wake you up. I'll stay with the truck."

"You sure?" The offer sounded good and Ryan hoped a nutritious meal, and maybe something to drink, would help.

"Yeah. Go on. I'll watch the truck."

Nodding his appreciation, Ryan reached for his wallet. "I'll come back as soon as I'm done, and then I'll watch the truck so you can get something before you take off." With a check for arriving vehicles, Ryan ducked his head and crossed between the gas pumps toward the doors of the convenience store.

Once inside the store, Ryan inhaled the smells floating throughout the store from the café. The aroma of fresh coffee shared the air with the smoky scent of grilled burgers. He headed toward the café, lifting a menu from the counter and scanning through the offerings.

"Did you want a booth, or would you like to sit at the counter?"

The voice lifted his eyes from the menu. A beautiful smile, nestled against striking Native American features, waited for his answer. The waitress looked familiar, and Ryan hesitated, trying to identify her face—her eyes. "Ah, neither. I have a friend waiting out at the truck, so can I just order something to go?"

As he spoke, his gaze shifted to her name tag.

Tallie.

A jarring thought shook his mind and he glanced back at her face while another name exploded into his brain. *Pikyavit.* She had to be Tallie Pikyavit. How many Tallies could there be in central Utah?

And if she truly was Tallie Pikyavit, that meant . . .

The name threw him back a decade, and he felt his stomach twist. Desperate, Ryan forced his mind to work fast, trying to erase the memory by force. He didn't want to remember, didn't want to face that part of his past.

Tallie didn't notice the slacking of his features or the paling of his skin. She merely voiced her approval for a meal to go, tipped her head sideways, and waited for his order. Her movement triggered another memory, and Ryan suddenly realized Tallie had been in the truck yesterday—the truck that stopped to help—the truck that held the kid from the airport.

Uneasiness pumped through his veins and Ryan tried to focus on the menu, tried to see it again. He struggled to recall what he had read from it before she approached, hoped she wouldn't notice the trembling of his hands. "I'll take a Chicken Monterey Sandwich, please."

"With avocado, tomato, and Monterey Jack cheese?"

"Yes." He didn't look up, struggling with a myriad of thoughts. He didn't like knowing her family identity. He also didn't like *not knowing* her connection to the kid from the airport.

"Do your want your chicken fried or grilled?"

"Grilled." Inside, his emotions churned through an alarming mix and he lowered his head more to prevent her from seeing his blue eyes. Even though it had been almost ten years, if she had a good memory, she might be able to identify him if she looked at him long enough.

Making a notation on her order, Tallie didn't seem to notice his unease. "Do you want it on a white, seven-grain, or Italian bun?"

Another delay, another question to answer. "Ah, seven-grain, please."

"What do you want for a side: french fries, chips, or a salad?"

He just wanted to get a sandwich and leave; not have to endure an interrogation! "Just a salad."

Tallie smiled with another question. "And your dressing?"

A cringe moved through him but he caught it before it settled onto his face and drew her attention. "Honey mustard or ranch, whatever you have." His voice grew quiet.

"And did you want something to drink?"

"No, I'll grab a milk from the store."

She wrote up the ticket. "Sounds great. It will be about ten or fifteen minutes. Did your friend want to come in and order something to go too?"

Ryan fumbled to return the menu to its original location. "No, he'll come in a little while."

"Okay. You can just pay at the front register if you want." She handed him his bill. Moving away from the counter, Ryan had entered the convenience store before he could breathe again. Strained, he snagged a quart of milk from the cooler and went to the cash register. There, he paid cash for his lunch, the milk, and one hundred and sixty-two dollars in gas. Returning his wallet to his pocket, he then forced himself to stay busy at a postcard display, counting the seconds with his breaths as he waited for his lunch.

Outside the convenience store, Jonathon and Severino returned to their ATVs parked alongside the building. Reaching his first, Jonathon straddled the seat of his machine and took another long drink of lemonade. "Think you can drive with one hand, or do you want to sit here until you finish your drink?"

Severino smiled. "I want to finish it. This is very good, *rico*, and I am thirsty."

Complying with his wish, Jonathon sat on the warm seat, drinking his own lemonade, enjoying the quiet. His gaze wandered over the parking lot. A powerful truck hitched to a flatbed trailer, sat at the pumps. A large wooden crate had been carefully secured to a trailer bed. Moving his eyes, Jonathon next scanned the valley that moved out away from them. Across the valley, the highway's concrete profile left a scar on the view that ran from north to south. To the east, mountains reared upward, sparse in their vegetation, dressed mostly in grass and sage.

Taking another swallow of his drink, Jonathon let his eyes return to the truck and trailer. A large, unmarked crate was well secured and a there was a tarp over the truck's bed covering a large collection of unseen items. For the first time, Jonathon noticed a man with brown hair leaning against the side of the truck, watching the store, waiting.

As he viewed the rig a second time, recognition moved through Jonathon and he leaned closed to Severino, his voice quiet. "That's one of the Spanish turtle guys. They're here. That's their truck right there."

Used to not drawing attention, Severino shifted only his gaze to look at the truck. His head gave no indication of the shift. "Where is the other one?"

"He must be inside."

"Think they found a gold mine yet?"

"I don't know. They found something, though. Look at the bed of their truck and that crate. I bet that guy is standing guard."

Severino pretended to take another swallow of his drink. "Wanna find out what they found?"

Lifting his own drink to his mouth, Jonathon smiled. "You know I do, but I get to look this time. Not you."

Stepping off the ATV and setting the last of his drink down on the running board, Severino shrugged. "Fine, I'll give you a distraction, but once he moves away from his truck, you won't have much time to check it out."

Grinning now, Jonathon set down his own drink. "I won't need much time. What are you going to do?"

"Act like a tourist."

A minute later, Jonathon walked around the corner of the building and passed the café's front door, moving toward the convenience store entrance. A few seconds after that, Severino approached the store with a digital camera in his hand. Intent on operating it, the Peruvian stopped on the sidewalk, pressed a few buttons, shut the camera off and on then looked around for help.

Next to the truck, the man noticed.

A smile of relief filled Severino's face and he crossed the parking lot toward the man. "*¿Señor, se puede tomar una foto para mí, por favor?*"

Startled by the Spanish and the approaching teenager, the man shook his head. "I don't speak . . ."

"*Foto*—photo," Severino managed in both Spanish and English. He motioned toward the mountain behind him with a wide sweep of his arm then held the camera out to the man, pushing it toward him until the man had to take the camera or drop it on the parking lot.

With a smile, Severino lifted a finger. "*Uno.* One."

Frowning, Steven shook his head and, again tried to refuse.

"*Por favor.* One photo please."

Reluctant, Steven activated the camera and nodded. "Okay. One photo."

Turning toward his ATV, Severino sent a handsome grin back at the man and pointed at the machine. Then, without waiting for the man to understand or refuse, Severino moved quickly toward the ATVs. Upon reaching the ATV, Severino straddled his machine and reached for his helmet.

Worried, the man stepped away from the truck. "No. I can't go anywhere."

Pointing again to the machine beneath him, Severino nodded and rattled off an explanation in Spanish, which included several elaborate gestures and another sweep with his arm at the mountains behind him. This time the man seemed to understand and stepped toward the machine. "You want a photo right here, on the ATV, with the mountains behind you."

"Photo. *Uno*," Severino smiled. Behind the man, Jonathon moved into place. He'd circled around the entire store and now crossed between the truck and the pump. The man did not notice.

Watching Severino, Steven lifted the camera. As he did, Severino held up his arms, stopping the man. "*Un momento!*" Taking another moment, Severino stepped off the machine and stood beside it, resting one foot on the running board. "*Así*," he nodded, proud of his new position. From beyond the man's back, Severino watched Jonathon lift the tarp to get a view of what lay beneath.

The man raised the camera to peer through the viewfinder.

"*Aye, mi pelo,*" Severino interrupted, stopping the photo session again. He reached up to finger comb his thick, black hair. "*Lo siento.* I am sorry," managing the apology in both languages.

The man exhaled but waited while Severino finished preparing himself for the photo. "Ready?" he finally asked.

"*Listo,*" Severino confirmed and he smiled broad for the camera.

When the man snapped the photo, Severino stepped toward the man. "*Gracias!*"

The man understood that much Spanish. "You're welcome," he said and handed the camera back to Severino.

Shrugging in confusion, Severino shook his head. "*¿A ver?* Please . . . may . . . I see?"

Realizing the Peruvian may not know how to run the camera, the man turned it back on and called up the photo. When it appeared, he tipped the screen to show it to Severino.

With the distraction working, Jonathon looked at the items under the tarp, no longer noticing Severino. Stunned by what he saw, his mind sifted through a million reasons but found only one explanation.

NINE

A FORCE grabbed Jonathon from behind, twisting his hand back toward his wrist, propelling him forward, against the truck. A hard voice hissed in his ear. "Do you want me to call the police right now?"

Jonathon's face tightened in pain, and he managed a look behind him. The blond man from the airport held him in a brutal restraint, his eyes livid. Demanding an answer with his strength, the man pushed again.

The physical attack and the items hidden beneath the tarp angered Jonathon. "Go ahead," he challenged. "I'd love to show them what you have in the back of your truck."

The teen's words enraged Ryan and he shoved in fury, his hand wrenching Jonathon's wrist upward, until Jonathon thought his bones would snap. Leaning sideways, the teen tried to relieve the pressure. A few yards away, Severino and Steven turned in shock at the sudden commotion, and both moved forward to help.

Ryan twisted harder. "Stop your friend."

"*Para!*" Jonathon gritted through the pain and Severino halted, watching, wary.

"You were trespassing on private property," Ryan growled. "The bed of a truck is as legally protected as the cab."

Sucking in a lung full of air, Jonathon spoke. "So is BLM land. I'm betting you took those artifacts from public land, judging by where I saw you guys yesterday."

Ryan's curse cut hot through the air, and he spun the teenager around, releasing his hands and driving him against the side of the truck, letting the metal bed bite into Jonathon's back. "You have no idea who you are playing with right now."

Just as tall as Ryan but lighter in frame, Jonathon stood bold and quiet in front of him. "I'm not playing. You probably don't have any documentation for those items, do you? Not a single letter of provenance, not a single signed permit; and even if you did, they're probably all forged. You can't take artifacts like that from public land."

The calmness in Jonathon's voice, the stillness of his face surprised Ryan even more than the teenager's knowledge. A muscle twitched high on Ryan's jaw and he studied the youth, seeing courage in the light brown eyes he hadn't expected. The teen wasn't looking for a fight or he would have shoved back as soon as both of his hands were free, maybe thrown a punch or, in some other way, expressed physical displeasure. Instead, the youth stood still, holding Ryan's gaze without fear or wavering, waiting for the man's response to the accusation.

For a moment, the two stared at each other, and realization began to swell inside Ryan. The kid had stared down threats before—serious ones. That's why he didn't cower now; the youth had faced worse.

Amazed, Ryan's gaze skimmed over Jonathon's face, searching for signs of doubt or regret, but he saw none and that bothered him. The teen stood in front of him, challenging him to respond, unconcerned about what could happen. Ryan noted the scar on the teenager's cheek and wondered if that had anything to do with the resolve the youth now displayed. He also wondered if the kid would become bold enough to push things further. If he did, that would cause problems.

New thoughts reeled through Ryan. As soon as Steven got the turtle out of town, Ryan planned to go after Cole and didn't need a couple of teenagers messing that up. He had to punch through the teen's courage, find some way to shut him down.

Only one way came to mind, and the knowledge tightened Ryan's gut. He didn't want to throw that card onto the table, but he also knew it was the only one that could make the youth fold; it was the only one that ever made Ryan fold.

Tensing his mind, Ryan stepped close, preparing to say the words that would stop the youth's world. "You think you're smart? You think as soon as you walk away from here you're just going to call the police?"

With eyes narrowed, Ryan moved his face to within inches of the teenager, days of stubble visible across his cheeks and jaw, dust and dirt layered on his skin. The man's voice now dropped to a dangerous whisper. "Well, I'll tell you what you're going to do. You're going to leave and you're not going to tell anyone about this because if you do, that pretty little girlfriend I saw you with yesterday, that waitress just inside the cafe, is going to get hurt."

It worked. Ryan saw a sudden flicker of fear cross Jonathon's eyes. To emphasize the threat, Ryan shoved Jonathon harder against the truck and kept his voice low. "I've been told Tallie has the wire map, and I personally know of a couple of wolves prowling around, just waiting to get their hands on it—and they won't care who they have to devour to get it."

"You leave Tallie alone."

Though Jonathon hissed the words in fury, Ryan saw resolve waver in the teenager's eyes. The unexpected comment had shaken the youth to his core, just as Ryan knew it would. A smile lifted one side of Ryan's face. "If you want Tallie left alone, you'll leave right now and keep your mouth shut. Is that understood?"

For a second, Jonathon hesitated and Ryan cursed, slamming his forearm against the teen's chest. "She's only a few yards away. If you want to gamble with her, go ahead. I'll play."

The last words worked and Ryan saw the kid fold when his gaze lowered. Knowing his hand had been well-played, Ryan stepped back and allowed the teen to leave, watching him turn away.

Though Ryan knew the teenager would not say a word, he felt his gut sicken. Inside he understood the turmoil he'd just embedded deep in the kid. He knew, because he had heard similar threats breathed against his wife over the years, and they never settled well. In fact, the last threat, just a few months ago, finalized Ryan's decision to accept the divorce. He cared about his wife too much to put her at risk—and Ryan knew this teen cared too much about Tallie.

Lifting his gaze to Steven, Ryan indicated to him to watch the teen. Without moving, Steven's eyes flicked to the youth's face, catching the expression he saw there. Then Steven moved to join Ryan, who leaned against the bush guard on the front of the truck, his hard arms folded across his chest, his cold eyes tracking the teen's retreating steps.

Back at his ATV, Jonathon swung onto the seat and pulled his helmet down over his head. With the face guard in place covering his mouth, Jonathon's gaze shifted to the man at the truck, and Severino heard a quiet string of Spanish curses from his friend—words Severino rarely used. Astonished at the emotion behind the words, Severino knew something serious had happened. He also noticed Jonathon's hands were shaking as he started the engine.

The two ATVs left the convenience store and headed up the road. A mile rolled away under their machines, then two miles. Then Jonathon turned onto a gravel road and pulled to a stop beneath a line of cottonwood trees holding a barrier between the road and an alfalfa field.

In the shade of the trees, Jonathon stopped his machine and stepped off the seat. Severino pulled up beside him and cut the power to his engine, just in time to hear Jonathon swear vehemently.

Ripping off his helmet, Jonathon grabbed it by the lower face guard and hurled the helmet across the road. It bounced off the gravel, spun up into the air and disappeared into the tall grass. "I shouldn't have looked in the back of that truck!"

Concern at the violent reaction propelled Severino off his own machine. "Jonathon, calm down. Tell me what happened. What did the guy say?"

Jonathon raked his hands furiously through his hair and turned away from the machine, his entire body shaking in rage—and regret. "He said he'd hurt Tallie if I said anything."

"What!" Stunned, the Peruvian looked back down the road. "Did he say how?"

"No. He just said he would if I told anyone what I saw!" Jonathon repeated in anger. Then a groan welled out of him, and he looked up at the bluing sky. "I shouldn't have looked."

Feeling his stomach wrench, Severino approached his friend. "Okay, okay . . . let's think this through. Tell me what was in the back of his truck. What is so important that he'd hurt Tallie to protect it?"

Jonathon drew a trembling hand down over the lower half of his face. "There were . . . there were a couple of old bits from horse bridles, ornate ones, and . . ." his mind sorted through the items he'd seen, trying to pull out the important ones from the shovels and ropes.

"And there were some round balls, possible lead balls or musket balls of some kind, and he had a couple of things that looked like iron arrow heads . . . and then he had something that looked like a piece of metal armor, Spanish maybe, I don't know." Jonathon shook his head in frustration. "He had some other stuff too, but I didn't see it all. I don't know where he got that stuff but he had a lot of it."

Pained eyes turned to Severino. "He knows about the wire map too. Severino, he *will* hurt Tallie if we tell anyone about this." Now he pulled out his cell phone. "I've got to warn Tallie" Jonathon punched in a few numbers and lifted the phone to his ear, counting each eternal ring. "Come on, Tallie . . . answer."

Still at the convenience store, Ryan looked at his partner. "Did the kid say anything to you or his Spanish friend when he walked past you?"

"No. He didn't say a word."

"How'd he look? Did he look scared?"

Steven shook his head. "No. He looked mad."

Stunned, Ryan turned to look at him. "Mad, really?"

"Yeah, he looked like he wanted to tear you limb from limb. What did you say to him?"

Ryan smiled and nodded. "He has guts. I'm impressed."

"What did you say?"

"I told him his girlfriend would get hurt if he didn't back off and shut up about what he saw in the back of the truck."

Now Steven whistled and looked up the road, as if tracking the teens' departure. "No wonder he's ticked. You don't threaten someone's girl."

"Sometimes it's the only way to stop them." Looking toward the store, Ryan smiled. If the teen had as much nerve as he appeared to have, Tallie would be getting a call or a text soon, warning her; and Ryan wanted her to see his face. He no longer wanted to hide. He wanted Tallie to look into his blue eyes and feel enough fear to keep Jonathon away.

"Come on. Let's go in that café. You need to order something to go, and I'm betting my sandwich is about ready."

"What about the truck?"

"I think we're fine for a minute."

Just finished taking an order to go, Tallie felt the vibrating of her phone. She tore off the ticket for a hamburger with bacon and pastrami and a side order of fries. After passing the order to the cook, she retrieved her phone and read the caller's name. Jonathon.

Stepping into the doorway of the kitchen, Tallie answered on the fourth ring. "Hello?"

"Tallie, it's me, Jonathon. Listen, there were a couple of guys at the store just now. One has blond hair and blue eyes and is about thirty years old. The other one has brown hair and is about the same age . . ."

She turned and looked toward the counter. "Yeah, they're here."

"They're there, *with you*? Are you okay?"

"I'm fine. They're both sitting at the counter waiting for their food. Did you need to talk to them?"

"No. Listen, Tallie, I want you to stay away from them, especially the blond."

She gave a partial laugh. "Why him? Does the blond guy have something contagious?"

"No, Tallie! I'm serious. I think he's dealing in illegal artifacts, and he knows you have the wire map."

At the mention of the map, Tallie scowled and turned back to the kitchen. "Did someone send out a tweet or post something on my Facebook? I don't have the wire map! Why does everyone think I do?"

"I don't know, but the guy is dangerous." Jonathon hesitated. "He had artifacts in the back of his truck, and he said he would hurt you if I told anyone he had them."

"So you decided to tell me he had them. Gee, thanks."

"Tallie! I'm trying to warn you. Just stay away from him. I don't want you hurt. We're coming back right now."

She looked toward the counter and noticed the blue-eyed man watching her. When their gazes met, the man gave her a nod, and she realized he knew about the phone call! Infuriated at the man's cockiness, she turned her back to him, lowering her voice into the phone. "You don't need to come back. I'm fine. I'm at work. Besides, I can take care of myself."

"Not against these guys, Tallie. My dad has often said that many antiquity thieves are tied to organized crime. It's the third-largest crime in the United States, right behind drugs and illegal weapons."

"No, it's not."

"Yes, Tallie, it is!"

"Then, if it is such a big crime, call the police."

"And have that guy come after you before the police believe some stupid teenager? No way!"

"You're not a stupid teenager, Jonathon. Paranoid, maybe, but not stupid."

He didn't appreciate her humor. "Tallie!"

An exhale escaped her. "Come on, Jonathon. You don't even know if the guy is serious."

"And you don't know he's not! I'm not going to risk it. What time do you get off work?"

"I have a lunch break at one, and I get off at seven."

"We'll be there both times to pick you up. Don't go anywhere until we get there. Don't even take out the trash." When she hesitated, he pushed her. "Tallie, promise me you'll stay there and wait for us."

When her eyes turned back to the man, he smiled at her, lifting his brows, waiting for her reaction. Her nerves tightened across her stomach and chest. Something about the man seemed familiar, as if she had seen his eyes before. "I promise," she whispered. "I gotta go. The guy's sandwich is ready."

Ending the call and closing his phone, Jonathon looked at Severino and spoke in Spanish. "She has a lunch break in forty-five minutes. We'll pick her up then and figure out what to do."

Still trying to reason some hope into the situation, Jonathon thought out loud. "When he had me pushed against the truck, I saw the total he had on the pump. He must have two tanks and filled them both up. You only do that when you're getting ready for a long drive and don't want to be stopping. Maybe he isn't planning on sticking around and will be long gone by the time Tallie gets off work."

Frustrated and worried, Severino looked at him. "I hope so."

Sitting behind the wheel, Steven watched Ryan climb out of the truck and move to a second truck. The blond unlocked the cab, set his packaged lunch on the seat, and reached briefly beneath the seat. The items he'd stashed earlier were still there.

Turning back, Ryan returned to the loaded truck and smiled. "Well, looks like you're on your own now, Steven. You know where you're going?"

Steven nodded and adjusted the visor, blocking the sun. "Yeah. It should take me about four hours to get there."

"Don't get in a hurry. I don't want anything damaged."

"I'll get it all there, safe and sound."

Ryan nodded then hesitated. "Listen, I want to thank you for your help. I couldn't have done this without you."

"No problem. Get some sleep while I'm gone. I'll be back tomorrow." He smiled. "As far as my wife knows, I still have another week of 'training'."

Ryan sniffed and rubbed his upper lip, remembering his earlier conversation. Steven would not be making it back. "Yeah, well, you better get going." Stepping away from the truck, he gave a nod of farewell and waited until Steven pulled away, heading for the freeway.

When the truck and trailer had disappeared, Ryan returned to the second truck. Climbing into the cab, he opened his cell phone. A dry breeze blew through the open door as he dialed the number. The call went through and a man answered after two rings.

"Yeah, it's Ryan again. He just left."

"He's bringing everything?"

Ryan thought of the items hidden beneath his seat. "He should have everything. I think we broke a shovel getting stuff out, but other than that, the truck and trailer are loaded."

"Good. I'll be waiting, and, Ryan, I made a couple of calls— Steven won't be coming back."

Even though Ryan requested it, the words stung and made him blink with regret. "Okay, thanks. Ah, listen, I need one more favor. There were some kids poking around in the back of the truck today and they saw some of the items."

"Did they take anything?"

"I don't think so but, just in case, I got the plate numbers on the ATVs they were riding. Can you find out who owns them, in case we need to go and retrieve a few items."

"Yeah, we might. I'll see what I can do."

When the call ended, Ryan sat still for a moment, gazing out at the nearby mountains. Then, he reached under the seat and extracted a cloth-wrapped bundle. Setting it on the passenger seat, he looked at the cloth for a moment before unwrapping the fabric from its ancient remains. Three Spanish artifacts lay in the cloth.

A smile came to his face as he fingered the items and imagined Cole Matthews's eyes when he offered the items—and more—to him for a price. Retrieving his cell phone, Ryan entered the number he'd intercepted on the plane. It would connect him directly to Cole's personal cell phone.

Coming into the house, Tallie tossed her keys into a bowl on the counter. "I can't believe you looked in his truck all by yourself."

Jonathon followed. "Okay, it was a dumb move, and I'm sorry."

With a yank on the refrigerator door, Tallie turned and smiled at him. "And you didn't even ask me if I wanted to come see what he had. He really had some old Spanish bits for horses? I would have loved to have seen those."

Stunned, Jonathon found himself speechless. A can of pop arced through the air in his direction. "Catch. I know you like root beer." While Jonathon scrambled to catch the offering, Tallie reached for a second can. "Do you want some, Severino?"

"Root beer, no. It tastes like medicine in Peru."

The comment surprised her and she straightened. "Really? I'd love a medicine that tastes like root beer. Oh well, what do you want?"

Uncertain, Severino shifted on his feet. "Do you have real milk, please?"

Again she looked puzzled. "*Real* milk?"

Jonathon popped the top on his can. "In Peru they only drink canned milk mixed with hot water. Severino has decided he likes *real* milk, and he likes it cold. If you want to put some ice in it, he'd love that too. They don't have much ice where he's from either."

"Okay, one glass of *real* milk, on ice, coming up." She opened the cupboard and retrieved a tall glass. A moment later, milk and ice cubes shared the same container. Severino smiled and thanked her.

"Actually, that looks good. I'll have to try it." Tallie made a second one and then moved from the kitchen, through a short hallway, to the living room. Jonathon followed, but Severino stopped at a framed picture in the hallway. The photo showed a young Paiute, crouched near the earth, his brown hands holding back a medium-sized dog that appeared ready to leap out of the photo with excitement. "Who is this?"

At the question, Tallie peered back and smiled. "That's my dad. When I moved in here, I brought his picture with me. There was a nail right there, so I hung it up. I love looking at it every day."

Severino studied the image. "It is a nice photo. You have his smile."

Drawn to the photo, Tallie stood beside Severino, looking at the image. "I've been told that many times. I've also been told I have his eyes."

With a turn of his head, Severino looked at her face. His dark eyes slid over her features, holding her in an almost intimate way with his gaze. "Then your father had very nice eyes."

The comment caused her eyes to brighten and her face to soften. "No one has ever said it to me that way. Thank you."

Jonathon felt the emotions shift, felt the walls of the hall become even more close and intimate. "Okay, guys. That's enough comparing. Let's figure out what we're going to do when Tallie gets off work."

"The guy is gone, Jonathon. He and his buddy left after they got their food and haven't been back." To distance herself from the conversation, Tallie crossed the living room and kicked off her shoes. The couch became her perch, and she settled deep into the cushions, taking a sip of her iced milk. "Hey, *me gusta*. I like it. This is good." She lifted her glass toward Severino in a toast as he moved to sit in a chair. "Cheers."

In response, Severino paused and tapped his glass to hers. "*Provecho,*" he smiled back.

Another deep swallow of cold milk seemed to satisfy Tallie, and she relaxed. She stretched her feet out in front of her, setting them on the coffee table, the butterfly tattoo resting on top of her crossed ankles. Across the room from her, Jonathon settled in a rocking chair. "Tallie, what if the guy comes back?"

"He won't."

"You don't know that. I want to make sure you're fine. Is there someone you can stay with tonight?"

Shock filled her eyes. "What? Are you kidding? I'm not leaving my house because some guy made a threat to *you*."

"Tallie . . ."

"No."

"Fine. Then have someone stay here."

She groaned and shook her head. "And who am I going to call, my mom? *Hey Mom, remember me—your grown-up, out-of-the-house, independent daughter? Well, I want a babysitter tonight.* Nope, sorry, not going to happen."

"We will stay here," Severino said quietly.

Jonathon and Tallie turned to look at him, stunned by the solution. Then Jonathon nodded his approval. "That's a great idea."

Tallie hesitated. "But you have your camp all set up. You can't just leave it like that. What if someone takes your stuff?"

Jonathon leaned forward. "Tallie, you're more important than a stupid tent."

She swirled her milk. "But I thought you had a couple of camp chairs up there too."

"Tallie, they'll be fine. We can crash out here in the living room. You won't need to do a thing. We can run up the canyon and grab our sleeping bags."

Now she frowned. "You came here to camp, not sleep on someone's living room floor."

"Tallie, I messed this whole thing up, and I'm sorry. I just want to make sure this guy is long gone and not going to bother you."

"And what about Severino?"

Seriousness held his eyes, his voice slow, searching for the right words. "I would not sleep there if I felt worry for you here."

She looked from Jonathon to Severino and back again. Finally, she nodded. "Okay."

Back from lunch, Tallie stayed busy with afternoon customers who came in for coffee, ice cream, and conversation. The slower hours gave the workers time to clean and prepare for the dinner crowd, and most were in the back working.

Behind the counter, Tallie noticed a new customer and set aside her work to move out onto the floor. Coming around the corner of the booth, she froze. Blue eyes looked up at her, and the man Jonathon worried would return greeted her with an unreadable smile.

For a moment, she looked around for another worker to take his order, but other responsibilities held their attention. Committed, Tallie pulled out her order pad and stepped forward. "Did you need something else to go this afternoon?" she asked, keeping her eyes focused on the pad.

"No, I think I'll eat here. I'm actually waiting for someone."

The words allowed her some room. "If you're waiting for someone, we can just wait . . ."

Not willing to let her retreat, Ryan stopped her. "No. I'd like to order now."

A controlled exhale brought Tallie back to the table. "Okay. What would you like?"

The closed menu sat on the table. "I think I'll just take a slice of pie. Peach, if you have it."

"We do. Did you want ice cream with it?"

"No."

"Do you want it heated?"

He smiled at the routine of questions, not bothered this time. "No."

"Something to drink?"

"Milk, please."

"Is that all?"

"For now."

Tallie retrieved the menu and pocketed the order pad. "It will be out in just a couple of minutes."

Ryan watched her walk away before shifting on his hip and extracting his wallet. Opening the leather billfold, he removed a twenty-dollar bill and slid the wallet back into his pocket.

True to her word, Tallie came back a few minutes later with a tall glass of milk and a slice of peach pie. She set the milk on the table, and as she started to place the pie down in front of him, Ryan leaned forward, the money extended between his fingers.

"I'll give you twenty dollars if you tell me your last name," he said quietly.

The unexpected offer caused her to tense and she held still, not knowing how to respond. Ryan narrowed the distance between them, his words quiet. "You can tell me yourself and pocket the money, or I'll just ask one of your coworkers or a customer here. Either way, I'll find it out."

The challenge angered her, and she lifted her head, turning to look at the small crowd at the café. "Excuse me, everyone," her voice carried over the noise of the café and people stopped and turned. Still holding the pie plate in her hand, she smiled at the waiting audience and motioned toward Ryan. "This strange man here just asked me for my last name, and, personally, that seems kind of creepy since he is almost twice my age; so, if he asks any one of you for any kind of information about me, please don't tell him. Thank you very much. You can go back to your meal now."

All eyes in the café shifted to Ryan as she smiled and turned back to him. A smug expression filled her face and she set the plate in front of him. "Enjoy your pie, sir." Then she returned to the kitchen.

For a moment, Ryan sat there too stunned to react. Her move had been bold, brilliant, even arrogant, *and it worked*. A smile of approval melted across his face. With three fingers, he folded the bill in half, stuffed it into his pocket, and cut off a bite of pie.

With the third bite on the way to his mouth, Ryan saw the door darken and sent his gaze in that direction. Cole Matthews entered the café. Without hesitation, Ryan set his fork back down on his plate and sat back in his booth. When Cole looked his way, Ryan removed his cap, turned it over in his hands, and returned it to his head. Cole caught the prearranged signal and came toward the table.

The older man slid his body into the booth across from Ryan, adjusted his clothes and took his first look at the man who called him. Scruffy, like he expected. It contrasted with Cole's clean appearance. "Well, Ryan, seems like you haven't seen a razor for a few days."

"Nope. I've been busy."

"Doing what?"

Ryan extracted his cell phone. "This." A few touches of his finger activated the screen and Ryan slid it across the tabletop toward Cole.

TEN

THE DISTINGUISHED man looked at the image then lifted Ryan's phone for a closer look. "That's interesting. What is it?"

"It's a bolt head, the iron tip from a Spanish crossbow, probably dated around 1550 or 1580."

"Hmm."

Ryan pressed another button. "And that is an iron dog collar from roughly the same time period. The Spanish crossed mastiffs or *molossar* dogs with *Alanos* and used them here in America for, shall we say, crowd control of the natives. The dogs were very effective, and a collar like this is a rare find. I have more things, if you'd like to see them."

Cole seemed under impressed. "Where'd you get them?"

"Private property near here."

He nodded. "You have the documentation to prove that?"

"Not with me, but I have it."

The answer did not seem to be the one Cole wanted to hear, and he started to move out of the booth, irritated. A casual switch on the cell phone screen by Ryan stopped him. "You haven't seen the best yet."

When the new image downloaded onto the screen, the older man stopped and reached for the phone, stunned. "That's a Spanish turtle! Where did you find it?"

"Out in the desert, west of here." A second photo appeared on the screen. "And that's a picture of me and my buddy loading it onto a truck."

"You stole it? You can't do that! Do you realize that turtle pointed to a treasure trove of Spanish artifacts, possibly even a mine!"

"Before we moved the turtle, we got a GPS bearing on where it was pointing and the exact coordinates are . . ." Ryan turned the screen back toward him, called up a third picture, and smiled, "Somewhere up there. The good ol' Pig on the Mountain. See the pig?"

Well-acquainted with the local landmark, a scowl crossed Cole's face. "It doesn't look like a pig."

"You're right, it doesn't, but folks here are so interested in seeing a pig up there that's all they see. No one notices the heart, which is probably good because . . ."

"The Spanish used hearts to mark their mines."

Ryan smiled. "You've studied your history. In fact, if you look close, there are two hearts up on that front range . . . one right here and the other right here." He pointed each one out on the screen. "Most people just think the hearts are simply rockslides or bald spots, but they are too symmetrical. In fact, the faces of these three mountains are covered with over a dozen rockslides that, coincidentally, look just like Spanish symbols. If you look, there is a snake, a couple of circles, a person . . . no other mountain face on this entire range has so many bizarre looking rock slides. Definitely not natural."

Casting him a disbelieving glance, Cole lifted the phone and stared close at the photos. Doubt washed away into shock, and the older man turned to stare out the café window at the mountains behind them, trying to see with his own eyes what the photo told him. The rock-slides *did* form Spanish symbols.

"You see, Cole, this place was so valuable that the Spanish wanted to make sure they found it again, so they carved out giant symbols across the entire mountainside." Now he smiled. "There's not just a mine up there; there is a *giant* Spanish mine in this area, and if I had to place my bet, I would say that mine runs through all three of these marked mountains. So, why don't you and I join forces and start looking."

The proposal brought some mental chewing from Cole. "I'm not going to do anything that could get me thrown in jail."

"Hey, would I ask you to break the law?"

"You obviously did it yourself when you removed that turtle."

"I just got the turtle out of the weather to preserve it. I'm just asking for your help in preserving a few other things. Maybe a whole mountain full of other things."

Angered, Cole stared at him. "You should let the authorities preserve those things. What if I decided to call them?"

"I'd pass you my phone and let you. I have their number on speed dial. I'm a good guy, Cole."

For a long moment, Cole didn't move. Then, to release some of the tension, he motioned toward a waitress, signaling for attention, and pointing numbly to the coffee mug waiting, upside down, on the table beside him.

When Tallie approached the booth, coffee pot in hand, Ryan saw a look of irritation hiding beneath the surface expression she wore. Though she knew Ryan watched, she ignored him as Cole turned over the coffee mug. As he did, Ryan saw Tallie's face go slack, saw the color drain from her complexion. Confused, Ryan wondered what had caused the sudden change and his gaze tracked hers . . . to the Tiger's eye ring Cole wore on his left thumb.

Though Tallie didn't seem to hesitate, Ryan noticed the stream of dark liquid trembling as she poured coffee into the cup. Cole also noticed it and he looked at the waitress, curious.

Unable to face the specter she had seen, Tallie started retreat but then stopped and turned back to Cole, her voice quiet. "Can I see that ring?"

Cole looked down at his thumb. "This ring?"

A tight-lipped nod came from Tallie. "It's a very unusual ring."

Giving a shrug, Cole slid it off his thumb and passed it to her. With her free hand, Tallie took the ring and turned it over, looking at it from every angle, noting the detailing as she rolled the ring over in her fingers. Finally, she handed the ring back to Cole. "Thank you," she whispered.

Cole returned the ring to his thumb and flexed his fingers as it settled back into place. Again, Ryan watched Tallie struggle with something, and again she seemed to battle herself, yet she managed to brave another question. "Can I ask how you got the ring?"

The older man frowned. "Let's see, it's been about ten years now. I own a car dealership in Southern California, and, as I remember it right, a man—an Indian—came into the dealership. Seems his truck had broke down and he needed it repaired. He didn't have enough money for the repair, but he had this ring. I liked the ring, so I agreed to approve a trade—his ring for the work. It took about a day, but we got his truck repaired and he and his girlfriend took off."

"Girlfriend?"

Cole smiled over at Ryan and chuckled. "Well, if you want to call her that. She was more the play toy of a man having a mid-life crisis if you ask me. She was pretty, blonde, and stacked and couldn't have been more than eighteen or nineteen." Now Cole looked back at Tallie, ignoring her pale complexion. "I guess I could see what he was attracted to—she was gorgeous. I didn't say anything, but every-one at the shop knew he had ditched a wife and maybe some kids somewhere."

With an expression of melancholy, Cole looked down at the ring and twisted it on his thumb. "I don't know, I probably should have called him on it, told him to go home to his wife and kids and spend as much time doting on them as he did his new girlfriend, but I didn't say a word, and I've regretted that decision ever since. In fact, I keep the ring because it reminds me of the worst business decision I ever made."

Tallie nodded, thought about what he said, and nodded again. When she turned away, Ryan saw deep hurt in her eyes. With her back rigid, she moved behind the counter, returned the coffee pot to its place, and disappeared into the kitchen beyond. When Ryan shifted his blue eyes back to Cole, he felt hatred increase for the man.

Not seeming to notice, Cole returned his attention to Ryan, a smile on his face. "A lot of people like the ring, until I tell them that story."

"Yeah, it's quite a story," Ryan muttered. Emotions churned inside him, and Ryan wished he had never heard it. Mostly, though, he was angry that Tallie had been subjected to the story.

Taking a careful sip of his coffee, Cole redirected their conver-sation. "So, you think this Spanish turtle is pointing to something significant?"

Pulling himself back to the deal at hand, Ryan nodded. "Something . . . um, but I'm running low on cash. I can't really exca-vate until I can find some way of funding my time."

Cole understood and leaned back in the booth, his cup lowering to the table. "So that's why you contacted me."

"No, I just knew you were a man who liked Spanish antiquities. I thought you would like to see what I'd found, maybe give me some advice on what to do next."

A flash of anger passed over Cole. "If you're looking for *funding*, look somewhere else. I don't fund other people, especially people stupid enough to get caught breaking the law." Pushing up, Cole left the booth and exited the café without looking back.

For a long time, Ryan did not move, his mind empty, his appetite gone. Several minutes later, he left. The pie sat, unfinished, on the table.

When Tallie came out to clear away the dishes, she found exact change for the pie sitting on top of the bill. She should have known that's all he'd give her. Irritated by the entire episode at the booth, she lifted the pie plate to clear it away and paused. A twenty-dollar bill sat where Ryan tucked it under the plate, along with a small piece of paper. Curious, she lifted the paper and read the simple note he'd left behind.

Tallie, your father, Charlie Pikyavit, was a good man.

Still too hurt and betrayed, Tallie crumpled the note with anger and shoved it into her pocket.

"I think Tallie will like this fishing spot," Jonathon called across the stream. Grass and overhanging branches protected the small pool, and a logjam deep in the water gave fish shelter and feeding opportunities. Beneath the warmth of the sun, Jonathon wove through the tangle of growth and crossed back to the opposite side.

"I think she will too," Severino noted.

Together they turned and scrambled up the short, steep slope out of the creek bottom. Gravel, sand, and shale tumbled and rolled away from them back to the bottom. At the top, the pair stopped and surveyed the canyon around them. Afternoon light shimmered on the rocks below them and shot a small reflection at Severino, searing his gaze. A shift in his weight broke the intense glare, and he searched the treacherous incline for signs of the object. The glare came again and this time he spotted the item, partially buried in the slope they had just ascended, kicked loose by their rapid climb.

Curious, Severino began to sidestep back down the rocky face. With his gaze locked on the spot, Severino dropped down, closing the distance until he stood over the item. He toed it with his shoe, feeling the hard, smooth surface.

"What did you find?"

"I don't know yet." Severino bent and brushed away the dirt. Clumps of caked earth broke away from the object. Lifting it up, he brushed it clean with his hand then wiped it on his jeans.

Jonathon climbed back down the slope. "What is that?"

Severino passed it to him. "I have no idea. Something metal."

Jonathon reached for the formed metal in his friend's hand. He turned it over and over, examining the hourglass shape of the metal. The bottom held a worn relief carving of a cross, encircled by the double outline of a shamrock. The flat top showed ancient hammer marks, and the entire piece fit in the palm of his hand with heft. Jonathon's fingers closed around the narrow part. "It almost looks like it was used like a stamp or something. Can you see the hammer marks on top?"

He passed the item back to Severino who took it and nodded. "I see them. This looks very old. Maybe even Spanish."

"It does."

"Think your dad would know what it is?"

"Probably. If not, he can find out. Let's take a photo of it with my cell phone, and we can send it to him as soon as we get back to town and have service."

In agreement, Severino held the object balanced flat in his hand while Jonathon extracted his phone and took a picture of it. He then turned the object so Jonathon to take a photo of the worn relief on the bottom.

"This is so cool. If it is Spanish, it's at least five hundred years old."

Amazed, Severino turned the object over in his palm. "What do you do with artifacts here in the States? In Peru, the government controls all of them for the people."

"Here it depends on where you find it. Because this is government land, it is government property, so we can't take it or we could be arrested. We need to leave it here and report it. If it was private land, and the landowner gave me written permission, I could keep it.

"So we just put it back?"

Jonathon nodded. "But let's bury it to make sure no one else sees it and takes it."

With a shrug, Severino returned to the spot where he found the item, dug a hole in the dirt with the heel of his boot and buried it beneath the soil. Jonathon moved a rock on top of it then set a smaller rock on top of the first to mark the spot. "There. Now we can find it again. Let's go get Tallie and send these pictures to my dad."

Filled with the same excitement to share their discovery, the two left the slope and hiked back to camp. As they crested a small ridge together, the terrain broke and tumbled away, the trees and cedar giving way to the grasses and hard-packed earth of their camp. This time, however, instead of two ATVs parked near their tent, a third one also waited, its rider sitting sideways on the seat.

The image startled the pair and concern filled Jonathon's voice. "Looks like we don't have to go get Tallie. She's already here."

"That's not good. That means she traveled here by herself."

"I know. I don't like that at all."

Together, the pair moved into a jog and crossed the remaining terrain, negotiating the rugged earth. Though they entered camp together, Tallie did not look up to greet them. At her stillness, more concern settled over them and they didn't stop until they arrived at her ATV. "Tallie, what's up? I thought you didn't get off work until later."

Lips pressed tight, Tallie glanced at them briefly, her face filled with emotion she could not express. The unexpected expression caused them to tense, and Jonathon straightened. "Whoa, Tallie, what's wrong?"

Sorrow glistened in her eyes and she hesitated—the words hard to share. A whisper finally came as her answer. "I found out what happened to my dad."

Both of them slowed in their movements, sensing deep hurt. "What happened?"

An indistinguishable head roll showed her anguish and the words lodged in her throat. Jonathon sank onto the ATV beside her. "Its okay, Tallie, we're your friends. You can tell us."

A long pause filled the camp and she fumbled with her thoughts and her actions. "He . . . ah . . . he left us for another woman."

Stunned, Jonathon looked up at Severino, mouthed the translation then looked back at her. "How do you know? Are you sure?"

A soundless nod came as her answer, and they saw a single tear slip over her dark lashes and slide, silent, down her cheek.

"*Tanto lo siento*, I am so sorry." Severino murmured. He sat down on the other side of her, put his arm around her shoulder, and drew her in a pained embrace. The move released her emotions in a choked sob and Tallie leaned against him for support. Hurt by her hurt, he laid his cheek against the top of her head and tightened his hold around her like a safe blanket. "Shh, it's okay."

Secure in his hold, Tallie began to speak, Jonathon translating the words she could not. "This man came into the restaurant today, and he had my father's ring."

Confused, Jonathon looked at her. "How do you know it was your father's ring?"

She wiped her eyes. "My dad made it. It is the only one like it in the world, so when this man came into the restaurant wearing this tiger's-eye ring on his thumb, I recognized it right away."

The translation made Severino remember another tiger's-eye ring worn on a man's thumb. Severino sat back and pointed to his thumb. "He wore it here?"

When she nodded, Severino looked at Jonathon and fought to find the right words, fast. "How do you say *tortuga*?"

"Turtle?" The odd request surprised Jonathon.

"Yes. His ring was like a turtle?"

Though the question further confused Jonathon, Tallie understood and shock washed over her. "Yes! How did you know that?"

"I rode on the plane with a man. He had a ring like a turtle, here." Again Severino pointed to his thumb.

Stunned, Jonathon looked up at him. "You mean the exact same plane with the blue-eyed creep?"

"Sí."

This new piece of information startled Tallie, and she looked at them. "What are you talking about?"

"The guy that threatened you apparently was on the same plane as the guy with your father's ring."

"They were together in the café," Tallie offered.

"What?" The unexpected news widened Jonathon's eyes.

"The guy that threatened me came back. He was with the guy who had my father's ring."

"They must be working together. Did the blue-eyed guy say anything to you?"

The question caused her to hesitate and Jonathon pushed harder. "Tallie, what did he say?"

"He wanted to know my last name. He offered me twenty bucks if I'd tell him."

"Did you tell him?"

"No, but he knew my last name anyway. And he knew my dad's name, and the guy with the ring knew my dad too."

"How'd they know all that?"

"I don't know!"

Enraged, Jonathon turned away from the ATVs and ran his hands through his hair. "You must have said something, Tallie. I told you to stay away from them!"

"They were at the café. I had to serve them."

"Oh, come on, Tallie . . . if a wolf steps in front of you, are you going to try to pet it?"

Not understanding all of their conversation but enough to understand Jonathon's building anger, Severino looked at him and spoke quietly in Spanish. "Jonathon, I know you're upset and worried about protecting her, but she needs a friend right now, not a bodyguard."

The truth sounded through Severino's words and Jonathon stopped, his anger twisting into a knot inside him. Inhaling deep, he waited.

A bit reluctant to let her go, Severino removed his arm from around Tallie and rose to his feet. A step toward his friend brought him to within inches of Jonathon, where he kept his voice quiet. "She needs to talk to *you*—without me slowing the conversation, so just listen. Let her tell you everything. Later we can worry about who the guys are and what they want. Right now, we just need to worry about her heart and how she's dealing with the news of her father."

Jonathon understood and gave a nod. Without a look back, Severino moved away to let them speak in the language of their upbringing.

Overhead, the sun shifted to the west, sinking low in the sky, lengthening shadows in the canyon, and sending a definite clip of coolness into the air. Still Jonathon and Tallie stayed at the ATV, talking. Without interrupting them, Severino started a fire and then, later, dinner. Soon the smell of garlic and onions lifted with the woodsy smell of the smoke.

Eventually, Jonathon stood up from the ATV and extended his hand to Tallie. Pulling her to her feet, he gave her a hug and the pair moved toward the fire, ready to move on with the evening and new emotions.

"It smells good," Jonathon commented.

Rising to meet them, Severino watched their advance. The expression on Tallie's face still showed pain, but she managed a smile as she crossed to where he stood. Stopping in front of him, she lowered her gaze. "Thank you," she whispered.

"It was nothing," he shook his head.

"It was something to me." Then she reached up and kissed him gently on the cheek. The action surprised Severino, and he lifted an uncertain gaze toward Jonathon.

Standing behind Tallie and pleased by the kiss, Jonathon gave two rapid lifts of his eyebrows, then let a playful smile fill his face. "So, it seems warm enough over here by the fire. Is dinner about ready?"

Grateful for the distraction, Severino managed to swallow the surprise from his throat and look down at the fire. An iron skillet embraced a watery dish that simmered on the coals. A second pot sat near the heat, its lid nestled firmly over its contents. "No. It needs more time."

Tallie looked down at the meal. "It smells wonderful. What is it?"

"It is *Carapulcra*. The food is very old."

At Severino's explanation, a bottle of pop stopped partway to Jonathon's lips. "Ah, you may want to say the *recipe* is very old, not the food." His gaze shifted to Tallie, and he smiled. "We just bought the food today."

The correction brought an embarrassed smile of his own to Severino's face. "My people, the Incas, made it five hundred years ago. In Peru, we use *papas secas*, you say dried potatoes, so today we buy American dried potatoes." Severino held up an empty box of Hamburger Helper with potato stroganoff. "I just used the potatoes," he grinned.

Charmed by his explanation, laughter bubbled out of Tallie, and she put her hand on Severino's shoulder in a gesture of support. "I love it! When it's ready, can I try some?"

"*Sí, sí.* I made some for you too."

"Good. Thank you. I'll be anxious to try American-style *Carapulcra*."

Across the fire, Jonathon's expression made a sharp change to excitement, and he lowered the drink bottle from his mouth. "Oh, I almost forgot. Tallie, you ought to see what Severino found today! It is so cool." Recapping his drink, Jonathon set it on the ground and extracted his cell phone. While Tallie stood close, he called up the images and showed them to her.

"What is that?"

"We have no idea." He clicked through the images. "The next time we're in town, I'm going to email the pictures to my dad and see if he can figure it out."

"Why don't you email him right now?"

"No cell phone service up here."

She looked at him. "There is down at the campgrounds."

"No, there's not. We go there all the time."

Now her smile brightened. "You just have to be a local. Only locals are allowed to have reception there."

The comment caused Jonathon to frown. "Uh-huh."

She laughed. "Not really. You can get reception there too. You just have to know where to stand. There's one little pocket of reception down there. Come on, I'll show you." Hesitant, she looked at Severino. "Is there time?"

He nodded. "You go. I will stay and finish dinner."

"You sure?"

"Sí."

Excited, Jonathon shoved his phone in his back pocket and reached for the large water jug. "I'll get some more water while I'm down there. We won't be gone long. Thanks."

At the campground, while Jonathon visited with his dad, Tallie drove the ATV over to the water spigot. There she unhooked the large, insulated cooler from the back of her machine and set it on the gravel beneath the faucet. As cold, fresh drinking water poured into the large container, it drowned out the sound of a vehicle approaching through the campground. Behind her, the engine powered down as a truck pulled to a stop.

"I would recognize the shape of those jeans anywhere."

The voice brought a grimace to Tallie's face, and, without even turning around, she knew the speaker. Her eyes rolled with disgust. "Hello, Halden."

Grinning, Halden leaned out the open driver's window of his truck. "So, why are you getting some water? Are you camping up here?"

"Nope."

"Who's it for then, your two boyfriends?"

"They aren't my boyfriends, Halden."

"You're spending a lot of time with them."

"That's because I want to."

"You could spend time with me."

Irritation caused Tallie to straighten, and, for the first time, she turned around and looked at him. "Now why would I *want* to do that?"

"Hey, our discussion the other day was cut short. We could pick up where we left off." With his eyebrows raised, he waited for her response.

A growl of annoyance came from her and she turned back to watch the flow of water. "I'm not interested in discussing anything with you."

The obvious snub made him laugh. "Even better. Why don't I grab a pizza and some drinks and show up at your place around ten tonight? It will be just you and me, and we won't have to discuss a thing."

Finished filling the first container, she secured the lid and lifted it onto the back of her ATV. "Don't waste your time."

From his side mirror, Halden saw a person walking toward them on the dirt road. Shifting the truck into gear, he smiled as he pulled away. 'Oh, it won't be a waste, believe me. See you tonight, Tallie."

Furious, she stared at the truck as he pulled out of the campground and back up onto the gravel road. A minute later, Jonathon walked up beside her and nodded at the truck. "Is that who I think it is?"

"The creep? Yes." She started to fill up a second container.

He heard the strain in her voice. "And what did the creep say?"

"Nothing."

"You're lying, Tallie."

"Fine. He said our last discussion was cut short, so he's going to bring pizza to my place tonight, and we can pick up where we left off or not say a thing. Take your pick."

"He said all that?"

"Yup."

"Mouthy little jerk, isn't he?"

"It's Halden. He's not a mouthy little jerk. He's a mouthy big jerk."

Reaching past Tallie, Jonathon shut off the water and lifted the last container onto the back of her ATV. "Well, he may show up tonight, but you're not going to be there. You're staying in camp with us."

When Jonathon and Tallie climbed off the back of her ATV, Severino could tell they were arguing through their helmets. Surprised, the Peruvian stood up from the camp chair and watched the pair.

In frustration, Jonathon pulled his helmet off his head and crossed the camp to Severino. "Tell her she's staying."

Tallie protested. "Jonathon, I have work tomorrow."

"Not until ten in the morning! Severino, tell her she's staying. She'll listen to you."

"Staying where?"

"Here. Halden showed up while she was getting the water and said he's coming by her house tonight with a pizza. I don't want her anywhere near that *maleducado*."

The news surprised Severino, and he looked at her for confirmation. "Is this true?"

The curiosity in his eyes caused Tallie to lower her gaze. "Yes."

"Hmm." Not ruffled by their argument, Severino reached for a paper plate and then lifted the lid off the small pot, uncovering the flat, white face of freshly cooked rice. Steam lifted into the air. He scooped up a serving of rice, placed it on the plate, and ladled the simmering dish next to the rice. While they were gone, it had thickened into a rich, reddish-brown creation. With a smile in his eyes, he offered the plate to Tallie. "Why eat pizza when there is *Carapulcra*?"

The technique worked. Anger melted out of her like steam disappearing from the food. She reached for the plate. "But I don't have a sleeping bag."

"Use mine," he offered quietly.

"And what will you use?"

"*Mantas*, blankets."

"But I don't have a comb for my hair."

"Use mine," countered Jonathon.

"I don't have a toothbrush."

"Use your finger." Jonathon's verbal reply happened at the same time Severino held up his index finger. The simultaneous response brought laughter to her face. "And are we all supposed to fit inside that tent?"

"No. You can sleep in the tent, and Severino and I will sleep outside."

"What about the mosquitoes?"

"We have bug spray. Tallie, we're doing this for you."

"I know." With a sigh she lowered herself to a camp chair. "If I stay and get the tent, then you guys get the sleeping bags. I'll take the blankets. If you don't agree, I'm heading back down the canyon right now."

"Fine. You can have the blankets."

ELEVEN

NIGHT PROWLED around the camp, a hungry beast intent on devouring everything with its darkness. Only the light from the campfire eluded it, the flames happily popping and crackling around a new log. Jonathon, Severino, and Tallie lounged around the fire, visiting and watching the stars appear in the sky's black coat. Around them, dark mountains surrounded their campsite, leering down on them like ominous giants.

"Anyone got any ghost stories?" Jonathon asked. Above him, a star fled its home, leaving a streak behind it as it fell. They all watched the dying light.

Tallie used a stick and poked at a log in the fire. It sent out a hissing shower of sparks in protest. "You don't need to tell stories up here. Wait long enough and you'll see stuff for yourself."

"What kind of stuff?"

"Weird lights, UFOs . . ."

"What is UFO?" Severino questioned.

Astonished at her words, Jonathon pulled his gaze away from her long enough to explain it to Severino. "In Peru you would call it an *OVNI*, an unidentified flying object." Finished, he looked back at Tallie. "Now you have to explain yourself. I think you have a few campfire stories to tell tonight."

She laughed. "People always see strange lights in the canyon. Most folks say the UFOs are just some new type of aircraft coming out of Douglas Proving Grounds. They're an army testing ground west of here, but I don't know. The animals always react to the lights in the canyons just like they do to the Death Light, and they don't react to an airplane or helicopter flying overhead."

The information about the animals intrigued Severino. "How do they react?"

She thought about it. "Dogs will howl; sheep and cattle will bunch up and stop eating or drinking."

"What do birds and snakes do?"

The unusual question caught her off guard and she hesitated before answering, thinking. "They act strange too, I guess. I don't hang around snakes, but the birds don't roost and they fly a lot, even at night."

Across the dancing, shifting light of the campfire, Jonathon looked at his friend. "You're thinking something, Severino. What?"

Using the language of his upbringing, Severino nodded his need to Jonathon. "There are volcanoes here that left many fissures and vents under the ground, deep in the earth. Because the plates that created the volcanoes are still moving and shifting underneath the ground, they are still creating heat, which is why you also have the warm springs here. The heat moves up through those vents and heats the water. Warm springs and hot pots always occur where plates are still moving. Plate movement also causes earthquakes, so this place is sitting on an active fault line." In Spanish, Severino's intelligence flowed, uninhibited, and Jonathon had to work hard to translate.

Surprised at his knowledge, Tallie looked at him. "Half of Utah is sitting on an active fault line. How do you know all this stuff?"

"It is the same where I live. Wherever you have volcanoes, you will have earthquakes. The colliding plates cause both. If the area also has natural warm water, you will have many quakes and tremors."

Interest brought Jonathon forward, his forearms resting on his knees. "I get the volcano-earthquake-hot springs connection, but what does all this have to do with UFOs?"

A smile creased Severino's face. "Not UFOs . . . lights. You have the Death Light out in the valley and unidentified lights here in the canyon. Before an earthquake hits, the shifting of land plates causes friction and electricity to build up inside the earth. That electricity can ignite pockets of gas under the ground. When that happens, the burning gas produces earthquake lights. These lights often appear just before an earthquake in areas where the gases can reach the surface. The lights can be stationary, or they can move on air currents until the gas is consumed and the fire goes out."

The explanation intrigued Jonathon. "You mean like air currents caused by a passing truck or animals in the area?"

"*Sí*; so it looks like the light is reacting to you, but it's really responding to subtle air patterns." To demonstrate, Severino moved his hand slowly in front of the fire. The flames reacted and waved, bending toward Severino.

Amazed, Tallie watched. "I always wondered why they said *smoke follows beauty* around a campfire! It is following the air current created by your body."

Even by holding his hand still, the flames seemed to sense the presence, and they leaned toward his outstretched palm. "*Sí*. Even if you are sitting still and you don't feel a breeze, the air is still moving around you because of your body heat. Different temperatures create movement, and that means the air flow will change, which attracts fire . . . whether it is a campfire or the fire of an earthquake light."

Jonathon nodded. "That makes sense."

Looking up, Severino lowered his hand. "It also explains why the animals know the lights are coming. Animals can sense earthquakes. Dogs howl, animals stop eating, snakes and earthworms come out of the earth. I have seen many animals acting strange before an earthquake in Peru. I have also seen the lights. Many people have. Before the big earthquake in Pisco a few years ago, hundreds of people saw and filmed earthquake lights. And just before the big earthquake and tsunami in Japan, the same type of lights were seen and videotaped."

"So you're saying this Death Light and the UFOs in the area may really be just earthquake lights?" When he nodded, Tallie questioned him more with a statement. "But we don't have that many earthquakes here."

A shrug showed Severino acceptance of her skepticism. "Not that you can feel. These mountains are granite, which means many earthquakes are being absorbed by the granite, so you do not feel them. But the friction and electricity generated by the shifting plates and their building pressure could still be igniting gases. When those gases make their way to the surface through the fissures and vents, you will see them. Most illogical things have a logical explanation."

A gray, wet morning seemed quiet, too quiet. In his sleeping bag, Severino sensed something different. No birds sang.

Years spent in the mountain told him of the approaching dawn, even without the call of the birds, because he could *feel* it in the air. The world changed just before the sun rose. Grass straightened, the air grew crisp, and even the breeze sensed the approaching day.

Yet while darkness still wrapped the morning earth, Severino sensed something else—something watching. Concerned, he opened his eyes and let his senses tell him of the watcher's location. Moving just his eyes, he glanced in the direction of the threat, and, as he did, he heard a low growl several yards away. The intruder could sense things too, and it knew Severino had awakened.

Next to Severino, Jonathon stirred, but Severino's hand caught his arm, holding him still. "Don't move," he whispered. "Something's in camp." Fog settled over the valley and shrouded the camp in a gray, eerie blanket.

"Where?"

The answer did not settle well with Severino. "By the tent."

"Halden?"

"No, it growled."

In answer, the threat growled again. This time, Severino rolled slowly onto his right side and focused his gaze through the gray darkness. In the fog, a large creature stood near the door of the tent, watching. As their eyes met, the beast lowered its head, a snarl on its fleshy face. Blond hair bristled across its shoulders and Severino saw powerful, tense muscles.

Behind Severino, Jonathon sucked in his surprise, peering through the mist. "What *is* that thing?"

"You don't know?"

"No! I've never seen anything like it."

The creature looked at them for a moment then turned back to the tent, lowering its hideous face to inspect the door, sniffing at the ground. From inside the tent they heard Tallie move, heard the distinct, harsh sound of the tent's zippered door opening.

"No, Tallie! Don't come out!"

Too late, the urgent warning snapped from Jonathon and cut through the graying light. Tallie pulled back the nylon barrier and froze in horror. Intense eyes glared at her from less than two feet away.

Wild kicks pushed Severino free of his sleeping bag and he scrambled toward the tent, running before he'd even stood upright. *"¡Salga!"* The command rolled out of his throat and filled the campsite. Behind him, Jonathon rushed to his feet and followed, fully expecting the wolflike creature to attack one of them.

At the noise, and the rapid movement, the creature vacillated, shifting its weight between the two rushing forward and the terrified face only inches away. Fury caused it to growl a warning and then the beast took a step *toward* the tent. In fear, Severino and Jonathon both shouted their protest and lunged forward to close the distance. The action worked and the thing changed its mind, snapped a tremendous assault in their direction, then bolted for the protective darkness of the fog-wrapped trees.

In the door of the tent, Tallie sunk to the earth. Hands covered her face, and her entire body shook in terror. Dropping to his knees beside her, Severino grabbed her and lifted her hands away from her face. "Are you okay?"

Dread caused her to draw back, still trembling, shaking her head in horror. "It was the Skinwalker," she whispered.

Not sure of what she had said, Severino called over his shoulder. "What was that, Jonathon?"

Coming back from where he'd chased it to the tree line, Jonathon kept his gaze shifting, searching the thick fog and the tight knitting of forest around them. "I don't know! It was too big to be a wolf, and it didn't look like a bear."

"It was a Skinwalker," she repeated. "Tate was attacked by one the other night. That's how he got so torn up. I saw the picture he took of it. It was the same thing."

In an effort to catch his breath and his nerves, Jonathon bent over and rested his hands on his knees, breathing hard. "What's a Skinwalker?"

With Severino's help, she climbed to her feet and stepped out of the tent. "It's bad to even talk about them."

With a quick step around Jonathon, Severino bent over the camp-fire, stirring up the embers, lighting the coals, building the flames back in the early morning. The fire would keep the animal at bay. All three kept a watch on misted trees. Around them, a breeze started to blow through the canyon.

Near the fire, Tallie huddled in fear, her arms folded tight. Severino saw her worry and took off his jacket, draping it over her shoulders.

"He's still out there. I can feel him watching me." Her voice whispered as soft as the smoke.

"Who, the Skinwalker? Is the Skinwalker a person?"

Tallie managed a swallow. "The closest thing you would have to it would be a demon that can change into an animal."

"You mean like a werewolf?"

"No. Werewolves don't exist. No one is ever going to turn into an animal simply because they were bitten by that animal. But Skinwalkers are different. They are evil men who know how to take over the traits of an animal. It's human-to-animal possession, and it's very real."

In the silent trees, ghosts and owls watched the lone campsite.

"Skinwalkers have the ability to talk and think like a human but also move like the animal they've become. They can scent their prey and track them anywhere. They can run on four legs faster than a car, climb trees with amazing speed, and leap great distances. They look half-human, half-animal while they are possessed, and they only appear in an area," anguish dropped her voice to a mere breath, "when they have come to kill someone."

"And you believe that?"

Fury turned her on Jonathon. "I just saw him! I just looked into his face! Jonathon, that thing was half-human, half-animal!"

Severino spoke quietly. "We have a similar creature in Peru. We believe there are witches who become so evil they make pacts with the jungle demons to become *Runapumas:* half-human, half-jaguar. They attack and kill humans and increase in evil and strength with each killing, until they can transform back and forth at will and become demons themselves."

Not wanting to accept an explanation of demons, Jonathon shook his head. "But you just said last night most illogical things have a logical explanation. I can't believe we just saw a Skinwalker. Maybe it was a cougar with mange."

The fire held Tallie's gaze. "Whether there are men evil enough to actually become animals, I don't know; but I do know there are men evil enough that they act like animals. That thing knew me. I saw it in his eyes. He came to the tent, looking for me." Then she gasped and looked up, horrified. "Jonathon, he had blue eyes!"

After saying good-bye on her driveway to Jonathon and Severino, Tallie watched the pair return back up the canyon to search for the creature. She did not agree with their quest but she could not stop them either.

As they disappeared back up the road, she moved across the drive and climbed up the steps to her back door. The morning sun had burned off the gray fog, and now long morning shadows crossed her yard and porch and stretched to the road. Coolness blanketed the back porch and the doorknob felt chilled beneath her touch. Intent on getting ready for work, she rushed through the back door and into the kitchen, where her rapid step slowed before the onslaught of a shocking sight. Her kitchen had been destroyed, and every cupboard and drawer stood open.

Uncertain about why her kitchen lay in tatters, she left the back door open—an escape route if she needed it—and stepped further into her house. Caution moved her into the living room where more destruction greeted her arrival. Pictures hung in disarray on the walls, end table drawers had been emptied, and cushions had been pulled off the couch.

Worry now moved her quickly into the hallway, where the same destruction awaited her; the spare bedroom and bathroom were the next victims she saw. A sense of uneasiness filled her, and she moved to her own bedroom. There her heart sunk. Each dresser drawer waited, open and defiled. The covers on her bed had been torn away, exposing the mattress beneath. Clothes lay strewn across the bed and floor. Even the surfaces of her dresser and end table had been swept clean, the décor broken on the floor.

A shadow stepped behind her. "I waited for you all last night, but you didn't come home."

The voice filled her with more dread than the sight, and she whirled at the sound. Halden stood in the doorway of her bedroom, his frame filling the portal.

Anger consumed her at his presence in her home and she stepped toward him, tense. "Did you do this?"

Halden shrugged. "I saved you some pizza. It's in the refrigerator."

"*I don't want any pizza, Halden! I want you out!* You have *no* business being here." Fury drove her forward, and she shoved him, hard.

Before her onslaught, Halden took a step back. "Tallie, what's your problem?"

"You came into my house and destroyed it! What's *your* problem?" Again, she shoved at him, but this time he braced against it, and she failed to move him. Enraged, she punched her fist against his chest. *"Get out of my house right now!"*

One hand moved to capture her wrist, and he smiled at her efforts. "Don't get mad at me. If you had been here and had *not* spent the night with your boyfriends, I wouldn't have made such a mess. In fact, I may have spent the whole night doing something else besides looking for the wire map."

Horror filled her and she stepped away from him. "You were looking for the wire map?" With new dread filling her, Tallie's eyes scanned the damage in the room.

"What did you think I was going to do while waiting for you to come home?"

Angered, she retreated to her bedroom and started scooping up her clothes. "I can't believe you did this. You went through my drawers!"

He followed her into the room. "Your closet too."

She growled her frustration. "I ought to call the police."

"But you won't."

Angered, she turned on him. "And why wouldn't I?"

A wreckless, lopsided grin greeted her. "Because you don't want them seeing your underwear."

Enraged, she threw her clothes at him. *"Get out, Halden! Right now!"* The decision came easy, and Tallie stepped toward the bedside table, scooping up the phone. Before she could call the police, Halden lunged for her.

The man pivoted in his computer chair and grinned up at the person who had just entered his private office. "Look what showed up in the morning mail." Turning back to the computer, the man typed in a few commands, and the message opened on the screen. The distinguished visitor wearing a tiger's-eye ring stepped around behind the desk to view the monitor.

Fwd: Re: need help identifying.

Hey, I'm hoping you can help identify an artifact my son found. He and a friend are camping in central Utah, and they discovered this yesterday. They sent me the picture last night, but I have no idea what it is. Can you help? Thanks, David

At the computer, the man opened the attachment, and a photo appeared on the screen. The image caused Cole to stop in shock. A Hispanic teen held a crude mint mark. The sight forced air out of Cole's lungs.

From the chair, the man heard the stunned exhale and smiled. "I thought you might like that." A few more commands opened a second photo and revealed markings across the bottom of the object.

"That's an old Spanish mint mark," Cole breathed. "This was found yesterday, in central Utah?"

"Yes. I called my friend who sent the forward and he gave me David Bradford's phone number. When I called Dr. Bradford, he said the kids are camping in the Fishlake National Forest down around Kanosh."

"That's right where my guys are! If these kids have located an old Spanish site, I want to know where it is. I don't want some teenagers ruining the site or taking anything from it."

"I already asked Bradford about that risk, but he said the site is fine. He said his son knows enough about artifacts to not do anything stupid, but he'll remind him the next time the kid calls. He said he'd send me any new information."

"Good. In the meantime, I'll give my guys a call." Already extracting his cell phone and his truck keys, Cole nodded. "I'm heading back down to Kanosh. If anything new comes in, let me know right away."

The phone vibrated in Halden's pocket. Irritated, he reached for the device and glared at the caller's name. The name caused Halden to stiffen and he hesitated. Cole Matthews waited on the other end of the line. The phone rang again. Swallowing, Halden managed to answer the call. "Mr. Matthews, what can I do for you?"

"Halden, I need you to find a couple of kids camping just outside of Kanosh in the Fishlake National Forest."

"Right now?"

"Yes, right now! Ask around. They shouldn't be hard to find. They aren't from around there, and one of them is Spanish."

The news caused Halden's gaze to shift and he glared at another person. "I know exactly who you're talking about. Why do you want me to find them?"

"They found an old Spanish mint mark yesterday. I just saw the pictures. I want you to find out where they got it, retrieve the mint mark from them, and have them take you to the site. Think you can handle that?"

"Yes, sir."

"I don't want any problems. This is too important of a find. Old mint marks were only associated with large mines."

"Oh, there won't be any problems. I've met the boys personally, and I'm sure I can get them to help out any way they can."

"Good. I'm leaving the university right now. I will be there in about three and a half hours."

"Yes, sir." The interruption to his plans left a scowl on Halden's face. Irritated, he closed the phone and looked at Tallie. "We're going to have to continue this later, but, since I don't want to have to *wait* for you to show up again, I'm going to make sure you don't disappear. You're coming with me."

Grabbing her by her arm, he wrenched her to her feet and forced her through the house.

As soon as he had reception, Jonathon called his dad. "Did you find out what it was?" he asked.

David exhaled. "Yes, I did, but first I want to know what you did with it. Did you remove it from the site? You remember the law, don't you Jonathon? Anything over a hundred years old is considered an archeological resource and cannot be removed from public land without a permit. You don't have a permit, Jonathon."

"Dad, I know the law. I didn't remove it from public land. I don't want to go to jail."

"That's good, 'cause I'd hate to have to visit you in jail."

"So, what is it?"

"Well, this morning I sent your photos to a friend of mine at the university. He forwarded it to some of his colleagues and I got a phone call. It appears Severino found a crude Spanish mint mark."

"What's that?" Excited to have an identification, Jonathon looked at Severino and gave him a thumbs-up sign.

His dad continued. "A mint mark identifies where the gold was melted and refined. Most mint marks are associated with official mints, and the closest Spanish mint was in Mexico, but my friend said they also developed simple stamps, like yours, to identify the gold from large mines outside of Mexico."

The news caused Jonathon to clench his fist with enthusiasm and pump it through the air. "Yes! Tallie said there was a lot of Spanish mining in the area."

"There was, and her people were forced to work those mines as slaves."

"I know. She told me that."

"The average life expectancy for a slave was three months."

"She didn't tell me that." The comment sobered Jonathon.

"It was a miserable life, what little of it they had. The slaves too young, old, or weak to mine the ore were put to work crushing the rocks by hand. Others ran the furnace and bellows. The healthy ones, even pregnant women, dug rocks out of the mines and carried them out on their backs. They had to bring up a quota of rocks every day and couldn't stop working until they met that quota. Most of the time the quota required that they worked nineteen to twenty hours a day, and then they had to do it all over again the next day."

Unsettled by the information, Jonathon took a deep breath to clear his lungs and his mind. "No wonder so many of them died."

"Some smaller tribes were completely wiped out and no longer exist at all. Other tribes, like the Paiutes, were reduced so drastically, it's amazing they survived. You can understand why the Native

Americans were leery of the pioneers and settlers when we showed up a hundred years later."

"Yeah, I'm not sure I'd want anyone ever setting foot on my land or near my family again."

"Exactly. Listen, Jonathon, because that's a Spanish artifact, I also forwarded the photos to Juan."

"In Peru?" At the news, Jonathon's voice brightened. He had stayed in close contact with the anthropologist since meeting him in Lima. Not only was Juan a good friend of his father but now was a personal friend of Jonathon. As the only person Jonathon ever told about his experience in the tunnels, Juan guarded that knowledge as closely as Jonathon.

"I thought he would enjoy seeing them, only he's not in Peru. He's in Dallas right now just finishing up the Conference of Anthropology for the Americas. Apparently he's one of the speakers. When he saw the mint mark, he got excited. He said the Spanish had a gold mint in Lima and silver mint at Potosi, which used to be part of Peruvian territory before the boundaries changed and it became Bolivia. Anyway, Juan saw it, sent the photo on to his bosses, and they gave him permission to change his flight and stop in Utah before heading home."

The news surprised and pleased Jonathon. "Really? He's coming here?"

"He is. He's going to catch his flight to Salt Lake in about half an hour, then I'm going to pick him up, and we'll both be in Kanosh later today. We want you to show us where you found that."

"We will. That is so cool!" Jonathon lowered the phone from his mouth. "Juan is coming to Kanosh. He and my dad both will be here this afternoon. They want us to show them where we found the mint mark."

A cocked eyebrow and half nod, showed Severino's approval of the news. David's voice drew his son's attention back to the phone. "So, did you find anything else?"

Not wanting to tell his dad about their effort to track the strange creature, Jonathon guarded his answer. "Um, yeah. We were there this morning. We found some rocks with distinct burn marks on them and some coins with crosses on them. They look like gold to me. I took some pictures of both sides of them. Hang on, I'll send them to you right now." Jonathon lowered the phone and typed in a series of commands, sending the photos through to his dad's email account.

A few moments later, David laughed over the phone. "I got them. They look great. I know exactly what these are. They're cob coins, from the Spanish word *cabo* or end. Once they melted the gold, they poured it into crude sand molds and, as it cooled, they'd remove the ingots, stamp it with that mint mark you found, and slice off both ends to make them even. Then, so they wouldn't waste the end pieces, they hammered them between a press to imprint them and make the coins. This is so cool. How many of those did you find?"

"Five. So, are they worth anything?"

"I'm sure they are, but I don't know how much. I'll forward these photos to that professor who called. He could tell you. But remember the laws, Jonathon. I don't want you two getting into any trouble over this, okay?"

Understanding his father's worry, Jonathon tried to assure him. "We aren't breaking any laws, Dad. We buried them back where we found them and marked each spot so we can show the 'big boys' when they show up. Now it's going to be you and Juan. That's neat. We're going to head back up the canyon and look for more stuff until Tallie gets off work."

"No. I don't want you looking around for 'more stuff'—you could damage something. Besides, you're not supposed to go poking around a known archeological site. It's—"

"—against the law. I know, Dad. How about we just go back up there and look for *unknown* archeological sites, then?"

David laughed and exhaled. "I can't tell you not to go up there . . . it is public land, but no more digging, okay? Wait until we get down there. And Jonathon, thanks for sending me the photos. This is a great find. Even that professor got really excited over these photos. He's been looking for proof of Spanish mines in that area for years, and it looks like you guys have given him some pretty solid evidence. I'll send him these coin pictures right away."

The phone rang three times before being answered. The man's voice flowed in rich Spanish over the phone, and Jonathon spoke back in rapid Spanish. "Juan, it's me, Jonathon."

Hearing the voice, Juan smiled and turned to find privacy in the busy terminal. "Hey, Jonathon, how's it going?"

"Great."

"Your dad sent me the photos of that mint mark. I see you've been digging in the dirt. I never figured you for the type."

Now Jonathon laughed. "Well, you know—monkey see, monkey do."

Smiling, Juan responded without hesitating. "Now, that's not nice to talk about your dad that way."

"I wasn't talking about him, Juan. I was talking about you!"

Chuckling into the phone, Juan smiled. "Oh, in that case, I'm absolutely flattered."

"Yeah, you would be," Jonathon teased back. "Man, it's good to hear you again."

"It is good to hear from you. Did your Dad tell you I got permission to come to Kanosh?"

The question brought a nod. "He did. He said you're going to be here this afternoon."

"I will. I'd like you to show me where you found that mint mark. Is that going to be problem?"

"No, not at all. We'd love to show you. We also found some other stuff too. Wanna see the photos?"

"You know I do."

A few minutes later, the photos passed between the phones, and Juan examined the images. "Those cobs are in amazing shape. You found them by the mint mark?"

"On the same slope, yeah, but they were several yards apart."

"There has to be an old Spanish mine near you somewhere—and your nose for money hasn't sniffed it out yet?"

"Hey, I'm closer to it than you!"

"*Verdad*. Do you have any more photos you can send me so I can grow increasingly jealous of your discovery while I'm on the plane?"

"*Claro que sí*. Every teenager has more photos on his phone than he first shows people."

"And should I tell your dad you said that?" The smile in Juan's voice came through the phone.

The unexpected question lifted Jonathon's gaze to the tree line, his mind doing a rapid mental inventory. "Ah . . . sure. Just give me a minute to delete a few things and—"

"You hadn't better delete anything."

Now the teen smiled. "I'm just kidding. Believe it or not, I have nothing on my phone I wouldn't show to you or my dad. Here, let me send you these photos."

"Good, because I really hate reading those airline magazines."

Within seconds, the first photo came through, and Juan opened the image . . . carvings, weathered by time, etched onto a black rock surface. Excited, Juan returned to the call. "Jonathon, where did you find these? Are they close to where you found the mint mark?"

Turning to the west, Jonathon shook his head even though Juan couldn't see. "No. They are about twenty-five miles from here, but Severino said some of them are Spanish."

"He's right, some of those carvings are definitely Spanish. I've seen similar ones in Peru. Just how much Spanish activity did you guys have in that area?"

"A lot, apparently. Enough that the Spanish used slave labor to run their operation."

The news caused Juan to exhale. "Oh, that's too bad. That means your indigenous people suffered greatly."

"Apparently they did, although I'm just now finding out about it."

An announcement over the loudspeaker pulled at Juan's attention. "Listen, Jonathon, they've just called my flight. While I'm on the plane, I'll look at these carvings and see what I can figure out. Sometimes they'll even tell you the direction and how many kilometers to the mine."

"That sounds great."

"If all goes well, I'll be there about four this afternoon."

"That sounds great. We don't have good cell phone coverage up here, so we'll just plan to meet you guys at the café this afternoon, around four. Dad knows where it is."

"Sounds great, *hasta pronto*," Juan finished.

"*Hasta pronto*," Jonathon concluded.

At the café, Cole's final commands to Halden drifted through the intercepted phone call. *"This is too important of a find. I'm leaving the university right now. I will be there in about three and a half hours."* Then the call ended.

Sitting at the café bar, Ryan removed the small earpiece and stared at his phone, stunned. He'd listened to the entire call and still struggled to wrap his mind around the conversation. Two teenagers had found some Spanish artifacts and Cole just sent Halden to find them.

Ryan's gaze shifted out the café window. Thoughts of the two teenagers he caught rummaging through the back of his truck yesterday consumed him, and Ryan realized he should have done more to chase them off. Now Cole had just thrown a big problem into the middle of his road.

Anger twisted inside him, drawing his muscles and nerve sinews tight. The snarl of possible troubles rolled through his mind. He had to get to the site first—before Cole or Halden—and that meant he had to find those kids.

With his first decision made, Ryan turned his attention back to his cell phone and began to text. *Two kids camping in Fishlake National found a Spanish mint mark yesterday. Someone at university has pics. I need to see those photos now. Find them!*

He pushed send.

Less than a minute later, his phone vibrated and he looked at the screen. *Haven't heard a thing. Will try to find info/photos. May take a while. Will send ASAP.*

The reply brought a groan of disapproval from Ryan. He didn't have time for it to take time; Cole would be here between one and two. Frustration sent his gaze away from the reply and down the bar to where a waitress placed clean glasses under the counter. There had to be another way to get the information he needed about the teenagers.

An idea flowed into his mind, and he knew what to do. One hand moved his cell phone beneath the counter and the other motioned toward the waitress. When he had claimed her attention, she moved toward him and Ryan questioned her. "Is Tallie Pikyavit working today?"

Whatever answer he expected, it did not include the surprise that passed across the waitress's face. In front of him, the girl shuffled through her mind for the answer. "She is supposed to work today, but she should have been here by ten. Are you waiting for her?"

Ryan looked at his watch and felt his stomach knot. The hands showed twenty after ten. "Sort of. Is she usually late?"

"No, she's usually early."

TWELVE

LISTEN, I'VE tried her cell phone. Can you call her house and see how much longer she's going to be?"

A smile of compliance moved the waitress to the nearby phone anchored on the wall. At his bar seat, he watched her lift the receiver and push the buttons. His eyes noted the numbers she pressed, and, beneath the counter, he entered those numbers into his own cell phone.

The waitress waited while the phone rang. After several unanswered rings, she hung up. "She must be on her way now. No one is home."

Nodding his appreciation, Ryan thanked her. "I'll just wait then. How long does it take her to get here?"

"Oh, only about five minutes. She should be here any minute."

"Thank you."

Ryan waited a full ten minutes, feeling his stomach knot tighter with each sweeping rotation of the second hand around his watch face. Finally, unable to wait any longer, he motioned to pay for his bill, left a tip, and exited the café. Outside, on the sidewalk, he opened his phone and used Tallie's number to do a reverse search. In seconds, he had the address of where she lived. Keeping it on his screen, he headed to his truck.

The GPS system led him to her home in less than five minutes. The small, older home sat back on a graded road, surrounded by alfalfa fields, irrigation ditches, cottonwood trees, and space. The nearest neighbor claimed their place half a mile down the road. The only signs of life were some horses in the corral, watching him.

A deep breath steadied his nerves and Ryan climbed out of his truck. Hope that his explanation would work battled with concern that she would see him standing in his doorway and slam the door. The lesson with the pie told him she had her own way of dealing with things, and she could catch him unprepared.

Worn, dusty boots carried him across the sidewalk and up the front steps. Two planters filled with flowers and ornamental grasses greeted him from either side of the door. The view caused a sudden twist in his thoughts that turned his emotions sideways. The bright, cheerful plants reminded him of his own front porch. He never planted flowers, but his wife always did. Even when they were first married and lived in a small apartment, she took care of a tiny pot of flowers in the kitchen windowsill. Then, when they bought their home, she planted flowers before she even painted the interior.

The unexpected thoughts caused Ryan to pause by the front door. Memories took him back to his own front porch, watching his wife plant flowers that first summer. She looked cute covered in dirt, a smudge on her nose that she didn't even know about. After that, every May he would find her on her hands and knees in the dirt, digging new holes, planting new flowers, and putting new smudges on her face.

Now, with a divorce shortly ahead, he wondered what would happen to those flowers, their home, and her.

The thought caused his feelings to gray and wilt. Tattered, his mind returned to Tallie's front porch, where the flowers waited in cheerful silence. For a moment, he stood still, trying to reclaim his hardened veneer. When he felt it lock down in place, he stepped between the two planters and rang the doorbell. The chime echoed through the house and then fell quiet, the same muffled silence that only exists in empty space. The home held no one.

Wanting to make sure, he waited several seconds then rang the bell again. The same response reverberated through the house and back to his ears.

A shift on his boots allowed him to look around the property and the silent road to be sure no one watched. Alone, Ryan crossed to the end of the porch, jumped to the ground, and walked around to the back of the house. At the rear entrance, he lifted his fist to rap on the door when he noticed the portal slightly ajar. Thinking Tallie may have gone outside to tend to the property or animals, Ryan looked around again. No movement came to his view.

Curious, Ryan returned his focus to the door and called out to the interior of the house. "Tallie, are you home?"

No answer.

"Tallie, your back door is open, so I'm coming in." When silence returned to his ears, he accepted it as approval and pushed the door open. It swung slowly inward, and sunlight fell across the messy kitchen. Not the housekeeper he had expected, but he'd seen worse.

"Tallie?"

Still no answer. He cautiously stepped over the threshold and into her home. Out of the morning sun, the lighting shifted and Ryan's eyes focused to the chaos around him. Cupboards stood open. Drawers, removed from their spaces, lay on the floor, their contents spilled across the worn linoleum. Containers of food spilled on the counters, drawers and papers lay strewn across the table and floor. In that moment, Ryan felt coldness grip him. Tallie's house had not been neglected; it had been ransacked.

Shock spread through him for just a second as he viewed the destruction. Then, realizing his own legal vulnerability, he backed out of the house. If she came home and saw him there, then he would be blamed, and he didn't need that! That would mean police and more problems than he wanted to face.

A quick retreat returned him to his vehicle. As he reached the front of his truck, a wave of frustration rolled through him and Ryan stopped. He couldn't leave.

Thoughts of Charlie Pikyavit rolled—unbidden—into his mind, and he lowered his head before the one truth he knew. If his daughter lived in this house, he'd want someone to go inside and check for her.

Frustration turned to irritation, and he jerked open the truck door with a groan of anger. "Charlie, you're going to owe me big-time for this." Reaching across the seat, Ryan retrieved his gun, released the safety, and turned back to the house. Then, keeping the revolver close to his body and out of sight, he made his way back to the open kitchen door.

Once again, he stepped back into the kitchen. Standing amid the destruction, he checked and listened for signs of movement within the house. Nothing registered. Ready with his gun, Ryan continued forward, selecting his path over the debris and through the kitchen.

At the end of the short hall, he let his eyes enter the living room first. More emotions turned inside him. This wasn't a normal burglary; the house had been searched. Couch cushions, twisted by a search, tumbled off the sofa. Magazines carpeted the floor. A throw blanket lay in a disheveled pile, but the end table and lamp disturbed him the most. Knocked over in a struggle, the end table lay on its side and the lamp lay in its own, shattered remains. Struggles meant someone had been in the house trying to stop the destruction. It meant Tallie had probably been there!

Lifting his gun, Ryan's mind shifted to Tallie, and he increased his speed, needing to see the rest of the house as fast as safety would allow. Swift strides took him across the living room. Standing in the arch of the back hallway, he peered to the right then the left. His path selected, Ryan moved into the first bedroom he saw.

Destruction filled the room. Obviously a spare bedroom, storage boxes had been opened and dumped on the floor and bed; the mattresses had been shifted as if someone looked between them for an object. Quick to search both sides of the bed, Ryan made sure no one lay on the floor, injured and out of sight.

In the bathroom, the linen cupboard had been emptied and Tallie's personal things thrown on the floor in piles. Hair accessories tumbled over makeup supplies, and bottles of shampoo leaked onto perfumes.

But Tallie's room suffered the most destruction. Clothes lay strewn across the room, ripped from the closet and dresser. Drawers, removed from the dresser frame and dumped onto the floor, left contents spread over the carpet. Destroyed bedding tumbled across the bed and onto the floor, and a toppled lamp lay denuded of its lampshade.

Fear and quick steps carried him to the far side of the bed, hoping he would not find Tallie on the floor. He didn't. For a brief moment, relief filled him, until he saw something on the bed that filled him with dread. A short section of rope lay on the mattress. A fresh, clean cut on one end told him the rope had been cut for recent use.

With his stomach twisted tight, Ryan extracted his cell phone and called the café. Sick with concern, he counted the rings, willing someone to answer. Finally a worker did, and he asked the question the rope had already answered. "Is Tallie there?"

"No, she hasn't come in to work yet."

Disconnecting the call, Ryan grimaced. "Tallie," he whispered, "what have you gotten yourself into?"

Outside, Ryan climbed into his truck and accessed the Internet through his phone. When he found the phone number he needed, he backed out of Tallie's driveway and headed for Kanosh. There he found a pay phone by the city park. With his truck engine still running, he got out and dropped money into the phone, dialing the number on his cell phone.

"Millard County Sheriff's department. How may I help you?"

"You'll find the back door open and the house burglarized at 12750 West Cedar Hill Road." Before the barrage of questions started, Ryan hung up, climbed back into his truck, and drove away. The house now lay in the hands of the authorities, but it didn't solve his original dilemma.

With his mind churning through more thoughts than he wanted to process, Ryan left the area. He still didn't know where the archaeological site or the teenagers were located, and now Ryan clearly understood he had an additional problem on his hands.

He had no idea where to find Tallie.

Rocks, wooden planks, and debris tumbled into the abyss, leaving behind a trail of dust. A look of surprise moved from Severino to Jonathon. "I thought your father said no more digging."

"Hey, I didn't dig this hole. I just found it!" With a playful grin, Jonathon turned on a flashlight and scooted close to the edge on his belly. The beam peered down into the chasm. Dust filtered through the beam in fingers of swirling smoke and particles.

As it settled, the cavern below came into view, and Jonathon jerked back as a rattlesnake, perched just below the edge, struck at his head. "Oh, geez! Snake! Did you see that?"

Rolling sideways, Jonathon grabbed a broken plank of wood, then returned to the edge. Using the wood, he flipped the snake off its perch. Released from its ledge, the sinewy body of the snake rotated in midair like a bird in flight, and the reptile disappeared from view into the bottom of the pit. "That was close. Too close."

With his light, Jonathon checked the edges for other snakes before retraining the beam on the bottom of the shaft. A second light joined the power of the first, and both shone down into the pit below them. In the swirling light, they spotted two, then three rattlesnakes. Even from their height, they heard the reptiles' displeasure with those who had disturbed their home.

Again Jonathon rolled back from the edge. "That settles it. I'm definitely not going down first."

"And you think I am?"

Jonathon laughed. "Maybe we can go get Tallie to do it. She'll do it if *you* ask her."

Now Severino sat back from the edge of the opening and smiled. "I wouldn't ask her."

"Even if I paid you five bucks?"

"Not even if you paid me six bucks." For emphasis, Severino held up a total of six fingers, his dark eyes dancing at his response.

Laughing now, Jonathon shook his head at the sight and shifted sideways. A five-dollar bill emerged from his pocket and he passed it to Severino. A picture of Abraham Lincoln peered up from the bill's face. "Ah, come on. You mean you like her more than you like that guy?"

Severino snorted at the image and handed back the money. "She's a lot cuter than that guy."

Taking a moment to study the bill, Jonathon shrugged. "Yeah. I guess you're right. Okay, I won't ask her to go in there for five bucks." He stuffed the money back in his pocket. "I wonder who's on a ten-dollar bill." Severino gave him a friendly shove, and Jonathon shook his head, joking. "Nah, I wouldn't send her down there for even twenty bucks. It wouldn't be fair to the poor snakes."

Together they peered back into the shaft, letting their flashlights cut through the dust and darkness. "I wonder how deep it is," Jonathon queried.

"It looks like it's about nine to twelve meters."

"So about thirty or forty feet?"

"I guess."

Jonathon moved his beam across the vertical sides, five feet away. "Think it's a mine shaft?" Jonathon asked.

"It looks more like a ventilation shaft to me." Severino focused his beam on a dark place near the bottom. "My guess is that's the opening to the mine shaft. So, do rattlesnakes live that deep under the ground?"

Using his cell phone, Jonathon snapped a photo of the discovery. "I don't think so. I'm guessing they either crawled in from the mine shaft, or were hiding under the wooden planks to get out of the sun when we kicked in the cover."

"They can survive a fall like that?"

This time Jonathon laughed in disdain. "They can survive just about anything." Scooting away from the chute, Jonathon looked at the new images on his phone. "I'm going to send these to my dad as soon as we're back in town." Then, looking at the time, Jonathon closed his phone. "If you want, we can head down to the café and get some lunch and show all the pictures to Tallie."

Their eyes met and Severino grinned. "Good. Let's go."

The day's growing heat joined them on the hike back to camp. They both felt relief as they topped the last rise, but that sensation vanished at the sight of Tate and Halden. Caution filled both of the teenagers and they entered camp with senses alert and wary. "What are you guys doing here?"

"Waiting for you." Comfortable in one of their camp chairs, Halden took a drink from a bottle of pop he had commandeered. Tate, still standing, looked down at his boots.

Sensing Tate's unease with the entire situation, Jonathon looked back at Halden, a bit more bold in his next question. "What do you want?"

A quick swallow of soda followed the question, and Halden extracted his phone. With one hand he pressed a few buttons. "It seems you boys found something yesterday, and I want to see it for myself." Standing, Halden turned the phone's screen around to show them an image of the mint mark.

Confused at seeing the image on Halden's phone, Jonathon frowned. "I sent that photo to my dad. How did you get it?"

"Small world. Did you know it is estimated our Internet distance from any person in the world is four and a half friends? That means forwards move fast. So, are you going to show it to me?"

A scowl crossed Jonathon's face. "No. You already have your own picture, thanks to your four and a half friends."

Halden didn't like the intentional slam. "I mean the actual

object. Where is it? It doesn't appear to be here."

With his jaw set, Jonathon glared at Halden. "I'm not going to tell you."

"You got it in your pocket?"

"No."

"Where did you hide it? Come on, I know you're going to try and keep it. You're teenagers."

"And that makes us artifact thieves?"

"It makes you stupid." Halden stared at him, challenging the younger kid. Jonathon remained quiet. "Now just tell me where it is and where you found it and let us professionals come in and take care of the site."

Snorting in disgust, Jonathon stepped back. "You're not a professional. You couldn't even handle a sandbox dig. You're just someone's lackey."

Halden bristled at the comment. "You don't know what you're talking about. I've already handled more digs this summer than you've seen years."

"Then show me your federal permit so I know you have authority to pursue archeological finds on government land; 'cause if you don't have a badge or a permit, I'm not going to show you where it is."

Next to Jonathon, Tate leaned close, his whispered words a warning to the teenager. "Don't get Halden mad. Just tell him, please."

"No, not unless he produces something."

Irritated by the teenager, Halden came to his feet and crossed to the tent. "You want me to produce something? I've got something right here that gives me all the permission I need." Jerking open the tent flap, Halden stepped partially inside and then emerged again, dragging something with him.

Jonathon and Severino froze as he jerked Tallie from the tent, her mouth covered in duct tape, her hands tied behind her back. She stumbled at the rough removal and both friends surged forward, but Halden pulled her away from them and shoved her into a camp chair. "So, you want to tell me where you found that mint mark?" questioned Halden.

Enraged, Severino stepped forward, his voice erupting low and angry. "*Supaypa wachasqa kanki*—" Jonathon didn't have to know Quechua to understand the fury on his friend's face.

Halden didn't need to know it either. He felt the threat and responded by pulling out a gun and pointing it—not at Severino—but at Tallie. The threat worked and Severino froze.

Stunned, Tate looked at his cousin. "Halden, what are you doing with a gun?"

"I'm getting that mint mark, and then I'm going to find out where they found it."

"Before Cole?"

"Especially before Cole!"

A frown of fear filled Tate's expression, and he shook his head. "No, man, this isn't worth it. You can't double-cross Cole. Put the gun away and let her go. Let the kids go. Nothing is that important. If Cole finds out about what you're trying to do, you know what will happen to us . . ."

"Shut up, Tate!" He shoved the muzzle of the gun beneath Tallie's chin and she shut her eyes at the pressure.

"*Por favor,* release her." Severino whispered.

Seeing the expression on the Peruvian's face change, Halden laughed. "You like her, don't you? Well, you know what? So do I. In fact, we've spent all morning together, haven't we, sweetheart?" In emphasis, Halden brushed Tallie's hair behind her shoulder, tucking it behind her ear. Furious, she tried to pull away, but Halden stopped her, gripping her shoulder with his hand and squeezing it until she submitted and her dark eyes winced in pain. The move brought another curse to Severino's lips who didn't understand all the English Halden used, but understood the actions.

Jonathon eased forward. "Halden, just calm down. If you want to know where it is, we'll tell you. We'll even show you. Just let Tallie go."

Halden refused. "I'm not letting her go."

Severino spoke in bargaining. "We found an old mine."

The news startled Halden and he looked at the Peruvian. "When, today?"

"*Sí,* just now."

"And how do I know you're not lying?"

Jonathon pulled out his cell phone. "We took pictures." His fingers retrieved a photo and he passed the phone to Halden.

Seeing the shaft, Halden smiled. "Looks like you're telling the truth. So you're saying you'll take me to both places, right?"

Jonathon did not shift his gaze from Halden. "Yes, if you let her go."

At the answer, Halden grinned and jerked Tallie to her feet. "You have a deal, but I let her go only *after* I have the mint mark and we get to the mine. She's my 'permit' and she's going to keep you two lackeys in line. Understand?"

Anxious to protect Tallie, both Jonathon and Severino nodded.

Pulling Tallie back a step, Halden waved the revolver at both teenagers. "Pick up those packs. They're filled with excavating equipment. I figured you'd agree to work for me and we'd find something more than a mint mark today. Now get moving."

Without a word said, Jonathon and Severino each lifted one of the heavy packs to their backs. Shrugging into the gear, a silent look passed between them at the sudden upheaval in their lives. The danger of the situation loomed around them, like the mountains narrowing the skyline above them. Somehow, they needed to get all three of them to safety.

Angered by their slow and quiet movements, Halden waved the gun at them. "Get moving, now!"

In compliance, Severino moved ahead of Jonathon toward the edge of camp, his path taking him near Tallie. He purposely met and held her gaze as he walked by, asking her questions with his eyes and reading the answers they gave back. No language could match the communication they shared in those short seconds. With Halden watching Jonathon, Severino gave her a soft nod. "*No te preocupes,*" he mouthed. "You'll be fine. I promise." And he knew, as he moved first out of camp, that he would risk his life to keep that promise.

A scan of his watch told Jonathon the time. Ahead, Severino stopped to wait, and Jonathon caught up to him. "We took Tallie down early to get ready for work, and Halden said he's been with her all morning," he whispered

"I know," Severino returned.

Behind them, Halden drove Tallie, like an animal, up the slope and Tate came last, burdened by more supplies. Concerned for Tallie, Jonathon watched her chained to Halden by his hard grip. "That means he's been with her for at least four hours. What do you think he's done to her?"

"Nothing."

Jonathon looked at Severino, desperate to believe him. "How do you know for sure?"

"I looked at her eyes. She's furious. If he'd done anything to her, there would have been hurt or shame in her eyes, but right now she absolutely wants to tear him apart. So far only her freedom has been controlled, nothing else."

Down the trail, Jonathon watched Tallie jerk her arm free from Halden and glare at her captor. A small smile lifted the corner of Jonathon's mouth. "That's my girl. Maybe it's a good thing—for Halden's sake—her hands are tied and she can't reach him."

Together they climbed a few more steps. Disquieted thoughts enwrapped Severino until they had to be given voice. "You know he's not going to untie her, Jonathon."

Climbing up onto a boulder, Jonathon looked over at his friend. The response came as a statement, not a question. "You've seen hostage situations before."

"Besides yours? Yes. If they blindfold you, you have a chance; but when they let you see where you are, who *they* are, and what is going on . . ." Severino could not finish, his expression heavy.

The words turned Jonathon's gaze back down the trail to Tallie, and he felt sorrow pass through him. Instinct told him Severino spoke the truth; Halden had made a decision he couldn't erase. "So, what are we going to do?"

"We need to think of someway to get her away from him." Severino affirmed, then a small smile lifted onto his face. "I've helped free at least one *Americano*, and I know you aren't too bad at devising unique escape plans yourself."

Memories flowed back into Jonathon's mind, and he returned a slight smile. "Yeah, I did free Carlos from the Shining Path with only a pop bottle and some cooking oil." Beneath the heavy pack, Jonathon shrugged his shoulders and shifted the weight on his back. "And it feels like we have a few more supplies to use this time."

The humming of his phone caused Ryan to jump in the cab of his truck. Shifting his weight and extending his leg, he slipped his hand in his front pocket and retrieved the phone and the new text.

Though still driving, his eyes scanned the message.

Here is the picture.

The four simple words sent the truck into a fishtail on the gravel road as Ryan pressed hard on the brakes. The powerful vehicle came to a reluctant stop. A quick check to his mirrors told Ryan no vehicles approached through the settling dust. Anxious, Ryan returned his full attention to the message, and he opened the attachment. A photo of a crude Spanish mint mark filled the screen and a satisfied smile pulled across Ryan's face. The contents of the photo showed nothing about the terrain, but he didn't need it to. If the teens had used a cell phone to take the photo, the image would be embedded with geotags. He just needed to access the tags to know exactly where they were standing when they took the photo.

Sitting in the cab of his truck, Ryan worked the keypad. The gamble paid off and a wide grin took his handsome face hostage. The exact longitude and latitude of their photo glowed across the screen. Putting the truck back into gear, he redirected the vehicle and headed toward the coordinates.

The road ended eight miles up Kanosh Canyon. At Horseflat Canyon, he parked the truck and began to load things into a small pack: a topographical map, binoculars, first aid kit, flashlight, matches, rain poncho, and space blanket. He shoved his gun and extra ammunition into his holster. Then he slipped his cell phone into his front pocket. Ready, Ryan moved through the wooden barrier that restricted access to the trail and kept vehicles out.

Half an hour later, still moving in the direction of the GPS codes, he slowed his hike. Ahead, a small camp hugged the canyon walls. Lowering himself into the bush, Ryan observed the camp. A two-man tent faced a small fire pit and four ATVs sat still near the woodpile, too many ATVs for the tent. That meant the campers had visitors.

He looked down at his compass and map. The camp stood about two-thirds of a mile from site of the photo. Chances were good this was where the teens were staying.

A few more minutes of observation convinced Ryan the camp stood empty. Still, he approached with caution.

In the camp, he took a moment to study items around him, especially the snack foods. His visual exam turned up typical camp food along with bottled water, pop, chips, and jerky. The campers were most likely men. Female campers selected sweets—especially chewy sweets like licorice and gummy bears or fruit chews.

The food choices, however, did not tell him the age of the campers. The clothes inside the tent would, though. Also, if this camp belonged to the teens who found the mint mark, their lack of creativity would limit their hiding places. He'd probably find the artifact in the tent too.

After scanning the canyon for movement, he approached the tent and ducked beneath the open flap. The sight inside stopped him cold. Sleeping bags and pads pushed and shoved around the small interior showed a struggle had taken place inside the tent. Then his eyes found a piece of duct tape cast to the side. Tense, he approached the tape. Even before he turned it over with his foot, he knew what he would see stuck to the other side.

When his eyes confirmed his fears, Ryan felt sick. Waist-length black hairs twisted and clung to the tape.

Tallie had been inside the tent, and she had not wanted to be there.

THIRTEEN

THE MINT mark retrieved and safe in his pocket, Halden pushed the group further up the canyon, toward the mine. Here, the terrain increased in steepness and rockiness. Climbing proved difficult. With her hands tied behind her back, Tallie stumbled and fell often, scraping the skin on her arms and legs and cutting her flesh on the rocks. Protests from Jonathon and Severino did not convince Halden to untie her. In fact, Halden responded by pushing Tallie faster up the slope. By the time they reached the shaft, Tallie's dark hair hung from her ponytail in a rumpled mess, and her shirt and shorts were stained with dirt and blood.

Exhausted and standing a few yards back from the shaft, Tallie tried to suck enough air into her lungs. The duct tape restricted her ability to breathe, and her nose seemed incapable of drawing in enough air. To compensate, she took rapid, short breaths.

Nearby, Tate shrugged free of his pack and coiled ropes and removed a bottle of water from his pack. Opening it, he approached Tallie and started to remove the tape from her mouth.

"What are you doing?" Halden demanded.

"She needs a drink."

"And what if she screams?"

Tate held his ground. "Who's going to hear her up here?" Without waiting for Halden's response, he pulled the tape from her mouth. The pain caused her to wince, and Tate apologized then lifted the bottle to her lips. Several long swallows made their way down her throat before Tallie lowered her head and thanked him. Tate then walked across the slope and extended the bottle of water toward Jonathon and Severino.

At the offering, Severino studied the quiet cousin before retrieving the bottle. Sadness filled Tate's expression, and Severino knew the younger cousin might be the key to helping them get out of this situation. "*Gracias.*" Only a soft nod came as response and then Tate lowered his head and returned to his pack.

Taking a few appreciated swallows of cool water, Severino passed the bottle to Jonathon and watched Tate pull some headlamps from the pack. Tate set these next to the rope coils he had carried up the trail while he continued to rummage through his gear. A moment later, Tate retrieved a small first aid kit, and Severino watched him return to Tallie. Tenderly, he helped her sit on the ground and, without a word, began to clean and bandage some of her wounds.

"Tate, what do you two think you're doing?" she whispered.

In response, Tate shook his head and used an alcohol wipe on her knee. "I didn't know he was going to do this, Tallie, I swear." She hissed at the alcohol burn but said nothing more. Opening a pack of gauze, Tate placed it over the still bleeding cut on her knee and held it in place with one hand while he reached for the largest bandage he had with the other. Then he hesitated. With only one hand to hold the bandage, he didn't know how to open the package.

Severino knelt beside him and held the gauze to Tallie's knee.

"Thanks," Tate whispered. He opened the large bandage, removed the protective barrier, and secured it to her knee. That wound addressed, Tate examined a long, wide scrape on her elbow. On the other side of her, Severino cradled Tallie's chin in his hand and brushed hair off her forehead. A scrape and swelling discolored her forehead above her right eye. Concerned, Severino's gaze shifted to hers. "*¿Estás bien?*" he questioned gently.

"Yes."

He pointed to the wound. "Do you have a headache?"

As he formed the simple question in English, Tallie shook her head. "No." The movement caused her to wince. "Maybe—just a little."

The admission turned Tate back to the kit. "I think I saw some painkillers in here." Several single-dose packets came into view, and he handed one to Severino, motioning for the Peruvian to give them to her while Tate stood to retrieve the remaining water from Jonathon.

Severino tore open the packet and poured the two pills into his hand. He lifted them to her mouth and helped her take them from his palm. When Tate returned with the bottle of water, he passed it to Severino. Carefully, the Peruvian lifted the water to her mouth, watching as she swallowed the pills with a mouthful of water. "*Todo,*" he admonished, wanting her to drink the rest.

Too thirsty to argue, Tallie accepted the last three mouthfuls. Finished, she caught her breath and looked at him. "Thank you," she whispered.

Behind them, Halden walked around the edge of the chute, looking down into the opening. "Ooo-weee, that looks deep. You two been down inside it yet?"

"No." Jonathon glared.

"So what's keeping you out? Afraid of the dark?"

"No. There are rattlesnakes down in the hole."

Clicking on a flashlight, Halden looked into the chute. "Oh, yeah. I see 'em. There's actually quite a few down there. Hey, look at that one. I'd say he's close to five feet. You'll have to go down and measure him for me."

"You can go down yourself. We told you we'd show you where the stuff is, and you said you'd let Tallie go. Now untie her."

Stepping back, Halden looked at Jonathon. "Maybe you've forgotten who holds the gun right now. I didn't ask if you wanted to go down. I said you will *have* to go down, so go get some rope and start heading down."

Jonathon straightened but did not move.

At the defiance, Halden lifted the revolver in a physical threat. Still, Jonathon did not move. He had stared down the barrel of a gun before, and his angry gaze did not waver now.

Seeing Jonathon's resolve, Halden partially cocked the revolver and stepped closer. "Get down in that hole."

The hot sun burned down on Ryan, heating his body and his clothes. Sweat trickled down the sides of his tanned face and marked his shirt in several places. Again he checked the GPS coordinates against the map and didn't like the reading. He stood where the boys had taken the photographs—but the canyon revealed nothing. No artifacts, no teenagers, and no Tallie. Now he had no idea where the teenagers had taken her.

Thoughts carried Ryan back to the destruction inside the tent. The clothes he found indicated that two teenage boys were camping there, and he worried about their reasons for taking Tallie hostage. She may have discovered they were digging for artifacts and called them on it. And, if the teenagers were part of a bigger ring of diggers and dealers, if they were digging for Cole, Tallie could be in a lot of trouble.

Ryan tried to swallow his frustration in an attempt to clear his mind, but the dryness of his mouth made the action twist and tear in his throat. From his pack, he pulled out a bottle of water. He twisted the lid, snapping through the seal and opening the container. In several long, deep swallows, he drew half the water into his system and scanned the canyon, searching for clues.

Experienced eyes searched the creek bottom and the steep slope. Then he noticed a hole scarring the side of the mountain, footprints and gouges marring the terrain around it. Interested, Ryan approached the wound and examined the mark. Something had been dug out of the earth recently, and the irritating sensation in his stomach told him they exhumed the mint mark from the site.

Frustrated, he looked around him at the vacant canyon, fighting his emotions. As he did, his eyes saw a single, upright stick a few yards away. For a moment, he stared at the twig, out of place for the area. Then, side-stepping across the slope, he moved to where the stick stood watch over a small patch of disturbed ground—a fresh burial ground. Curious now, his hand brushed away the dirt, removing centuries of dusting. As the item came into view, amazement filled him. An old Spanish cob coin lay in its earthen safe.

Stunned that it had been reburied and marked, Ryan looked around him for some type of visual explanation. None presented, but only three feet away he saw a second upright stick buried in the hillside, marking another recent mound. At the second location he uncovered two cob coins, well pressed and in excellent shape despite the centuries.

A minute later, Ryan turned up two more coins, each location marked in the same manner as the others. More mystified, he struggled for understanding. Someone had been here, found the artifacts, and—rather than pocket them—reburied each item and marked their locations. No artifact thieves that he knew of would go to that much work or that much risk. They would take their find and leave the area.

The heft of the coins in his hand felt solid to him. With his fingers, he turned over each coin and examined their markings. Almost perfect. For another minute, Ryan tried to understand the unusual events, then he accepted his find and slid the coins into his pocket. After all, he didn't want to leave them here and tempt someone to break the law.

Though he still didn't know their location, the geotags in the photo told him where the teenagers had found the mint mark. Several other artifacts in the area had been marked as well. The site appeared to hold quite a treasure. He just couldn't understand why the mint mark would be taken and other, easier-to-carry artifacts had been left behind.

Frustrated, Ryan tipped back his head and took several more swallows of water, then choked as his throat suddenly closed. Gagging, Ryan leaned forward and spat the water to the ground and wiped his mouth with the back of his hand. Almost unable to breathe, he stared at the mountain and saw nothing.

All this time he assumed the teenagers were stealing artifacts, but what if he was wrong?

Churning through the possibility, Ryan looked at the hole dug to remove one artifact and the four sites marked to protect other artifacts. Could the teenagers be trying to protect the site while someone else came through and robbed it?

A quick turn allowed Ryan to survey the slope again, and he recalled the teenagers had taken photos of the mint mark and sent the images to someone at the university. Thieves didn't do that!

With his throat still tight, Ryan sought for more understanding. Yesterday, the one teen had been visibly upset at seeing artifacts in Ryan's truck. The kid actually knew the laws and challenged Ryan to produce the proper permits. Now Ryan stood at the location where several cob coins had been left behind, their earthen beds marked with small twigs. Someone wanted to preserve the find, not take it.

Like snow melting into water, more understanding trickled through Ryan's brain. The teenagers weren't involved in anything illegal. They were trying to mark, share, and protect the artifacts they had found. They had probably put the mint mark back and marked it, but someone else came along that knew its location.

Halden.

He must've been sent by Cole to find the teenagers and the mint mark and Halden accomplished both. That would explain the extra ATVs at the camp.

Burdened by a collection of unfinished thoughts, Ryan rubbed his temple, trying to figure out how Tallie fit into everything. She had been with the two teenagers in the truck; and at the café the American had shown genuine concern for her and even left to protect her. Yet an obvious struggle took place in Tallie's house. Ryan had found duct tape with long black hair on it *inside* the teenagers' tent.

Thoughts struggled to piece together in his mind, to give him understanding of what had happened at both locations.

Then the intercepted phone call returned to his mind and ice filled Ryan's veins. When Cole told Halden to find the teenagers, Halden sounded confident he could *and* that the teenagers would be willing to work with him.

Not wanting the truth to fit together in his mind, Ryan still felt realization wash over him and he swayed in his boots. That's because Halden used Tallie to find the teenagers and get their cooperation. Halden took Tallie hostage at her home and brought her to the teenagers' camp to force them to comply!

And, if that was true, it meant there were three hostages now, not just one!

Not knowing what other direction to pursue, he started hiking back toward his truck.

Time stood still on the mountain as Halden pointed the gun at Jonathon. From the rocks, Severino, Tallie, and Tate all came to their feet, watching the standoff in fear.

His eyes hard, Jonathon glared at Halden, his voice calm. "If you start shooting people, who will go down in that hole?"

Breaking away, Halden smiled and eased the hammer back into place. Then he stepped beside Tallie and grabbed her arm. "Maybe I won't waste a bullet on you yet. Maybe I'll just spend some time with her. How would you like that?"

Everyone but Halden bristled in fear at the suggestion.

"I will go down."

Stunned, Jonathon turned to Severino and spoke in Spanish. "You can't! No one can! There are rattlesnakes down there!"

Scooping up the coiled ropes, Severino approached the edge of the shaft and dropped the rope at Jonathon's feet. Keeping his voice low, he lifted a short rope from the pile. "There are snakes up here too. You stay with Tallie and keep *him* away from her."

"Severino, you're crazy. You'll get lost—"

"I know caves better than you do."

Tate rose to his feet. "Halden, he'll get bit."

Not waiting for arguments to settle, Severino walked to a nearby cedar tree and slapped it with his hand a couple of times, testing the solidness of the inner trunk. Then, taking a step back, he kicked the flat of his foot against the trunk. The tree did not move. Satisfied it would hold the weight of two people, Severino passed the rope around the tree, tied a clove hitch, and turned the tree into an anchor.

Looking up at Tate, Severino spoke as much as he could in English. "I need *guantes.*"

Uncertain, Tate looked at Jonathon for help. "Gloves," Jonathon translated. "He needs a pair of gloves. Do you have some?"

Quickly, Tate moved to his pack and retrieved a pair. He passed them to Severino who moved toward the shaft and motioned for Jonathon to join him. At the edge of the opening, Severino handed the gloves the Jonathon. "Put them on. Have you ever been *un asegurador?*" he asked in Spanish.

Understanding the word but not the meaning, Jonathon stared at him. "Have I ever been an *insurance agent* before?"

"No." Severino shook his head and tried to find a better Spanish word. "Have you ever been a *freno* or *ancla* before?"

"A brake or an anchor? What are you talking about?" Jonathon knew each of the Spanish words but they weren't making sense to him in the mountains.

Tallie understood enough to figure it out. "Belay. He wants to know if you've ever belayed a rock climber before. They act like a human anchor or brake on the rope."

"No. What do I have to do?"

"Hold still while I tie this rope around your waist." With Jonathon's arms stretched out from his sides, Severino reached and passed the rope around his hips three times. This he secured with another knot and anchored Jonathon to the tree.

Halden snorted with delight. "Hey, I like that. Maybe I'll just leave him tied like that."

This time, Severino intentionally ignored him and retrieved one of the longer ropes. "Sit," he told Jonathon, directing him to face the shaft and put his feet against an imbedded rock for tension. Then Severino ran the new rope about Jonathon's hips and back, placing one end in Jonathon's right hand and the other in his left hand.

"Never let go of this rope. This is the rope that holds me. The tree is holding you, but you are in charge of holding me. Which is your strongest hand?"

"My right." Still holding the rope, Jonathon lifted his strong hand. Nodding with understanding, Severino tapped Jonathon's left hand. "Then this is your guide hand."

Next, grabbing Jonathon's stronger right hand and holding it firmly, closed around the rope, Severino met his gaze with seriousness. "And your strong hand is your brake hand. The most important thing you can do with this rope is stop me if I start to fall."

"If I can't see you, how will I know if you're falling."

Severino gave a half smile. "I'll yell *caigo*."

With a shrug, Jonathon nodded. "That will work. But how am I supposed to stop you?"

Severino grabbed the excess rope. "This way. Pass the rope across the front of your body, like this, and hold it there, *tight*, with your braking hand. At the same time, lean back, push back on the rock with your feet if you have to, and tighten your grip on the rope with your guide hand to stop it from sliding through. Let me see you do it."

Jonathon followed the instructions and Severino nodded his approval. "Do it again."

Jonathon complied. Satisfied, Severino looked over Jonathon's shoulder at the tree. "With the tree as your anchor, you will be able to hold my weight, even if I fall. You won't be dragged over the edge, but you have to understand you are my anchor. Even if it hurts, you can't let go of the rope."

Tallie struggled to her feet and came and stood beside them.

Without understanding all their Spanish, she knew their plans. "Don't do this, guys. Don't go down there."

Though he heard her words and her worry, Severino shut off his emotions and stayed focused on teaching Jonathon, showing him with his hands and explaining with his Spanish what he needed. "Now, when I tell you to lower me, all you need to do is loosen your grip on both hands just enough to let more rope feed out. If you're letting it out too fast, I'll call for more tension. Just slow the feed by tightening your grip and leaning back. Understand?"

Grim-faced, Jonathon nodded.

"Now, when I'm ready to come back up, it's a bit different. As I climb up and give you slack in the rope, you will need to draw up that slack as quickly as I give it to you, but you still can't let go of the rope. Always keep your brake hand on the rope. If you have to itch your nose, use your guide hand but *never* let go with your brake hand. Your brake hand will be holding my life the entire time I am on the rope, even when I'm climbing back up. Do you understand?"

Jonathon nodded

Next, Severino showed him the technique for drawing up the slack and keeping the rope controlled while he climbed out "Grab both ropes together with your guide hand, slide your brake hand back along the rope toward your body, and pull the slack around. Grab, slide, pull. If something goes wrong and I lose my grip and fall on the way up, just wrap that brake line back across your body and set it hard like before."

"You're not going to fall though, right?"

"I hope not. But if I do I'm not going to hit the bottom, right?"

The question fed through Jonathon with force and he realized the weight of his job. "No. I won't let you hit the bottom." Then he smiled. "Not hard anyway."

Smiling, Severino straightened and left Jonathon to get a feel for the rope. At the other end of the rope, he created two medium loops and tied a double-eight knot.

Tallie stepped close to him, speaking in quiet English. "Severino, I don't want you going down there. I'm worried about the snakes."

With his voice low, he looked over at Halden then back at her. "I am worried about other things right now." He stepped into the loops and slid them up over his jeans until they were snug against his upper thighs. Next, he slung the rope over his shoulder, letting it hang in front of his chest. Then he removed his belt, and, still standing in his rope harness, he wrapped the belt around his chest and secured it over the rope. The simple chest harness wasn't the best, but it would help hold his body upright and in line with the rope in case he slipped.

Looking over at Jonathon he nodded. "Take up all the slack between me and you. Let it coil behind you in a *neat* pile. That's important."

Jonathon did, practicing his hand technique.

"*Caigo,*" Severino tested, and Jonathon locked the rope across his body. Severino nodded. "*Muy bien.*"

With the slack out of the rope, Severino walked to the edge of the shaft. "I'm going to need a *linterna.*"

"A flashlight," Jonathon translated.

Tate lifted a headlamp and passed it to the Peruvian. Severino snugged it into place over his forehead.

"You guys were prepared for this, weren't you?" Jonathon observed.

"We're always prepared to send someone else into a mine for us," Halden taunted. Then, to Severino, he smiled. "Hey, *amigo,* if you see that big snake, the five-foot one, tell him '*hola*' for me."

Severino responded to this English and glared at Halden. "I am not your friend," he growled.

Jonathon looked at Severino, his warning coming in rapid Spanish. "When you get down there, the first thing you are going to need to do is kill those snakes."

"And how should I do that? I don't have a gun or a knife."

Turning back to Tate, Jonathon spoke in English. "He needs someway to kill the snakes."

Without hesitation, Tate retrieved a folding shovel. This he brought to Severino and showed him how to open and lock it into position. No words passed between them as Tate closed the shovel and clipped it onto one of Severino's empty belt loops.

More rapid advice flowed from Jonathon to Severino. "Remember, rattlesnakes can strike two-thirds of their body length, and, I didn't tell you this before, they will strike even after they are dead, so make sure you use the shovel to cut off their heads after you kill them."

"*¡Aye, caramba!* Thanks for telling me now." A glance back at Tallie shifted Severino's eyes for only a second, and he returned his gaze to Jonathon, his Spanish moving fast and quiet. "Take care of Tallie. If he tries anything, even if I'm on the rope, you let go and help her, understand?"

"I'm not going to drop you."

"Don't argue with me about this!"

"Severino, I can't do that."

Their eyes met, and Severino knew he was forcing Jonathon into a difficult position. Still, he needed some kind of assurance. "Jonathon, please. At least yell *fuera seguridad,* and I'll grab hold of the first thing I see, but you keep her and yourself safe, okay?"

Still Jonathon hesitated.

Severino stepped toward him, his eyes concerned. "I'm serious. I need your word."

Reluctant, Jonathon finally nodded. "Okay, but let's hope I don't have to make that choice."

Stepping back to the edge Severino nodded. "When you're ready and braced, let me know."

Jonathon settled in, took up the last inches of slack and nodded. "*Listo.*"

Severino leaned back on the rope and pulled, letting Jonathon feel his weight. Then, confident Jonathon had him, he stepped back over the edge.

FOURTEEN

THE SMILE on David Bradford's face vanished as he saw the expression worn by Juan. The anthropologist moved down the airport escalators two stairs at a time, his hand working a cell phone. Juan lifted the phone to his ear, listened for a minute to the ringing of the phone and David saw his mouth move in a curse. Concerned, David stepped forward in the baggage claim area to greet him.

"*¿Juan, que tienes?* What's wrong?"

"I can't get ahold of Jonathon. I've been trying ever since we landed." Juan's fingers redialed, and, again, the phone rang five times then went to voice mail. The lack of connection caused Juan to groan, and he looked upward at the terminal ceiling.

David tried to calm him. "He knows we're coming, Juan. Whatever it is, you can tell him yourself in about two hours."

"Two hours may be too late." Juan turned the phone around and called up the images of the petroglyphs. "You son sent me these before I boarded the plane. I didn't have time to look at them right then because we were boarding, but this image, right here . . ." He called up the image and zoomed in on it. David peered at a carving that looked like a bear.

"Yeah, what about it?"

"It means a rock trap was placed in the area of the mines." Now his finger pointed to the image of a snake on the screen. "And this one means poisonous serpents were placed inside the mine. The Spanish often did that when they had to leave a mine for a while, to deter thieves."

Now Juan retrieved another image. "But this one worries me the most." He zoomed in on the carving, a crude image that looked like ancient weigh scales or balances. "This one means death—not danger—death. It is an ancient alchemist symbol for poison."

Juan looked up at David, worry eating at the brown in his eyes. "It means that somewhere, in or around that mine, there was a deadly poison. It could be arsenic intentionally placed on the floors of the mines by the Spanish, or it could have been a naturally occurring poison—but this symbol says it is toxic enough to kill."

The rope held as Severino descended into the shaft. Sunlight warmed the rocks and he held on as he worked to place his feet safely. Slow and cautious movement allowed him to place his hand in cracks and handholds, always looking for snakes first. With calls for slack or tension, he worked his way down the rough sides.

The shaft, only about six feet across, smelled of dirt and rocks. As the earth closed around him and took away the light and sound from above, he better heard the occasional dry sound of a snake moving across a hard surface beneath him. Clicking on the headlamp, he continued his descent. The entire time he looked and listened for snakes and tested the air. Underground, he knew he could die from bad air long before a snake bite killed him.

Unlike a snake, bad air did not give a warning sound. Its death came with silence, but Severino had learned years ago to listen for changes in his body—a headache or dizziness, shortness of breath—anything that would indicate the presence of harmful gases in the air. Almost to the bottom, his lungs and body responded well to the shaft air.

Movement from below again claimed his attention and Severino paused. Two snakes retreated from the light of his headlamp, disappearing in the small, confined space. He didn't like not seeing them. The others had probably retreated into the tunnel and he knew there could be more inside the dark lair . . . a lot more.

Looking up at the circle of light that marked the only sky he could see, Severino called for Jonathon to brake the rope. He felt the tension increase, and he stopped, dangling above the shaft floor. Letting the headlamp shine across the darkness, he studied the floor and walls for more snakes while he carefully unhooked the shovel. Suspended, he turned slowly on the rope, rotating in free space while he opened the tool and locked it into place. Beneath him, a snake coiled and rattled a warning. The thing, he knew, could strike almost the full width of the pit. Ready now, Severino looked up the rope and called for more slack, then he slowly descended to the floor.

"Off belay!" Severino called up the shaft.

When Jonathon felt the rope lighten and give him back slack, he waited, wanting to make sure his friend stood safely on the ground, and then he rose and untied himself from the tree. His muscles had cramped, not from exertion but tension, and he worked them now, trying to release the stress they held.

Opening and closing his hands several times, Jonathon also shook his arms, rolled his shoulders and stretched his back. Then he stepped to the edge of the shaft.

"You okay?"

"Sí."

"Any snakes?"

The ring of a shovel on rock echoed up as an answer.

Halden chuckled at the sound. "Sounds like a 'yes' to me."

With the path temporarily cleared before him, Severino leaned down and peered into the smaller opening. His only way out now was back up that rope or through the mine entrance. A snake scooted rapidly away, disappearing into blackness. Wary of the dangers he faced and the dangers his friends faced, Severino entered the smaller tunnel.

Already his mind worked on an escape plan. Any mine that had an air shaft had at least one entrance and Severino needed to move fast if he wanted to find it and go for help without raising Halden's suspicions.

The narrow tunnel angled downward, and he emerged from the hole into a larger shaft. Stunned at the find, he straightened and looked around him.

The shaft, hollowed out of dirt and rock, drifted in a downward slope and disappeared into the darkness. The smoothness of the floor told him this had been a main tunnel at one point. The shaft above rose seven feet and the ceiling, braced beneath wooden beams, shadowed the floor ancient and silent. In the tunnel, the circular light of his headlamp cast eerie shadows on the cavern that fled in two directions from the beam.

With the choice go uphill or downhill, Severino chose to move up the slope. Before leaving, though, he used the shovel to dig together a pile of earth—a marker on his path. Then he moved up the main shaft.

Every ten steps he stopped to build another earthen pile, keeping all of them on the same side of the tunnel. Often he looked behind him, seeing the mounds in the wavering light: his way back. Ahead, in the heavy darkness, he hoped he'd find his way out.

Despite the need for haste, Severino proceeded with caution, often bending low to move beneath wooden beams without touching them. Their age and decay, he knew, made them dangerously unstable and that could lead to a cave-in. All around him, his headlamp illuminated dirt walls, punctuated by small streams of dust and dirt that trickled to the earth with his passing. He didn't like the sight. That much dirt in the walls and ceiling meant instability. Rock walls were more stable. When tunnels cut through dirt, a sound or even a hard footstep could be enough of a vibration to cause portions of the wall and ceiling to collapse.

Only a few minutes up the tunnel, Severino saw a hole, gapping in the floor, partially covered by rotting timbers. Knowing floor shafts often had unstable edges, he stayed back. A fist-sized rock on the ground became his means of exploration and he tossed it into the shaft. The rock bounced and rolled and Severino could not hear when it stopped. The sound merely vanished in the darkness, leaving Severino concerned about its size and depth. Not able to see a safe way around it, he made the decision to go back and try the other direction.

As he retreated, Severino erased his mounds and smoothed them back into the tunnel floor. Back at the narrow passage he first crawled through, he began to follow the shaft downhill, moving slowly and carefully. He knew, from the ancient Inca tunnels he protected in Peru, that bad air and lethal gases sank, and just the act of walking through an unseen accumulation could stir the poisons into the air.

The tunnel moved downhill over rocky terrain and around bends. More timbers braced the walls. As he continued to move downhill, he passed several other passageways. At each opening, he stopped and entered, studying the wall and floors, looking for signs of use. Tunnels with rough-hewn walls and floors that showed little wear, caused him to back out and continue on his original course. If the newly discovered shaft appeared larger, with signs of heavy use, he followed it. He knew the closer he got to an entrance, the more wide, worn, and smooth the tunnel would become.

Always, he left piles of earth behind him.

Finally, up ahead, he saw pinpoints of light and felt relief flood him. He had found some type of entrance. With quick steps, he approached. A wall of rocks stood between him and the dapples of sunlight shining through.

A careful search of the rock pile did not reveal any snakes, and Severino set aside his shovel. Still wary of an encounter with the deadly creatures, Severino looked for snakes before reaching down to grab the first stone. He tossed it off the pile and grabbed another one. As he removed the fifth stone, the pile shifted slightly, and Severino froze. Through the rocks he saw a long, stone beam, lying horizontal in the pile, the space around it large enough for the beam to shift sideways. Each time the beam moved, the entire pile shifted slightly.

Lowering himself to view the entire stone, Severino traced it with his eyes. The beam pressed up against a second smaller stone, precariously perched beneath a tremendous boulder. If the beam shifted and applied too much pressure on the smaller stone, it would displace the boulder.

His eyes lifted to study the boulder, and he realized the mighty stone held back a wall of rocks and stones. If the boulder was moved, not only would its tremendous weight come crashing down, killing anyone who stood in its way, it would start a deadly cave-in.

The mine's entrance had been rigged with a death trap.

He backed away cautiously, and, for several minutes, Severino studied the design. With limited light he could not see well enough to find a safe way around the rocks, nor could he see how to brace the boulder in case the stone lever shifted. Unless he had more light, it would be impossible to escape through this opening. Only the ventilation shaft held an exit for him now.

Looking back in the direction he had come, Severino felt pain inside. He didn't want to disappoint Tallie and Jonathon. He needed to find some way to get them to safety. Maybe he could go back and explore some of the other tunnels, find a secondary exit . . .

Time too was a factor, and Severino realized finding this entrance had eaten a lot of his limited time. Frustrated, his gaze shifted back to the death trap as a new plan began to form in his mind.

Though he didn't know what the mine entrance looked like from the outside, Severino hoped there could be a way, from that side, to maneuver around the trap and get *into* the mine. If he could get Jonathon and Tallie safely *into* the mine and then release the trap, the cave-in would drop a protective wall between them and Halden. Then it would just be a matter of retracing his steps and escaping out through the ventilation shaft.

Though risky, he also knew the plan might be their only chance.

He needed to be able to find this entrance from outside, though. Shrugging out of his shirt, Severino placed it on the tip of his shovel and moved it through one of the smaller openings, shoving it out into the sunlight, hoping he would spot it as he hiked the ridgeline.

Now, backing away from the rocks, Severino began to study the ceiling, trying to determine the size of the collapse. The braced rocks would tumble and roll for a ways, and he calculated they would have to be standing at least fifteen feet back from the trigger rock. With his shovel, he dug a trench across the tunnel shaft to mark the safe point and then stopped to study his decision.

He smiled. Even though it was dangerous, it just might work.

"*Estás asegurado!*" Jonathon's voice called down the shaft, and he braced his feet against the rock, leaning back. A second later, he felt Severino's weight on the rope. In quick response, Jonathon began to work the rope as he had been taught. The cable pulled at his hands and body, challenging him more than the descent. Determination filled him, and Jonathon continued to labor for his friend. A few minutes later, Severino emerged over the edge of the shaft, shirtless, sweaty, and covered with dirt. Hoisting himself onto solid ground, Severino stepped away from the open shaft.

Relief filled Tallie, and she moved close. "I was worried about you. You were gone for over an hour."

Tired from the climb, his lungs still trying to claim their first easy breath, Severino only nodded and draped his arm around her shoulder in a reassuring hug. From the action, he realized her hands remained bound behind her back. Irritated she had been tied for so long, Severino turned her around and reached for the rope. He started to tug at the knot.

Halden moved forward and jerked her away from him. "She stays tied!"

Stepping after her, Severino spurted his rage in Spanish, but Jonathon caught him, holding him back, whispering to him in Spanish. "You don't want to do that, Severino."

Again Severino responded with a phrase in Spanish. Finding protection behind the gun, Halden shoved it at Tallie while he held her arm with one hand. "What did he say?"

Jonathon shook his head, not wanting to translate. Severino repeated it, louder.

Angered, Halden raised his voice. "*What did he say?*"

"*Digale,*" Severino hissed.

"No," Jonathon returned with a growl.

"I *want* you to tell him!"

"Severino, you can't do this," Jonathon whispered in Spanish. "He's got you by three or four inches and twenty-five pounds."

"I don't care."

"That's what I'm afraid of. You could get hurt. I need you to help me figure out how to get Tallie out of this."

Furious at their Spanish conversation, Halden pointed the pistol toward the ground and pulled the trigger. The powerful explosion sent up a blast of dirt and caused everyone to jump. "Tell me what he said right now or I put the next one through her foot!" Fury twisted Halden's face, and the pistol now held a dangerous aim over Tallie's foot.

Jonathon tried to calm the situation. "Okay! Just move the gun."

"What did he say?"

Licking his lips, Jonathon struggled with the words. "He said for you to man up, put the gun down and take him on right now. Just you and him."

Halden laughed. "Man up? Is that really what he said?"

"*Sé hombre*. Yeah, that's what he said."

"Well, you just tell him I don't have anything to prove, the gun makes me the real man here, and that's all, nothing else."

Again, Jonathon hesitated to play translator, and Halden again pointed the gun at Tallie's foot. "Tell him what I said!"

Worried, Jonathon spoke to Halden. "Okay, okay. Just don't shoot that thing again." Keeping his eyes on the gun but directing his voice toward Severino, Jonathon spoke in Spanish. "Um . . . he wants me to tell you it's only the gun that makes him a real man and nothing else."

Startled, Severino shifted his gaze to Jonathon, questioning him with his eyes before looking back at Tallie. Across the distance, she understood the intentional mistranslation and started to smile. The three friends exchanged glances in a triangle of mirth and Jonathon tried to swallow a snicker.

"What did you tell him?"

"What you told me to tell him. Hey, it's not my fault if things don't translate straight across."

Not in the mood to be mocked, Halden shouted at Jonathon. "You little . . ." He never finished the comment. Fury drove him forward and he threw a hard fist across Jonathon's face, energy and anger increasing the power.

The unexpected blow caused Jonathon to stagger backward, toward the shaft. Horrified, Severino grabbed his friend as Jonathon teetered on the edge and managed to pull him forward, away from the abyss. Blood erupted from Jonathon's mouth and nose, and he doubled over in Severino's arms.

Before they'd even braced, a cry of alarm from Tallie caused them both to look up. Halden stood, his face twisted in hatred. The pistol, held in both hands, now pointed straight at Jonathon's head, and everyone saw the brutal intent in Halden's eyes.

With only an instant to react, Severino stepped in front of his friend and spoke in broken English. "I found an opening."

The words worked and Halden lowered the gun. "Where?"

"*Norte* . . . north. My shirt is there, marking it."

"You'll take me there?"

"*Sí. Te llevaré.*"

Angered, Halden pointed the gun at Severino this time. "Stop speaking in Spanish, I'm tired of it! Only English!"

"Okay. Okay. Only English. Yes, I will take you there."

Momentarily soothed by the deal, Halden stepped back and gave Severino freedom to turn to Jonathon, who stood, bent back over, letting the blood drip to the earth.

"You okay?" Severino whispered.

Feeling his face with a hand, Jonathon winced but nodded. "Yeah. I think so. Thanks."

"Let's get headed for the opening!" Halden snapped.

Straightening, Severino unbuckled the belt from around his chest and released the rope. Then he stepped out of the harness and cast the end of rope, still anchored to the tree, behind him, listening to it drop down the ventilation shaft. If his plan worked, they would be able to climb up that rope and escape.

When he looked at Tallie, he saw fear in her eyes and knew she now realized the truth of their predicament. Halden had left only one outcome for all of them. Emotion surged inside Severino, and he moved toward her to comfort her, but Halden again claimed her and pulled her with him.

The group headed north, looking for Severino's shirt. Severino led them through the rugged terrain, estimating the distance and direction he had traveled, searching for his shirt. Every moment he could, Severino whispered bits of his plan to Jonathon in Spanish until he had revealed the entire idea.

When Severino led them down an incline into a new canyon, Tallie stopped, her eyes recognizing the canyon floor hundreds of feet below them. "This is Hell Hole Canyon." Recalling the night Tate was attacked by a Skinwalker, her eyes shifted to Tate and she saw him blanch. The canyon laid painful memories into his mind. Panic filled her and she looked toward Halden. "We can't go down there."

"I am not in the mood for you or anyone else telling me what we can and can't do. Now shut up and get moving."

"Halden, this is where that thing attacked Tate just a few days ago."

"You mean the Skinwalker?" Halden teased.

She winced at his disrespect. Halden toughened his voice. "Are you really afraid of some stupid Indian legend? Get down there!" He pushed her down the slope and, with her hands still tied behind her back, she scrambled to keep her balance.

Jonathon managed to catch her as she stumbled down the slope past him. He righted her and helped her get her feet securely back under her. Without moving his lips much, he whispered to her. "Tallie, just hang tough, and we'll get you out of here."

"He's going to kill us, Jonathon. I've never seen him like this before."

Pretending to brush dirt from her shorts and legs, Jonathon gave a slight shake of his head. "No, he's not. Just keep your eye on us. Severino has an idea so when we tell you to move, *move*."

Uncertain, she glanced down the slope where Severino had stopped, waiting. Their eyes met, and though he had not heard their conversation, he knew Jonathon had told her. Without a visible movement of his head, he gave her a sign of agreement.

The strength she saw in his eyes and the conviction in Jonathon's voice allowed resolve to flow back into her. She nodded her own understanding in return. Behind them, Halden moved down the slope. "Get your hands off her and keep moving. She's a big girl. She can walk down the hill by herself."

A rock overhang concealed the outside of the mine entrance. Cool shadows and stone made it a perfect retreat for rattlesnakes. Halden shot one within the first minute of arriving. The body of the snake writhed and twisted on the ground before it died, leaving a scalloped path of splattered blood everywhere it passed.

Carefully, Severino reached for his shirt and pulled it out through the opening. Shaking off the dirt, he pulled it on over his head and looked at the trap, finding it even better concealed from the outside. Yet they only needed to create a small passage, big enough to allow one person at a time to crawl through to safety.

"Get moving those rocks," Halden demanded.

"Snakes," Severino warned in English.

"If a snake tries to bite me, I'll shoot it. If it tries to bite you, I'll let it. It's that simple. Now get digging."

Unable to understand enough to protest, Severino looked at Jonathon and motioned for him to work on the left side, removing rocks.

They bumped each rock with their foot, listening for warning rattles, watching for a shifting of the pile. If neither occurred, they moved the rock aside. Working their way into the mine entrance, Jonathon and Severino continued to move careful and slow.

Outside, in the overhead sun, Halden looked at Tallie, sitting beneath a cedar tree, trying to stay in the shade. Without shifting his gaze from her, Halden called over his shoulder. "Tate, why don't you keep a lookout just in case someone is coming."

Stepping back from the entrance of the mine, Tate looked at his cousin. "But you told me to watch these guys."

"They're not going anywhere. Get up there, above that big rockslide, and keep your eyes open. If anyone comes, roll a few rocks down the hill."

Frustrated, Tate turned and looked up the mountainside, marked by multiple rockslides. "Which one?"

Irritated, Halden turned around and motioned with his hand. "The one right there that looks like a hammer."

Tallie and Tate both looked up and saw a horizontal slide that replicated an old hammer. At the sight, Tallie's eyes narrowed and memories flooded back to her. Somewhere, in those memories, she remembered her father telling her it wasn't a hammer. The rockslide represented a mining pick. The Spanish made the Indian slaves build it to mark a mine—yet her father said the real treasure lay hidden just to the east of the giant mine pick.

Still searching her memories, Tallie turned eastward, studying the rest of the mountain. Other giant slides marked the face, including a massive butterfly. "Butterfly Mountain," she whispered in Paiute.

Along the mountain face, she saw images form a story, a story she remembered her father telling her one warm afternoon. Comforted by the memories, she retreated in her mind to a fishing trip with her father the year before he disappeared. Once again, in this very canyon, she could feel the sun's warmth on her father's shirt as she leaned against his side, eating lunch. She could smell the scent of his cologne and hear the soft tones of his voice.

Looking up toward the mountain, Tallie's father spoke to her.

"That mountain holds great *puha*, Tallie. Do you know what *puha* means?"

Following his gaze, seven-year-old Tallie shook her head.

"It is Paiute for spiritual power. In fact, that is such a sacred mountain that the Great God left behind a story and a promise on that mountain for everyone to see. Can you see it up there?"

"No."

Directing her gaze, Tallie's father pointed to the first image . . . a giant patch of earth wormed across the face of the mountain. "That is a caterpillar," he said. "Many years ago, the Creator was watching his daughters play in the sunshine. They were beautiful and happy and laughed because of the joy they felt at being alive. But the Creator felt sad because he knew that the earth held sorrow for them. The brilliant flowers they picked in the fields would fade in color. The leaves on the trees would shrivel and shrink with time. Even his daughters would grow up and then grow old. The color would fade from their beautiful hair until it was only gray and lifeless. They would feel their bodies weaken with age and begin to wrinkle and grow fragile, like the wrinkled, brittle leaves of summer. Even those around them would grow gray and wrinkled and all would lose their youthful beauty. It was part of the way of earth."

Enthralled by the story, Tallie leaned closer against her father and he continued the legend. "All these thoughts made the Great Creator's heart heavy. Soon a little caterpillar came across the ground and looked up at the great Creator. The caterpillar saw the Creator's sorrow and asked what had turned his face so sad. The Creator told him he sorrowed for his daughters. He worried that a lifetime of seeing things grow ugly and fade in beauty would turn their hearts ugly and make their joy fade.

"The little caterpillar spoke to the Great Creator and told him that, even though he was small and crawled through the dust, he would do anything he could to help the Creator keep his daughters happy."

Smiling at the story, Charlie rubbed Tallie's tiny back. "That tiny offer to help filled the Creator's heart with great gladness, and he knew what to do. He asked the caterpillar to spin a tight blanket around itself and stay there while he gathered the things needed to make his daughters happy."

"He asked him to spin a cocoon," Tallie interjected with excitement.

Her father smiled and leaned down so she could see the mountain. "Yes, he did, and that cocoon is right there, just above the caterpillar. Do you see it on the mountain?"

"I do!" The sight caused her to sit up with excitement. A second rockslide waited above the caterpillar, shaped like a chrysalis. She forgot about her sandwich and listened to her father's words.

"So the caterpillar made a blanket all the way around his body. The Creator told him he may have to stay in that blanket for a very long time, but it would be worth it. So, the caterpillar trusted the Creator and he stayed there, waiting. Sometimes the wind blew and the caterpillar felt afraid. Other times rain and snow fell and the tiny creature shivered with cold."

Her dad lowered his voice to a whisper and held his finger to his mouth in a gesture of silence. "When predators came by, his branch he held very still, hoping they would go away. Worst, though, were the times the darkness seemed to be unending. Wrapped inside his little cocoon, the caterpillar worried about ever returning to the light. But always the caterpillar stayed there, trusting in the Great Creator's return.

"Then, one day, the caterpillar heard the voices of young women approach his branch. The Creator's daughters had grown up. The caterpillar was so excited to surprise them and make them happy that he wiggled in his little cocoon. When the daughters saw it, they just thought it was a faded leaf, curled and diseased. Then the Great Creator came and told them the cocoon held a beautiful promise for anyone who felt small or alone or ugly or sad. He called for the caterpillar to come out of its cocoon and the little creature did but this time . . ."

Excited, Tallie cut him off. "This time he was a butterfly!"

Her father laughed. "Yes, he was a beautiful butterfly. The Creator had painted him with all the colors of the flowers and all the beauty of the trees. He gave him wings so he could dance through air like the Creator's daughters danced on the earth."

Squeezing her shoulders, her father pointed up to the mountain. "Now, Tallie, do you see it? Do you see the gift he gave them up there?"

Excitement lifted Tallie's eyes to the mountainside, searching. When Tallie saw it, recognition slowed her response and Tallie breathed out her amazement. "A butterfly!" On the other side of the cocoon stood a massive collection of rocks and boulders that formed the four wings and body of a butterfly.

Charlie kissed the top of her head. "The butterfly is the only thing he made that grows more beautiful with age. It is a promise that he can take even the smallest, most lowly creatures and make them breathtaking—all because the caterpillar was willing to do whatever it took to make another person happy. Remember that as you grow up. Always try to make others happy. Do what it takes to become more and more beautiful, like the butterfly, okay?"

She nodded her conviction. With his voice gentle in her ears, he looked up at the story told in rocks. "Some people call this place Hell Hole Canyon, but I like to think of this as *Ts'oa pu* Mountain. This is a special mountain, Tallie. It can change people's lives. Like the butterfly, there are promises here you can't even begin to image. One day, when you're older, you will understand the power of this place."

Her father never got the chance to explain any more. He disappeared the following summer, and now she felt that loss even more.

"What have you been staring at?" A shadow fell across Tallie's face, pulling her back from her memory.

The voice and form, so close to her, caused her to jump, and she looked over, to see Halden squatting beside her. "Nothing. I was just remembering my dad. He brought me fishing up here once."

Halden shifted his weight at the news. "To this canyon?"

"Yes."

He looked around, glancing up and down the stream, thinking. Finally, his eyes returned to hers, hard. "Well, that was dumb."

"What?"

"That was dumb of you to sit here thinking about your dad. Why would you ever do something like that?" Annoyance filled his voice.

"Halden, he's my father! He brought me here."

"Yeah, well, it's probably the last thing he ever did for you. He hasn't been anywhere near your house in ten years! You need to just get over it! Stop sitting here thinking he just lost track of time."

Unable to respond with anything but a bewildered expression, Tallie stared while Halden continued his rant. "What do you think? Maybe he got drunk at the bar and forgot where he lives and as soon as he sobers up, he'll stagger home. Oooh—I know, he found another squaw and set up his wigwam with her, but one morning he'll wake up, come to his senses, and show up on your mama's front porch like a runaway dog, his tail tucked and a stupid grin on his face, hoping everyone will forgive him. Is that it?"

The tender memories of her father still fresh on her mind, the pain of her father's choice only recently revealed to her by a stranger, and the sting of Halden's insensitive words violated everything she held sacred about her father. In rebellion, she rocked back, away from him, away from everything that hurt, and she thrust a volley of kicks in his direction. "You jerk! Get away from me! Get out of my life. *Leave me alone!*"

Straightening, he stepped around her and reached down and grabbed her bound arms with his hands, jerking her to her feet. "Knock it off, Tallie!"

But she continued to fight him, twisting and kicking, dropping down then surging back up again to try and break his hold. "*Let me go!*"

"Stop! You're being an idiot!"

"You know nothing about my father!"

Still trying to control her, Halden struggled to enchain the bending and jerking of her body. Words growled out of him in anger. "I know he's *not* coming home."

The words infuriated Tallie, and she erupted with more vengeance. This time Halden grabbed her hair and twisted it around his hand, shoving her head down, bending her over. "You *will* stop."

FIFTEEN

THOUGH HE snarled the command and wrenched her hair hard for control, she continued to fight. Even doubled over, she sought to reach him, to do damage any way she could.

Only a little way up the hill, Tate heard the eruption and turned back. When he saw Tallie explode into a fireball of fury, he dropped back down the slope. A raining slide of rock and dirt marked his rapid descent. Hitting the bottom, he managed to keep his footing and rushed to the pair, grabbing Tallie in his arms and turning her away from his cousin. "I got her! *Tallie, stop*—just calm down!"

The noise penetrated the mouth of the mine and brought Jonathon and Severino out into the sunlight. The unexpected battle caught them off guard. With his strong arms wrapped around Tallie, Tate tried to keep her from reaching Halden, yet she arched back, kicking out, twisting, and trying to break free.

Fear for Tallie drove the pair up the slope to help, but Halden saw them coming. A fluid move brought his pistol up, and he fired a wild shot in their direction, bringing them to a stop.

The sound of the gun exploding only inches away contorted Tate's response, and he turned Tallie away, shielding her with his body. For several seconds, everyone held still, wondering where the bullet hit then, slowly, movement returned to the canyon.

Cautious, Tate lifted his upper body. "Okay, *everyone* stop! What just happened?"

Still lashed in Tate's arms, Tallie straightened, glaring at Halden. Rage coursed through her entire body, and she shook with violent emotion in his arms. With her hair disheveled and her clothes twisted, she stood defiant, ready to resume the battle. Fury filled her eyes. "He was talking about my dad." Before Tate could think of a response, her chest heaved out a new wave of emotions, and she sagged in his arms. "He said maybe my dad forgot he had a family, maybe he got drunk at the bar or found another woman, and that's why he disappeared." Pain glistened in her eyes and lowered her voice. "My dad didn't forget us. He never drank, and I can't believe he would run away with another woman."

"I know, Tallie. I know." Lifting his own pain-filled eyes, Tate looked at his cousin. "Halden, you gotta lighten up. This is the canyon where her dad was . . . last seen. You know that." The words lodged in Tate's throat, and he struggled to get them out through his emotions.

Stiffening in anger, Halden glared at his cousin. "You shut up. Just . . ." The rest of his words froze in his mouth, and Halden's eyes widened with horror as he looked over Tate's shoulders to the slope behind them.

At the look of pure fright in Halden's eyes, Tate turned. From the rocks, a gruesome face stared back, twisted in a snarl of hate. Tate recognized the face—he would never forget it. "That's the thing that attacked me!" he breathed. "*That's the Skinwalker!*"

Jonathon and Severino turned and saw the hideous creature from their camp. Daylight illuminated the awful features, and the beast bristled its anger at them.

When Tallie turned and looked, the beast shifted its eyes to her, and their gazes locked. Then the thing took a step forward, and she realized the Skinwalker had come for her. Fear ran through Tallie, and her knees buckled in Tate's hold.

Overcome by the sight, Halden shouted his defiance. "There is no such thing as a Skinwalker!" In emphasis, the gun blasted its own deadly protest, the bullet's invisible path toward the beast marked by a rock that exploded into fragments near its head. Shards flew as the demon disappeared into the rocks.

Turning to his cousin, Tate shouted in anger. "If it's not a Skinwalker, then you tell me what that is because it's not a bear or a wolf, and it certainly isn't a mountain lion. I've never seen a face like that."

"You tell me. Get up in those rocks and go find it."

"No way!"

This time Halden turned the gun on his own cousin, his icy voice without compassion. "You get up there and look for it, *now*!"

Tallie regained her footing and strength in her legs. "Halden, don't. Don't send him up there."

"Shut up!"

Concerned, Tallie glanced toward Jonathon and Severino, her eyes begging for help. Of all the threats they faced, Tate had never been one of them.

Jonathon hesitated for only second before he stepped forward. "Halden, I'm sure the thing is long gone—you chased it off when you shot at it. You don't want to send Tate up there. We need his help opening the mine. There's some rocks in there we can't lift."

The final appeal worked, and Halden lowered his weapon and glared at his cousin. "Fine. Get in that mine and help them."

If Cole was coming from the university, interested in finding the teenagers, interested in ancient artifacts somewhere up Kanosh Canyon, there was only one road he could take. Ryan waited there until he saw the familiar vehicle, then, angling his own truck across the road, he forced Cole to come to a halt.

With only seconds of time, Ryan moved fast. Bailing out of his cab he crossed the gravel road, jerked open the truck door and pressed a gun against Cole's face, just below his ear. "Get out!" To emphasize the command, Ryan grabbed him by the arm and physically hauled him out of the truck.

Startled, Cole held up his hands and complied as Ryan roughed him around and shoved him against the bed of the truck. "Okay, take it easy. Just calm down. What do you want, money?" He started to reach for his wallet.

Furious, Ryan lunged at him, pressing the gun under his chin and tipping Cole's head back. "I want my stuff back!"

"What stuff?"

"My mint mark and cobs!" he lied.

"I didn't take them."

"No, but I bet you know where they are! *Tell me where my stuff is!*"

"What makes you think I know . . ." The sound of the hammer being cocked made Cole cringe. "Whoa, whoa. Wait a minute," he said nervously.

"Some guy named Halden spouted off at the café that two teenagers had a mint mark—my mint mark—and he was being paid big bucks to go find them. Since I know you're the only one in the area with the big bucks to find artifacts, I figure you have to be paying Halden or the teenagers or both." Angered, Ryan shoved Cole again. "Those two kids took that stuff right out of my dig, and I want it back!"

"I don't have . . ."

"Give me your phone!"

"What?"

"Your cell phone; give it to me right now!"

Cole motioned with his hands to lower the gun. "Okay, just put the gun down so I can reach it without worrying about a bullet taking my head off. If those kids stole from you, I want to stop it as much as you do."

In an angry gesture, Ryan tipped the gun away and lowered the hammer into place. "I want your phone. Not your sympathy."

"I'm getting it." Cautious, Cole leaned across the front seat of the truck, moving slow so he wouldn't agitate Ryan.

"Keep your hands where I can see them!"

"It's right here, on the center console. See?"

Ryan saw the phone and motioned with his gun. "One hand."

Holding his left hand away from his body, Cole reached in to lift the phone out of the console with just his right hand. "Okay, just take it easy." Cole's hand slipped around the device, his fingers also finding a small nail he knew rolled around in the console. Still leaning across the seat of the truck, Cole passed the phone into his left hand but kept the nail hidden in his right. Moving slow and easy, he offered the phone to Ryan. "Here."

The gun trained on Cole, Ryan opened the phone. "What tracking service are you using?"

"I don't know what you're talking about."

"Don't be stupid. Dealers who want to keep track of their diggers all upload a GPS tracking program onto a cell phone, hand the phone to their diggers, and tell them to use it to stay in touch. That way they can track the location of all their diggers. After all, you can't run the risk of those diggers going rogue on you and disappearing with your artifacts, can you?"

Irritated, Cole mocked him. "Sounds like you should have used a program like that on those teenagers."

Ryan's blue eyes glared hard. "You can play this hard or easy. Remember, I now have your phone."

"My phone is password protected."

Undeterred, Ryan touched a few buttons. "Ah . . . lookie there. Like most people, you didn't use your password to lock it." A few more touches to the screen and Ryan smiled. "And there's your user history and . . . bingo . . . there's your tracking program."

"You need a password to access it."

"I just need a phone number to track." Switching screens, Ryan located Halden's phone number in Cole's contact list, switched back to the other screen, and typed in the number. The program accepted it and began a search for the phone's location. A few moments later, the search returned with nothing. A sense of frustration and disappearing time began to tick inside Ryan. "When was the last time you heard from Halden?"

"I have no idea who Halden is."

"Don't give me that. I just took Halden's number from your contact list and put a track on it."

A smirk crossed Cole's face. "And you didn't locate anyone named Halden, did you?"

"That's because he's either out of the area or turned off his phone. Did you tell him to leave the area?" Without waiting for an answer, Ryan continued. "Sounds to me like he's trying to scam you. You sent him to find my mint mark, and I bet he doesn't want you to locate him, so he turned off his phone because he is planning on selling my mint mark instead of giving it to you. If I was Halden and had an artifact like that, that's what I'd do."

"Yeah, well, that's you."

Not liking the answer, Ryan glared at Cole and made another harsh demand. "I want your two-way and your GPS. I'll find them with that."

A scowl filled Cole's face and he reached back inside the truck with the same cautious movement. Passing the devices from his right to his left hand, he delivered them to Ryan, still guarding the nail and keeping it from sight. "What you're doing is illegal."

"Ha! You're one to talk." Without looking away, Ryan tossed the new devices through his truck's unrolled window. They landed on the seat.

Cole glared at him. "You have no idea who you're crossing right now."

With the gun, Ryan gave a mock salute and backed around the front of his truck. "Oh, I know exactly who I'm crossing right now. It's you who doesn't have a clue." He opened the driver's door and swung inside. Through the open passenger window, he smiled. "Thanks for the phone and radio and the GPS system. When I find Halden and the kids, I'll get my stuff back—but you won't."

Fury drove Cole forward, but Ryan brought the gun up in a fluid motion, its deadly aim sighted on Cole's face. "That's close enough. Keep your hands up where I can see them and back away from my truck."

Cole hesitated, his hand still working below Ryan's line of sight— working to press the nail between the tire treads of Ryan's truck.

"*Now!*"

This time Cole complied. He didn't look down at the passenger tire but he hoped the nail would stay imbedded in the tread until Ryan rolled forward. If the nail didn't twist out, the weight of the truck would press it completely into the tire, start a slow leak, and leave Ryan stranded with a flat tire somewhere. Then Cole would make sure he got his stuff back.

In the car, Juan sent another text to Jonathon. *Contact me or your dad ASAP.* Anxious for a response, he held the phone in his hand, waiting for a reply. Every twenty minutes on the drive down, he had tried to reach Jonathon by phone call or text and he'd failed each time. After seeing the petroglyphs, he worried that just being in the area of one of the mines could prove deadly.

David signaled right and exited the freeway, passing some haystacks and corrals, then slowing to a stop at the bottom of the rural ramp. Just as he signaled to turn toward Kanosh, his own cell phone rang. The sound caused him to jump and grab for his pocket. "I hope it's Jonathon!"

He opened the phone without looking at the caller. "Hello?" The voice on the other end did not belong to his son and the disappointment David felt quickly changed to surprise. "Mrs. Pikyavit, hi. What can I do for you?"

As the news came through the phone, David lifted stunned eyes and stared at Juan. He spoke to the woman. "Say that again? Are you sure? When did this happen?" Earnest, David turned the car toward Kanosh, increased urgency holding his expression. "Okay. We're in Kanosh, we just pulled off the freeway. We'll be there in ten minutes." Ending the call, David pressed his thumb against the number three and speed-dialed his son. "Come on, Jonathon. *Pick up!*"

The phone rang five times then went to voicemail. Breathing out his dismay, David shook his head and closed his eyes for a brief second.

"What's wrong?"

"A girl named Tallie Pikyavit was supposed to go to work today and never showed up. Then the police got an anonymous tip this morning that her house had been ransacked. Now no one knows where she is. She isn't answering her cell phone either."

"Does Jonathon know this girl?"

"They've grown up together, and they've been together every day since he got down here."

"Would she help them look for the mines?"

A nod came from David, starting slow but growing in conviction. "Tallie would help them look for a bear. She's got grit. In fact, she's one of the strongest girls I've ever met, both physically and mentally. I think Jonathon only started pinning her in wrestling matches a couple of years ago. Yeah, she'd have no problem at all searching for a mine or even going inside one. And, if the guys hesitated at all, she'd go in first."

Digesting the news, Juan pressed his lips together. He didn't want to add the worry of a girl to his mind. Glancing out the window, Juan didn't see the scenery change as they drove toward the small town. "So you think she is with them right now?"

Leaning his arm on the window ledge, David rubbed his temple, his face pressed into a frown. "I don't know. And I can't figure out why anyone would break into Tallie's house. This is Kanosh. It doesn't happen here." More road passed beneath them and David shook his head. "I really hope they are all just out of cell phone range, goofing off somewhere, but now this break-in." He shook his head. "I'm trying to tell myself it has nothing to do with the two of them not answering their phones, that it was just random, a coincidence . . ."

"But your *instinto visceral* tells you different."

"Yeah, my gut instinct is telling me something way different."

While Halden scanned the rocks for signs of the Skinwalker, Tate guided Tallie inside the mine entrance. There he found a boulder and helped her sit.

Away from Halden's threat, Jonathon approached, his voice low. "Think you can untie her?"

"I don't dare. Halden's on edge as it is."

Tallie looked up at him. "Tate, what's gotten in to you two? This is crazy. You can't keep us here forever."

"Tallie, Halden wasn't supposed to handle things this way."

"Well, just what was he *supposed* to do?"

Tate winced. "He was just supposed to find out where Jonathon and Severino found that mint mark. That's it."

"Find out for who?"

"I can't tell you." A cant of his head lowered Tate's vision to the ground for a long time. "Tallie, we didn't start this. You guys were just in the wrong place at the wrong time, and so was I, and so was Halden—years ago. Believe me, Halden and I are tied up in this mess just as much as you are."

The comment bristled Jonathon and he stepped closer. "Why? Who's forcing you guys to do this? Does he have blond hair and blue eyes?"

Turning to the all of them, Tate ignored the question. "Do you guys have any water you can give her?"

"No. Answer my question."

"I can't." He nodded back at Tallie. "She really needs some water."

"Then ask your cousin. He's been guzzling plenty."

Tired, Tate rubbed the back of his neck and stared toward the rock pile that blocked the entrance. "I wish there was some way I could help you guys. I really do." Now he laid his head back and stared at the ceiling above. An exhale of complete frustration left him. "I wish it would have been me ten years ago." He blinked at a shimmering of tears. "I've got nothing left."

Concerned for her friend, Tallie frowned. "Tate, what's going on? Talk to me."

He gave her a sad smile. "I wish I could."

Before she could press him more, Halden's voice entered the entrance of the mine. "Think you're all on vacation? Get working. Tate and Tallie get out of there, now!"

Startled, Tate looked at Tallie, his eyes telling her to stay while his voice carried back to his cousin. "Halden, she needs to stay out of the sun for a while. I think she's got a bit of heat exhaustion. I'm going to go get her some water."

"Fine, but not the guys. They don't need any water. They're not working hard enough."

Lowering his head, Tate turned to exit the opening. "I'll be back," he whispered. Halden followed him out.

Remaining quiet, Jonathon and Severino watched them go, then Jonathon kicked at the earth. "Something big is going on that he's not telling us."

"But he wants to help us," Tallie protested. "I know he does."

"That may be . . ."

Severino spoke quietly. "He's a man who has died. He feels he has lost his soul." Turning to Tallie, Severino watched her face. "How much would he do for you?"

"Anything. He'd do anything for me and my family. Why?"

Jonathon turned to his friend, whispering in quiet Spanish. "Are you thinking we should tell Tate?"

"Tell him what?" Tallie questioned.

Realizing she understood his Spanish question, Jonathon smiled and tried to distract her. "Wow, you don't look so good. Your hair is really messy."

"Gee, thanks. Tell him what?"

"Turn around. Let me get this ponytail out of there."

"Jonathon." Not about to let him forget her question, Tallie frowned while she turned on the rock and he released the last of her thick black hair from the elastic band. As her hair tumbled around her shoulders, he removed the bobby pins and smoothed her tresses as best as he could, then he stepped back. "There. That looks better."

Shaking her hair away from her eyes, she met his gaze and returned to her original question. "So, what are you thinking about telling Tate?"

Jonathon grinned and removed his cap, sliding the bobby pins onto the side. "You know, you really should wear your hair loose and tangled more often." With his fingers, he combed his own hair back against his scalp and tugged the cap back into place, hooking it behind his head and pulling it low over his forehead. He slid the ponytail holder into his jeans' pocket.

"Jonathon!"

Reaching out, he tugged some of her dark hair in front of her eyes. "It will keep you from seeing too much."

Frustrated, Tallie shook her head, pulling away from him. Dark eyes flashed her growing irritation, and she blew at the displaced locks through her lower lip.

Severino stepped close and gently lifted away the hair. Then, lowering himself in front of her, he brushed back the long hairs, feathering them away from her face. "This entrance has a *trampa*."

"A what?"

Looking back at Jonathon, Severino asked silently for his help. Jonathon gave it. "The entrance has been booby-trapped."

"By who? By you?"

"No, by the Spaniards or the Native Americans. We're trying to dig through the rocks enough to get *behind* the trap before we spring it."

At the plan, Tallie looked up, terrified. "You guys are going to spring the trap?"

"Yes."

"While you're *inside* the mine?"

"Yeah."

Horrified, she looked between them. "But that's suicide! You'll get trapped inside the mountain!"

To calm her, Severino laid his hand on her knee. "Things will be fine."

A step forward brought Jonathon close to her. "Severino knows the way back to the ventilation shaft. He's marked the trail and left the rope hanging down inside the shaft. As soon as we're separated from Halden by a wall of rocks, we're going to race back to the chute and climb out before he even knows what we're doing."

Then Jonathon's voice sobered. "But, Tallie, we don't want to leave you here with Halden. We want you to come with us."

Stunned, Tallie looked between her friends, uncertain about their seriousness. Neither one wavered.

Licking his lips, Severino met and held her gaze. "Tallie, you can trust me. I see the ceiling and walls and know how the rocks will fall. I put a mark in the dirt. If you stand by that mark, you will be safe when the rocks fall."

Her face filled with anguish, and she looked at him, afraid of the answer before she even asked. "And who will stand near the entrance and make the rocks fall?" Severino understood her question and did not look away. Seeing the quiet resolve in his eyes caused sudden hurt to seize deep inside her and her voice quavered. "It will be you, won't it?" Behind the pair, Jonathon realized the one factor in the plan he had not considered, and he looked away, fighting his own hurt.

A furious headshake showed Tallie's disapproval, and she leaned back. "No. I won't let you."

Movement darkened the entrance of the cave, and Severino rose quickly to greet the arrival. Tate returned, a single bottle of water in his hand. Stepping close, he passed the bottle to Tallie, but then, positioning his back to the entrance, he reached under his shirt for a second water bottle and extended it toward Severino. "It's all I could take."

Relief filled everyone's faces and Severino reached for the second bottle. "*Muchísimas gracias.*"

"Keep it hidden. If Halden sees . . ."

Jonathon nodded. "We understand."

Tallie leaned toward her older friend. "Tate, this mine has been booby-trapped, and Jonathon and Severino are planning to set it off so they can try to escape." The news, blurted from her mouth, startling everyone and they stared at her.

"Tallie, what are you saying?" Shock filled Jonathon's voice.

"Is this true?" Tate asked.

Tallie pressed her only advantage to protect her friends. "If they set it off, Tate, someone is going to get hurt. You can't let them do it."

More forceful this time, Tate looked at Jonathon. "*Is this true?*"

The teenager stared at him in silence, unable to answer, unwilling to lie. In the confined space, no one spoke.

Tate's eyes turned to study the precarious rock pile. His chest rose and fell while his mind struggled with the news. He ran a hand through his hair, opened his mouth to say something, then stopped. Finally, he turned to them, his eyes calm. "I guess you don't have to tell me how you're planning to escape. I can see why you wouldn't trust me, but I don't want anyone to get hurt."

Sad, Tate began to move toward the entrance and then hesitated. "If I can help, just let me know. I'll do what I can." Then he disappeared out into the bright sunlight.

For a moment the three held motionless, then Jonathon turned to Tallie. "Can we believe him? Will he really help us?"

A quick nod was the only answer Tallie could give.

Working quickly, knowing Halden could come in and retrieve Tallie at any moment, the pair moved rocks and set them aside, digging through the left side of the opening. After fifteen more minutes, Severino heard a rock tumble to the earth into the tunnel beyond, and a small opening yawned through the barrier. "We are through."

Careful not to displace any rocks, the pair worked to enlarge the opening. When it became large enough for a person, Severino turned on his headlamp. "I'm going through." While Jonathon watched for Halden, Severino bellied his way into the hole, dropping onto the back side of the wall. There, the cavern remained largely undisturbed. Smiling, he returned to the opening.

"This will work. Hand me the water bottles and the shovels."

Jonathon passed them through the opening and Severino placed them on the floor in the safe zone, and then he wormed his way back through. "If Halden asks, we can tell him we need to work from the back side too. Now we just need to find a way to get Tallie through here."

As Severino extracted his body from the hole, Tate appeared quietly in the mouth of the mine. He studied the Peruvian and the hole. "You're going to make a run through it back to the airshaft, aren't you?"

Unsure of what Tate said, Severino looked at Jonathon. Tate stepped closer and looked at the rocks. "Halden will just follow you."

"The trap will cause the entrance to cave in. He won't be able to follow us."

Remaining quiet, Tate looked at the rock pile and contemplated the outcome. Then he gave an accepting nod. "It just might work. What can I do to help?"

"Really?" Jonathon looked at him.

"If you think you can get out and go get help for Tallie, yes."

Jonathon hesitated. "We plan to take her with us into the mine." The news lifted Tate's eyes, and he looked around at all three of them. With a need to explain, Jonathon stepped closer. "We don't want to leave her here with Halden."

"Will she be safe?"

"She'll be safer in there with us than out here with him. We just need some time to get her through the rocks and spring the trap."

"How much time?"

"Three minutes."

Tate nodded with resolve. "I can get you that."

Lowering his voice, Jonathon talked to Tate with his words and his face. "Listen, Tate, if you help with this and Halden thinks you crossed him . . ."

"I'll worry about Halden. You guys just need to get her out of here. I can distract Halden. I'm going to go outside and whistle for his help somewhere away from the mine entrance. When you hear my whistle, that will be your signal. Wait till he leaves, and then get her through the mine and out of here."

Tallie stood up and stepped in front of him. "Thank you, Tate."

His eyes shifting back and forth over hers hesitantly, appearing as if he wanted to say more, but something held him back. With his gaze lowered in defeat, he turned aside in silence and left the mine.

Just above Corn Creek Campground, Ryan could no longer ignore his truck's pull to the right. Getting out of the truck, he walked around the warm hood and saw the front passenger tire, flat. A curse rolled out of him. He didn't need this. Not now! Going back around the truck, Ryan shut off the ignition, pocketed the keys and began the grungy task of changing a flat tire in the hot, dry summer; on a dirty gravel road; in a narrow, breezeless canyon.

A truck rolled by, heading up the canyon and leaving a thick curtain of dust in the air. The filth settled back on Ryan, coating his sweat as he wrenched off each lug nut. A few minutes later, another vehicle moved down the canyon, sending up a second layer of fine silt. Focused on his task, Ryan set each bolt into the hub cab and pulled off the heavy tire and set it on the ground.

A blow connected with his shoulder and skull, making him stagger sideways. Flesh split open, bones cracked, and Ryan tumbled into the gravel, gasping to breathe and to understand what just happened.

The silhouette of a man blocked out the sun and Cole stepped over him with a tire iron. "Need a little help changing that tire?"

Even the curse Ryan felt could not escape his mouth through the pain. He curled up and reached for the back of his head, feeling the intense pain and the wet, warm blood. Then darkness eased over him and he lost consciousness.

Cole smiled and bent over him, rifling through Ryan's pocket. There he found Ryan's cell phone and opened it. Mockery filled Cole's voice when he accessed the menu. "Ah . . . lookie there. Like most people, you didn't use your password to lock your cell phone." Calmly, Cole scrolled through the menu until he found a string of texts that interested him and began to open them.

That ATV is registered to Dr. David Bradford, senior archaeologist at the museum. The kid you think is a punk is probably his son, Jonathon. Can't buy the dad or the kid. Despite what you saw, Jonathon seems pretty solid. Last year, he got lost in Peru and survived for a month in the mountain jungles. Made national news, but he handled the spotlight well. His grades improved, and he's on the varsity rugby team, did some national talk shows, and actually saved the appearance fees—so if he is involved in all this, it's not for glory or the money. And, no, he doesn't have a girlfriend, so he's not trying to impress anyone either.

Cocking his head with interest, Cole opened another text.

If the house is ransacked, stay out. We don't need cops messing this up.

The next one appeared on the screen. *Here are the pics.*

Another. *Did you get the girl yet?*

Still another. *I know you don't want Steven involved in this anymore because of his family, but I called him back in anyway. He's on his way to help you, but it will still take him three hours to get there. Until then, just follow Cole and see what he does.*

The sight of his name in the last text, caused Cole to look down at Ryan, surprised. With his interest turning personal, he scrolled to the next message. When it opened, Cole froze.

Don't try it. Pull out now! That's an order! Down the case. I know you've been working this for ten years, but we don't need this arrest. We'll go after Cole later.

"Down the case?" he whispered. Angered, he turned to the man, bloody and still at his feet. "You're an undercover agent!" Cole's curses disappeared beneath the onslaught of his boot connecting with Ryan's chest and stomach, again and again.

SIXTEEN

THE WHISTLE cut sharply through the still, hot air. Severino stepped to the edge of the cave and watched Halden leave. Moving back, he lifted Tallie to her feet and helped her climb toward the hole. She slid her upper body into the opening.

Already on the other side, Jonathon reached up and grabbed her under her arms, pulling her through the small tunnel and into the enclosed mine shaft. Setting her on her feet, Jonathon moved her back behind the line of safety and started to untie her hands, letting the light from his headlamp illuminate the rope in the darkness.

Severino slid through the tunnel feet first and moved toward the keystone. "Stay back," he ordered. Then, with his back braced against the mine shaft, he lifted a leg, placed his foot against the stone lever and pushed. The lever slid sideways and the boulder wobbled, but nothing happened. Severino lifted both feet to the lever and pushed. Again, the trap refused to trigger, and Severino realized the trap had been set up to stop people from going into the mine. Rapidly, he moved back to the opening.

Stunned, Jonathon stepped toward his friend. "Where are you going? What are you doing?"

"It was set up to fall when someone tried to come into the mine. It has to be triggered from the other side."

A horrified protest tried to stop him. "You can't do that! You have to stay in here. Halden will kill you when he realizes what you did."

"Just take care of Tallie. Get her out of here."

"*No!*"

"Jonathon, what's happening? What's he doing?" English and fear mixed with Tallie's words.

"He's going back outside. He's going to release the trap from out there!"

Terror filled her and she stepped toward him. "No, Severino. You can't. Jonathon, tell him we'll find some other way. Tell him . . ."

The grating and grinding sound of rocks stopped all three of them and they looked toward the sound. The lever shifted, being moved from the other side. "Get out of here," a man groaned as he shoved hard against five hundred years of inertia.

"Tate?"

Then the boulder tipped sideways, falling into the wall of stones, sending rocks and debris tumbling into the cave. Rocks roared down from the sides and above, raining onto them. Jonathon spun and shielded Tallie from the cave-in.

Beneath the downpour of rocks, Severino stumbled sideways, reaching to catch his balance as he fell into the dirt. "Run!" he shouted. In the chaos, rocks and stones bounced and struck him on the ground. A sharp pain snapped through Severino's forearm, and he pushed himself off the floor. Rolling to his feet, he looked in desperation for Jonathon and Tallie, yet his headlamp cast only a narrow beam of light through the dust and darkness.

Through the swirling storm of rocks and dirt, Jonathon grabbed Tallie's hand. With only the light from his headlamp, he raced into the corridor, pulling her with him. They had to make it back to the shaft and all get out before Halden realized what they were doing. Ahead he saw a small pile of dirt, the mounded markers Severino told him about. Still guiding Tallie, he rushed toward it, worried he wouldn't find another one, but a second earth pile came into his view, and he sprinted forward.

Pain and consciousness returned to Ryan at about the same time. Dried blood covered his face and clothes, and, for a moment, he struggled to identify his location. Then the truck bounced its way across a stream bed, and ricocheting pain told Ryan he lay in the backseat of a truck. Grimacing, Ryan tried to move, but PlastiCuffs kept his hands bound tight behind him.

"Ah, you're awake." Cole spoke, watching him in the rear view mirror. "I found the handcuffs you planned to use on me, but I thought they fit you better." The truck rocked and swayed up the rugged road, and Ryan again winced at the jostling. In the driver's seat, Cole didn't care. "So, who do you work for? The FBI, BLM, Forest Service?"

"I don't know what you're talking about."

"Don't lie to me. I've been reading your texts." Cole held up Ryan's cell phone. "You didn't lock it with your password," he scoffed. "I know your partner, Steven, is on his way here right now, so we don't have much time. I also know your handler told you to pull out and down the case about an hour ago, but you ignored him—probably because you're worried about this kid . . . a Jonathon Bradford."

"I'm not worried about him."

"Well, you should be." On purpose, Cole drove the vehicle through a deep dip, jarring the truck. Without his hands to brace himself, the movement threw Ryan against the side of the truck.

"Oops, sorry about that," Cole taunted.

Pain throbbed through Ryan's entire body, and he knew he had taken a serious beating at some point. Though he knew Steven was coming in with backup, they would go to Ryan's last known coordinates. Ryan had no idea where he was now.

The truck drove up and dropped off another large boulder, slamming Ryan around inside the cab. In the rearview mirror, he met Cole's glare, and Ryan wondered how long he had to live.

"Crawl through!" Severino shouted.

The darkness ahead of them condensed into a smaller shaft and Jonathon dove inside, arm crawling through almost twelve feet of narrow passage. Right behind him, Tallic crawled.

The tunnel emerged into the ventilation shaft on the other side. Free of confinement, Jonathon helped pull Tallie to her feet. Then he spun and looked for the escape rope.

Sunlight filtered down the shaft, illuminating the bottom of the pit and the two snakes Severino killed. On the walls, angles of light glistened against the steep dirt sides, but nothing revealed a rope.

"The rope!" Jonathon cried out. "It's not here!"

Tallie turned around in the bottom of the shaft, searching every side, looking upward. "Where's the rope?"

From up above, several large stones tumbled over the edge and Jonathon lunged backward. "*Rock!*"

Tallie heard the crashing sounds tumbling down. Without time to look up, she ducked, covering her head and neck as the stones rained around her. Above, she heard the sound of laughter. Halden had beaten them to the shaft.

In angered protest, Tallie cried out, straightening in the shaft. "Halden!"

A form peered over the edge. "Yes, my dear?"

"You stole the rope!"

"I didn't steal it. It's my rope."

From behind, Jonathon heard a soft sound and turned. Through the narrow hole, Severino emerged and winced in pain. Emotion twisted his face, and he gripped his forearm tightly. Once he got his feet under him, Severino turned in a half circle, the sign of pain. Legs bending, he sank to the ground and leaned back against the shaft wall. There his chest rose and fell with strain. Instant concern filled Jonathon, and he moved toward his friend.

Still standing in the center of the shaft, Tallie glared upward. "How did you know we were going to be here?"

"Figured it out. I'm not stupid. When Tate whistled me away from the mine, I saw him double back and go inside, so I knew something was up. I got back just in time to watch him trigger the trap. I heard him tell you guys to get out of there, and I knew there was only one way out of that mine. While you guys had to run through dust and darkness, I just hoofed it over here in the bright sunlight."

As the memory returned, Tallie gasped and covered her mouth. "Tate—where is he?"

"Still in the mine I guess. I don't know how anyone could have survived that cave-in. Half the mountain face came down on top of him."

Tallie cried out and stumbled backward. Jonathon caught her. "Tallie," he whispered.

"Did you hear? Tate didn't make it out."

"Tallie, I'm sorry, but Severino's hurt."

"What?" The news jarred her with the force of a slap, and she questioned Jonathon with her eyes.

"It's bad."

She turned and saw Severino leaning against the shaft wall, his face tight, his hand covering his forearm. Moving toward him, she knelt in the dirt. "*¿Severino, que tienes?* What happened?"

With his head supported by the shaft wall, he shifted his gaze to her and shook his head, his teeth clenched against the pain. Carefully, she reached for his hand to uncover the wound, but his grip tightened. Uncertain now, she looked at Jonathon for help. "What happened to him?"

Jonathon swallowed, trying to find the words. "He was bit by a rattlesnake."

Horrified, Tallie shook her head to refute the words but Jonathon could not erase the truth. "When the shaft caved in, it must have dislodged a snake from somewhere. It bit him when he fell."

"And he ran here!" Countless emotions seemed to overwhelm her. "We've got to get him out of here, now!"

"How, Tallie?"

"I'll get him out of here." Coming to her feet, Tallie called up the shaft. "Halden! *Halden!*"

Irritated at the tone of her voice, Halden peered over the edge. *"What!"*

"Severino's been bit by a rattlesnake. He needs to get to the hospital."

"I wonder how he's going to do that since I have the rope and the other entrance is effectively *closed*."

"Halden, stop playing games. Give us the rope."

"Oh, Tallie—I've never been playing games. This has all been very real."

"I'll give you the wire map."

Her words stunned everyone, including Halden, who looked down, surprise evident on his face. "So you *do* have the wire map."

"Yes. I know exactly where it is. You get us out, and I'll show you the wire map myself."

The news roiled through Halden for a few moments before he

could respond. Then he sat down on the edge of the shaft above them and swung his feet back and forth against the pit walls. "I don't know. One map for three people? I don't think that's really a fair trade. You probably ought to try sweetening the deal a little bit more."

Exasperated, she looked up at him, shielding her eyes from the dust his feet kicked loose. "Fine! What do you want, Halden?"

A grin crossed his face and he looked up at the blue sky overhead. "Oh, let me think . . ."

Jonathon growled at her. "Don't do this, Tallie. Don't make any deals with him."

Frustration turned her to Jonathon. "Severino needs to get to a hospital."

"But this isn't the way to do it."

Pain and deep hurt filled her eyes. "What other options do I have?"

"Tallie, even if you go up there and give him the wire map—and everything else he wants—do you honestly think he's going to allow us to go after all he's done? He's looking at major prison time, and he knows it."

The truth of his words cut deep and Tallie choked on her emotion. "But what are we going to do, Jonathon? I don't want Severino to die."

In response to her need, Jonathon drew her into a close embrace. "We're going to get out of this some other way and we're going to get Severino to a hospital, okay? I'm going to head back and try to dig out through the other opening."

"But Halden will stop you. He doesn't need to guard us here. We're stuck. We can't climb out so when he sees you're gone, he'll know where you're headed."

A slight shift of his weight took Jonathon back a step. A smile, meant to give her courage, appeared on his face. "Then maybe I'll dig out another way. I've got a shovel, and I know how to use it." With his hand, he lifted her chin and looked into her troubled eyes. "In the meantime, you stay here with Severino. Keep him quiet. And don't make any deals with the devil, no matter what he promises you, okay? Severino is going to need you down here more than Halden needs you up there."

Feeling numb, she managed a nod, her heart in turmoil.

Jonathon slid his hand into his pocket and withdrew her elastic ponytail holder. "Try not to use a tourniquet on him—it will cause more damage than it will prevent. Use this instead. Put it on his arm above the bite. It won't be as tight as a tourniquet but should slow the poison." When her trembling hand took it from his grip, Jonathon saw her fear and gave her a hug. "Keep his hand down, lower than his heart, and keep your chin up. We'll get out of here . . . all of us will." Then he crawled back through the access hole and into the mine.

Sunlight beat down on the bottom of the shaft, but it did not compare to the fire burning inside Severino's arm. The intensity caused his body to shake, and he pressed harder against the bite, trying to stop the pain or at least create a different one he could handle. With her emotions gentling, Tallie knelt beside Severino and showed him the ponytail holder. "I need to put this on your arm." Words and gestures help her explain.

"Why?"

"We need to slow the spread of poison." Lifting his bitten arm, she looked at him. "This is going to hurt." Despite the language barrier, he seemed to understand and nodded his consent. With care, she stretched open the elastic band as much as she could and slipped it over his swelling hand. It grazed his flesh and pain shot up his arm, radiating through him, causing him to draw in a sharp breath.

"I am so sorry," she grimaced.

"You are fine," he managed. Though he tensed, he controlled his response as she worked it up over his elbow.

"Almost there," she soothed.

Once above his elbow, she eased it into place against his bicep. The tightening pain bit hard, and he growled, pressing his head back against the wall. New sweat glistened on his skin. Not knowing if the heat radiated from the poison or his race to the shaft, she touched the side of his face. "We need to get you out of the sun. Can you move into the mine shaft?" She pointed toward the small tunnel, hoping he would understand.

Severino did and nodded. With effort, he climbed to his feet, holding his arm tight. Already Tallie could see redness spreading out from around the bite. Distressed, she slid an arm around his waist and whispered through her fear. "Come on. Let's get you where it's cool."

Inside the cooler shaft, Severino sat with his back braced against the wall, his arm held low. To conserve his strength and slow the spread of the poison, he did not move or talk much. Half an hour later, Jonathon returned and found them there. Though Severino still held his hand over the bite, Jonathon could see he struggled to keep his grip tight.

Relieved at his return, Tallie rose. "How's the entrance? Can we dig out?"

"No."

"What if I go and help?"

"No, Tallie. It will take a bulldozer to break through."

"Did you find Tate?"

Jonathon's answer came softer. "No." He passed two bottles of water to Tallie. "But I found these. We left them behind."

"Oh, thank you." Opening a bottle, she passed it to Severino. "Here, you need to drink some water." He gave no argument but, instead, reached for the bottle. The movement forced him to release his arm. Beneath his hand, Tallie saw his forearm starting to swell. Bruising began to darken around the bite. The damage worried her and she turned pleading eyes to Jonathon. "Let me talk to Halden," she whispered.

"No!"

"Jonathon, I can show him the wire map. I have it."

"You heard him, Tallie. He wants more than the wire map now."

"I don't care!"

A new voice broke into the conversation. "I care, Tallie. Please no." The quiet plea came from Severino.

Protest turned her to him. "But you need to get to the hospital."

Dark brown eyes watched her. "I am Inca. I do not need a hospital. I need my friends to be okay."

The gentleness in his voice caused her eyes to moisten and she looked down. "But what about you?"

"I will be fine. Just talk to me. Keep my mind busy."

"Talk about what?"

A tired smile managed to come across his face. "About where you hide this wire map from Halden."

His slow English and curiosity brought a smile to her features. "I don't hide it. It's always in plain sight." Quietly, Tallie settled, cross-legged, onto the tunnel floor and pointed to the butterfly tattoo on her ankle. "That's it."

Stunned, Severino lifted his dark brows. "*That* is the wire map?"

"Yes. Isn't it cool? All those lines in the butterfly wings are actually directions on the map."

The announcement brought Jonathon to the ground beside her, staring at the tattoo. "No way!"

"Yes, way."

Jonathon looked up. "So, why does Halden want the map so bad? You said it doesn't lead to *Carre Shinob* so just where does it lead?"

"It doesn't really lead to anything."

"You mean Halden has been chasing a worthless map?"

"It isn't worthless." She stroked the tattoo on her ankle, her mind lost in deep thoughts. "But to understand this map you must know the story of my people."

Without interrupting, Jonathon and Severino let her continue. "The Paiutes believe in Tobats, the great God who had many sons and daughters, including Shinob, his beloved son." A smile softened her face as she told the story. "Shinob was kind and helped his father create this earth. Shinob was always willing to sacrifice all he had to help his brothers and sisters. He loved all of Tobats's children, whether they lived on the earth or in the Heavens, whether they were Paiute or Hopi. All were the same to him."

Tallie brushed her hair off her face. "But not all Tobats's children loved Shinob. He had a jealous brother named O'onuput, who killed Shinob in anger. Our elders tell us that when Shinob died, the entire earth shook then went dark with sorrow. For days the sun did not shine."

A nod came from Severino, and he responded, letting Jonathon help him with the words he did not know. "We have a legend like that in Peru. The Incas say the earth shook with grief over the death of a beloved king who was the son of a god. When he died, it is told that the rocks cracked together, and the sun didn't shine for days until all the people thought they too would die."

Surprised, Jonathon looked at them. "How could there be two legends like that? One in America and one in Peru?"

"There are some legends so universal, they have to have been borne in truth." Severino gave a tired half-smile. "Maybe a great earthquake happened, or an eclipse covered the Americas, I do not know. But something affected North and South America."

Tallie nodded. "For the Paiutes in America, the shaking and dark-ness happened so fast that loved ones were out hunting or gathering and they became instantly separated and lost. The ground changed and new mountains rose. In the darkness, no one knew how to return home or find each other, and they all cried for their loss. No one could light a fire or even strike a flame. The darkness was so thick for days that it snuffed out everything."

Softness lowered her voice to a whisper. "Sometimes I feel that way. I know what it is like to lose a loved one. Sometimes I feel like things are so dark, I can't even breathe. I have cried many tears for my father."

The two watched her, their thoughts quiet.

Trapped in her emotions, Tallie stroked her calf, her mind strug-gling. "For three days and three nights my people wept. During that time, all the people—from all the tribes—were fearful and sad. They worried they would be separated from their loved ones forever. All they wanted was to be together again."

The story too poignant, Tallie stopped and rubbed her tattoo, moving over the inked butterfly again and again. Then her shoulders straightened and she continued. "In the middle of their loneliness and despair, Tobats spoke to them from heaven. He said Shinob's memory would always be with them to help them. He told them to call to their family members and walk with outstretched arms. When they found someone, even if it wasn't a family member, they were to hold that per-son's hand tightly and form a living chain. Then, together, they were to keep searching for more lost people. When they found a group of people, they were to hold hands with that group and not worry about their differences. In this way, they would grow in their size and ability to find more lost people in the darkness."

"Pretty smart. I like that idea," Jonathon agreed.

Thoughtful, she ran her thumb across the butterfly. "I do too. So Paiute joined hands with their enemies, and, working together, they were able to help each other be united with their own families. It took them days of searching in the dark, but eventually all the people, from all the tribes, were united into one great chain. Then, and only then, when all the world was joined together as one, did Tobats pierce the darkness with his sacred arrows and bring light back to the world."

The end of the story made her smile and she lifted her gaze. "When they could see again, all the people were standing together, united, and they could see the power of that unity and of working with each other in love, like Shinob had taught them. That is when the different tribes decided to build a temple—to always remember that sacred time when the gods helped all people be reunited with their loved ones."

Looking back at her tattoo, Tallie's voice seemed small again. "So we buried our weapons of war deep in the earth as a sign of faith; and peace reigned among all the tribes for many generations. Together the tribes built *Carre Shinob* deep inside the Sacred Mountain where Tobats stood and restored the light. They filled it with gifts of gold and records of what they learned; and buried their great religious leaders there. Inside the Sacred Mountain there are Paiute and Navajo buried side-by-side, Ute and Comanche leaders resting together in peace. Tribe does not matter. We are all one because of Shinob."

Curious, Jonathon leaned forward. "So is your tattoo a map to the Sacred Mountain?"

She gave an instant head shake and refuted the question. "No. Everyone knew the location of the Sacred Mountain. They didn't need a map to get there."

"So what is this a map to?"

Now Tallie tipped her head to the side, her eyes downcast. "It isn't a map to anything. It's a map *through* the Sacred Mountain."

Sitting back, Jonathon tried to wrap his head around the information. "Wait. You're saying this map on your ankle shows you how to get *through* the Sacred Mountain?"

"Yes. My father said the Sacred Mountain was carved to represent life. And just like life is filled with right and wrong choices, the mountain was purposely filled with right and wrong paths. If you did not take the correct paths, you would never find your way through the Sacred Mountain."

Puzzled, Severino thought about her words for a long time, then looked up, his English slow. "Why did your father know so much about the Sacred Mountain?"

The question made her hesitate and struggle with her answer. "When the people built *Carre Shinob* inside the Sacred Mountain, with all of its pathways, they called one trusted family from each tribe to act as the guide for that tribe. My family was chosen to show others the way through the Sacred Mountain. My father learned the path from his father—but he disappeared before he could share the information with any of his children. Now that information is lost forever."

Slowly, Severino leaned his head back against the mine wall. "That is like the Incas in Peru. They pass their knowledge of sacred things down through their families."

Frustrated, Jonathon looked from her tattoo to her face. "But, Tallie, you have the tattoo! You have the map through the Sacred Mountain, so just go to the mountain and learn the path yourself."

A shrug of pain lifted Tallie's shoulder. "I told you, my father died before he was able to pass on that information. I don't know where the Sacred Mountain is." Tears glistened in her eyes. "I worry the location of *Carre Shinob* and the Sacred Mountain has been lost forever."

Sitting back, Jonathon shook his head. "No, Tallie. I'm sure someone, somewhere knows where the Sacred Mountain is, and then you can use your butterfly tattoo to find the right path through . . ."

Tallie gasped. "*Ts'oa pu!*"

"What?"

"*Ts'oa pu*. It's Paiute for butterfly!" She shook her hands with emotion and looked around her at the stone walls. "My father loved *Ts'oa pu* Mountain and told me it was very special. I thought it was because of the butterfly." Tallie came to her feet, pacing in a tight circle. "Why didn't I see it before?"

"See what? Tallie, calm down. You're not making any sense."

Overwhelmed, she bent over, trying to catch her breath. Her hands rested on her knees. "It's the butterfly. Butterflies are the only thing that can change from something ugly into something beautiful. My dad always told me the Sacred Mountain could change a man for the better!"

Concerned, Jonathon climbed to his feet. "What are you talking about?"

"The Spanish didn't put those symbols out there on the mountain. My people did."

"What symbols?"

"The butterfly symbols on the side of the mountain, the rock slides that look like a caterpillar, cocoon, and butterfly. That's why my father brought me here years ago. This is it!"

"This is what? Tallie, you lost me."

"We're not lost." With bright eyes, she looked at Jonathon. "We can get out of here. This is the Sacred Mountain—Butterfly Mountain. This is *Carre Shinob*." For assurance, she clutched her butterfly necklace. "My father knew! And years ago he gave me the very map that will lead us through this mountain safely!"

Cole looked at the coordinates in the GPS system and then lifted his eyes to the canyon around him. "So, where did the kids find the artifacts?"

Spitting out fresh blood, Ryan sat on a rock and tried to support his body. "I'm not going to tell you."

Furious, Cole moved back with rapid stride. A single hand reached down and grabbed Ryan's jaw and twisted the man's face around to stare at him. With his other hand, Cole shoved the cell phone into Ryan's view. Rage darkened his face, and he leaned close. "I have your entire life in my hands. I know every single contact you have, and I know your wife's name and phone number. If you want to keep her safe, you *will* tell me what I want to know."

Only inches away, the smiling photo of his wife—the one he stored as his cell phone's background photo—stared at Ryan. Joy captured her face. He could almost hear the laughter that sparkled in her eyes, and Ryan felt his entire soul ache. The pending divorce told him how his wife felt about him—but he couldn't deny how he still felt about her.

Ryan shifted his gaze away. "She's not my wife anymore. We're getting a divorce."

The news piqued Cole's interest. "And who filed for that divorce?"

"*I did!*" he lied. "I don't care what you do to her. I'd probably pay you to do it."

The words snapped out of Ryan with force and made Cole straighten. Methodical, the older man retrieved his own phone and started working the keypad. "Well, we'll just see about that."

A knot of fear grew inside Ryan. "Who are you trying to fool? There's no cell phone service up here."

"Oh, that's right. The government doesn't give you guys satellite phones, do they? They're too stingy with their funds. Don't worry, I have one. Just let me make a call to a couple of twiggers I know." He looked up from dialing, pushed send, and the call went through. "I'll put it on speaker so you can hear."

The sound of a phone ringing traveled through the stifling air and Ryan's stomach twisted. He knew that twiggers dug for artifacts to support a drug habit; and he knew too, that made them very dangerous. The phone rang again, and Ryan felt his mouth turn dry. On the third ring a man answered. "Yeah?"

"Hey, you know who it is. I got a job for you and your pal. I'll pay you three times what I paid you for your last find."

The voice grew interested. "Sure, what do you want?"

"This time I want you to find a lady . . ."

"Okay!" Ryan burst. "I'll show you. Just call off your guys."

A casual push of a button disconnected the call, and Cole gave a cold grin. "There, Mr. Government Agent, it wasn't that hard to come work for me now, was it?"

SEVENTEEN

DAVID WALKED nervously around the truck. Raised on a jack, the vehicle tipped toward the road. A flat tire lay on the ground, the bolts stored in the hubcap, waiting to secure the replacement. Checking his phone for service bars, David shook his head. "I can't call from here."

They'd seen the truck up on its jack with the tire on the ground and had stopped to help. David also planned to ask if the driver had seen three teenagers in the canyon. Neither of them expected the story that unfolded before them when they walked around the other side of the vehicle.

Squatted on the side of the road, looking at the ground, Juan now lifted his gaze but saw nothing that could explain the scene inches from his feet. Troubled eyes carried Juan's gaze back to the earth near his boots. A darkened puddle of blood soaked into the earth and stained the rocks.

"It could have been a cut hand. Working with vehicles always causes a lot of cuts and scrapes," David offered, unease in his voice. Around them, insects clicked and buzzed in the heavy air, and both men churned through private thoughts. They knew the amount of blood indicated that more had happened here than a simple cut.

"Do you think it may have something to do with that girl who is missing?"

A frown showed David's concern. "I don't know. I hope not."

Rising to his full height, Juan looked again at the blood. "You said they found a newly cut rope in her bedroom Any cut rope in this truck?"

The question caused David to turn and look through the open windows and in the bed. Without touching anything he made a quick scan. "I don't see any." He looked up as Juan moved away from the road, toward the brush. "Where are you going?"

"To look for an injured person."

"Watch out for rattlesnakes," David warned. Again he checked for cell phone service. Nearby, Juan moved slow through the grass and bush. Then the Peruvian stopped and lowered himself for a closer look at something.

"I think I've got something."

"What?" Worried his friend may have found Tallie, David rushed around the truck.

"Is that girl a blonde?"

"No, she has black hair. What did you find?"

Looking up, Juan's hand motioned to a tire iron. The metal rod lay in the hot sun, dried blood holding several blond hairs to the crimson-stained metal.

The sight of the hair caused David's stomach to turn. "That's not good. It looks like someone or something was hit with that thing. Maybe a dog?"

"No, those aren't dog hairs."

David's eyes dropped to his phone. Frustrated when the bars refused to disclose service, David shut the device and made his decision. "I'm going to head back down the canyon to call the police and tell them about this."

"I'll stay here and keep looking. If someone's been hurt . . ."

"Good idea. I'll be back in a minute."

Seriousness filled Tallie's face. "Let me find the way out. I have the map on my ankle."

Jonathon stopped and looked at her, his expression a clear refusal of the offer. "And I can use your necklace. Besides, I've done this before. You haven't."

Still she protested. "Let me help."

This time Jonathon's gaze shifted toward Severino, who sat against the cave wall, his eyes closed, pain written on his face. Poison darkened the skin on his arm and the swelling spread toward his elbow. "You can help. You need to stay with him, Tallie. He needs you more right now than anyone." Stepping closer, Jonathon lowered his voice. "He's going to fight this for you, more than for me." Her eyes showed her confusion and Jonathon gave a half-smile. "It's a pride thing. Guys can't let a girl see them defeated by anything." Next he tucked her hair behind her ear. "Tallie, stay with him. Keep him fighting this. I'll bring help as soon as I can."

"At least take the water, then."

"No, Severino is going to need it. His fever is only going to get worse."

From his berth against the wall, Severino heard their conversation. "Take the water," he growled.

"Severino, you need to drink."

"And if you have to dig, you will need to drink." Still Jonathon hesitated and Severino pushed forward, his voice gentling. "Jonathon, I need you to get us all out. Take the water, please."

The plea caused Jonathon to relent. "Okay, but just one bottle."

"Fine."

Jonathon picked up a bottle of water and reached for the shovel. "Got any advice for me before I go?"

Trying to control his breathing, Severino nodded and spoke slow, "Always leave a trail of dirt piles so you know where you've been. Try to stay out of low spots and away from standing water. Both places can collect bad air. It may not smell different, but it will feel different. If you find yourself breathing faster or your heart starts to beat faster, get out. Turn around and come back. Don't push it."

"I won't."

"If you get into bad air, you can die within minutes and not even know what is happening to you. That is why you have to pay attention to the little warning signs. If your mouth feels dry or it gets an acid taste, you're breathing bad air even if you think you're in a safe tunnel. If you get a headache or start feeling dizzy, clumsy, sleepy, or slow, you're already in big danger. Don't go any further. Turn around and come back."

"I will."

Severino swallowed against the pain and tingling feeling in his lips. His words were hard to form. "In mines all wood is rotted and all openings in the floor are dangerous. The earth can crumble away beneath you, even if you're several feet back. *Never* jump over one."

"So how do I get around them?"

"Sometimes you can't. If you can't, come back and we'll see if we can figure another way out."

"What about booby traps?"

Severino shifted against the wall, sucking against the pain as he moved. "I can't tell you about those, only warn you that they are here. Just be careful. Most of all, if something *feels* uncomfortable, trust your instincts."

Jonathon tried to help him move into a more comfortable position. Severino braved a smile. "So, do you have any advice for me before you take off?"

"Yeah. Stay calm, don't move, keep your arm lower than your heart, drink the water Tallie gives you, and *don't die*. You have a sister I want you to set me up with when we get out of here, and she probably won't like me very well if you die while you're here."

The last comment surprised Severino and he looked at Jonathon. "My sister, huh?" Thoughts processed Jonathon's comment for a moment, then Severino gave a quiet smile. "She'd like that. *Tienes un trato*—you have a deal."

A grin came in response. "Sounds good. I'm holding you to it."

"Okay."

Rising to his feet, Jonathon turned to Tallie, his face somber. "Take care of him, Tallie."

"I will. Take care of yourself." Then, because she knew of no other way to say good-bye, Tallie gave Jonathon a quick hug before stepping back and watching him move down the corridor. The light cast by his headlamp moved through the tunnel and then disappeared.

"You can go with him if you want."

Tallie turned around. Severino slumped against the wall, his eyes closed. "I'm going to stay here with you," She said. To emphasize her words, she moved and sat down next to him. The fever from his body radiated against hers.

"There is nothing you can do."

Without Jonathon around, she struggled to answer him in

Spanish. "I can help. I can talk. I can help you *rayar*."

Severino turned his head to look at her. "Did you just say scratch?" His hand movement made a scratching motion.

Horrified, she shook her head and, this time, answered him in English. "No, no! I mean laugh, ha-ha, not scratch! I can help you laugh."

"Ah . . ." An understanding grin moved across his tired face. "You meant *reír*, not *rayar*." Then a soft chuckle eased out through his smile. "Well, you just did that. You helped me laugh." Comfortable for a moment, Severino laid his head back against the wall. "Okay, you can stay. I will even let you scratch, if you want."

"Gee, thanks."

In the dim light from the air shaft, she pressed her lips together and looked at him. Sweat shimmered on his skin, and she could see the rapid pulse of his heart pounding blood through the vein on his neck. "What can I do for you?" she asked, reverting to the language she knew best.

Tired, Severino managed to find simple words and answer in her in English. "Just keep talking. Help me forget. Jonathon said you will go to college. What will you study?"

"Probably medicine."

He managed another smile. "My sister too."

"What do you want to study?"

A tired roll of his head came with his answer. "I have no plans for college."

"Why not? You're smart."

"I have told you—my father."

"Yes, but you should go to college. I think he would want that more than he would want you running with the sunshine guys."

More laughter rolled out of Severino but this time it brought a rush of pain. Against the tunnel wall, he clutched his arm and fought to bring both his laughter and his pain into control. "They are called the Shining Path."

"They don't seem very shining to me if they kill good people and keep minds like yours under their control." The comment puzzled him and he could not understand what she said. At the sight of his confusion, she tapped the side of her own head. "They control you—your mind."

This time he did understand and his expression changed. "They do not control me."

"They do too because you let them. You let them take away your future."

The words drew no response from Severino, only his quiet eyes watching her.

Tallie lowered her gaze. "I'm sorry. I said too much."

"You spoke your feelings. That is never too much."

"I'm just worried about you—and what will happen when you go back to Peru."

"I will be fine." He shifted his gaze away from her and exhaled. "Maybe one day I will go to college."

"If you do, what will you study?"

"I do not know. Maybe life?"

The response made her smile. "I think you have experienced enough of that already." Her hand offered him the bottle and he took it with his good hand, lifting it to his cracked lips and taking in just enough to wet his mouth. A metallic taste filled his mouth and his hands and lips tingled.

"How are you feeling?" she asked.

"It is harder to breathe and I feel different in my mouth and hands." He passed the bottle back to her, working his good hand, moving the fingers, trying to work the sensation out of them. Fire burned in his swollen arm and fever throbbed at all his joints.

"Different? How?"

"I cannot say in English."

"Does it hurt?"

He tried to answer her, to explain the tingling, the numbness, but his tongue stumbled and his mind struggled to function in English. Inside, he felt a tightening and rolling in his stomach and knew he was also growing nauseous. "Just different," he breathed.

"Don't worry about it. I'll accept different." Concerned, she brushed sweaty hair off his face and watched him. "You don't look good."

"I do not feel good," he admitted. Braced against the cave wall, his breathing grew more rapid and shallow. The numbness in his hands and face increased. Suddenly his face paled. "Things just got bad." A deep breath lifted his chest once, and he lurched forward, rolling to his knees, balancing on his good arm.

"Severino, what are you doing?"

Before he could answer, before he could rise to his feet and move away, his body rebelled against the poison and he heaved hard, vomiting onto the cave floor. Tallie scrambled beside him and touched his shoulder in support, just as he retched again. Weak and sick, he swayed on his knees, close to collapse, his bitten arm cradled against his upset stomach. "I am sorry," he whispered.

"Don't be." She handed him the water bottle, helped him shift his weight, and let him rinse the vomit out of his mouth. Then she guided him to a cool spot against the hard stone wall and he laid down. To keep his heart higher than his arm, she sat on the ground next to him and lifted his head and shoulders onto her lap.

For a long time Severino lay still, his eyes closed as he tried to keep control of his stomach and his mind. In pain, he tried not to feel the fever that burned through his body, leaving him hot on the outside and ice cold on the inside.

Blackness colored his lower arm. Thick as his calf, it lay useless at his side, the swelling and bruising well past his elbow, moving beyond the restricting band and toward his shoulder. Blisters began to fill with fluid around the bite and his fingers had swollen so much he could not move them.

Overwhelmed by the increasing damage, Tallie closed her eyes and began to sing a song. The song, learned from her grandmother, filled the desolate cavern with the melody and distinct intonation of the Paiute language. The words rolled off her tongue, and Tallie rocked her upper body with the song, wishing she could sing away the poison like her grandmother had been able to sing away so many of her hurts and fears.

Even though he did not understand the words of the song, Severino knew she sang for him—and he knew she sang a prayer of healing and strength. Too sick to move, he tried to swallow a lump in his throat, but the dryness only hurt more. Above him, Tallie sang the song again, stronger the second time, pleading for his relief; then her voice fell and she finished in a whisper.

"I thought you did not know Paiute," he managed.

"I only know a few things. When I was little, my grandmother used to sing me that song whenever I was sick. It always made me feel better."

"It still works. Thank you." Dark brown eyes opened and found hers. "You should learn more Paiute."

"Not many people speak Paiute anymore."

"Then you should learn." He struggled to speak, to find the words for his thoughts. "When a language . . . dies, the rest of that . . . that *cultura*—"

"Culture," she offered.

"The rest of that culture dies too. It cannot live long without its *voz*, its voice."

In her lap, Tallie saw him try to swallow against the hoarseness. With her hand, she lifted his head and held the bottle to his cracked lips. He managed three small sips and no more. Tallie blinked back her concern and tried to distract herself. "Paiute is difficult. You know how many mistakes I make with Spanish."

"And I make mistakes with English." He tried to draw air into his lungs but even they felt weakened beneath the crush and burn of the poison. "Tallie," he whispered, "until you learn someone's language, you will never understand their soul, their *alma*. That is why I learn English—to understand you and Jonathon, not for me." In respect, she listened to him speak despite the pain, saying words he felt deep inside. "If you want to truly understand your own people, your *patrimonio*, your *cultura*, you must learn to speak with the Paiute voice. Only then will you truly understand."

Beneath the afternoon sun, David and Juan moved on foot up the ATV trail. Urgency hastened the trek; concern for Jonathon and Severino propelled their steps into the canyon.

"Do you think the police will have trouble finding the truck?"

"No. I told them where it was, and they have my number if they need to get ahold of me or ask me any questions. But they also know I'll be up the canyon, out of cell phone range for a while."

Juan took a deep breath and nodded just before stopping. The canyon had opened to reveal a solitary campsite.

"That looks like our tent," David affirmed, moving faster. "Jonathon! Severino! Are you here?"

The men entered the camp, moving quickly through the supplies, looking for the teenagers. David ducked into the tent and then withdrew. "They're not here."

"Are you sure it's their camp?"

Nodding, David pointed to a helmet hanging over the ATVs handlebars. "That's Jonathon's helmet. This is their camp."

"Then, if they left the ATVs parked here, they have to be on foot. That means they have to be close. Whose ATVs are those?"

David shook his head. "I don't know. I really hope one belongs to Tallie and that she is up here safe with them." Again the men called for the teenagers, and again only the mountains returned their echoes.

Frustrated, David ran his hands through his hair. "Where are they!"

A warm breeze moved through the canyon and rippled the tent flap, revealing the contents inside for just a brief moment. It was enough. Juan notice the mess—the disheveled sleeping bags pushed to the sides of the tent.

Behind him, David moved toward the vehicles. "I'm going to get the plate numbers and have the police run a check on them. They can tell us who the ATVs belong to, and at least we'll know who they're with."

Another breeze moved the flap, and Juan again saw the unusual chaos inside—as if someone had been searching for something. Curiosity pulled him toward the tent

Again the flap billowed out of the way, and this time, Juan saw something gray. Pushing back the flap, he saw the duct tape, crumpled and discarded on the ground, the prize of long black hairs still stuck to the adhesive.

As he recognized the object, he instantly pieced several bits of information together and then he froze. The ransacked house, the tent, the blood and tire iron . . . and the missing girl. Now Juan knew she had *long* black hair.

"David, I think the kids are in trouble. That girl has been here, and I think she fought whoever brought her up here."

Horror moved David to Juan's side, where he noticed the duct tape and the destruction inside the tent for the first time. "Maybe there is a logical explanation for this."

"And for her house? And the truck down the canyon? And the duct tape? And your son being off the radar?"

David shook with emotion, and he turned away from the tent. "I don't know! There has to be a simple explanation. I *need* there to be."

"David, I know what you need, but right now I don't think all those events are coincidences. I think something is going on here and the kids got caught in the middle of it." Juan motioned at the interior of the tent. "Someone was looking for something both here and at the girl's house."

"But what would the kids have that anyone would want?"

"The mint mark."

The words jarred David's memory, and he looked up at Juan, stunned. "That's right. Jonathon said he thought someone was in the area stealing artifacts! If someone knew the kids had found some Spanish artifacts . . ."

Worried, David turned to scan the canyon, looking for movement. "But where are they now?"

"Maybe they just wanted the kids to show them where they found the artifacts. Do you know where the kids found them?"

David frowned and began to move up the canyon. "No. They never said. They could be anywhere!"

"Within hiking distance." Quick strides brought Juan to David's side. "Look, you go down, get the police and bring them up here. I'll keep looking up here and see what I can find. I'll study those petroglyph photos again and see if I can find any clues."

"It will take me over an hour to get down there and back."

"If they are with artifact thieves, we're going to need the police."

The wisdom of Juan's words pulled David off his search. Reluctantly, he turned and headed down the canyon, while Juan increased his pace and moved deeper into the gorge.

Burdened by concern for his friends, Jonathon moved at a brisk pace. The tunnel led him downward, spiraling through the mountain. Every tenth step, Jonathon dug a new hole and piled the dirt into a small mound. Severino's idea had merit, and Jonathon wished he'd known it before, when he was in the secret tunnels of Peru.

Another marker finished, he checked Tallie's necklace. Silver lines traced their trails through the intricate teal-green wings. Variscite,

Severino called it. The stone made the perfect canvas for the silver designs.

Again he studied the main trail. In the necklace, and on the ankle tattoo, the path had not seemed very far, but he knew—from personal experience—the tunnels could wander a long way through the earth. The silver designs might represent a few hundred yards or several miles.

Though the tunnel continued downward, Jonathon did not change his direction, trying to follow the direction of the large lines on the necklace. He hoped the lines on the necklace matched the tunnels in the mountains. Tallie said her father explained that man sometimes found himself caught up in the small, insignificant paths of life and that those detours would take them away from the larger, more important things—always with consequences.

The tunnel continued its descent, growing colder and more damp. The warning about bad air collecting in low spots and near stagnant water haunted Jonathon with each descending step, but a glance at his watch brought a renewed anxiety to his mind for Severino. With each passing minute, he knew the poison was doing more damage to his friend. Concerned, Jonathon increased his speed until he jogged between each digging stop. At least the headlamp made it easier. The first time he'd traveled through mountain tunnels, he'd only had the light from his watch and a small gaming system.

The tunnel sloped sharply downward into a long turn. Confused, Jonathon looked at the necklace. It didn't show a turn.

Forced by the steep incline to slow to a walk, stress pounded Jonathon's mind, and he rubbed his fingers against the side of his head, unsure about the unmapped turn. Memories tried to replay through his mind and Jonathon struggled to remember what Severino told him about the tunnels. Had he said if something *feels* uncomfortable—or if something *looked* uncomfortable—to turn around?

Jonathon couldn't remember which—in fact, he couldn't remember anything Severino had told him! Throbbing dulled his thoughts and filled the inside of his head. With a wince, Jonathon moved forward. Nothing looked wrong. Tallie's dad couldn't put every turn into the necklace. He probably just marked the main tunnels.

A swallow of water did not ease the dryness of his mouth or erase the taste of bitter earth that rested on his tongue and wrapped around every tooth. He'd been digging too many mounds of dirt, and the dust must have settled in his mouth.

Deciding he didn't need another mound so close to the first, Jonathon worked his way down the slope and through the long, sweeping turn, the shovel loose in his hand. In fact, he didn't see the need for another mound at all. No matter where he stood in the tunnel, he had to follow it.

On the far side of the turn, the tunnel opened up, disappearing into the darkness to the left. Ahead of him and to the right, his headlamp bathed a cavern filled with creamy, gleaming formations. The sight, crystalline and milky, stopped him with its iridescent beauty.

All around, water dripped from stalactites onto slowly mounding stalagmites. In other places, time had united the formations into vertical columns, striped pink and yellow and brown. Above him, the entire ceiling seemed filled with soda straws—long, icicle-like beginnings of stalactites. On the far side of the cave, just beyond the reach of his light, flowstone covered the walls in sheets of wet, waxy-looking formations.

Amazed, he stepped forward, and the ground beneath moved. He looked down, startled to see the rippling movement of water beneath his boots. Surprised at the sight, he directed his beam across the floor of the room and discovered it entirely covered with water. Water reflected the color of the formations and dazzling crystals sparkled in the beam of his headlamp.

Captured by awe, Jonathon took a step and felt the cold water seep through his hiking boots and into his socks. The sensation caused Jonathon to grumble. He didn't want wet feet. For a moment, Jonathon stared at his feet, watching the leather on his boots darken in the water, trying to remember why he was here, ruining his boots— but not a single thought came to his mind. He swayed as he watched the water ripple around him, and he spread his feet to hold his balance. Something didn't seem right, but he didn't know what.

Lifting his eyes and light to the giant room, he saw nothing but beauty around him and felt as if the cavern could shift around him— move around him because of his dizziness. Had Severino said something about feeling dizzy?

A pause allowed Jonathon to rub his brow, trying to recall an image of Severino and remember a face with the name, but he failed. Jonathon wanted to sit down and try to get his mind to work better, but he couldn't sit down in the water. It would get his pants wet.

A sense of cold burning entered his mind, and he looked down again, realizing his feet felt wet and hot at the same time. The water around his hiking boots surprised him. He couldn't remember walking into the water. He needed to go some place dry.

Somehow, when he looked over his shoulder at the tunnel, Jonathon didn't want to go back. He knew he was trying to move *away* from the tunnels. Again he swayed on his feet. Was he back in Peru? Jonathon struggled to find an answer—couldn't find an answer.

Turning his light back across the cavern, he saw a ledge on the far side, above the water line. He could sit there, out of the water.

Short of breath, Jonathon moved toward the ledge. Clumsy splashes soaked his jeans with water. Soon his lower pant legs, socks, and boots felt heavy and wet. The water began to irritate his skin. Angered, he swatted his lower legs, trying to drive away the burn. More water splashed against his hand, but still the burning encircled his lower legs.

Each step in the water disturbed the surface, sending ripples against each other and out across the room. Each step took him deeper into the water until the water encircled his knees, then his thighs.

His hand started to burn, and he wiped it, with annoyance, against his shirt. Still it burned, and Jonathon stopped in the water to look down. The back of his hand had turned red. The burning sensation in his legs traveled upward, grating against his skin like the sting of a thousand ants.

Confused, Jonathon stood in the cold, thigh-deep water and wondered why it burned so much.

Then, somehow, Jonathon realized the water caused the burning. Jumping back as if bit, he tried to get away, but the water splashed upward, arcing across his face. He stumbled on the slick surface beneath the water and almost fell. More water splashed his hands and arms and his face. Somehow he remembered the ledge and pushed rapidly through the water toward the formation. It rose above him at chest height. He scrambled to climb but his hands found no grip on the water-slick surface. Again, he tried to exit the water, using his feet to climb out, his knees, his hands—nothing worked. He felt the burn left by splashed water across his face. His hands burned and his legs felt raw.

He felt the shovel against his hip, unaware that he had hooked it on his belt. Despite the fuzziness of his brain, Jonathon realized the importance of that tool. Fingers, thick and awkward, groped to find and release it. Bringing the shovel around in front of him, Jonathon swung it at the flowstone, trying to break open a hold. The rock broke away in sheets. He struck again, releasing more of the ancient formation and finding a foothold. With his boot gripping the edge, he climbed up, reaching higher. This time his hand found a stone, and he grabbed it, lifting himself out of the water.

Still straining, the stone as his anchor, he pulled his body upward. Tensed against a slip, he inched higher. If he fell now, he knew his entire body would fall beneath the water and that couldn't be good.

The ledge leveled out, and Jonathon slung his left leg over the edge. Shifting his weight, he leaned heavy on the stone, trying to pull the rest of his body up onto the ledge. Then without warning, the stone broke away, tumbling down into the water below and releasing a gushing torrent. Icy water throttled his chest and face, threatening to push him backward, off the ledge. Desperate, Jonathon grabbed for another anchor, claiming a tight grip on a new rock.

More water continued to roar out of the opening, pounding his body, drenching him with its freezing flood. The rush of liquid slammed against him and took away his breath. Turning his head to the side, he choked and gasped for air. Beneath him, the still pool churned into a cauldron of froth and foam as the fresh river of water tumbled into the chemical-rich cesspool.

Determined to lift his entire body onto the ledge, Jonathon reached still higher, finding another hold. He managed to pull his body up through the coursing water, then onto the ledge. Exhausted, he collapsed and lay on his back, shivering with cold and his head pounding with pain. Closing his eyes, Jonathon needed a moment to rest.

Beneath him, the clean water stopped rushing, abating to a steady flow, then to a smaller trickle. Though he heard the water subside, he did not care. Fatigue filled him and his muscles felt weak.

Breathing deep to catch his breath, Jonathon tried to remember why he was so wet and so tired, and when he had left his bed. A struggle to open his eyes ensued, and when Jonathon finally claimed victory, he did not recognize his location. Around him he saw the strange formations, thought he was back in the tunnels in Peru, and thought Carlos would come through the dark with a flashlight.

Tired, and just wanting to sleep, he closed his eyes. He didn't worry about the Peruvian mummies and the gold. The mummies were probably sleeping anyway. And the bugs would protect the gold.

Even though his thoughts did not make any sense, Jonathon didn't worry about that. He'd sort everything out when he woke up. Heaviness claimed his body, and despite his wet clothes, he felt warm. The burning had stopped. Letting his body sink deeper toward sleep, he felt his muscles relax.

Time passed.

A sound moved through the darkness.

His mom must be doing the laundry.

Another sound entered his hearing. This one sounded deep, like a growl—a warning.

Wondering, Jonathon blinked and opened his eyes. Seconds passed before he could focus his mind and his gaze. At the edge of his headlamp's beam, he saw a movement, a shadow slipping by in the darkness. He blinked, staring at the shadow. Something told him the shadow stared back.

A feeling of unease filled him, and Jonathon rolled onto his hands and knees. He forced one leg beneath him and managed to rise to unsteady feet. Why did he feel so weak? Then he noticed the shovel he held in his hand and remembered something . . . rocks and dirt and water.

Staggering forward, Jonathon only made it five steps before he sunk to one knee and then the other. He groaned, his head pounding from front to back. A sharp pressure filled the space between his eyes and a tense ache at the base of his skull made it painful to raise or lower his neck. He just wanted to rest.

Easing his body against a pillar, he closed his eyes. He'd get up for dinner later, when his mom called. Right now, with his room blanketed in semidarkness, he just wanted to go to sleep.

Seconds later, he heard his little brother enter his room and walk toward him. Then Jonathon felt a hand on his chest, the soft whisper of a movement, and he wondered why his brother pushed him.

Then a deep growl and popping sound caused Jonathon to open his eyes, and he cried out in horror. In the beam of the headlight, the eyes of the Skinwalker stared at him. Only inches away, its horrific nostrils sniffed at his shirt.

EIGHTEEN

THE MASSIVE creature glared at Jonathon. Blond hair framed its face and bristled across its back and down its shoulders. Blue eyes stayed fixed on Jonathon, and its half-human, half-wolf face twisted into an angry snarl.

Groping for the shovel, Jonathon swung at the beast and yelled out in fear and protest. The Skinwalker jerked its head to the side and caught the shovel's handle in its mighty jaw. Shaking only once, the powerful creature wrenched the tool from Jonathon's sluggish hands, and it clattered to the cave floor.

Without protection now, Jonathon scrambled backward and tried to get to his feet to escape the awful hallucination that had taken a very real form. Yet the thing advanced, and a terrible sound rolled out of the creature's throat. It snapped at him, so close that Jonathon saw the saliva arc from yellowed fangs and smelled the stench of its breath.

Turning onto his hands and knees, Jonathon rushed up the ledge, but the fiendish being followed him, growling deep, and snapping in fury. Each time Jonathon looked back, the blond monster charged him in rage, snarling and cracking its teeth together, coming within inches of closing its powerful jaw onto Jonathon.

Fear propelled Jonathon upward. He felt his heart pound with exertion, and sharpness pulsed through his head until he felt his vessels would burst with blood. Pain rasped at his lungs as he sucked hard for air.

At the top of the chute, the earth widened, and Jonathon spun to face the hideous tormentor. With a powerful lunge, the creature surged up onto the flat and circled around Jonathon, watching with his blue eyes, and sniffing the air. Twice the thing made a complete circle around Jonathon, and then on its third pass it stopped and faced him. The thing lowered its head of gray flesh and blond fur, and Jonathon could see the bristling of hair across its back. Muscles rippled beneath the short coat, and Jonathon knew he would be helpless against a direct assault.

Breathing heavily, still trapped on the ground, Jonathon watched the standoff and waited. As his chest heaved with fear and adrenaline, Jonathon's mind sharpened to the situation, and he knew that, without the shovel, he needed to find something else to use as a weapon. He moved his hand in slow motion across the ground, feeling for a rock, anything he could use to strike the beast.

The Skinwalker saw him move and seemed to know his intent. A warning growl slid out of its throat, and it backed up a step.

Jonathon used the retreat to his advantage and reached further. As his hand came in contact with a large stone, the beast snarled, snapped his grotesque jaw one more time, and then, before Jonathon could lift the rock and hurl it, disappeared to the left.

Afraid the thing would circle behind him, Jonathon swung his head and let the beam from his headlamp track its path. Several feet away, the Skinwalker looked back at him once more, then vanished into an opening in the cave.

Silence dripped through the cave like water. When the beast did not return, Jonathon sagged back against the cave wall and took a deep breath. Clean air filled his lungs and his heart slowed to a more normal pace. The pounding in his head lessened, and Jonathon lifted the rock, balancing it in his hands, his fingers no longer clumsy and inept.

Rolling the rock over in his palm, he realized he felt better up here on the ledge—breathing came easier, his mind and body no longer felt as fuzzy. And the burning sensation had stopped.

A shiver of cold rolled through him, and Jonathon realized the water that rushed out of the rock had saturated him and his clothes, diluting any acidic compound from the stagnant water below.

Then all of Severino's warnings about bad air returned to his mind, and Jonathon looked up, stunned. Down in that grotto he had come close to dying in a pocket of bad air. Even after he escaped from the water, the poisoned air threatened to put him to sleep permanently.

The danger of his situation washed over him, and Jonathon started to shake, not from cold but from reality. Looking toward the direction the Skinwalker took, Jonathon realized if it had not attacked him and chased him from that chamber, he would have died there.

Then Jonathon realized the beast had not sunk his teeth into him. It snapped and growled all the way up the ledge, but it never bit. It hadn't come to *attack* Jonathon. It had come only to drive him out of the lower chamber!

Amazed, Jonathon again looked in the direction the Skinwalker went and, just as suddenly, he knew which path to take.

He needed to follow the Skinwalker.

A canyon breeze ruffled Juan's shirt and hair. He looked at his watch, marking the time. Again he called for Jonathon and Severino but heard no answer. With his gut twisting around inside of him, he increased his pace up the canyon, following the creek. Ahead he could see a split in the trail and knew he would have to take one path or the other. Without knowing which way the teenagers had gone, Juan felt a hesitation over the decision. He climbed further up the canyon sides, hoping to see something that would tell him which way to go. He studied the terrain for a long time, searching for movement or clues. He saw nothing yet something continued to pull his vision to the west, to the rockslides on the face of the mountain.

Then his vision began to unravel at what he saw, and Juan made out the image of a butterfly too large and symmetrical to be natural. Stunned, he broadened his gaze, taking in more of the mountainside, until he saw a worm or snake figure made out of rocks—no, a caterpillar! There were other symbols up there, and though he didn't recognize them as Spanish symbols, he knew they were man-made markers; and he felt that he would find the teenagers near that mountain.

Over the last hour, several additional bouts of nausea left Severino empty and weak; yet his stomach still sought to rid his body of the poison. Only capable now of rolling onto his side, he fought through a new wave of dry heaves while Tallie held him. Each powerful retching fit twisted his body and wrung strength from his frame. It hurt. It raked through his muscles, his lungs, and even his head; but he couldn't stop the vomiting motion until his system became convinced of his empty stomach and finally released his body. In agony and relief, he sunk down into her arms.

"Do you want some more water?" she asked.

A weak shake of his head became his only answer. More water may trigger more vomiting. He wanted nothing in his stomach.

Tallie poured a small amount of water into her cupped hand. This she used to wipe across his brow and sweated hair, trying to cool his fever. In response to the comfort of her touch and the coolness of the water, he rolled his head toward her. The water lessened the fever that burned across his face, neck, and chest.

Beside him, his bitten arm lay straight and useless on the ground. Swelling had spread his fingers apart and puffed his hand to such an extent, she wondered if the skin would start to split. The rest of his arm looked even worse. Almost the size of Tallie's lower leg and swollen to his shoulder, the skin had turned a dark, bruised-black color, like death. She shifted him in her lap and tried to keep his heart higher than his arm, but she didn't know that it did much good.

Severino slipped into unconsciousness several times. During one of those times, she eased away from him and entered the air shaft. There she called up to Halden. No longer did she care what Jonathon and Severino thought. She would make any kind of deal with Halden he wanted, just to get Severino out of the mine and to a hospital; but Halden did not respond. He'd left them to die in the shaft without even a rope to help themselves. Fighting tears, Tallie returned and took Severino back into her arms, hoping Jonathon had made it out of the mine some other way.

Almost an hour passed since Severino had spoken. The poison ate away at his strength and he lay still, motionless. Tallie brushed his hair off his forehead tenderly and let her eyes study the strong, angled planes of his face. In silence, she wondered about his life in Peru, what his dark eyes had seen. They had probably seen more than he would ever tell anyone. A depth filled his eyes that only came to those who had seen a great many trials. Jonathon returned from Peru with that same depth in his eyes, and she wondered what he too had seen and endured that gave him that maturity.

Using a little more water, Tallie bathed Severino's heated brow and spread the cooling liquid down the side of face. His lips, cracked and dried from the poison, moved slightly at her touch. At the movement, she wondered what made him smile or laugh in Peru. In the States, she knew laughter came easy to him. Often she saw quick brightness rise to his eyes and an impish grin pull at the corners of his mouth, expressions that told her he thought far more than he ever said.

Reflecting on their time together, a smile softened Tallie's face. Though he didn't say much, in either language, when he did speak, she noticed kindness in his words—a calmness. She wondered if a girlfriend back in Peru heard and appreciated that same gentleness.

Thoughts that he may have a girlfriend made her feel uncomfortable, and she looked away from Severino, sending her gaze down the empty tunnel shaft.

A pale blue light slowly approached.

NINETEEN

T HE LIGHT moved in measured passage up the tunnel.

"Jonathon?" she called. The sound of her voice echoed through the empty shaft and did not bring back an answer. Nervous now, she called louder, the tone of her voice demanding a response. "Jonathon!"

This time, the light quivered in the tunnel and held still, but still no sound emerged from the shaft—no footsteps, no rustling of clothing or equipment. Willing her sight to penetrate beyond the light, Tallie tried to identify feet or arms in the glow that would indicate a person held the light aloft. Only the glow of the light returned, shining off the tunnel walls.

"Severino, wake up," Tallie whispered.

Severino heard a voice and sensed fear. Deliberate, he tried to force himself away from the darkness that claimed his thoughts and body. He blinked twice and recognized the voice, knew that it held fear.

"Someone's here."

Severino worked to focus his mind on Tallie and tried to sort through the reasons behind her concern. "Who is here?" he questioned. His eyes found her looking into the mine shaft.

"I don't know. They aren't answering."

"What?" The words made no sense to Severino, and he turned his head in the direction she looked.

Thirty yards down the shaft, a glowing orb held still, suspended in the center of the shaft. "Is it Jonathon?" he asked.

"No."

"Halden?"

"That's what I'm afraid of."

Even though weakness claimed his body, anger filled Severino's mind, and he rolled to his side. Realizing his intent, Tallie caught his shoulders. "No, stay down."

"Tallie, if that's Halden, he is not here to help."

Suddenly Tallie cried out and ducked. In the tunnel, the light dropped to the ground and skittered up the slope toward them, a tongue of rolling fire. Severino cursed and, through his weakness, wrapped his good arm around Tallie, pulling her down to protect her. The bluish light made a hissing and popping sound as it rushed forward, and then it disappeared only a few feet away from them, leaving the tunnel black.

Terrified, Tallie grabbed for the remaining headlamp and snapped it on, casting the beam down the tunnel. The tunnel stood empty. No one stared at them in ominous silence, and they heard no sounds of retreat through the mine. Deep fear took hold and she used the beam to search every inch of the tunnel. "*What was that?*" she demanded.

"*No sé.* I don't know." Yet Severino worried he did know, and that meant they were in a lot of trouble.

Moments after the first light disappeared in a streak of ground fire, a new light emerged in the same place, starting as a dim glow and gaining luminosity until it again filled the tunnel, hovering in midair, moving as they moved, seeming to sense their movements.

"What is that?" she whispered. "Am I seeing things?"

"No." Severino felt her fear and reached for her hand, trying to force his mind and his voice to work together. They had seen many snakes in recent days, and this morning, fog filled the canyon and a horrific beast came close to humans. "Tallie, has anyone seen the Death Light recently?"

Confused, she stared at him while her mind sorted through her memory. "You mean the Death Light out in the desert? But this isn't the desert . . ."

"Tallie, think!" A tightening in his stomach caused Severino to tense. He didn't want to vomit again—not now. They may not have much time. A grimace forced itself across his face.

"Ah . . . I can't remember."

"Try! *Es importante*."

The stress in Severino's voice sharpened her memory and she nodded. "Two days ago, some guys at the café said a couple of men from out of town had seen it a couple of times this week—they were asking about it because they didn't know what it was."

"They saw it *this* week?"

"Yes—"

A groan rolled out of Severino and he pushed to his feet, fear growing on his face. At the movement, the blue light swung wildly and crackled loudly. The noise caused Tallie to recoil but Severino ignored it and extended his hand toward Tallie. "I need the headlamp." Tremors shook his body as he waited for the light

Concerned, Tallie set it in his hand. "What are doing? You need to sit down." Clicking on the light, Severino moved deeper into the tunnel, *toward* the light. Fear gripped her and Tallie climbed to her feet. "Severino, where are you going? What are you doing? Stay away from it!"

Undeterred by her fears, Severino scanned the walls and ceiling with the arc of the headlamp in his hand. The mysterious blue light quivered in protest and backed away. Seeing the light respond to him, Tallie stepped toward him. "Severino—"

She said no more, for at that moment, the light shuttered, crackled, and then exploded into a shower of fiery sparks and orbs. Tallie cried out while Severino ducked. The rapid movement almost put Severino on the ground in pain and he sagged against the cave wall. The light vanished from the tunnel.

Fear filled her voice. "Please stop. Come back."

"*Granito*," he breathed.

"What is *granito*?"

With his good hand, he felt the tunnel wall, inspecting the rock as he moved through the shaft. Worried he had become delirious, Tallie stepped after him, watching the deeper tunnel, expecting the light to reappear.

A few feet ahead, Severino lowered himself to the ground, his voice sharp. "Here!" He dug frantically in the dirt with his good hand, scraping debris out of a large crack that ran upward through solid rock.

The crack disappeared through the rock. Inspecting the opening with the light, Severino found no snakes. Turning back to her, Severino motioned to the water bottle. "Drink all the water but one inch."

"What?"

"Drink the water or I will empty it."

"But you need it!"

Not waiting, he retrieved the bottle and he started to pour the precious liquid onto the ground. Horrified, Tallie tried to stop him. "Don't!"

He did not stop.

"Half," she offered in desperation. "We'll both drink half."

Now he shook his head. "It will only make me vomit."

"Fine, but that's the deal, the *trato* . . . if you want me to drink half, then you have to drink your half first or I won't."

Watching the seriousness in her eyes and wanting her to have at least some of the liquid, Severino lifted the bottle and took several large swallows, forcing it into his upset stomach. With his obligation fulfilled, he passed the bottle to Tallie who drank the rest, leaving only a small amount in the bottom.

"Is that enough?" she questioned.

With the bottle retrieved, Severino supported himself against the wall and lowered his exhausted frame to the ground. Though weak, he held the bottle between his thighs and used his good hand to scoop up the sandy soil and pour it carefully into the bottle.

Stunned, Tallie sat beside him. "What are you doing?"

"Making a warning."

"What are you talking about?"

Intent on completing his task, Severino scooped up more sand, his hand shaking from the poison as he worked. Not understanding his purpose but seeing his need, Tallie reached for a scoop of dry dirt. "Let me help. What do I do?"

Accepting her help, he leaned back against the cave wall, resting, trying to stay focused. "Pour it in the bottle until I say stop."

She poured several small handfuls of dirt into the water, until the soil rose above the water level. Then he stopped her. "Now I need two small rocks that will fit inside."

Motions from him showed her how to tip the bottle so the rocks rolled down the side and didn't drop onto the sand. When the two rocks were inside the bottle, resting on a bed of sand, she looked at him. "Now what?"

"We wait." Deliberate in his actions, Severino took the bottle and set it on a flat spot. Then he stared at it. Tallie worried the fever had affected his mind.

The water in the bottle did not move but the water in his stomach roiled. Severino fought to keep the liquid down, his breath quickening as his body argued with him. Fever and cold shook through his limbs and new sweat glistened on his forehead. When his mouth also started to rebel, Severino tried to swallow. A surge of his stomach announced his failure and he turned to the side, vomiting forcefully onto the cave floor, heaving water and stomach acid into the dirt. The action took the last of his strength, and he slid down onto his side, curling into a ball. "Tallie, if I do not make it, you need to know . . ."

"You're going to make it."

"Tallie—" He cut her off, not having the strength to argue. Somehow, he found the words, blending English and Spanish to tell her the truth he feared. "The light is an earthquake light. It means an earthquake is coming here, under the ground."

Horror filled Tallie. "But we are under the ground."

"Sí."

"Are . . . are you sure?"

Tired, his mind and body strained almost to defeat, he kept his eyes closed. "When earthquake lights come near granite, many times they are blue and make sounds, like this one. And this morning there was much *niebla*—how do you say it—clouds or smoke on ground." Words failed him.

"You mean fog?"

"Sí. In areas with much granite, fog often comes before an earthquake."

"So granite is bad for earthquakes?

"No," he whispered. "Granite is good. It gives earthquake lights and fog to warn us. Granite is also very strong and does not move in an earthquake. This granite can protect us." Weak, he nodded toward the crevice. "When I say so, you need to go inside."

"What about you?"

"I will come too."

Feeling nervous, Tallie crawled up and sat beside him. "Do you think we will have an earthquake?"

He put his good arm around her, drawing her close. "Yes," he breathed quietly. "I just do not know when." Without much strength, he motioned now to the bottle of dirt. "That will tell us."

"How?"

"When the earth shakes, before we can feel, the dirt inside the bottle will move, the water will come to the top, and the rocks will fall. We call it *licuefacción* in Spanish. What do you call it in English?"

"I don't know. I don't know anything about rocks or geology. How do *you* know so much?"

Severino, tired, found rest behind closed eyes. "Inside the Inca tunnels I have seen lights before earthquakes. I have seen many things inside the tunnels . . . Jonathon too."

Though she had not heard of the Inca tunnels before, Tallie knew he spoke the truth. "I believe you," she whispered. A gentle brush of her hand moved sweaty hair back, away from his forehead and temples. "Keep your eyes closed and rest. I will watch the bottle."

Fury drove Halden to throw a large rock at the ground. It smashed against a boulder, and rock shards chipped away, into the air. To protect his face, Tate could only close his eyes. Rocks pinned his body into a small space and pain further restricted his movements.

"I saw you do it, Tate! I saw you start that cave-in. Why did you do it, huh?"

Breathing hard, Tate tried to push on a rock and gain some freedom, but pain again stopped him short. "What you are doing is wrong."

"What I am doing is right! I deserve every thing this mine holds and you do too. After all Cole has put us through—he doesn't deserve a thing! This is payback!"

"I don't care about payback, Halden!"

"Well, you should. You should want to make Cole bleed as much as he made Charlie Pikyavit bleed. He shot him, Tate. Cole shot Tallie's dad, and you were standing right there when he did it! *I was standing right there*, and he shot him anyway. He doesn't care who he kills or who's watching, and we're probably next on his list!"

Furious, Halden looked at the jumble of rocks and swore in

frustration. "Now, thanks to your stupid move, the mine entrance is buried! I could have been getting stuff out of the mine to pay me back for all that Cole put us through for ten years and to get us some money to get out of here and away from Cole. But you went and buried it."

Now anger turned Halden to his cousin. "You buried them too, Tate. You buried Tallie and her boyfriends. Now they're probably all dead or dying just on the other side of these rocks, and it's all your fault. Do you hear me? It's your fault!"

The words hurt Tate, battered and broken, worse than all his pain, and a tear slid down his cheek. Lifting his gaze, he pleaded with his cousin. "Please, Halden, help me help them. Go get help—if not for me, then for Tallie and her friends."

A sour laugh escaped Halden's lips and he backed away. "Nope. No way. You got yourself into this mess, you get yourself out."

"I can't. It hurts. Halden, please. I can't move the rocks, or I would . . ."

"Well, if you can't get out, I guess you'll just have stay there and I'll come back and check on you in, oh, three or four weeks. I'll figure out something to tell Cole. Then, when he's back in California and you're dead, I'll just come back up here and mine it alone." Halden turned and left the entrance. "Maybe the Skinwalker will find you and you'll be dead by tonight."

Desperate, Tate called after him. "Halden, don't. Don't leave!"

Halden did not turn back and let Tate's petition echo off the canyon walls.

Without his shovel to leave markers on the ground, Jonathon hastily dug the heel of his boot into the earth, carving an X every few feet. They would be harder to spot than the dirt piles, but they would still lead him back if he needed to return.

The trail he followed formed a natural chute that only went in one direction. Several yards into the narrow opening, Jonathon wondered if the Skinwalker had led him here on purpose, to trap him. A confined area left him more vulnerable than a large area where he could maneuver and find weapons. Here, he could barely move, and weapons in the smooth tunnel were nonexistent. Now Jonathon wished he had kept the rock or risked the bad air long enough to retrieve his shovel.

In the chute, Jonathon paused to recall how Severino told him to trust his instincts. As crazy as it seemed, his instincts told him to continue to move forward. Though he didn't know where the path would lead, he knew the Skinwalker got in and out of the mountain, and he would follow the creature until it killed him or until he emerged into the sunlight.

Caution accompanied Jonathon along the narrow chute. At the end, it angled almost straight up. To proceed further, Jonathon hoisted himself upward, into the unknown. Like a gopher, he emerged from the chute into a new opening and cast his light around, searching for the Skinwalker; but the area held only rocks and darkness. Lifting himself out of the chute, Jonathon climbed to his feet and moved slowly through the larger room.

With his headlamp, he tried to find a trail, a footprint—anything that would show him his next direction. He scanned the ground slowly, sweeping his gaze back and forth until he found one faint print in the dust. Amazed at the size, he squatted beside it, holding his hand next to the image. The footprint loomed in the earth, as big as his fist, and he knew the beast he followed weighed as much as a full-grown man.

Proceeding forward, Jonathon found a second print and then a third, and he knew that, at some point, the creature had passed this way. Still worried about an ambush but trusting his instincts, Jonathon eased forward. Every sense prickled inside him and Jonathon slowed as he entered a small chamber. The musty odor of animal and the mottled smell of death twisted through the long and narrow room. He felt the Skinwalker close by.

Easing his pace, Jonathon advanced only inches at a time. Instinct heightened beneath unseen eyes, and he knew he moved in the presence of a creature that could kill him. As he progressed forward, his light caught a presence to his left . . . a human presence. The dark image startled him, and Jonathon whirled to face the threat, the beam of his headlamp cutting into the darkness.

A corpse—dressed in blue jeans and a T-shirt—stared back at him.

TWENTY

SHOCK AT the sight drove Jonathon backward, and a chok-ing exclamation bubbled out of his throat. All thoughts of the Skinwalker disappeared before the decayed specter.

Until the beast stepped out of the darkness and into the light.

Head low, shoulder muscles tight, the creature growled a warning at Jonathon and moved slowly across the beam toward the skeleton. Then, positioning itself in front of the corpse, the beast braced for an attack, forming a protective wall between Jonathon and the dead man.

"Easy," Jonathon whispered.

The animal growled a warning.

Jonathon spoke again. "I'm not going to touch a thing. I just want to get out of here."

In the limited light, Jonathon shifted his gaze between the deformed creature and the decomposed corpse. The skeleton he'd found in Peru had been centuries old, most of its clothing decayed away. The skel-eton, ensconced behind the Skinwalker, had spent less time trapped in the underground world. Hiking boots encased the feet, blue jeans, covered in the dust and dirt of many years draped over what remained of the man's legs. A T-shirt hung loose over a rib cage and shoulder blades.

Decay had eaten away the muscles holding the lower jaw in place and it sagged downward, against a collarbone. The head, tipped to the right, held a crown of short, dusty black hair. In all aspects, the skeleton looked dressed for a Halloween horror, but the large, gaping hole that destroyed the left side of the man's face demanded Jonathon's attention. Jonathon knew only a bullet could leave that kind of a wound.

Glancing back at the creature, Jonathon noticed the Skinwalker had a similar deformity on the same left side.

A sense of unease descended over Jonathon, and he backed up another step. Then he saw the remains of a watch on the man's wrist. A painted butterfly held a faded place on the leather band. Overwhelmed to see the butterfly, Jonathon reached behind him for support. "Charlie?" he whispered.

At the sound, the creature shifted his ears forward, recognizing the name, and new realization overwhelmed Jonathon. The deformed creature in front of him was Charlie's dog.

From across the years came a single name: Po'ohe. It meant "blue" in Paiute. Charlie named the dog Po'ohe because of his blue eyes, but Charlie always just called him Po.

Unable to draw much air into his lungs, Jonathon spoke again. "Hey, Po. Is that you?"

At the sound of his name, long silent for so many years, the dog stopped growling and closed his malformed muzzle. A nervous tongue flicked out to lick the furless side of its face.

"Po, do you remember me, boy? Come here, boy."

To Jonathon's relief, the dog did not advance, but he saw its wise blue eyes studying him. "What happened to you, huh? You look pretty messed up. You been up here, all this time, protecting Charlie and waiting for him to take you home?"

The dog continued to watch, still tense but not aggressive.

"I've been with Tallie. Do you remember Tallie? Maybe you can smell her on me, huh, Po? I've got her necklace with me. Maybe that's why you came and chased my butt out of that place with the bad air." The dog, much larger than any dog he'd ever seen, did not respond but merely watched the human intruder now with curiosity.

Hoping the sound of his voice would soothe the animal, Jonathon continued to speak. "I don't know if you remember Tallie or your name or anything like that, but I do need to get out of here. Tallie needs my help and so does my friend. Can you show me how to get out of here?"

Just then, something seemed to distract the dog and Po looked away from Jonathon into the darkness. Then the mighty creature whined in fear.

A lump of concern filled Jonathon's throat. Anything that worried a creature this powerful had to be dangerous. Looking around him in the dark, Jonathon searched for movement, shadows, eyes watching him. But Po did not search for anything. Instead, the dog lowered his ears in submission and turned in a quick circle in front of the skeleton. Then, to Jonathon's astonishment, the dog lay down and placed its mangled head on Charlie's thigh. A whimper of concern rumbled out of the dog's throat.

Not left with time to question the motion, Jonathon looked up as trickles of dirt began to spill from the ceiling and shadows in the beam of his headlamp moved and danced. Then the earth began to lift and fall, rising and undulating like a snake. Next it started to shift direction, shaking back and forth, from side to side—and Jonathon realized the dog had sensed an approaching earthquake before it hit.

When the water in the bottle began to rise above the sand, Tallie questioned her vision; but then the rocks began to sink into the sand and she knew the items in the bottle were reacting to sensitive movements in the earth she could not yet feel. She touched Severino's good arm.

"Severino, the rocks are sinking and the water is rising!"

The concern in her voice lifted his alertness, and he tried to pull himself back to reality to understand her English. He managed to raise his body. Through distorted vision, he saw the bottle and knew an earthquake approached.

"*Adelante*," he directed, motioning her toward the opening. "Go inside, now." He struggled to his feet, and she rushed to crawl inside the crevice. Once beneath the protective canopy of granite, she turned back to him, beckoning for him to join her, but Severino had known all along the opening could not hold both of them. Instead, he used his body to seal the opening, becoming a human door to protect her. As he did, the earthquake unleashed its fury into the tunnels.

Rocks, stones, and dirt rained down from the ceiling, falling in the tunnel like hail stones, bouncing off the earth and striking Severino as they fell, his frame reacting to each blow. In front of her, he jerked hard beneath a blow—once, twice, three times—then his body collapsed away from the opening in a final shower of dust and darkness.

The earthquake shook the chamber, sending boulders and stones bouncing to the ground. Rocks pounded Jonathon's body. Dust swirled, choking out the air and trying to strangle the light from his headlamp. To protect himself, Jonathon curled into a ball, his arms wrapped around his knees, his head buried against his jeans and tucked under his arms. Across the cave, the dog yelped in pain, and the sound lifted Jonathon's head. In that instant a stone fell in the darkness, bounced off the cave wall, and hurled back at Jonathon. Through the brown murk, he saw a flash of tan just before the rock smashed against the side of his face and knocked him to the earth. Unconscious before he hit the ground, Jonathon lay exposed to the rest of the quake.

A cry of despair erupted from Tallie when Severino collapsed, but her words were buried by the tumult of the quake, her efforts to reach him were ineffective. The tunnels filled with staccato *booms* and high-trebled *snaps* echoing out of the darkness. The bending and shifting of the earth held her prisoner in her granite cell, and she could only wait for the mighty trembler to pass. Then the earth seemed to sigh in relief, exhaling the last bit of pressure and then returning to silence.

Desperate to reach Severino, Tallie scrambled from the tiny hollow, letting the headlamp beam cut through swirling clouds of dust. Severino lay on his stomach in the dirt, his bloodied face turned to the side, his eyes closed. Not sure if he was still alive, Tallie knelt beside him and laid her hand across his back. His back rose and fell weakly. In fact, the movement had been so slight that she felt for it again to make sure. His back lifted in respiration and then dropped. Anxious, she bent close to his face. "Severino, can you hear me?"

He gave no respond.

"Severino, please answer."

Nothing.

Afraid to move him, worried his spine may have been damaged, Tallie looked around for something . . . someone to help . . . but the shaft only shared its darkness with her. Tears burned in her eyes, and a new fear filled her. If Jonathon was still in the mountain somewhere, he may be as badly hurt as Severino. If so, none of them were going to survive unless she found a way out.

When the debris settled and the dust began to thin, movement returned to the cave floor. The dog stood up, shook dust from his coat, and then started to whine. The sound reached across the small cavern to where Jonathon lay, a coating of broken earth across his back. The light from his headlamp illuminated tendrils of dust, lifting like smoke from the earth. It also shone on the blood that moved slowly through the dirt.

The world slowly and quizzically returned to Jonathon's senses. A wince accompanied the opening of his eyes and Jonathon reached for his head. The sound of whining continued to grate on his mind and he sat up slowly. He groaned in protest at the movement.

Removing his hand from his head, he saw blood paint his palm and fingers red. The sight brought a deeper groan from him, and he leaned forward, pressing his hand against the pain.

The dog continued to whine, but this time, a new sound registered in Jonathon's hearing. Captured by the unusual sound, Jonathon forced himself to look up. The dog clawed at a stone, digging frantically beneath it. It had fallen on the skeleton's lower leg, and the dog wanted it off his master. Determined, Po continued to dig and whimper his anxiety.

Worried about aftershocks, Jonathon pushed to his feet and stumbled to keep his balance. Ready to leave the dog to his task, Jonathon staggered across the cavern, intent on finding an exit before another earthquake buried him alive. The dog saw his departure, vocalized a sharp protest, and looked at Jonathon.

Stunned, he stopped. "You want me to help?"

The dog dug some more and then moved back, away from his master and again directed worried blue eyes at Jonathon, waiting.

Jonathon looked at his bloody hand then back at the dog. "You know, this isn't really what I need to be doing. Severino was bit by a rattlesnake and he's stuck in a tunnel with Tallie and earthquakes always send out aftershocks and . . ."

Po sat down on the earth and looked at Jonathon, The appearance of the hideous face, waiting for assistance, brought a sense of sympathy to Jonathon. "Okay, fine. But if you bite me, the deal is off. You got that?"

Slowly, cautiously, Jonathon approached. He realized the feral dog may not tolerate the close presence of humans, especially so near to his master. To calm the dog and himself, Jonathon spoke as he eased close. "Okay, Po, it's just me. I'm not going to hurt you or Charlie. Easy now."

As Jonathon got close, the dog grew unsure and lowered his head. A growled warning caused Jonathon to hesitate. "I used to give you my beef jerky when I was little, remember? It's okay." Again, the dog growled, but his hair did not bristle. With caution, Jonathon put his hand on the stone. "See, I'm only going to move the stone, get it off Charlie."

This time the dog seemed to understand and bent its head and, once again, began to dig at the base of the stone. Jonathon used that time to give the stone a steady push, but the weight of the rock kept it in place. Jonathon pushed harder. The boulder swayed a bit but did not move.

"Um, I'm going to have to use both hands," he said. Shifting closer, he put his second hand on the stone and pushed. This time the stone tumbled off the leg and into the dirt. With effort, Jonathon pushed it further away. Then he turned back and sat down on the floor of the cave to catch his breath and watch the dog.

With the obstacle removed, Po again lay down and placed his head on Charlie's lap watching the stranger in his cave. Jonathon smiled. "That's why you wanted it moved. So you could lay down, isn't it?" The dog's ears perked at the human voice. Touched by the loyalty, Jonathon nodded. "You're a good boy, Po. Charlie would be proud."

The two eyed each other for a long time then Jonathon climbed to his feet. "Well, it's been interesting, but I really need to get going. Any chance you could show me to the door?"

The dog did not move; it did not even lift its head from Charlie's lap. It was content to stay right there.

"Okay, fine. I'll see myself out. I know there's an entrance around here somewhere because you're getting in and out." Quiet words shadowed him as he moved around the formidable creature. "I probably won't try petting you good-bye. Hope you're not too offended by that." Only the dog's gaze followed Jonathon.

A few feet away from the skeleton, Jonathon spotted a well-worn trail leading through the chamber and began to follow it. It twisted around but seemed to be climbing.

About thirty yards later, he saw light filtering through the darkness and grinned. Just as he quickened his step and the opening came into view, Po bounded ahead of him, up the slope and into the sunlight.

Outside, Po shook earthquake dust from his fur. As Jonathon emerged into the sunshine, the dog trotted down to a nearby creek, took a drink of water to wash the coating of dirt out of his mouth, and returned to the cave. At the entrance, he stopped and looked back at Jonathon before disappearing into the dark and returning to his master's side.

In the canyon there appeared to be no evidence of an earthquake. The trees still stood, water still flowed. Even a few birds flew by. Jonathon knelt by the shallow stream and rinsed the blood from his hands. When he lifted the icy water to his forehead, the cold hurt then soothed the wound. Finished, he opened his bottle of water and drank half before recapping the container. Kanosh, he knew, lay west of the mountains. If he followed the creek in that direction, it would provide a trail through the canyons.

With time so vital for Severino and now worried about the how his friends had survived the earthquake, Jonathon came to his feet and broke into a jog. A sense of urgency filled him, and he knew he needed to listen to his instincts.

The rugged terrain challenged his body and jarred his head with every step, but soon Jonathon felt his frame begin to respond and numbness took over his head. Oxygen moved easily in and out of his lungs, and his muscles settled into his pace.

The tempo of his stride continued for a quarter mile. The creek became his guide, leading Jonathon around bends and twists. Sometimes the best path took him through the water, and other times he ran on the bank.

A half a mile down the canyon, he splashed through the water and didn't hear the call. Moving up the bank, a sharp whistle penetrated the sounds of his running. Stopped in surprise, Jonathon turned around. Higher up the canyon, he recognized the man waving his arms, then watched as Juan began a rapid descent through the rocks.

"Jonathon! Your father and I have been worried about you." Coming close, Juan saw Jonathon's swelling features and the blood on his face and clothes. "Looks like we had reason to worry. What happened?"

"Earthquake. Did you feel it?" Bending over, Jonathon tried to catch his breath.

"*Sí.* You okay?"

"Yeah, but Severino's been bit by a rattlesnake."

A quick lift of his eyes caused Juan to scan the area. "Where is he?"

"Stuck in the mine. I gotta get help and get him out. Where's my dad? Is he here?" Jonathon had already resumed his swift trek down the ravine.

Juan fell into step along side him, keeping pace. "He's back down the canyon, getting the police. When we got to your camp and saw your tent . . . we thought something was wrong."

"You thought right."

"So, what's wrong? There's a truck down the canyon with a lot of blood around it, and there's also a girl missing from Kanosh. No one can find her. Your dad said you know her?"

"Yeah, it's Tallie. She's technically not missing. But I don't know anything about the truck or the blood."

"Technically *not* missing? Is that like technically not shot or technically not dead?" Juan looked at the teen before he could answer. "Jonathon, what is going on? And is it something your dad is going to want to hear?"

"Probably not. Juan, some guys kidnapped Tallie and brought her up to our camp then forced us to dig out a mine for them."

"Is this something *I* want to hear?

"You need to hear it. I need your help. Both Severino and Tallie are trapped inside the mine, and we have to get them out. One of the guys who helped us escape may be dead, and Tallie's dad *is* dead, inside the mountain. I know, because I just saw his body and . . ." Overwhelmed, Jonathon stopped and looked up at the cloudless sky. "I can't do this, Juan."

"You don't have to. Just tell me what you need. Where are Severino and Tallie?"

A wave of his arm, indicated the direction. "They're over there a couple of miles, in Hell Hole Canyon, but you'll never find it. They're down a forty-foot air shaft."

"What about you? Can you find it?"

"Yeah, we found it the first time. Severino rappelled down inside the shaft, but Halden took the ropes, and now they can't get out."

"Who's Halden?"

"The guy who kidnapped Tallie."

"Is he over there?"

Jonathon looked toward Hell Hole Canyon. "I don't know."

"Then you need to come with me. We'll head down the canyon and tell the police . . ."

"No! I can't leave. You head down the canyon and tell the police. I'm going back to help Severino and Tallie."

The plan worried Juan and he stopped. "What would you have done if you hadn't met me?"

"Head down the canyon."

"Then let's go together and stay with your original idea."

"Juan, you're here now. We can separate. You go get help, and I can get Severino and Tallie out of the mine. It will save time. Just send the crews up to Hell Hole Canyon."

Juan exhaled. "Look, Jonathon, I understand your logic. I do. But I don't see it as sensible. If this Halden guy is still there . . ."

"When have you ever known me to be sensible!"

"Technically?"

"Come on, Juan. Severino was bad when I left him almost three hours ago. Now with the earthquake . . ."

Frustrated, Juan turned away, chewing on the inside of his cheek. "If I leave you up here on your own, do you know what your dad will do to me?"

"Kill you?"

"That will be the easy part."

A grin brightened Jonathon's face; he knew Juan was caving. "I'll come to your funeral."

"Yeah, and I'll haunt you for the rest of your life."

"Deal."

A sour look covered Juan's face, but it didn't hide the smile in his eyes. "Somehow I still think I got dealt the low card."

"Hey, in some games, that's good."

A dimple pressed into the side of Juan's cheek. "And, is your dad going to like knowing you know about poker?"

"Probably not but we'll have that discussion later. I'm going back to help Severino."

"Fine, but you play it tight. If something looks dangerous, you fold and get out of there, okay?"

"Okay. And, Juan, thanks."

Just then a voice drifted through the canyon. Worried, Jonathon lowered his frame and motioned to a covering of cedars. Juan followed. A second voice floated along the slope. At least two men were ahead of them, in the narrow ravine.

Moving slow, quiet, Jonathon positioned himself deep in the trees to watch. Juan eased his body down next to Jonathon. Grateful to have Juan beside him, Jonathon shifted his gaze back to the brutal scene several yards ahead. He recognized the handcuffed man, and a quick rush of relief filled Jonathon to see the man captured, yet a second twisting took hold of his stomach. Something wasn't right. Something *felt* wrong.

On the sun-heated earth, Ryan lay still, his eyes closed, his battered body trying to save the last of his strength. Handcuffs held his hands prisoner behind his back and his short blond hair carried both dirt and blood. His swollen face showed the blue-black discoloration of heavy bruising.

Digging another cob coin out of the dirt, Cole smiled. "You know, you could have made a lot more money off artifacts if you'd played your cards differently—but, no."

Anger and pain hissed out of Ryan. "Is that *all* you can think about—money? We just had an earthquake. People could be dead right now, and we should be going back to help, but all you care about are your stupid artifacts!"

Mirth disappeared from the face of the older man, and he approached the downed man, shoving him in the shoulder with his boot. "You're the stupid one! You made the mistakes, not me, and now you're the one wearing handcuffs. Ten years of your life wasted. How does that make you feel?"

"I'm not worried about me right now!"

"Then let me give you enough information so you do. I'm going to leave you up here to rot and, by the time they find you, *you* will be the artifact!" A boot to the gut punctuated the man's statement, and the blond coughed out a sound of pain, curling tight to protect his body. Ryan tried to calm his body and his mind. The power of the quake worried him, and he wondered about damage along the Wasatch Front—and especially about the safety of his wife.

Still trying to catch his breath and his heart, Ryan closed his eyes. Pain from his emotions hurt more than his body. He wanted to call his wife to check on her. Mostly, though, he wanted to tell her he loved her and was sorry for all the times he thought only about his job— about all the stupid, self-absorbed times he left her feeling unnoticed and undervalued. Never had she been either to him, but she didn't know that.

Cole went back to scanning the area with a small, handheld metal detector. "You know, if you don't want to become a human arti- fact, you can change all that. In fact, you could start making obscene amounts of money, like I do."

Cole swept the small metal detector carefully across the slope. "Did you know that artifact theft is so profitable it comes in right behind drugs and guns? Did you know that?" Cole snorted as he looked for changes in the readings. "Yeah, you probably did. The problem with you is you aren't connected to the right people in the business."

Now the older man looked up and smiled. "I'm one of the right people. I don't work with the local dealers. Nope, I sell only to a list of international buyers. With a small, local buyer these cob coins will get you a hundred dollars, tops; but I know guys who will pay thousands of dollars for the right coin and the right story to go with it. And that is pocket change."

A new reading on his detector caused Cole to squat on the earth and sift through the soil. "Last week I turned down seven and a half million dollars for the mummified remains of a Hopi woman buried in her wedding shroud. *Turned it down* because I can get more—a lot more. And what would you do with a find like that? You'd turn it in to your handler, get a pat on the back and a 'good job,' and receive the same measly paycheck two weeks later, because you're not the one in charge. You're just a drone—you're expendable, you're cheap . . . and your talent is being wasted."

"It's the life I chose."

"Well, you should choose a different life now. You can come work for me and get a fair cut of those millions and millions of dollars I pull off the international market. What do you think?"

"I think I'll rot first."

Stunned, Jonathon looked at Juan. Without a word, they both read each other's gazes and knew the silent thoughts. The men were talking about antiquity theft, international theft! Absorbed in their thoughts, neither one saw a shape step out of the trees behind him.

"You almost made it," the voice behind them taunted. Startled, Jonathon turned fast and then froze. Halden stepped closer, balancing the gun with one hand. "Where's Tallie? Did she get out too?"

"I don't know." Jonathon's voice came in a quiet hiss, not wanting to alert the men ahead of him in the canyon.

Not noticing, Halden shifted on his feet and motioned to Juan. "Who's this guy?"

"Some strange guy I found."

"You found him, like a lost puppy on the trail?"

"Something like that." Jonathon kept his voice low.

"So you won't mind if I shoot him, then? I don't like stray puppies."

"Figures you'd be the kind to hate puppies."

Enraged, Halden released one hand from the gun and shoved Jonathon on the chest. "You know, I'm really getting tired of you!"

Jonathon rolled his eyes. "*Iqual*, Halden, *iqual*."

In an attempt to deflect Halden's anger, Juan eased forward yet intentionally spoke Spanish. "*Me llamo Juan*."

Looking at Jonathon, Halden sneered. "In the habit of naming your stray puppies?"

Defeated, Jonathon made a flat hand motion. "Juan, *te presento* Halden. Halden, Juan. There, are you satisfied? Now you can send each other Christmas cards."

Furious, Halden backhanded Jonathon and the butt of the revolver split open Jonathon's lip. Turning away and catching his face, Jonathon felt irritation take hold of him as new blood began to flow. "Would you stop it with the hitting!"

"When you stop it with the mouthing off. Where's Tallie?"

"Probably right where you left her." Again Halden raised the gun to strike, but Jonathon waved him off. "Halden, it's the truth. I left her and Severino there in the chute. I haven't seen them in almost three hours."

"How'd you get out?"

"I followed the tunnel."

"There's another opening?"

"Obviously."

"So where's is it?"

"I don't know. I probably won't be able to find it again."

Out of patience, Halden pointed the gun at Jonathon. "*Show me!*" he shouted, and Jonathon felt his stomach churn. The men had to have heard that.

A second later, his ears confirmed his instinct. The older man shouted through the canyon. "Halden, get over here now!"

Startled by the intrusion, Halden looked up the slope. "Who's up there?" he snarled.

Touching his fingers to his bloody lip, Jonathon scowled. "Well, I'd offer to introduce you, but the last time I made introductions, it didn't go very well for me." Halden cursed at him.

The man called down again. "Halden, I suggest you get up here *now*; and bring your buddies with you."

Cornered, unable to leave, Halden looked at Jonathon and motioned him and Juan up the slope. The sick feeling in the pit of Jonathon's stomach increased as they moved away from one gun into the muzzle of another.

The blood and bruising on Jonathon's face intrigued Cole as the teenager came into view. From the ground, the sight of the teen brought a different response from Ryan. For a brief moment, their eyes met, and it looked to Jonathon like Ryan was disappointed to see him—as if Ryan had failed at something.

Irritated, Cole pointed a gun at Halden. "Why didn't you answer any of my radio messages? Are you trying to double-cross me?"

Visible fear showed in Halden's expression. "No, sir. I was having trouble with this guy and his new friend."

Shifting his gaze to Jonathon, Cole studied the young man. The blood gave credence to Halden's claim. "What kind of trouble were you giving Halden?"

"I wasn't."

"He says you were."

Jonathon shrugged but said nothing else.

"Let them go, Cole." Ryan spoke as he struggled with the new situation.

"Shut up, Ryan."

"You don't want to involve anyone else, especially not a kid."

"Don't tell me what I want to do." A quick shift of his gaze locked Cole's eyes on Halden. "Put your gun down. I have them now." When Halden hesitated, Cole's eyes hardened and his gun lifted. "You don't want to test me."

The warning worked, and Halden lowered his weapon.

Cole stepped forward and looked at the bloody youth. "You must be Jonathon Bradford." Though the sound of his name surprised him, Jonathon did not waver in his gaze.

A cell phone lifted in Cole's free hand. "I have a text telling me all about you. You're a tough kid, survived the jungles of Peru—impressive. I've been there. They're not nice. This your dad?"

When Jonathon did not answer, Cole pocketed his phone and grabbed a handful of Juan's hair. Jerking the man's head back, he exposed Juan's neck. "*Is this your dad?*"

Jonathon's eyes met Juan's and he vacillated, not sure he wanted to say anything. "No."

"Who is he?"

Again Jonathon hesitated. "Halden seems to think he's a stray puppy."

A brief lift of Cole's eyes showed surprise at the answer. On the ground, Ryan wore the same expression. Finally, Jonathon shifted his weight. "He's a friend."

Cole returned his gaze to Jonathon. "I thought your friend was a teenager."

"Hey, I have more than one friend," Jonathon defended. From the ground, Ryan started to chuckle.

Furious, Cole kicked Ryan, and the blond man's smile turned to a grimace. Jonathon tensed with concern for the man bound and unable to defend himself.

Walking toward him, Cole glared at the teenager. "Where's the mint mark?"

"What mint mark?"

"Don't push me. I also have texts and photos that show you and a friend found a Spanish mint mark yesterday, in this very area, but it's not here now. What did you do with it?"

"Nothing."

"Don't lie to me."

"I'm not lying. What do you want me to say, that I buried it and Halden came and dug it up later without telling you?"

A slight pause held Cole still and he processed what Jonathon just said. Deciding it must be true, Cole turned to Halden. "Where's the mint mark?"

"I don't know. He's lying."

"I don't think so."

Worried, Halden plead his case. "Mr. Matthews, I've worked for you for over ten years!"

"If you want to make it ten more, you need to find my mint mark before the end of the day."

Before Halden could protest, Cole turned back to Jonathon. "Do you realize that you found more things yesterday than Halden has found all summer long? I think I have a job for you. It has great benefits, and, for the right items, I pay very well."

"I'm not interested."

"Did I mention that one of the benefits of working for me is that I'll let you live?"

To Cole's surprise, the threat didn't frighten the youth. Rather, it hardened Jonathon's gaze. "I didn't bring an application."

Cole draped his free arm around Jonathon's shoulder, rubbed the back of Jonathon's head. "You're going to be fun to work with." Then his face grew stern and the rub turned into a shove. "Sit down. You don't need an application. I just hired you."

The words caused Jonathon to stiffen but he didn't move. Stepping behind him, Cole jarred the back of Jonathon's knee with his boot, forcing the leg to buckle. "It can get worse," he warned.

In physical compliance, Jonathon eased his body to the ground and sat forward, knees up, arms resting on them, staring out at the site from beneath the bill of his blood and dirt marred cap.

A few feet away, Ryan forced his body into a sitting position and watched the teenager, noting the set of Jonathon's face—angered, not scared. He also noticed the two bobby pins that hugged the side of the cap Jonathon wore. The sight caused Ryan to shift closer.

Cole pointed the gun at Juan. "You, sit down."

"*Sientate*," Jonathon spat the rapid instruction to Juan, then to Cole, "He speaks Spanish."

The information accepted, Cole gave an angry motion for Juan to sit. As Juan eased himself to the ground, Ryan saw the two friends exchange quiet glances, and the blond knew Juan understood English.

Anger turned Cole to Halden. "Besides losing my mint mark, where have you been all day and what have you been doing?"

The swing in Cole's attention allowed Ryan to lean close to Jonathon, his words a mere breath. "My name is Ryan Polson, I'm an agent with the BLM."

Skepticism turned Jonathon's brown eyes to Ryan and the agent continued, quietly, urgently. "I need you to take the plastic tips off the ends of one of those bobby pins on your cap and pass me the bobby pin."

"Why?"

"So I can get out of my handcuffs. Then I can go after Cole. He has a satellite phone."

For a moment, Jonathon looked at Ryan. The heavy beating the man took gave him reason to hesitate. "Looks like he pretty much owned you the first time around. What makes you think you can handle him now, and why should I believe you?"

"You don't have to believe me about anything, but you do have to believe Cole is dangerous and we all need to get out of here."

Cole turned back around, his voice interrupting the silent conversation. "Bradford, get up!" At the command, Jonathon scrambled to his feet, wary while Cole approached. "Halden says you found an opening to a mine."

Angered by the sellout, Jonathon looked at Halden. "It caved in."

A harsh glare emerged from Cole. "I don't care. You're going to take me there anyway and start digging. That's part of your new job description."

Defeat sighed through Jonathon's voice. "Look, my friend needs medical help. I just want to get him to a doctor. If you let me use your phone to call for help, I'll show you everything you want."

Cole extracted Ryan's cell phone and waved it back and forth in his hand. "There's no cell phone service up here."

"What about that phone?" Jonathon nodded toward the phone snug in a leather case against Cole's hip.

"That phone doesn't work either."

Removing his cap, Jonathon toyed with it, his irritated and distrustful eyes on Cole. "Don't lie to me. I see the ring on your thumb. You have Càrn hiking boots on your feet and an Omega watch on your wrist. You have a *lot* of money. You didn't come up here with a cheap cell phone like the one in your hand. That's probably not even your phone. I bet it probably belongs to this guy." A nod of Jonathon's head directed his words at Ryan. "Your personal phone is on your belt, in that fancy leather case, and, with your obvious money level, I'm betting it's a satellite phone. So use it." Finished with his demand, Jonathon raked his hair back into place and returned the cap. Only one bobby pin hugged the side.

The bold challenge made Cole smile. "You don't miss much, do you? I like that."

"I like money. I always have. You call in help for my friend, and I'll take your right back to the mine . . . and we split everything we find fifty-fifty."

"And if I don't call for help?"

"You don't see the mine."

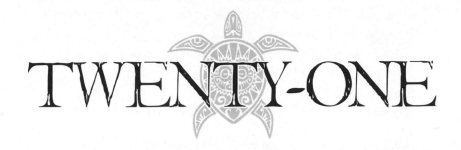

TWENTY-ONE

JONATHON SAT back on the ground and waited for Cole's answer. Though he appeared to be resting with his forearms on his knees with hands clasped together, Ryan saw the teen had the bobby pin concealed in his hands, his hidden thumbs working to pick off the plastic tips.

Furious now, Cole leaned close to the teen. "You aren't in a position to bargain."

Jonathon held his hands still, his face unmoved by the gun or the man. "The mine entrance that Halden so readily told you about is completely closed. No one could dig their way through it. But I was inside the mine when it caved in. Now I'm outside. So, as the only person who knows *another* safe way in and out of that mine, I am the only person here in a position to bargain."

Ryan stared at the youth, dumbfounded. His words had just hog-tie Cole.

The news turned Cole back to Halden. "You didn't see him get out of the mine?"

"No."

An exchange of glances from Jonathon to Ryan came with a slight nod from the teenager. Then Jonathon turned away and raised his voice in anger, speaking only Spanish. "*Hey, Juan, parece que ellos no nos entienden.* So that means we could talk about anything we wanted and they would just think we are arguing."

Juan nodded, his own voice growing hard. "We could do that, couldn't we? So, what did you want to argue about?"

"Oh, how I think the older guy is *un culero*."

"You would think that!"

"Yes, I would!" Jonathon snapped back in mock anger.

"That shows how little you know!"

"And what would you call the old man?"

Bristling, Juan yelled back at him. "Maybe something more harsh, like . . ."

When the word spat out of Juan's mouth, Jonathon jumped to his feet. "That just proves the old guy has no idea what you're saying! If he had understood, he would have taken your head off right now!"

Juan too came to his feet but Cole stepped between them. "Knock it off, both of you!"

Switching to English, his voice still raised, Jonathon snapped at Cole and pointed an accusing finger back at Juan. "Do you know what he just called Halden?" Before anyone could respond, Jonathon continued in English, his voice angry. "He called him nothing, absolutely nothing! Do you know what that means in Spanish?"

Irritated, Cole barked at them. "*I don't care! Now sit down!*"

This time it worked and the two eased back to the ground. Still speaking Spanish, but in subdued tones, Jonathon mumbled quietly. "When I create a diversion, I want you to make a break for it. Try to get down the canyon."

"What about you and the other guy?"

"We'll be fine. Besides, the guy seems to want one of my bobby pins. . . ."

Not in the mood for more Spanish, Cole stepped close. "*Quiet!*"

Eyes lifted in explanation and Jonathon shrugged his shoulders, returning to English. "I'm just telling him where to go." His gaze caught Ryan's and he gave an affirming motion with his eyes.

Cole didn't see the silent communication. "Yeah, well if you don't say it in English, I don't want to hear it."

"You probably don't want to hear it in English either," Ryan growled, watching the teenager closely.

Purposely keeping the tension high, Jonathon turned to the

battered man. "Do you want to keep your busted nose out of this?"

"Hey, I have a stake in this too, punk."

"Not in my book you don't, *cholo*."

"Everyone, shut up!"

Silence fell over the group and Cole straightened with his fresh victory. Jonathon gave a soft tug on the bill of his cap and nodded his eyes at Ryan before looking away.

Not willingly to let Halden off easily, Cole turned and questioned him. "Do you know of any other way into the mine?"

Before the man's onslaught, Halden shifted, nervous. "There is a ventilation shaft . . ."

In haste, worried what would happen to his friends if Cole and Halden showed up, Jonathon cut him off. "You mean the one with a forty-foot drop and a hole full of rattlesnakes? Yeah, I've been there too, but the opening I used doesn't have either."

"So, you do know a better way in?"

"Yes, but like I said, you have to promise me a cut of the action. I don't care what you're paying anyone else here. I want fifty percent."

The comment gave Ryan an opportunity to move. A curse erupted from the battered man as he came to his feet. "You little sellout! Keep your mouth shut about the mine!" Even though cuffs restrained his hands behind his back, Ryan dove at Jonathon, knocking the teen sideways into the dirt.

When the man's weight hit hard, Jonathon slammed into the earth. Before he could respond, Ryan claimed the advantage and pinned the teen beneath him. Desperate, Jonathon twisted for freedom, surprised at the man's strength and speed. His hands grabbed Ryan's shoulders and Jonathon shoved back, propelling the man off him. At the same time, he turned to Juan. "*Corre!*" he shouted. Behind him, Juan bolted for the trees and help.

In a swift move, Jonathon rolled to a squat, then dove forward, driving his shoulder into Ryan's stomach and thrusting him backward. In the fall, Jonathon managed to wrap his arms around Ryan's waist, controlling the man.

The tackle threw Ryan to the ground and he landed on his side, hard. Pain ricocheted through him. Before he could catch his breath and shift away, Jonathon released his hold around Ryan's waist, lunged forward, and pushed the man's back into the dirt. A scramble and quick swing of the leg put Jonathon across Ryan's chest.

Now straddled over Ryan, Jonathon drew back to strike, but a sharp blow to the back of his left thigh jarred Jonathon from the waist down. Pain shot down his leg and across his hip and Jonathon felt his entire limb go numb. Stunned, immobilized, he fell forward, off Ryan.

"Enough!" Cole shouted. Pointing his gun at Halden, he shouted, "Go after the man!" Halden rushed down the slope.

The blow left Jonathon on the ground unable to move, his left leg entirely paralyzed, his hip and abdomen in sharp cramps. Air tried to wheeze through lungs locked tight by the blow. Motionless, the distraction cut drastically short, Jonathon struggled to draw air into his body, tried to understand what had just happened.

Rolling him over with a shove, Cole glared at the teenager. "I told you it could get worse." On the ground, Jonathon could not answer, could not breathe.

Slowly Ryan rose to his feet, his own breath heavy. Concerned, he looked at the teenager, reading the youth's expression. Jonathon lay bewildered and paralyzed on the ground, unable to breathe, sucking for air but not getting any. "What did you do to him!"

"Sit down!"

"He can't breathe!" Unsure of what he could do with his hands bound and useless, Ryan still took a step toward the youth.

Irritated at the agent, Cole shoved the agent sideways. "I told you to sit down!" The force caused Ryan to stumbled across the earth.

On the ground, the blow's numbing shock dissipated enough to free Jonathon's lungs, which managed a desperate gasp for air. Ryan heard the hard rasping sound and turned toward the teen.

As oxygen entered back into his body, so did the pain. A deep groan expelled from Jonathon and he rolled sideways to clutch his useless leg. No effort brought a response from his leg; only his hands could move the limb. Fear that the damage might be permanent exploded into his thoughts. "What did you do?" he hissed through the emotional and physical pain.

"I hit a pressure point. Don't worry, the pain and paralysis will pass, but I could have killed you." Cole lowered himself next to the youth and, with a single knuckle, pressed another pressure point on the outside of Jonathon's injured thigh. Pain exploded into agony and Jonathon arched away, crying out in protest. "I still can," Cole warned.

Releasing the pressure, Cole stood. Instantly, Jonathon rolled toward his paralyzed leg, gripping his thigh against the pain, gasping for breath and control.

Disdain filled the older man's voice and face. "As soon as you can move, we'll get going."

Quiet, Ryan settled onto a rock and watched, his hands bound behind him, the bobby pin held in his closed fist. The unplanned pass between them had worked. Jonathon managed to press the bobby pin into his palm during his tackle. Right now though, Ryan didn't care about the bobby pin. The teenager held his full attention and concern. He knew the youth thought quick, reacted fast, and showed tremendous intelligence and resourcefulness, yet none of that was helping Jonathon in a battle against extreme pain. The teenager, he knew, just had to tough it out.

On the ground, a second tremulous moan emerged from Jonathon and he lay back, staring up at the blue sky, willing his body to recover. Within a minute, the slowing of Jonathon's chest showed sign of the dissipating pain. Soon Jonathon's breathing became regular, his body relaxed, and his leg loosened, easing flat onto the ground.

Cole looked up from examining his gun. "You ready to get up?"

"Give me a minute."

"I'll give you another blow to your leg."

At the threat of more pain, Jonathon rolled over. "Okay, okay, I'm up." A push up with his hands brought him to his feet but he held most of his weight on his right leg.

"Get moving," Cole ordered.

The knowledge that he could not outrun a gun carried Juan down the slope and straight toward the creek. Rocks tumbled and rolled down the hill, leaving an easy trail to follow. It was what he wanted.

Knowing he would not have much time before someone came after him, Juan's mind raced ahead of the situation. As long as Cole wanted to get to the mine, Jonathon would be kept alive. And if Jonathon could just find ways to stall for time . . . .

His initial path set, Juan then cut hard to the right and moved *up* the steep slope, weaving his way with care through the rock formations that pillared the mountainside. This time he did not want to leave a trail.

No sooner had he lowered himself between the sandstone columns when Halden appeared. The man rushed toward the creek, following the path left by Juan.

When the trail disappeared, Halden continued to follow the creek, taking the same path of least resistance as the water. Juan watched him pass fifty feet below him and continue down the valley. Then, easing himself out of his hiding place, Juan looked for a new path to take.

Trapped amid the earthquake's carnage, Tallie continued her monologue, trying not to look at Severino's arm. Blisters bubbled and oozed around the bite and the swollen limb carried colors of black and purple, red and blue. Even the sockets around his eyes looked swollen and dark to her.

Face down on the tunnel floor, his eyes had not opened since the quake.

In an effort to hold back her fear and keep up her spirits, Tallie rambled about her family, her first memories of Jonathon, her favorite teacher, even her embarrassing first kiss; but Severino did not respond to any of it. On the cold floor, he lay still, unmoving except for the faint rise and fall of his back.

Finally, her throat sore from talking around a lump of emotion, Tallie could not bring herself to continue. It felt futile. Defeated, she slowly slid down onto her side and eased herself as close to him as she dared. Tears glistened in her eyes and she touched his face, trying not to hurt the bruising, fingered his hair. For several minutes, she stayed close to him, watching him, trying to engrave his face into her memory.

"I don't want you to die, Severino," she whispered. "You still have to practice your English, and I have to learn Spanish."

"Paiute," he whispered.

Startled, Tallie drew back and looked at his eyes. When they flickered and opened partway, tears ran over her dark lashes and left wet trails down her cheeks. Emotion trembled her fingers as she again touched his face, looking into his tired eyes. "You're awake! How do you feel?"

"*Mal.* Everything hurts."

Talking took most of his air and he started coughing. The new pain twisted through his lungs. She put her hand on his back to calm him but he made a sharp sound of protest at her contact and she recoiled, her face pale. "I am so sorry!"

"It is okay," he whispered. "Is Jonathon here?"

"No," she managed in sorrow.

Severino processed the answer, accepted what that meant, and closed his eyes. "Forgive me, Tallie." he asked.

She touched his hair, fingering it off his face and brow. "There's nothing to forgive."

"I promised you would be safe . . ."

At his words, she saw a swallow move down his throat and he tried to lick his cracked lips. The movement gave her something to focus on. "You need some water."

Tallie turned and reached for the bottle but stopped. The bottle held only sand and mud and rocks. Inside, her heart sank. "We have no more water."

"*Esta bien.*"

"No," she snapped. "No, it isn't fine! None of this is fine. You shouldn't be here. You shouldn't be bit by a rattlesnake. Halden should have helped and not turned psycho." Furious, she pushed to her feet. "You need water and I'm going to get you some."

Not understanding all her words but clear on her intent to go somewhere, Severino protested. "No, Tallie. Don't."

She ignored him. "I'm going back to the cave-in. Maybe I can find another bottle."

"It is dangerous."

"I don't care!"

"I do."

Despite the pain, he tried to move, to stop her, but she stepped back, away from his hand, her voice shaking with emotion. "Severino, don't you understand? I have to do something!"

"You have already done much."

"I've been talking! That's it. A parrot can talk! I want to *do*!" Then, before she faced any more of his protests, Tallie turned and ran down the tunnel, letting the headlamp and the dirt mounds guide her path. Behind, in the shaft, Severino called for her to stop, but she willed herself not to hear him.

Fifteen minutes later, she returned, her hands empty, her heart drained. Overcome, she sank to the earth next to the granite crack, drew her knees to her chest, and closed her eyes against the tears. "I can't help you," she whispered. "I can't even get you any water."

"You have helped *bastante*, plenty."

"No. I have failed you, Jonathon, and myself. I shouldn't have been so stubborn with Halden. I should have showed him the map long ago. Then none of us even would be here."

"Tallie, you did the right thing."

"How can you say that? You are hurt. I don't even know if Jonathon or Tate is alive!"

To offer her comfort, Severino moved his good arm through the pain and managed to take her hand in his. "What is right is not always easy, but what is right is always important."

"What is important is that you get to a hospital and Jonathon and Tate are safe."

"And if that doesn't happen, what you did was still right. *El color de la pintura no cambia las bases.*"

In the tunnel, Tallie sounded out his words. "The color of the . . . paint . . . does not change . . . the bases?"

"Los sólidos cimientos."

The words gelled in her mind and she looked up with understanding. "The foundations. The color of the paint does not change the foundation!"

Tired and in pain, he still smiled. *"Sí.* When your decisions are right, it does not matter what color life paints around you. Your foundation will always be strong. You chose right. You will be fine, Tallie."

In the desolation of the tunnel, Tallie smiled and leaned close to kiss the back of his hand in appreciation. The movement lowered her into a small whisper of air and she felt the cool movement against her back and neck. The flow halted her movement and she looked toward the flow, Severino's hand still in hers. "I feel a breeze."

"What is that?"

"It's air . . . moving air." Excitement caused her to release his hand and move toward the wall, feeling with her hand, trying to locate the incoming air. Again, a whispering of air current moved her hair, in gentle caresses, across her face. Holding out her hand, she caught the movement against her palm and followed it forward. The tiny blast of air emerged from the sheltering granite crack and she wondered if it had been there before the earthquake.

"Is the air cold or hot?"

Startled by the question, Tallie looked at him. "It is cold, why?"

"That is good. Warm air from the outside is pushing the cold air down."

"You mean there is a warm air opening to the outside somewhere?"

"*Probable*. Where is it coming from?"

"The crack."

Curiosity directed her headlamp into the crack. In the back of the crack, fresh dirt lay on the floor. She reached in and pressed it with her finger. More dirt crumbled away, releasing more air through the narrow crevice and Tallie knew some type of space lay on the other side of the crack.

Excited, she started to claw at the dirt with her hand. The earthquake had loosened years of compaction, and clumps of dirt broke away freely. Sand, rock, and debris tumbled to the ground and Tallie found her digging quickened as the hole enlarged. Cool air now blew against her neck and chest. "I'm getting more cold air!"

As the hole enlarged, Tallie grabbed the remaining shovel and crawled into the space, scraping and digging her way forward, moving the dirt out of the way. Then the wall of packed dirt gave way completely, and an opening loomed in front of her. Shocked by the sight, she sat back and stared at the carved space in front of her.

Almost afraid to make a sound, Tallie announced her find to Severino. "There is a new tunnel here."

"Are you sure?"

"Yes. It may be a way out. I'm going to follow it."

Unable to move and needing to know more, Severino grimaced. "Not yet. Tell me about it first."

With renewed courage, Tallie leaned forward and let her headlamp illuminate the stone walls. "It's big—bigger than the tunnel we're in."

"The walls and floor, are they dirt or stone?"

"I think stone. They are very smooth."

When her headlamp panned to the left, Tallie froze. Nothing could force words out of her throat, and no explanation existed in her mind. Unable to do anything else, she lifted a hand to cover her mouth in shock.

The abrupt stop in her speaking filled Severino with fear. Though he could not see her, he could feel her emotion and did not understand it. "Tallie, talk to me!"

Still she could not respond.

"Tallie!"

Finally she managed a whisper, barely audible. "There's a door here."

"A what?"

"There's a man-made door in this tunnel."

"The mine entrance is just ahead." The whisper emerged from Jonathon. "If you're going to get out of those handcuffs, now would be a good time."

"I can't do it while I'm moving," Ryan returned in a quiet voice. To avoid suspicion, Ryan continued up the slope until a distance of three or four yards separated them. At that point, he stopped and turned back, breathing hard, fighting the pain in his body, watching the others.

In the rough canyon terrain, Jonathon leaned over and massaged the top of his thigh. "I need to rest. My leg still hurts."

"You don't need to rest."

Ignoring Cole, Jonathon sank down on a fallen log. "Just give me two minutes. Your other guy up there could use a rest too. You beat him up pretty good before you cuffed him." Both of his hands rubbed his leg.

A glance at both of his hostages told Cole they weren't going anywhere for a moment. "Fine," he growled. "You have two minutes."

Grateful for Jonathon's ploy, Ryan sank to the dirt above them and his fingers began to rotate the bobby pin into the right position. To release himself from the handcuffs he only needed to free one hand yet, unable to see or even maneuver his hands and fingers, Ryan fumbled to accomplish the first blind task—spreading apart the bobby pin.

Twisting and bending, he worked and angled the small metal clip, while his fingers distinguished the smooth side from the rippled side. Because he did not have much play with his hands or fingers, Ryan then used his thumb and fingers to turn the bobby pin around and inch it slowly upward, toward the locking mechanism on the cuffs. The bobby pin needed to become a shim inside the square mechanism so he could push the small locking bar back and away from the cuff straps. Then he could pull and push the ribbed strap backward through the mechanism and loosen one side just enough to slip free.

Though he had never freed himself from handcuffs with his hands restrained behind his back, on slow days, he and the other agents would cuff each other, hands in front, and have contests to see who could get out of them first. The stupid game passed the time and brought them some good laughs, but now, he hoped, it would save their lives.

Perched on a fallen log, Jonathon rocked backward and massaged his thigh, playing up his need, trying to buy Ryan a little more time. Not sure he believed Ryan yet or even if he thought it possible to escape from PlastiCuffs with a bobby pin, Jonathon had decided if the guy only requested a two-cent hair accessory and some time, he could give it to him.

Up the hill, Ryan got the flat side of the bobby pin inserted into the locking mechanism. With his fingers bent, he tried to work it between the bar and strap, pressing the tiny metal tool upward. His finger slipped, and he bobbled the insertion, almost dropping the bobby pin. Catching it with his forefinger against the pad of his thumb, Ryan managed to press the bobby pin tight against his palm to keep it from disappearing into the dirt.

After a breath to calm himself, he tried again, rolling the bobby pin back into an upright position and easing it toward the locking mechanism. This time the pin stayed inserted, and Ryan pressed upward, hard, with his fingers, forcing it into place.

Cole moved toward Jonathon and jerked him to his feet. "Your two minutes are up. Get moving."

Bouncing on his good leg to keep his balance, Jonathon glared at the older man. "That didn't feel like two minutes to me. Maybe your expensive Omega watch isn't as accurate as you think."

"Shut up."

"I was just wondering, 'cause if I'd paid that much for a watch, I wouldn't want to lose even a second of my time."

"You may lose a lot more than that if you keep irritating me. Now get going." Anger shoved Jonathon forward.

With a pronounced limp, Jonathon climbed the slope to where Ryan still sat. When he drew even with Ryan, he stopped to catch his breath.

"Your boot is coming untied," Ryan noted loudly enough that Cole heard.

A glance down at his boots told Jonathon they were fine, but he took the opportunity Ryan gave him and knelt on one knee. Focused on retying his boot, he spoke quietly. "You get it?"

"I think." Ryan responded in the same silent way, sending his gaze up the slope and away from Jonathon. "When I shout, duck out of the way. I'll take Cole."

Finished tying his boot, Jonathon switched to retie the other one. "You sure you can take him out?"

"I've wanted nothing else for ten years."

Promising Severino she would return soon and that she would be careful, Tallie now hesitated inside the new tunnel—not out of fear but in awe. The giant door towered to almost ten feet. The heavy, stone barrier had been carved with intricate designs, and Tallie found herself touching the images in reverence. Etchings of the sun, moon, and stars shared the door's façade with carvings of men, animals, birds . . . and butterflies.

The delicate creatures drew Tallie's full attention, and she caressed the stone wings. Butterflies. She felt connected to the symbol. Somehow she knew the Pikyavit family was connected to this door.

In the mighty tunnel, the portal stood slightly ajar. Tallie did not know if the earthquake had shifted the mighty door or if it had stood partially open for years. Whatever stood behind the barrier no longer frightened her as it had the first time she saw the mighty door. The carved butterfly spoke to her of safety and of promise.

Pushing against the mighty stone, it pivoted easily away from a new space and she stepped forward. Before the headlamp's beam, the area beyond the door did not gape dark and ominous. Instead, her tiny lamp illuminated walls of sunlight. Everywhere she looked, a brilliant glow returned to her eyes. Amazed, Tallie entered into a great room with walls and a ceiling of gold.

Lost in the middle of the mighty room, she found she could not— did not want—to move deeper into the space. Instead, she turned in a slow circle, watching her light arc and dance in the magic around her. Deep inside the mountain, the sun shone, shimmering and gleaming, reflecting and refracting off a golden world.

Seven great pillars, each covered in gold, supported the mighty ceiling. Around the room, breathtaking creations of gold, silver, and gemstones filled every space. Around her she saw Paiute emblems resting alongside Hopi, Ute alongside Navajo, and all of them joined together, resting for centuries unharmed in one great room. Tallie moved into the room, looking at the ornate décor left to beautify it.

Weapons of war, emblems of might and power, lay on tables— given away as tokens of peace. Then she stopped. The sight brought tears to her eyes. Never had she seen anything more beautiful or more hallowed than the laying down of weapons, the sharing of trust. Respect moved her forward, her fingers brushing in whispered touches over the weapons, long removed from anger and hate.

Traveling deeper into the room, she touched other objects, caressed the sacred, and stroked silent history. She saw it all yet could not comprehend even a small part of it.

And then she knew, absolutely knew, she stood inside *Carre Shinob*.

A lift of awe-filled eyes brought her to a complete stop. Unable to move forward, she stared, her heart pounding in her chest.

On the wall hung a large butterfly, its intricate wings of blue-green variscite encased beneath a silver design, in every way identical to the butterfly necklace around her neck.

Stunned, Tallie approached the butterfly, touched the wings of stone and silver and knew her father once stood inside this very room. Overcome by emotions she could not explain, Tallie sunk to the earth, feeling her father's presence near, feeling his great love for her. Whether he crafted the butterfly on the wall or merely copied it, she did not know but she now understood what he tried to tell her that day. More than gold existed inside the Sacred Mountain. The room, the temple, the entire mountain held the love of her father, her family—her entire people.

She did not know how long she stayed there, but when her mind returned to Severino, Tallie found new strength. She knew where she stood and that meant she knew exactly where she needed to go. Her father had given her the map years ago.

Easing back through the granite crack, Tallie returned to Severino. She found him on the tunnel floor, the poison and his injuries taking the last of his consciousness. Kneeling at his side, Tallie brushed the hair off his face, but he did not respond.

She knew the way the home. The path had been clearly marked by her father in butterfly wings and daylight waited only a few minutes away. Yet she also knew she would have to leave Severino to help him. Leaning down, Tallie whispered close, and, as she spoke to Severino, she felt her father's voice whisper the same words to her. "I need to go now, but I promise to get you help. I know the way out, but you're going to have to hang tough without me, okay? I love you and I will see you soon, I promise."

Kissing his hair gently, Tallie grabbed the shovel and squeezed back through the small crack into the true tunnel system of *Carre Shinob*.

Ten minutes later, sunlight warmed her face and her heart as she left the Sacred Mountain and headed for help.

Motion came through the trees, and the group turned anxious eyes. Halden moved through the cedars, alone. Out of breath, sweat staining his shirt and face, he joined back with the group, his gun holstered.

"Where's the man?" Cole demanded.

"He's gone."

"Gone, how?"

The harsh jolt of Cole's voice caused Halden's eyes to shift toward Jonathon. "I took care of him."

"Like you took care of the girl?" Cole taunted.

"No."

"Then how did you take care of him? Did you kill him?"

Halden shifted his weight. "Yeah."

At the answer, Jonathon took a step back, horrified. Cole ignored the teen's reaction, pushing Halden for more information. "How did you kill him? I never heard a gunshot."

Nervousness caused Halden to lick his lips. "Because I didn't use my gun! I didn't want to attract attention."

"So where is the body?"

"At the bottom of a cliff. People will think he fell."

"Are you sure he's dead?"

Defensive, Halden's muscles grew tight. "Yes, I'm sure he's dead! You wanna go back and check, 'cause I can take you right to him."

Angered, Cole stepped toward Halden. "If you messed up, you'll be at the bottom of a cliff before nightfall." Cole waved his gun, motioning for Jonathon and Ryan to keep moving.

Relieved to see Cole move away from him, Halden stepped alongside the teenager and grinned, his voice a wicked hiss. "How does that make you feel, half bean?" Fury tightened Jonathon's jaw. Halden laughed drily and moved away, leaving Jonathon to grapple with his anger and his grief.

Head down, voice quiet, Ryan limped beside the teenager. "Everything about that guy tells me he's lying. He has no idea where your friend is. I'm betting your friend is still alive."

It had taken Tallie a moment to gain her bearings, to decide her location in the canyon, and then she headed toward help. Her trek through the shale and sage-strewn gorge filled the air with sound and she worried Halden might catch her unaware. At times, she slowed, watching, searching before moving forward again. Though her heart pounded with fear at each stop, she knew she didn't have time to be taken captive again. Severino didn't have time.

She wove her way down the canyon with increasing urgency. Soon the landmarks indicated she was drawing near to camp, and to the ATVs. Only a few more minutes and she could head down the canyon and call for help.

From all around, a thumping sound filled the canyon, and Tallie lowered herself into the bushes, watching for mechanical movement. She hated the way sound echoed and bounced off the canyon walls, making it difficult to pinpoint the sound. Then the sound vanished almost as fast as it came, and for a long time, Tallie held still, wondering if she had mistaken the pounding of her heart.

As she moved forward, a hand reached around her face and clamped down over her mouth. Terrified, startled, and furious, she spun to fight her captor. A twist of her body rolled her away from him, but the man moved just as quick, keeping her mouth covered, wrapping a strong arm around her waist, trying to pin her to the earth.

Grunting in protest, she rolled beneath him and arched away, but he shoved her backward to the ground, hissing something she did not hear. Not willing to be captured again, Tallie hooked her leg up against his hip and slid one hand under his arm. Clasping her hands together behind his back, she shoved her elbow under his face, lifted his head with her forearm, and cranked down on his shoulder. The move broke the strength of his hold and his ability to tighten down on her further.

Again the man spoke, and she almost thought she heard her name. Still not ready to be taken hostage, she shifted her hips to the side and swung the weight of her entire body against him. Pressing him down into the dirt hard, she shoved her knee into his shoulder toward the earth and scooted out from under him, broke free, and scrambled to her feet.

"Tallie, stop." The man rolled away and held a finger to his lips, his voice soft. "I'm a friend of Jonathon's."

The whisper stopped her and she looked back into the dark eyes of a stranger.

"There are men down in the camp," he breathed quiet. "They just came in by helicopter, but until we know for sure who they are, we need to stay out of sight."

Startled, she looked from the stranger, shifting her gaze further down the canyon. She could not see anything but hesitated, trusting the man's words. He rolled to his feet, rubbing his shoulder. "David said you beat Jonathon in wrestling all the time. I know why."

Juan pushed his hand through his hair and met her eyes. "I'm Juan. I'm an anthropologist and . . ."

Shock filled her and she looked at him. "You're from Peru!"

"You've heard of me."

"You saved Jonathon's life in the hospital!" Looking around her, Tallie searched for her friend. "Where is he? Where's Jonathon?"

"Right now he's being held by two men with guns."

"He's out of the mine?"

"Yes, but we've got to get him help." Juan's dark eyes held hers. "And we've got to help Severino. Jonathon said he'd been bit by a snake but right now I can't get help for anyone. I can't leave the canyon. Some men just showed up at the camp and they're blocking my exit. Do you know of another way out of this canyon?"

Concerned now, Tallie moved toward the man. "Who are the men?"

"I don't know, but they are searching for something—and they have guns."

Tallie did not take the news well. She shook her head in helpless frustration. "No. We have got to get help or Jonathon and Severino will die!"

Jonathon and Ryan, still held hostage, moved through the canyon with their own pains and their own thoughts. Branches scraped their skin and dead leaves crunched under their boots. As the group passed, squirrels chattered their displeasure and birds startled from their roosts. Protesting bird wings beat the cooling air as they lifted out of the canyon, announcing the intruders. Below them, a thin stream passed in gentle ripples over the still rocks.

Jonathon did not advance further. "The mine opening is down there."

Curious, Cole stepped forward and peered down the slope. He saw the stream and the opening. Nearby, Ryan sensed a growing urgency to be free. They'd found the mine. Cole no longer needed either one of them. With his hands still bound behind his back, Ryan began to twist and roll his wrist back and forth, trying to pull the ribbed cuff backward through the shimmed mechanism.

Near Cole, Halden glanced at the quiet scene. The landmarks below held silent memories for him and fear fell across Halden's face. "We can't go in there."

Irritation turned Cole back to Halden. "Why not?"

"Don't you remember?" Halden shifted, nervous.

"Obviously not."

Filled with unease, Halden brushed his hand across his upper lip. "We were here, about ten years ago."

"Who's we?"

"You, me, and Tate, remember?"

Stepping closer, his voice and eyes firm, Cole glared at Halden. "No, I don't remember. This is the first time I've ever been here."

Halden didn't understand the tone of his voice or his hard

expression. Fear held the younger man hostage. "You heard there might be an old Spanish gold mine up here, so you flew all the way in from California. It was the first time you hired us to dig for you." Halden hesitated again and looked around, shaking now. "This isn't good. Things didn't go well in this canyon. We can't go back in there."

At Halden's obvious fear, understanding began its slow growth inside of Jonathon. Brought forward to answer his own suspicions, Jonathon pried for more information. "What didn't go well here, Halden? Why are you so afraid to go in there?"

Cole turned to Jonathon. "He's not afraid of anything. Why should he be afraid? You came out of that opening and through this area and you didn't see a thing."

Jonathon lifted brow in confidence and he looked at the older man. "I didn't say that. I just said this was the way I got out."

Halden's gaze shifted toward Jonathon. "You saw something in the cave?"

Not interested in playing games or bargaining anymore, Jonathon looked at both of them and nodded. "Yeah, I saw something in the cave. I saw a skeleton in there. In fact, I saw the skeleton of Charlie Pikyavit about eighty yards in. Someone shot him in the head. Half his skull is missing."

Eyes wide with horror, Ryan stopped trying to escape. For all the unexpected events that had happened during the day, this one caused him the most complete and unmanageable shock. He reeled visibly at the news.

Anger emboldening him, Jonathon stepped closer. "Since I know Charlie disappeared about ten years ago, and Halden just said you were both here at that same time, and you happen to be wearing a ring I know Charlie made, I'd say you probably know exactly who's inside that mountain . . . you both do."

The news produced a sound of protest from Halden and his face paled. Stepping backward, he looked at Cole. "I knew it," he whispered. "I knew someone would find him."

"Keep your mouth shut, Halden!"

The news made Ryan's mouth go dry and he stood, tense and hurting over the news of his friend. *You killed Charlie Pikyavit?*

At the question, Halden protested. "No, not me! We were just up here to find a new dig site and ran into Charlie. He was up here fishing.

Charlie knew Cole and had dug artifacts for him before, so Cole told him to join us. But Charlie refused. He wouldn't dig."

Angered, Ryan stepped forward. *"He wouldn't dig because I told him not to!* Charlie was working for me, trying to get evidence for me on someone buying local artifacts illegally. It was getting dangerous, so I told Charlie to back out and forget it. He had a family and I didn't want him getting hurt. *And you killed him anyway!"*

Shaking, Halden continued. "It wasn't my fault. Charlie said this canyon was sacred to his ancestors, so Cole thought that meant there were Indian graves nearby. He tried to force Charlie to dig, but Charlie never wavered. That's when Cole shot him. Didn't give him a warning or anything. Just told Charlie he could go join his ancestors . . ."

As the truth tumbled forward, Cole's gun rose in a fluid motion and pointed at Halden, his face livid. Jonathon saw Cole's finger pull back on the trigger, knew Cole planned to kill Halden the same way he'd killed Charlie: without warning.

From behind, Jonathon heard Ryan's yell—heard the rage, the hurt, and the triumph in Ryan's voice. That one sound, that tone, told him the agent was free.

Without stopping to look, Jonathon surged into action, hitting Halden in the stomach with his shoulder. The tackle propelled both of them backward to the earth, beneath the aim of the gun.

The abrupt shout and movement startled Cole, who spun, swinging the gun in front of him. Released from the cuffs, Ryan charged forward, covering the ground to Cole in two swift strides. Without time to aim, Cole pulled the trigger by instinct.

Gunfire exploded through the remote canyon, filling the air with a thunderclap. Even as the sound bounced and echoed its way across the cliffs, a single brass casing ejected from the pistol. Still hot, it spun through the air, flashing in the setting sun. The light ricocheted off its metal jacket like ball lighting.

Birds erupted from the trees with disapproval, but the bullet did not pursue any of them. It already found its target. Ryan's body lifted off the ground as the force of the bullet pitched him backward.

Four guns raised in unison, but did not fire, as the teenage girl marched down the hill and into camp. Beneath the watch of the deadly barrels, she didn't slow, crossing the campsite toward the ATVs. Though fear pounded inside of her, she thought of Severino's words to her and knew she was making the right choice.

"I don't know who you are, but my name is Tallie Pikyavit," she announced, her quest focused on reaching the four-wheeled machine. "One of my friends has been bit by a rattlesnake, and the other is being held hostage. I'm going to get help so you can give it or you can shoot. If you shoot, trust me, someone from the lower campground will hear the shots and will call the police. If you want to give it, then I suggest you lower those guns."

One man tipped the muzzle of his pistol toward the ground and eased off the trigger. Relief filled his face and a slight smile at her boldness lifted his mouth. He brushed at his dark hair and felt the tension leave. "Tallie, my name is Steven. I'm with the BLM. I'm here to help, and I'm really glad to see you."

Jonathon heard Cole's gunshot echo through the canyon, saw Ryan jerk at the impact and fall in a crumpled heap to the earth. "No!" The protest tore from his throat like the bullet that tore through Ryan.

Across the creek, a mangled dog also heard the shot, recalled the sound from years ago, and rage filled its frame. Fury drove the dog, without hesitation, out of the cave. It raced through the water and toward the shooter. Teeth bared, the animal lunged up the slope. The scent of the man with the gun entered what remained of his nostrils, and memories returned. This time, almost one-hundred and fifty pounds of blond hackles rushed to avenge a master, slain more than a decade earlier.

A second bullet tore through the air as the dog hit its target, but the shot went wild. Beneath the onslaught of the hideous beast, Cole screamed and fell to the ground. The brutal enemy attacked with savage teeth that spread blood and destruction.

Time to think did not exist for Jonathon, only time to react. "Po," Jonathon called, "Po, stop!"

The dog refused.

Jonathon turned back and swept Halden's gun off the ground.

Braced to shoot, the teen stepped toward the battle on the ground, watching as the dog ripped and tore at the man he hated for so long. Beneath the savagery, Cole fought like the animal he had become. Again, Jonathon called for the dog to stop.

Not yielding to his commands, the animal continued, teeth latched onto Cole's arm, his mangled head shaking and biting. The carnage tore the gun from Cole's grip, and it clattered to the ground. Hurriedly, Jonathon kicked it away, his gun still poised.

With more force, Jonathon tried to shout the dog down. "No, Po!" He did not want to kill the dog, but he did not want Cole torn to pieces either. The dog showed no intentions of stopping and Jonathon raised the gun, braced it with both hands, and drew up the slack in the trigger.

"*Po'ohe, cach!*"

The command, spoken in Paiute, rang out over the sound of the butchery, and the dog heard. Recalling the language from long ago, Po obeyed and stopped ripping and tearing, his teeth still sunk deep into Cole's arm. Then as the memories returned, the dog relaxed his powerful jaw and released the man.

Jonathon looked up and saw Ryan, trying to rise, pressing a hand hard to a wound. The injured officer spoke more Paiute, and the dog backed away. Lifting the second gun off the ground, Jonathon rushed to Ryan's side. "What do you need? What can I do?"

"Call for help." Ryan breathed. One hand came forward, the plastic handcuffs still cinched to his wrist. "Then get these off me and put them on Cole. Just don't let him have a bobby pin." A smile managed to escape through his pain.

On the ground, Cole tried to move, but the dog bristled in hatred, his intentions coming out in a warning growl. Ryan saw the movement and snapped at the man and at Halden. "Hold still, both of you, or I'll send him after you again, and this time I won't call him off."

Held captive beneath two guns and the waiting dog, neither man moved. Cradling his injured body, Cole did not protest as Jonathon retrieved the satellite phone from his belt and backed away. "Who do I call?" Jonathon asked.

Tired, Ryan managed to answer, his body sinking to the ground. "My handler—my boss." Then he shook his head, a new thought coming to him, one he did not want to argue, and he tried to keep his emotions under control. "No. Call my wife first. She's more important. Tell her I love her and that I'm sorry, and, if she'll give me another chance, tell her I *really* want it."

Jonathon nodded his approval as he typed in the number Ryan recited and then moved the phone close to Ryan, holding it close to the man's ear. "How about you tell her that yourself. Then I'll call your boss."

TWENTY-TWO

FATIGUED, A doctor entered the private waiting room to deliver the news. Several rose in unison from the chairs and couches, waiting.

"Severino is stable and in the ICU, but he's in critical condition." The doctor sank onto a couch to rest. "He has a punctured lung and damaged spleen, along with several broken ribs, a dislocated shoulder, and bruising from top to bottom."

Tallie felt her emotions turn grim at the news. Jonathon drew her close to his side.

As if he could wipe away the last several hours, the doctor rubbed his hand over his face. "The lung has reinflated, so that's good. We've stitched him up, and we'll keep monitoring him to make sure everything goes well. We've already given him several doses of antivenom but that was a nasty bite. His arm is so swollen that we had to do a fasciotomy to try and save it."

"What's that?" David asked.

"It's where we cut down through all the layers of skin and into the fascia—the protective tissue that wraps around the muscles. By doing that, we can relieve pressure caused by the swelling and allow circulation to be restored to the muscles. We had to cut open all his fingers and his arm to almost his shoulder." The doctor showed them on his arm where the cut had occurred. Tallie turned away at the mental image.

Juan stepped forward. "Will it work? Will he be able to keep his arm?"

Affirming the seriousness of the situation, the doctor continued. "I think so. The arm will have to stay open like that until the swelling goes down, and then we'll have to see how much tissue has died. In the meantime, the big risk is infection, so you won't be able to see him for a while. After the swelling goes down, if all looks good, we'll put a skin graft over the area. Unfortunately, he'll always have an ugly scar there—they don't heal neat and straight either. The inside of his arm will look like he went through a windshield, but that will be better than losing it."

Relieved at the news, Jonathon looked at Juan and grinned. "I can see Severino milking that one. A big, long scar on his arm."

"His American souvenir," Juan teased.

"So, what do you think, Tallie? Think the scar will make him more *guapo*?"

"I don't care about *guapo*. I'm just glad he's going to live."

"Think other girls will find him more attractive because of the scar?"

A backhanded slap across Jonathon's stomach announced Tallie's opinion and made both Jonathon and Juan smile.

The doctor nodded his acknowledgment to Juan and David. "Well, if other girls find his scar attractive, that's just fine. At least he'll have a scar. He would have died if he hadn't have gotten here when he did. Good thing the BLM already had that helicopter in the canyon. His body was already close to shutting down when we gave him the first dose of antivenom."

"How soon before we know if it is working?"

"It's already working, and the swelling has stopped, which is good. But it will take days, even weeks before the swelling goes down completely; and he will suffer tingling in his arm for months, or maybe even the rest of his life. Rattlesnake bites are not like they show on TV. They don't just produce two little holes and a red area. They cause tremendous damage."

The memory of Severino's bruised and blistered arm returned to Tallie. "I know. I've never seen anything like it before."

The doctor looked at her. "You were with him in the cave?"

"Yes."

"Then you must be Tallie. Just before we put him under for surgery, he asked me to tell you *gracias*—and you too." He nodded at Jonathon. "He wanted me to thank both of you. From what I hear, all you kids have been through a lot."

Jonathon shifted forward. "We're not the only ones who have been through a lot. How are the others doing that were brought in here?"

"I've been told the man attacked by the dog has been taken into custody and transferred to a hospital up north. He'll have some of his own scars to deal with.

"What about Tate and Ryan?"

"Is Tate the one who was caught in the cave-in?"

"Yes."

"He's going to be fine, although he won't be able to walk or move very well until all those bones heal, but his doctor expects a full recovery."

"And Ryan Polson, the agent they brought in here?"

"He's still in surgery. Apparently the bullet and the beating tore him up inside, but he has one of the best trauma surgeons working on him right now. Wish I could tell you more."

"What about his wife, did she come?"

The surgeon nodded while coming back to his feet. "Yes, she's here, waiting with Steven, Ryan's partner. She got here just before Ryan went into surgery, and they let her visit with him briefly. She told Ryan she wasn't going anywhere. She was going to stay right by his side for a long time."

The news brought a smile to Jonathon's face. "Good. I'm glad to hear that. Thank you for everything."

Two weeks later, Jonathon sat on the seat of his ATV, waiting and watching. On a rock near the creek, Tallie sat patiently; a pile of nearby dog food and meat scraps attracted flies while it warmed and dried in the sun. From beyond the stream, a mangled dog watched with caution, sniffing the wind, his ears cocked in interest but his feet keeping him back.

After half an hour, Tallie turned and hiked out of the ravine. At the top, she joined Jonathon to watch. Below them, Po advanced toward the food, testing the air.

"So, did Tate get to look at the pictures you took of Po?" Jonathon questioned.

"Yeah."

"Does he think Po is the creature that attacked him?"

She nodded. "He's sure of it. So sure, in fact, that he's not coming back up into the canyon until Po is gone. He figures Po remembers him from the day Cole shot my dad."

"He's probably right." Breathing deep and calm, Jonathon watched the scene below. The deformed dog approached the food with caution. "Did the vet ever get a look at the photos?"

"He did."

A shift in his attention directed Jonathon's gaze at Tallie. "Did he say why he thinks Po got so big after he was shot?"

The breeze blew long hair across her face and she brushed it away. "Without being able to examine him, he's not sure, but he thinks the bullet could have damaged the pituitary gland. Even though it is located in the center of brain, he said it can be damaged by severe facial or cranial trauma."

"Well, Po has definitely suffered that."

"The vet said the gland regulates the growth hormone, and if it is damaged, it can cause all sorts of problems—including gigantism, which causes big feet and huge jaws."

"Sounds just like Po." Jonathon smiled. Then he nodded toward the creek. "He's eating."

Below them, the dog snatched a meat scrap and darted back to eat it in a more secure position a few feet away. Tallie shook her head. "I'm amazed he survived being shot and then managed to live in the wild this long."

"Hey, he's a Pikyavit. He's tough, and he's smart."

She liked the comment and smiled. "Yes, he is."

Jonathon settled deeper in the seat of the ATV and looked at Tallie. "And what about your dad?"

"I'm okay with him staying in the cave. The whole family is. Besides, if we took him out and buried him, it would destroy Po."

She blinked and looked at the new rockslide over the opening. "Thank you for closing the opening and leaving only a hole big enough for Po. I like knowing he's up here still taking care of my dad."

"And you're going to be up here taking care of Po until he dies."

"Yes I am, and one day I'm going to text you and tell you he ate out of my hand."

"Don't you dare text. You *call* me with that news."

Tallie laughed. "I will."

They both watched Po take another piece of meat off the pile. "You know, without a body, it may be hard to get a murder conviction," Jonathon mused.

The comment brought a shrug from Tallie. "I know that. We all do, even Ryan, but I think we all want him to stay here so we aren't telling anyone where he is. Tate said he will testify and do what he can to help us get a conviction, even if it means more jail time for him. He's tired of being scared and quiet. But we all agree that Dad's body just needs to stay right here. It's where he belongs. He doesn't need to be caught up in a long court battle."

For a long time, neither spoke. Instead, they watched Po take another piece of meat. Then, heavy emotion coated Jonathon's words and he looked at her. "How do you feel about Tate after all this?"

A sigh escaped her. "I'm worried about him. Right now, he's only facing charges of excavating without a permit, so I hope he doesn't get any jail time. The police say he was as much a victim as everyone else. He was younger than you when Cole shot my dad in front of him. He didn't even know Cole had a gun, and the whole thing terrified him. Then, when Cole threatened Tate and Halden and our family, Tate didn't know what to do."

The news turned Jonathon to look at her. "Cole threatened your family?"

"Apparently. In fact, Tate said Cole's threats against us scared him more than anything and that's why he kept quiet. I honestly don't think he cared about what happened to him after my dad died, but he did care about us. He always has."

Jonathon digested the information. "And what about Halden?"

The question set a frown upon Tallie's face. "He's up on all sorts of charges, including kidnapping. I don't know how he's going to come out of this, and I'm not sure I know how I feel about it. If it hadn't been for Halden, Severino wouldn't still be in the hospital."

"He's getting out tomorrow."

"That's good, but he'll still have to go back in for several surgeries."

"At least he'll being staying in the States a while longer."

"I'm not sure that's how he wanted to extend his vacation."

Jonathon laughed. "Probably not."

Still watching the dog, Tallie started asking the questions. "Have you heard anything about Cole?"

Quiet, Jonathon nodded. "Ryan said they have enough evidence to convict Cole of all sorts of federal violations."

"That's good. How's Ryan doing?"

"He's home and doing good. Still recovering, but he's spending time rebuilding his relationship with his wife."

Pleased by the news, Tallie smiled. "I'm glad to hear that. You know, I remember Ryan now. He came to the house a couple of times before my father disappeared. He was always nice to me. I guess my dad was the one who told Ryan about some guy from California stealing artifacts in the area."

"Cole?"

"Yes. My mom said my dad and Ryan started working together— my dad would help Ryan gather information and even met with Cole to get more evidence. Anyway, my dad and Ryan became friends and started spending time fishing together, with Po, of course."

"So that's how Ryan knew to speak to the dog in Paiute."

A smile creased her lips. "Ryan always liked Po. It's a good thing he remembered how to speak Paiute."

Jonathon laughed. "It's a good thing the dog remembered how to obey it!" The two returned their gaze to the animal below. After a minute, Jonathon shifted on the seat of his ATV. "And *Carre Shinob*?"

"It is still protected. I filled in the crack." She fingered her butterfly necklace. "It was beautiful, Jonathon. I wish you and Severino could see it."

"Maybe someday, but for right now, you just keep it sacred." Leaning slightly to one side, Jonathon extracted something from his back pocket. "Here is something else you need to keep sacred."

The tiger's-eye ring settled into Tallie's palm and she gasped. "How did you get this?"

Jonathon smiled. "Even before the authorities made it up the canyon, Ryan had your dad's ring back. He gave it to me just the other day and said it belongs to your family. It never belonged to Cole. Never even fit him. He wasn't man enough to wear it."

Tears slid down her cheeks, and Tallie closed her hand around the ring, securing it in her grip. "Thank you so much. This means the world to me. And thank Ryan when you see him again."

"I will."

Near the creek, all the meat consumed, the dog now crunched his way through the dry dog food. Jonathon smiled. "Watching him eat that food reminds me we ought to go. By the time we get back, my grandma should have dinner about ready."

Tallie smacked his shoulder. "That's an awful thing to say about your grandmother's cooking. She's a good cook."

"Yes, she is, and I'm starved." He settled into position to start the ATV. "You ready?"

In answer, Tallie climbed onto the seat behind him.

David Bradford stepped forward, glancing at his watch. "Hey, guys, it's almost time for Severino to get heading through security."

At the airport, the reminder brought frowns to three faces. The friends looked at each other, not wanting time to advance. Time in the hospital recovering from the bite and follow-up surgeries kept Severino in the States for almost three months. During that time, the trio had been almost inseparable. Now their time together ticked to an end faster than they wanted. None of them wanted to be in a busy airport.

The sorrow of the moment lifted Severino's gaze. "I will be back for the trial," he offered, his English improved. "Plus, the doctors want to check on this. *Mi recuerdo Americano.*" A lift of his arm showed scar tissue from the recent skin grafts, still pink and healing.

"Ha! Juan said you'd call it that!" Tease glistened in Jonathon's eyes and he looked at Tallie. "So, what do you think? Think it makes him look more *guapo*?" Severino watched her and nodded, encouraging her response. Still teasing, Jonathon continued. "Think other girls will think so too?" This time Severino shook his head in a quick, refuting way, watching as Tallie frowned but said nothing.

Stepping close, Severino looked at her. "I'll wear more long-sleeve shirts if you want."

The comment worked, and she finally laughed.

Jonathon pulled a piece of paper out of his back pocket and handed it to Severino. "Before you go, this is for you."

"What is it?" The Peruvian opened the paper and tried to read the English, not sure of what he saw.

A glance at the paper caused Tallie to lift astonished eyes to Jonathon. "It's a bank statement."

Jonathon nodded. "The first few days after all this happened, there was a media frenzy. You don't remember it much, Severino, but you were a big hero. The news carried updates every night about the teenager from Peru who was held hostage and forced to work as a slave in an old Spanish gold mine."

"They said nothing about the snake?" Severino teased.

A chuckle emerged from Jonathon. "Oh, they loved the snake part and the fact that even after you were bit, you still managed to save a cute girl during an earthquake with a bottle of sand. Everyone wanted to know how you were; so when the media found out you had no medical insurance, things just went crazy. The doctor waived his fee, and people were sending in donations from all over the country. I think the story went out over the wire and even made the Yahoo news page. Anyway, some of the money was used to pay off all your medical bills, and the rest is right there, in that account. That's your money."

"Mine? And this is American dollars?"

"*Sí.*"

Drained, Severino looked up. "Do you know how much money that is in Peruvian soles? I can't take this money."

"You can and you will. The people who sent that wanted to help you and thank you for what you did, and apologize for what was done to you. So, to show your appreciation, you go back to Peru and enroll in college. Since you don't want to take our money, now you can use yours. There is more than enough money to pay for your education, but we still want to pay for Delia's, okay?"

Severino stared numbly at the paper, unable to speak. Jonathon urged him along. "Severino, you're too smart not to go back to school."

"But what will I study?"

"Juan wants you to study anthropology or archeology. He said he'd help."

Tallie smiled. "How about geology? Figure out how to predict earthquakes with more than just a bottle of sand and two rocks."

Again Severino lowered his eyes to the figure on the paper. "This is a lot of money."

Able to feel Severino's uncertainty, Jonathon encouraged him. "Use it for good, Severino. This is a chance to change your life . . . to make it the life your father always wanted you to have."

Blinking, he lifted his eyes. A nod of growing conviction came. "I will go to school on one promise."

"What's that?"

Dark eyes shifted to Tallie's and held her gaze. "While I am studying in the university, you are studying Paiute."

Jonathon laughed at the bargain and looked at Tallie. "Sounds fair to me."

With her eyes lock on Severino she smiled in agreement. "Sounds fair to me too. You have a deal—*un trato*."

Approval brightened Severino's face. "Good, now learn to say it in Paiute. I want to hear Paiute when I come back for the trial."

Over Severino's shoulder, Jonathon could see his father point to his watch. "I hate to be a pest, but Severino, you really need to get going."

Severino nodded and slipped the bank statement into his backpack. For a moment he looked at Jonathon, trying to decide how best to say good-bye. Jonathon made the decision easier for him. "I remember you said a couple of times that Americans hug too much, so how about a handshake?"

The answer brought a smile to Severino. "Sounds good." The two shook hands, firm and long, then Severino turned to Tallie. "Handshake?" he teased.

A smack to his shoulder told him of her opinion. "No way." Then she stepped in for a hug.

As Severino slid his arms around her and drew her close, the busy airport vanished. Tallie returned the embrace, burying her head against his neck—fitting perfectly into his arms—not wanting to let him go.

A few inches away, Jonathon looked at the ground, at Severino's backpack sitting nearby, back at his family, and then at his watch. Finally, he leaned in and whispered quietly. "Remember once when I said Peruvians kissed too much? Well, right now I don't think they kiss enough."

The comment pleased Severino and he drew his head back, looking at Tallie with soft brown eyes. "*¿Puedo besarte?*"

She didn't need to know perfect Spanish to understand his request. The question brought a smile to her face. "I was wondering when you'd finally ask. *Sí*, you may kiss me."

Pleased, Severino smiled and gently found her lips with his. Surrounded by hundreds of people, they disappeared into their first kiss. Between them passed a silent, powerful language that needed no translation, no blending of words. They knew from their kiss that leaving would now be harder than ever; returning more sweet.

Next to them, Jonathon turned away and this time did not watch the clock.

When they finished, Severino gave Jonathon a gentle push on the back to get his attention. As Jonathon turned back around, Severino lifted the backpack to his shoulder and said his final good-byes. Just before he disappeared through security, Severino turned back and waved. Then he headed home, to Peru.

For a long time, Tallie didn't move. She stood there watching, quiet tears slipping down her face. Jonathon nudged her shoulder with his. "Hey, he'll be back."

She managed a laugh through her tears. "I know, but it just feels like he's going to be gone for so long."

Together the pair turned away, joining Jonathon's family on the walk back to the parking lot. Tallie wiped at her tears, and, again, Jonathon pushed against her with his frame. "I have an idea. Severino still owes me a date with his sister. How about you and I save up our money and head down to Peru over Christmas break? That's only a few months from now. You can see Severino, and I can see Delia."

The idea brightened her countenance. "I would love that! Maybe we can double?"

Jonathon laughed and put his arm around her shoulders. "Maybe we can."

ABOUT THE AUTHOR

WRITING HAS BEEN PART OF T. LYNN ADAMS'S CAREER SINCE SHE was a teenager. At the age of fifteen, she walked into a newspaper business with a story idea and was challenged by the editor to write it for them. She did and has been writing for newspapers ever since. She has also been published in many national and international publications. Currently, she is the editor of a regional agriculture newspaper.

T. Lynn Adams lived in Peru for eighteen months and deeply treasures that experience, the people, and the culture. While there, she learned about the secret tunnels of the Incas. She also had many encounters with members of the Shining Path, but like all Peruvians she met, they treated her with courtesy and respect despite their reputation.

T. Lynn Adams and her husband are raising six children, and she openly admits to enjoying their teenage years, their friends, and *most* of their music. Her teens love to tease her about not being able to fry an egg and about the time she burned a bag of potato chips in the oven. With the bag hidden there to keep it from being devoured by her teenage sons, she didn't remember the chips until after she turned on the oven. Since that episode, she has discovered the best hiding place in the entire house is *(shhh!)* the dishwasher. No teenager wants to get near one!

Her family is one of the most influential things in her life. They love to spend time together, and even though they are not perfect, the most common sound in their home is laughter.